THE HERITAGE PAPER

BY DEREK CICCONE

OTHER BOOKS BY DEREK CICCONE

Officer Jones (a JP Warner story)

Huddled Masses (a JP Warner story)

Painless

The Trials of Max Q

The Truant Officer

Kristmas Collins

"The problem with the gene pool is that there is no lifeguard on duty"

- Rodney Dangerfield

CHAPTER ONE

She lay still in her bed with her hands clasped close to her chest, pretending to sleep. The darkness was penetrated only by a trickle of moonlight sneaking through the curtains. But she could feel his presence.

The man was not the Grim Reaper, but she knew he'd be the last face she saw in this life.

"Has the great Nazi hunter come for me?" her voice sputtered and creaked. After nine decades of life, turning it on was like starting a car in a frigid Munich winter. She could no longer read an eye-chart without the assistance of a telescope, but she could still sense the surprised look on the man's face. He had no idea she knew.

"Hello, Ellen," he spoke in a hushed tone. "Think of me as a gypsy moth that has come to defoliate your evil family tree."

"How did you figure it out?" she played naïve. She didn't know if she'd fooled the man, but she sure had convinced her own family that she was a dementia-stricken loony tune. The most damning evidence occurred when they found her wandering the grounds in the middle of a cold night, and claiming to have spotted aliens.

"When I was a medical student, a wise doctor told me a story. It was about a young prostitute he treated in Munich named Etta. She had been impregnated by a German soldier and feared for her life if she elected to have the child. The pregnancy was further complicated by Etta's lifestyle, which had included contracting a severe case of syphilis.

"The doctor risked his own safety to hide out Etta and nurse her to health ... and she eventually gave birth to a baby girl. It wasn't until many years later that this doctor realized he'd helped spread the seeds of evil—a knowledge that led to his murder."

"And this is relevant to your presence here tonight?"

"You see, that child he delivered was named Ellen."

She tried to smile, but the muscles in her face no longer cooperated with her demands. "There are those who claim that you no longer have the passion—that you've been diverted by your wealthy American lifestyle. But I can tell that the fire still burns deep inside you. It's why I chose you."

She strained through her foggy cataracts to see the surprised look on his face. But there was no time to savor small victories. She pointed sharply at the small end-table beside his chair, causing a painful tingle in her arm.

He pulled the chain on a desk lamp and a dull light illuminated the table. A gold cross glistened in the light.

The Nazi hunter appeared mesmerized as he took it into his hands, paying particular attention to the engraved symbol $v^\wedge 988v^\wedge$. On the back was Ellen's Apostle name of Andrew. Like the original, and more famous Apostles, there were twelve of them.

"I've seen this before—when we captured Bormann in South America, almost a half century ago. He told us if we ever saw the symbol again, it would mean the Reich was on the verge of regaining power. I thought he was just using it as leverage because ..."

"You and your partner were about to kill him," she finished his thought.

He said nothing, his silence admitting his guilt. That is, if killing a swine like Martin Bormann, the Führer's personal secretary, could ever be associated with an emotion like guilt. Not only did he betray the Apostles, but he hurt Ellen in the most personal of ways. His Apostle name of Judas was fitting.

The Nazi hunter continued to peer at the cross. For all his "big game hunting" that took him across the globe, those he most dreamed of having stuffed on his mantle were right under his nose. But the ironies were just beginning.

"What does this symbolize?" he demanded.

"Why are you dragging this out? You came to kill me tonight—so get on with it," she bristled at him.

"If you don't answer me, I will not only eliminate you, but the rest of your family."

His threat was laughable. He'd already begun to "defoliate" her family, and once the gypsy moth began spreading its larvae, it wouldn't stop until the tree was dead. She did find it interesting that his threat to kill her family was synonymous with the Nazi tactic of *sippenhaft*. She always found it fascinating that victims seeking revenge often ended up resembling those responsible for their pain.

"It symbolizes the seeds that grew into a tree, and eventually became a forest—one that would one day spread over the land. And that day is here."

"Why would you tell me this?" he asked, still staring at the cross.

"Because I believe you're the only one who can stop it."

He tried to conceal his surprise. "Why would a Nazi like you want to stop the expansion of this forest, as you call it?"

"The struggle has led to nothing but suffering for my family. My children have been taken from me, and now with the moment so close, I fear an even worse fate for those who remain."

"Any suffering you faced doesn't remotely compare to what you've inflicted. The only way to stop another generation of evil is to remove the tree at its roots."

"Evil is not passed on like brown hair or the shape of a nose—it is taught. Using your philosophy, you would kill all the flowers in the garden just to ensure there are no weeds. But all you would accomplish is to steal beauty from the world. Are you saying that all those SS men were genetically inclined to murder? And if so, why did most return to peaceful lives when the war ended?"

"What your family perpetrates is far greater than the acts of the common SS man, no matter how vile he was. Because you have the ability to transfer it to others and inspire them to spread your hatred."

"Was my grandson transferring evil when you murdered him? He was an innocent victim—a father, a husband—just like those you claim to seek justice for."

His tone remained cold and unyielding. "Once I learned of his heritage, there was no other option. He wouldn't have been able to help himself … it was his nature."

Ellen didn't have time to advance the 'nature versus nurture' debate. It had been going on long before they arrived on this planet and would rage on long past their deaths. Besides, her plan wasn't to dissuade the Nazi hunter from his beliefs—there was little chance of that—what she wanted was his assistance.

She pointed to the drawer of the end-table. He was now under her spell, and followed her instruction. But when he slid out a piece of paper from the drawer he looked disappointed. This object was not gold, nor did it have historical significance. It was an invitation to witness her great-granddaughter present her Heritage Paper to her sixth grade class.

"If you want to protect your family, as you claim, why would you provide me such access to them?"

The irony caused the smile to finally appear on her face. "Because if you're going to stop the Reich from returning to power, you will need Maggie's help."

"You will use any lie or tactic to save yourself. How else can you explain hiding out all these years under the cover of being a persecuted Jew? As if the actions of you and your fellow Nazis were not depraved enough!"

"I've lived many lies throughout my life, many of which I'm ashamed of. But I never lied about being Jewish."

"More lies! Your deception can't save you anymore!"

"My mother's name was Etta Sarowitz—a *Jewish* prostitute from Munich. Perhaps your doctor friend failed to mention that part in his story. History tends to pick and choose the truth, depending on whether it fits the narrative of the author. Without a father around, I took her surname of Sarowitz—the name I used upon coming to America, and until I married. While many of my fellow Apostles took aliases to survive, Ellen Sarowitz was my given name."

It was a good thing the Nazi hunter was sitting, or he might have fallen and broken a hip. He searched her face for a lie, but the deep lines told an ugly story that couldn't be hidden. She spoke the truth, and he knew it

"But if you're Jewish ..."

"Then it's the great ruse of history."

As the Nazi hunter tried to wrap his mind around the bomb she just dropped, Ellen bit down on the glass vial she'd hidden behind her dentures.

The room turned hazy and began to spin. She never used drugs, so she finally was getting to experience the '60s, a time her children were so enamored with.

The Nazi hunter called out, "No!" But his voice seemed miles away. He was too late.

A beautiful painting filled the canvas of Ellen's mind. She was back on her first date with her husband, Harold Peterson—he'd taken her to Central Park for a picnic lunch. It was late October and a stiff wind was blowing the fall foliage off the trees. The leaves looked like a rainbow as they floated to earth.

She focused on one large oak tree with a stout trunk. The vision was so clear that she felt she could reach out and touch it. But slowly the picture turned blurry, as if she was looking at it through the steamed glass of a shower door.

She said her final prayers, but they weren't for herself—she knew her judgment would be harsh. She asked for compassion for Josef and Harry Jr.—her innocent children who were given burdens they couldn't handle—along with her grandson, Carsten. All taken too soon.

But most of all, she asked to give Maggie and Jamie the strength they'd need to end the cycle, and for the Nazi hunter to guide them with his experienced eyes.

Her mind flashed back to the tree in the park. The stiff wind picked up, continuing to blow the leaves off the branches until they were almost bare. She watched them float downward in slow motion, and when the last leaf hit the ground, everything went dark.

CHAPTER 2

"Maggie, c'mon, you're going to be late," Veronica Peterson shouted up the stairwell to her twelve-year-old daughter. She waited a moment, still no reply.

But there was no time to dwell on it. She swooped into the kitchen and caught nine-year-old Jamie about to douse his sister's cereal with jalapeño sauce. She grabbed the jar out of his stunned hands on her way to the toaster.

"Haven't you poisoned enough food this week?" she asked, while hastily buttering a piece of toast.

Jamie smiled his "can't be mad at me" smile. Her husband used to say it was like Mariano Rivera's cut-fastball—you knew it was coming, but it would still get you every time. She wasn't a big baseball fan, but understood the power of Jamie's smile. And it worried her.

"I'm sorry, Mom. I thought it was sugar. You know how Maggie likes sugar on her cereal … and with her project this morning …"

Yeah right.

The Maggie reference served as a reminder to check on her again. While Jamie was impossible to remain mad at, Maggie was quite the opposite. Veronica was convinced that she thrived on it—acceptance was the enemy.

Maggie had worked so hard on her Heritage Paper, trekking over to her Oma's place a couple times a week to interview her about the family history, or at least Ellen's version of it. Veronica was so proud of her effort, and thought she was finally starting to integrate into her new school, but on the day of the presentation she wouldn't even get out of bed. She was such a mystery.

"Maggie—I'm not kidding," Veronica yelled again up the stairs. "It would be a shame for you to put all this work in and then not show up."

No response.

All she could hear was Jamie crunching his cereal.

"What did I tell you about closing your mouth when you eat?" she asked on another walk by.

"I'm sorry, Mom."

Yeah right.

She hurried up the stairs to Maggie's room. She stared at the unfamiliar door, plotting her next move. The house was a lot different from their apartment in the city. It wasn't that Veronica disliked it; it's just what it represented.

She wanted to knock down the door like in one of those TV cop shows, but with her luck she figured she'd end up breaking her foot. And on top of that, Maggie never responded to threats. She perpetuated a stubbornness that always made Veronica's mother make snide comments about acorns falling near trees. There were rumors about Veronica having a similar stubborn streak during her youth.

She lightly knocked, then waited … nothing.

Maggie was likely playing her music too loudly through her headphones, in defiance of Veronica's warnings about deafness.

Passion for music was another handed-down trait, although their tastes differed greatly. Maggie had recently converted from bubblegum pop to a mishmash of loud and angry, which corresponded with her latest personality twist. Veronica preferred the classics—if 1980s "glam metal" was considered to be classic.

Suddenly the hairs on the back of her neck stood up. Something was wrong. She twisted the door handle—surprised to find it unlocked—and burst into the room.

Maggie was nowhere in sight.

Veronica performed a quick reconnaissance, her focus settling on an art easel in the center of the room. Maggie was a talented artist—better than Veronica ever was, even though she was no slouch with the brush. It seemed like a different lifetime when Veronica was the fresh-faced art history major at NYU, back before Carsten Peterson swallowed up her life. But now Carsten was dead, and she needed to find the old Veronica.

She checked Maggie's latest masterpiece, which was as angry as her taste in music. A mother cradling a bloodied child as bombs burst around them. *Was it concerning the loss of her father, the looming war, or maybe both?*

Veronica snapped back to reality. She couldn't believe with her daughter "missing," she'd slipped into a momentary daze. As a single mother she had to think for the three of them, but sometimes wondered if she could even care for herself.

She noticed the cracked window—the same one she caught Maggie sneaking out once before, by shimmying down the gutter. She ran to it and felt immediate relief when she spotted her daughter. But what was she doing? Maggie, wearing her typical ponytail and *Kingston for President* T-shirt, was digging a hole in the backyard with a rusted shovel.

"What the …"

Veronica bounded down the stairs and through the kitchen. "Jamie, leave the cat alone."

"Mom, I was just …"

Yeah right.

Veronica put on her down coat and stepped out into the chilly November air. She then headed toward the likely confrontation that would spoil the morning. "Maggie, what are you doing?"

"I'm almost done," she said, without looking up.

"What did I tell you about burying bodies in the backyard?" she asked, forcing a disarming smile.

"Jamie's class will be so excited that he's bringing his comedian mother for Career Day."

The twenty hours of labor, the late night feedings, the trips to the emergency room for the asthma attacks … *for this?*

"Now that I've humored you, maybe you can tell me why you're digging up the backyard?"

Maggie let out an angst-filled sigh. "It's part of the Heritage Paper project. We have to bury a time-capsule that can't be dug up for thirty years. Oma and I put it together."

"My Bon Jovi shirt isn't in there, is it?" Veronica asked. She checked her watch—they were getting late.

"That shirt is a dark family secret that should remain buried."

Veronica tried to keep a straight face, but couldn't hold it. Neither could Maggie, who began to laugh at her own wittiness. It was one of those rare moments that made all the negotiations and mental gymnastics worth it. There hadn't been a lot of laughs since Carsten died, but then again, there wasn't a whole lot of sunshine at the end of his life either.

Veronica took off her coat and draped it over Maggie's shoulders. "Your brother and I will be inside eating breakfast when you finish."

"Thanks, Mom."

A cease-fire. Things were looking up for Veronica, but she knew with two kids it could start going the other way at any moment.

CHAPTER 3

Veronica returned inside, again catching Jamie in the act. "What did you do to your sister's cereal?"

"Nothing—why would I do such a thing to Maggie? She's my role model."

"Then you eat it."

Jamie squirmed.

"Go ahead—as a reward for being such a good little boy."

"Thank you for the offer, Mom, but I'm not that hungry."

"I didn't think so," she said and tossed the contaminated cereal into the sink and rinsed the bowl.

She tried not to look at him, but how could she help it? He looked cute-as-a-button adorable in his mini police uniform, his normally floppy hair slicked to the side. He had inherited her blond, blue-eyed features. Carsten had the dark, Slavic look of his Jewish grandmother, which he passed on to Maggie. Veronica hoped he hadn't passed on the cheating to either of them.

A loud knock rapped on the front door. Before she could respond, Eddie Peterson rushed into the house. This was the way Eddie always entered, which Veronica didn't mind because Eddie was family, and since Carsten died, he had graduated to "godsend."

Today was no different. He was filling in for Career Day. She still couldn't believe the school scheduled Career Day (3rd grade) and Heritage Paper (6th grade) on the same day. Veronica complained about it to Principal Sweetney, but all she got in return was a lecture that focused on the many angry phone calls she'd received after Jamie pulled his latest stunt.

Jamie ran to give his uncle a hug. Eddie was Carsten's half brother, and both were raised by their grandmother, Ellen, after their mother died.

Eddie featured a bald shave on top—he claimed it was his preferred style and he could grow it back whenever he wanted, but Veronica doubted it—and a gut that was synonymous with his retro "bringing back the doughnuts" approach to law enforcement. He was NYPD, normally undercover in plain clothes, but for Career Day he was decked out in the full uniform.

He kissed Veronica on the cheek and scraped her with his stubble. "I like your shirt," he said, referring to her fraying concert shirt that had survived since her teenage years. Back when her life goal was to follow the band across the country. She still wasn't sure when exactly she became a thirty-seven-year-old paranoid mother.

"Thanks—I didn't know you were a Def Leppard fan."

"I'm not. I like the way it hugs your boobs," he said with a laugh.

Jamie joined the laughter, which received a glare from Veronica, instantly quieting him.

"It's surprising that a charmer like yourself has never been married," Veronica said as she made a return trip to the kitchen.

Eddie followed her, making a pit-stop at the refrigerator and removed a slice of last night's dinner.

"Isn't it a little early for pizza?" she asked as she poured a round of orange juice.

"I just finished my shift. My hours are a little off."

"*You're* a little off."

Jamie laughed, which reminded her. She subtly nudged Eddie to have the talk she'd wanted him to have with her son. She did her best, but sometimes a boy needed a strong male figure to deliver the news. The topic was the reason she had to meet with his principal this morning.

Jamie could always sense a potential ambush, and was already plotting his retreat. "Can I go see the police car, Uncle Eddie?"

"Not until you tell me what happened in school."

Jamie shrugged. "It was just a misunderstanding."

"I don't know who you think you're messing with, kid. I get gang members to flip on drug kingpins, so I ain't afraid of no suburban mama's boy."

Jamie smiled like it was a game. Before Veronica had kids she was convinced it was all about "nurture"—children were a blank canvas to be molded. But the more Maggie and Jamie had begun to resemble her and Carsten, specifically the traits that she'd gone out of her way to shield them from, she was starting to re-think it.

"Since you seem to have a bad case of amnesia," Eddie continued with the interrogation, "let me review the facts of the case. You, Jamie Peterson, nephew of esteemed NYPD Lieutenant Edward Peterson, assaulted your classmate, Fife Logan, by putting ex-lax in his food and making him crap all over himself in front of the class."

Jamie looked astonished by the accusation. He stood with palms up and an open-mouthed look of disbelief.

"What do you have to say for yourself, young man?"

"I say it was your idea, Uncle Eddie, so I don't know why I'm the one who's getting in trouble."

Eddie was immediately hit with Veronica's glare, and he tried to plead his case, "C'mon—I didn't think the kid would really do it. And besides, this Fife Logan character was picking on him, and if you don't stand up to a bully, you'll end up getting bullied for the rest of your life."

She wasn't impressed.

"And what kind of name is Fife Logan? His parents must have known he'd get his ass kicked when they gave him that name."

"If you wanna keep digging yourself a deeper hole, I know where to get a shovel."

Eddie owned the same ability to veer from oncoming trouble as Jamie did, and turned the tables. "So I heard someone had a hot date last night."

She squirmed. "I don't know what you're talking about."

"Do I need to give you the kingpin lecture?"

"Jamie, why don't you go help your sister," she instructed.

He didn't budge.

"Jamie, if you want to go to Career Day I suggest you go help your sister," her voice raised.

"Your wish is my command, Mom."

Yeah right.

When Jamie left, Veronica hesitantly asked, "Do you have a problem with it?"

Eddie shook his head. "My brother has been dead over a year. I think it's time to start boinking again."

"Have I mentioned I'm surprised a woman hasn't locked you up?"

"But that doesn't mean I don't get to be the overprotective brother-in-law. So where'd you meet this guy?"

"It's bad enough I live next door to my mother. I really don't need this."

"You know I've gotten drug kingpins to …"

"Fine—I met him at one of my classes at Pace."

"Class? Like a student—how old is he?" Eddie asked, smirking.

"Age is all relative."

"That means he must be *real* young. Let's put it this way, could he legally drink or did you have to order him a Shirley Temple?"

"He's twenty three … are you happy?"

Eddie began choking on his pizza. Veronica was pretty sure he did it for effect, but if he really needed a Heimlich he wasn't getting it from her. He miraculously survived long enough to say, "Maggie's mom has got it going on. You could be his mother!"

"If I had him when I was fourteen. Are you finished?"

"I work in the South Bronx. By fourteen, most chicks already have two kids in prison. So where did you and Sparky go on your date?"

Veronica didn't waste her breath with another in a long line of PC-scoldings; he was a lost cause. "It was just a date. There was a film festival at the Jacob Burns Center and then we had dinner at that Japanese place, Hanada. No boinking."

"Very disappointing," Eddie said, seemingly losing interest. "So where's Maggie?"

"She's out in the backyard burying a time-capsule for her Heritage Paper that she put together with Ellen."

Eddie jumped off his seat. "This I gotta see."

CHAPTER 4

Veronica watched as Eddie came up behind Maggie, and shouted, "Freeze, Maggot—you're under arrest for being late to school!"

Maggie turned, and a big smile came over her face. She tossed the final shovelful of dirt onto her time-capsule and ran to Eddie. The kids were always so affectionate with him. Maybe because in so many ways he was still a child himself. She even let him call her Maggot—nobody else got away with that.

"Did you see the pictures I sent you?" Eddie asked.

"Yeah—they were great. Blood spattered everywhere!"

Veronica cringed, not liking where this was going.

Maggie pulled out her phone—the one Ellen bought for her last Christmas, despite Veronica's insistence that she was too young—and they studied the images that Eddie had sent her. He turned to Veronica. "Couple of dead drug dealers we found in a loft apartment last night."

Most parents worried about their kids text messaging too much with their friends—her kids got dead bodies. No wonder she was constantly meeting with their principal. "You sent my children pictures of dead people?"

"Not people—drug dealers. Best anti-drug commercial going. You should thank me."

Eddie's focus changed back to the time-capsule, and he began peppering Maggie with questions about it.

She swelled with pride as she went on a tangent about the contents. Eddie tried to get a sneak peak, but Maggie warned him that it couldn't be opened for thirty years. This made him all the more eager to see inside, but Maggie didn't relent. She did give him a rundown of the contents—family photos, copy of the Heritage Paper, family tree, and a memoir of Ellen's life that they wrote together, expanding beyond the scope of the Heritage Paper. A record of her life that according to Maggie, Ellen hoped to pass down to future generations of the Peterson family.

Eddie began laughing. "Memoir? Only Oma could be narcissistic enough to think that anyone would want to read the story of her life. Who wants to read about some whiny housewife from New York?"

"She had a very interesting life," Maggie contended. "I think you'd be surprised."

It was almost two different lives, Veronica thought. As a young girl, Ellen had survived a concentration camp in Nazi Germany. Then when the war ended, she came to America, where she married a policeman named Harold Peterson. They had one child named Harry Jr., but when he and his wife died tragically, Ellen took in her grandchildren, Carsten and Eddie, and raised them. Maybe it wasn't worthy of a movie, but she would have to agree with Maggie, it was in interesting life.

But the Ellen that Veronica had known since she began dating Carsten was more along the lines of Eddie's description. She was a curmudgeonly woman, who was constantly complaining, and morbidly pessimistic. The only time she seemed happy was when she was around Eddie and Carsten. And in turn, they would do anything for her. Veronica suspected her downward cycle this past year was connected to Carsten's death, even if the doctors were convinced it was part of her natural decline.

"I'm giving a presentation on her life today, but everyone seems to be too busy to attend. So I guess you'll never get to find out," Maggie said.

The words might have been directed at Eddie, but Veronica knew the attitude was meant for her. "Mags, I'm going to try to make it. As soon as I get done with Jamie's principal," she said.

"Whatever."

CHAPTER 5

The final battle of the morning would be to get Maggie to change her outfit. Politically based shirts were banned in school, and one trip to the principal's office a week was Veronica's limit. After a brief but spirited fight, Maggie relented, and returned in a simple head-to-toe black ensemble of sweater and jeans, perhaps mourning life in general.

Veronica threw a professional suit jacket over her concert shirt that she wore with stylish jeans and heeled boots. She had maintained enough Manhattan style to pull it off, but she still hadn't got used to her new, short, blonde-bob hairstyle—a sharp departure from shoulder length style she'd worn since college. She figured if Jon Bon Jovi could cut off his hair, then so could Veronica Peterson.

But that change didn't compare to moving back to Pleasantville. And while it was culture shock for everyone, Veronica was convinced that she'd made the right decision. It gave the kids a bigger yard to play in and the schools were quality. And of course, finances played a big role. Like a lot of thirty-something couples, she and Carsten hadn't prepared for death. Carsten made good money as an executive at Sterling Publishing, but it was 'own a Saab and take an exotic vacation once a year' money, not 'manage a hedge fund and own a villa in Italy' type. So she quickly found out that raising two kids on the Upper East Side of Manhattan without a steady income caused their savings to hemorrhage.

And if those weren't reasons enough, there was no shortage of built-in babysitting. Which reminded Veronica—her Uncle Phil had been feverishly campaigning to fill-in for Career Day, but Jamie ruled his pharmaceutical sales career as "too boring." So they needed to get out of here before he realized that he'd been bumped by Eddie.

Veronica rounded up Maggie and Jamie, and headed off for school in their oversized Chevy Tahoe. Eddie had loose ends to tie-up concerning his dead drug dealer, and would meet Jamie at school. Mr. Charisma campaigned to ride in the "cool cop car," but was turned down. While Eddie was the infantile jokester around Veronica and the kids, he was obsessively professional when it came to his police work. It was always interesting for Veronica to see that side of him.

She drove through their secluded neighborhood, known as Usonia. It was named for the modernist, open-style homes made famous by Frank Lloyd Wright—typically small, single story dwellings made of environmentally sustainable materials. They were green before it became trendy.

Veronica's family had bought up many of the hillside homes off Bear Ridge Road back when they were built in 1948. This included the L-shaped Usonian that Veronica and the children now lived in, which was wrapped around a garden terrace at the rear of her mother's house. Uncle Phil and Aunt Val lived two houses down from them.

They maneuvered through winding hills until they arrived at the busy Bedford Drive, which was the "main drag" in town. Veronica flipped on her play-list of 1980s power ballads.

Maggie was not a fan—probably not angry enough. "Mom, can we put the news on about tomorrow's election?"

Maggie had carried on her father's passion for politics, and sounded eerily like him when she debated complex topics that should be beyond kids her age.

The election was contentious, to say the least. And at the heart of it was a potential conflict brewing in the Middle East. If war broke out, many experts predicted that it would last for over a decade, which caused Veronica to have horrible nightmares about her children coming in contact with roadside bombs ten years from now. So she was voting for Theodore Baer, who opposed US involvement.

Maggie had a different idea, and it had a lot to do with one of her strongest ideals. It always came down to loyalty with her.

"Israel is our friend, and you and Dad always told me it's right to stand up for our friends. Dad wouldn't vote for Theodore Baer if he was here."

That was a low blow. "Well, he's not," Veronica responded tersely.

Jamie decided to chime in, "If I was in a war I'd shoot everybody!" He then performed a machine-gun sound as he sprayed bullets around the backseat from his imaginary gun.

God help us all, Veronica thought with a shake of her head.

"If you have any thoughts of riding in Uncle Eddie's police car, then you'll be quiet. I'll call him right now," Veronica threatened. She picked up her phone and pretended to dial.

Jamie quieted, but Maggie moved on to her next point of angst. "I can't believe you're blowing off my presentation. Oma and I worked really hard on it."

"Do you really think I'd rather meet Jamie's principal than see your presentation?"

"If it was the other way around, I'm sure you'd reschedule it."

"I had no choice. Your brother can't participate in Career Day until I meet to discuss his punishment. So you can thank your brother and Mrs. Sweetney."

"Whatever."

Veronica knew appeasing Maggie's surly attitude would set a bad precedent, but despite their many quarrels, she had a soft spot for her first-born. The fact that she brought up Carsten after not uttering his name in months, meant she was feeling very wounded. And Veronica wanted to reward her for the job she did on this project. Maggie would take the train to Chappaqua after school, a couple times a week to meet up with Ellen. They'd work until Veronica would pick her up after her night class at Pace, and she'd often have to drag Maggie home.

So she turned on the election news. The big story was centered on controversial comments made by Theodore Baer yesterday. With only one day to go, Baer was dropping like a rock in the polls. Seemed like Maggie might get her wish.

They pulled up to Underhill School, which was separated into two campuses—K-4 and the 5-8 middle school. The first drop-off was Maggie.

"I'll try to make it back in time for your presentation, sweetie."

"Whatever."

Door slammed.

Maggie burst out of the car like it was on fire. She went straight for her one friend, fellow outcast TJ Chester.

As Veronica watched Maggie, a knock on her window startled her. It was TJ's father, Zach. She rolled down the window and he handed her a Styrofoam cup of coffee.

"If you were up half the night finishing the Heritage Paper like us, then you'll need this," he said and flashed his perfect smile. His eyes matched his dark suit.

"Maggie wouldn't let me near her project, which might have been a good thing," she responded. "And thanks again for all the assistance TJ gave her with the video."

He laughed. "Yeah, he spent more time on Maggie's than his own—I think he has a crush on her. That's why we were up half the night cutting and pasting the Chester family low-lights."

Veronica glanced at Maggie in the distance, who sent back a disapproving look. She wasn't sure if it was connected to her conspiring with her friend's father, or because she might miss her presentation, or perhaps it was that she was twelve and her mother was her natural enemy. Probably a combination of the three.

"I'm sure TJ did a great job, he's a smart boy."

"We just left out the part about his mother being in jail. Sometimes I think family secrets are best left a secret for a reason."

Veronica had heard the small town gossip about the good-looking journalist who moved to town without his imprisoned wife. But she never asked him about it. What was she supposed to say—*I'll pick up TJ and Maggie, and by the way, why is your wife in the joint?* She knew the etiquette when it came to divorce or death … but jail?

"Are you coming?" Zach asked between sips of coffee.

"No, first I have to meet the principal over at the K-4."

"The ex-lax thing?"

"Was it broadcast on the news?"

"Small town—everybody knows what color underwear everyone is wearing. I better go before they start gossiping about us," he said with a smile and moved toward the school.

She watched as he headed off into a sea of pre-teens. "Thanks for the coffee," she shouted, but he didn't hear her.

One down, one to go. Veronica drove around the building to the K-4 area. She waved at Teri Burkhardt and her perfect daughter Haley, who didn't poison other students. Jamie tried to make a run for it, to join Haley and the rest of his friends.

Veronica clicked the locks shut. "Don't even think about it. You're coming with me to meet with Mrs. Sweetney."

"I don't know why you're calling her that, since she's not more sweet than you, Mom."

Yeah right.

CHAPTER 6

Veronica walked into the principal's office like she was the one in trouble. The perpetrator stood beside her, still looking adorable in his police uniform.

Helen, Principal Sweetney's longtime secretary, ushered them into her office. Veronica hadn't seen the stone-faced woman smile in years, yet Jamie was able to bring one to her face.

"She'll be with you in a few minutes," Helen informed them.

A "few minutes" turned into fifteen, and then twenty. Veronica kept looking at her watch, knowing every minute that went by meant she was closer to missing Maggie's presentation, and heading for a week of dirty looks and "whatevers."

Ten more minutes crawled by before a boxy blonde woman strutted in, wearing a purple blouse and gray slacks. As usual, she overdid the perfume, attempting to cover up the smell of cigarettes. She looked like Veronica, except lately she'd begun to look like two of her. This scared Veronica, since people had always commented on how much they resembled each other. It brought her back to the whole nature (slow metabolism) or nurture (binge eating since the divorce) debate.

"Sorry I'm late, I've been trying to clean up your mess. I guess the more things change the more things stay the same," she greeted them without so much as a hello.

Veronica wanted to "go-Maggie" on her with a heavy sigh and a roll of the eyes, but instead she just said, "Hello to you too, Mom."

"Aren't you going to say hello to me, Grammy?" Jamie perked up.

"First of all, in this room I am Principal Sweetney. And secondly, I have a lot to say to you, young man, but none of it is in the form of a pleasant salutation."

Jamie tried his killer smile. The one he saved for times when he'd dug himself an especially deep hole. "I love how you know all the big words, Principal Sweetney."

"That won't work on me."

He looked confused, rarely having to go to a backup plan.

Veronica took the comment as: *like it works with your mother, who by the way, can't match up to me.*

"I just spent the last hour with the parents of the child you assaulted," she went on, holding a stern gaze on Jamie.

"Don't you think 'assaulted' is a little strong," Veronica responded like an over-matched public defender, and was quickly dismissed. She felt like she was sixteen again. But on second thought, the sixteen-year-old Veronica wouldn't have cowered like the Veronica of today.

Her mother lit a cigarette—prohibited on school grounds—moved to the cracked window and exhaled the smoke outside.

"The good news is that I was able to convince the injured parties not to sue the school. But the not-so-good-news for you, Jamie, is I promised that the school—and by school, I mean me—would take swift steps to punish the defendant. This will serve as the first step in ensuring that no further diabolical acts occur on school grounds."

"Diabolical? It was a prank for goodness sake," Veronica fought back. The fights during her teenage years were legendary, usually about choices in

men, music and college majors. *Art history is slang for no money,* her
mother would always say. It was impossible to win an argument with her—
Veronica's father finally gave up trying about five years ago. They got
divorced, and he now lived with his girlfriend in Charleston.

"Let me define diabolical," her mother responded calmly. "A
premeditated act in which a student smuggled in a substance that he used to
poison and embarrass another student. An act for which he still has shown
no remorse."

As much as Veronica hated to give an inch in these battles, she knew
her mother was right. If Jamie continued to charm his way out of these
incidents, what might they lead to?

Still facing the window, Principal Sweetney asked between drags, "So
what do you have to say for yourself, young man?"

Veronica could tell that Jamie was not ready to surrender. "I think
smoking is bad for you, Grammy, but you do it even though you know it's
wrong. Sometimes people do stuff they know is wrong because they just
can't help it."

That was about as close as Jamie would get to throwing himself at the
mercy of the court. He glimmered a smile.

Helen's voice came over the intercom, sounding flustered—phone calls
and messages were starting to pile up. Having Heritage and Career Day on
the same morning made no sense, but Veronica kept quiet—even sixteen-
year-old-Veronica would've realized she didn't have much leverage at this
point.

The judge informed Helen that she needed a minute, and then rendered
her decision, "You will be suspended until after Thanksgiving break. We
will meet again at that point to determine if you have realized your mistakes,
and have acquired the proper remorse. Any time missed from school will be
made up during the summer."

Jamie looked sheepishly happy. Visions of jumping into leaf piles and Xbox marathons likely dancing in his head. Not to mention all the gadgets Veronica bought him out of guilt after Carsten died.

But the judge wiped the smile off his face. "I've arranged for you to spend your suspension with your Uncle Phil and Aunt Valerie. They have *a lot* of chores lined up for you."

Jamie looked perplexed. "But they're no fun."

She pointed at him. "Exactly."

Jamie turned accepting—he was retreating. But Veronica knew his mind was already plotting a way out.

"Now get to Career Day before I change my mind and add another week to your punishment," Principal Sweetney belted out like a drill sergeant.

Jamie began to stroll toward the door, his shoulders slumped like somebody just stole his lunch box.

"And one other thing," she barked, just as he reached the door.

He turned, looking hopeful.

"The police are supposed to help people. Not hurt them ... or poison them."

He played with the toy badge pinned to his chest as he digested the words, and then exited through the door, head down.

Veronica grabbed her purse and stood.

Her mother pointed her back down, "You and I aren't done yet."

"Can't we do this later? I'm late for Maggie's presentation."

"Sometimes our children are better without us mothers hovering over them. And besides, we've put this off too long. I'm worried about them."

"They're kids—and they've had a tough year. Losing their father ... a new house ... a new school. I think they're just blowing off some frustration."

"It's more than that."

"I guess you know my kids better than me."

"I know you think I didn't like Carsten."

"Carsten?" Veronica was caught off guard. "It doesn't matter anymore. Where are you going with this?"

"It does matter. And you were right—I didn't like him. I should have been thrilled that my daughter found this seemingly perfect guy who was so smart and charming. And anybody with half a brain could see he was totally in love with you."

"But you never acted that way."

"When I met him I was unaware of his family situation, so that had nothing to do with my apprehension."

"Let's stop beating around the bush—his mother killed his abusive father. That's a little more than a *situation*. What does this have to do with anything?"

"There was something in his eyes that I could never shake. Behind his charismatic smile was this look that said he was capable of doing very bad things."

Veronica shut her eyes. She visualized the look in those eyes that night in the kitchen when everything changed for them.

"Honey, I've seen that same look in Jamie's eyes, and I think it's important to stop it right now before it's too late."

CHAPTER 7

Zach Chester was still smiling from his brief encounter with Veronica Peterson. They had gotten to know each other through their kids—TJ and Maggie had no other friends, so their parenting paths had crossed on numerous occasions—and she never failed to make him smile. The part he couldn't understand was why he felt guilty about it. Sara was the one who did the cheating. And sadly, that was the least of their problems.

It all started when Zach got his dream job at *Newsbreaker Magazine* and they moved to New York. All was right with the world; at least until Sara began acting erratically and forgetting to pick up TJ at school. There were times when she seemed like a completely different person, but he wrote it off as the stress of trying to adjust to a new life in a new city. But she sure didn't appear to be stressed-out on the surveillance tapes—the ones taken by the cameras they'd installed in their brownstone for security purposes, including their bedroom, where she seemed to be doing a good job of making new friends. The thing that struck him was how brazen she was. She knew the cameras were there—it was like she didn't care.

Zach moved out, so he wasn't present weeks later when Sara was arrested for running a crystal-meth ring out of their basement. And she was so hooked on the stuff she no longer recognized their son. The news helped explain her dramatic behavioral shift, but it sure wasn't easy to explain to

TJ. And being a supposed award-winning journalist, he couldn't believe that he never picked up on the signs. It still haunted him.

He remained married, but no longer had a wife. And for all intents and purposes, he was now a single parent. He'd moved to Pleasantville so TJ could be close to the Bedford Hills Women's Prison where his mother now resided. He was forced to leave his job at *Newsbreaker,* and now wrote for the *Hudson Valley Times*, a small local paper.

The students and assorted relatives were led into a classroom. Desks were set up in a semi-circle, facing a podium where the Heritage Paper presentations would be made.

Many of the children had brought a grandparent to accompany them with their presentation, so the room had the feel of Bingo Night at the local senior center. Zach was fairly new to town, so he didn't recognize many, but two of them he did, and was surprised by their presence.

He knew the elderly men from a story he did for *Newsbreaker* on the sixty-year anniversary of the end of the Holocaust. Aligor Sterling, head of the Sterling Center, was the most recognizable because of his political activism, including being presidential candidate Jim Kingston's biggest contributor.

Ben Youkelstein wasn't a household name like Sterling, but he was well known in the underground world of Nazi hunting. The two of them had relentlessly tracked Nazi war criminals across the globe the last half-century, attempting to bring justice to an unjustifiable event. Zach wasn't sure why they were here, but his best guess was that they had grandchildren in Pleasantville. He figured that some kid was going to have an interesting presentation.

After welcoming everyone, their teacher Mrs. Foss explained why they were packed like sardines into a sixth grade classroom. The mission of the Heritage Paper was to trace one branch of the family tree, using a living relative as the chief source, to see it through their eyes, and then present it together. Mrs. Foss had the kids pick an order out of a hat. TJ would be second to last, which meant Zach would have to stick around for the whole thing.

The first two presentations went by fairly quickly, as the nervous students talked a mile a minute. They were bland and generic, which made him feel better about TJ's presentation, which would be purposely vague.

Maggie Peterson was now up. Zach checked for Veronica, but it didn't look like she would make it. Instead of a relative, Maggie brought a television on a cart. Mrs. Foss announced that Maggie's great-grandmother, Ellen Peterson, was too frail to attend, so they had made a video. Zach remembered TJ helping out with the recording, or something along those lines.

Maggie read off index cards, explaining that her great-grandmother had come to America following World War II and lived in New York until she moved to Sunshine Village in Chappaqua, a couple of years back. And without further ado, Ellen Peterson appeared on the screen. She eerily reminded Zach of the old lady in the *Titanic* movie.

"My name is Ellen Peterson, but my maiden name was Ellen Sarowitz. I was born in Munich, Germany in 1918. Before I get into the events of my life, I have a confession to make. This project is about family and heritage, and I have not been truthful about my past with my own family."

This got Zach's attention. A little scandal might not be a bad thing, he thought, perhaps livening up the tedious school project. He looked at TJ, searching for a hint of inside information. TJ just shrugged. Zach wasn't sure what it meant, mainly because TJ responded to most things these days with a shrug.

Ellen continued, "I came to America as part of the underground railroad that helped deliver persecuted European Jews to the safety of the West. But I came under the false pretenses of being a survivor of the Terezin concentration camp."

Zach noticed a tear on Ellen's overly blushed cheek. He glanced again at Youkelstein and Sterling; now wondering if their presence might be connected to this confession.

"My mother, Etta, had been a prostitute, so my formative years were surrounded by drug abuse and my mother's loose morals. Strange men would gravitate to our apartment and would often beat and rape my mother. They would also try the same on me, so I had to learn how to defend myself at a young age."

Mrs. Foss looked shell-shocked—rape, drugs, and prostitution probably wasn't what she had in mind when she concocted this project. *That's what you get for opening up the scary can of worms called family,* Zach mused.

"I came to think of our ghetto as hell on earth, and the Jews who lived there were the devil's children, even if I carried the same blood as them. When I was around Maggie's age, my mother began to show the symptoms of a deadly form of syphilis. At the end, she couldn't get out of bed and I became her caretaker.

"It was the fall of 1932 when a young man running for German Chancellor came through our neighborhood on the campaign trail. He stopped by our home to see my sick mother to help promote his plan for national health insurance, building on the system that began with Prince Otto von Bismarck, after Germany united in the nineteenth century. The candidate was so taken by our plight that he openly wept and promised my mother he'd care for me when she died. And unlike most political candidates, he lived up to his campaign promise.

"That man's name was Adolf Hitler."

CHAPTER 8

Veronica watched them march one by one into the principal's office and be seated like a jury. The last person to enter was Maggie—the defendant. Her face was rigid, ready to fight authority. She had rebelliously removed her sweater, displaying her against-the-rules political T-shirt supporting Jim Kingston.

Maggie's teacher had a look on her face like she signed up to teach sixth-grade social studies only to find herself tricked into a ponzi scheme.

There were also two older men in the line-up. One that Veronica had never seen before, while the other she was well aware of.

The mystery man was rail-thin with a wispy mustache, and a few snowflakes of white hair on top of his head. He reminded her of the Obi-Wan Kenobi character from the original *Star Wars* movie, sans the beard and goofy robe, and had traded his light saber for an umbrella. Veronica found this odd considering that no rain was anticipated, although, a few unexpected thundershowers had already interrupted her morning. The umbrella matched his dapper black suit, which reminded Veronica of her father's look when he used to work at Reader's Digest, back when it was headquartered in Pleasantville.

The man she knew was named Aligor Sterling. He was Carsten's boss when he worked at Sterling Publishing. In fact, he was everybody's boss—

he was the founder, owner, and overall head honcho. She didn't know him that well—mainly from the annual summer party where they'd meander around Manhattan on his luxury yacht—but Carsten practically worshiped him. She did however feel indebted to him for his help the week following Carsten's death. He didn't just write a check for the funeral, he put in the time, providing her with much-needed comfort. And he was under no obligation, since Sterling Publishing had no liability in his death. Carsten had died of a stroke.

Aligor waved to her from his wheelchair. Despite being north of ninety, he still had a full head of hair that he dyed black, and wore his trademark oval-rimmed glasses. But she noticed that he wasn't sporting his usual gentle smile.

There was a pleasant surprise in the room—Zach Chester and his son TJ. Zach walked directly to Veronica's side, her eyes searching him for some clues as to what this was all about. When she found none, she asked.

"You wouldn't believe it if I told you," he whispered back.

Not very reassuring. "What does it have to do with Carsten?"

Zach looked puzzled. "Carsten?"

"My former husband. He worked for Sterling Publishing. I thought that's why Aligor Sterling is here."

"No, I believe he's here because Ellen invited him."

"Why would she do that?"

"Because he's a well-known Nazi hunter."

Veronica's face scrunched with confusion. She had no idea what that was. "I'm not sure I understand—I thought Aligor Sterling ran Sterling Publishing."

"While Sterling is best known for his political activism and his publishing empire, after the war he started an organization with intent to bring justice for the Holocaust survivors. His partner was named Ben Youkelstein—the guy standing beside him. For decades, they tracked down war criminals that had escaped after the war. But rumor has it that they had a nasty breakup this past year."

"They look more like a couple of guys who wandered away from Sunshine Village."

"Don't be fooled by the grandfatherly facades. I did a story on them a few years ago when I worked at *Newsbreaker*. It's rumored that Sterling has Martin Bormann's skull displayed in his office."

Before Veronica could ask why anyone would keep this Martin fellow's skull on display, or how it was connected to Maggie's project, her mother entered the room like the Tasmanian Devil, speaking rapidly into a phone. Veronica hadn't heard this many apologies from her mother in her life. Someone was in big trouble, and Veronica had the feeling it was Maggie.

She abruptly ended the call and eyed the group suspiciously. Zach was her first target. "I see you've taken it upon yourself to join us, Mr. Chester. Are you planning a story for your newspaper?"

"No, ma'am. My son TJ helped Maggie on her project and I'd like to get to the bottom of this as much as you. My son is very good at using Photoshop software, which I think might have played a role in many of the altered photos displayed during the presentation."

Her mother sat down behind her desk, looking out of sorts. Veronica could tell she was craving a cigarette. Veronica didn't smoke, but a shot of bourbon would have hit the spot right now.

She pointed at Sterling and Youkelstein. "Did you two get lost on your way to a hearing-aid convention?"

Sterling cleared his throat with an attitude, as if to say he shouldn't have to introduce himself. "Ellen Peterson invited me. I will always make time for Holocaust survivors, even with the election so near, and so much to do."

Seemingly unimpressed, she turned to Obi-Wan. "And you Mr. ...."

"Youkelstein. I also received an invitation from Ellen. She mentioned in her video presentation that she believes Aligor and I can assist in stopping a group called the Apostles, who's aim is to return the Reich to power."

"And when we're done with that, we can all fly to Mars for lunch. Do either of you have a previous relationship with Ellen?" she continued, while holding a stare at Maggie. To Maggie's credit, she peered right back. "Since invitations were supposed to be given to family or close friends *only*, I'm confused by your presence."

"I've known Ellen for years. My organization helped many people like Ellen who survived concentration camps. And her grandson, Carsten, worked for me at Sterling Publishing. That is why I didn't hesitate to come when I received the invitation," Sterling answered quickly.

Youkelstein added, "I would consider myself neither family or close friend, but she indicated to me that she was a fan of my books, which I assume was the reason for my invitation. She stated that she'd reveal secrets of Nazi Germany that would astound me, and she delivered."

Principal Sweetney leaned back in her chair and sighed. "So let's review the facts. During the Heritage Paper presentation, Maggie played a video of her great-grandmother, Ellen Peterson, in which Ellen confessed to lying about being a Holocaust survivor, and went on to claim that she had been taken in as a young girl by Adolf Hitler, who raised her in a hideaway in the Bavarian Alps.

"She later partook in a group calling itself the Apostles, which included a who's who of Nazi war criminals such as Himmler, Rudolf Hess, and Heinrich Müller, the latter she claimed to have a child with named Josef. And not just any child, but one who was anointed as the 'chosen one' who would help return the Reich to past glory. This led to an orchestrated plan that has been in place since these Apostles infiltrated America after the war. Now sixty some years later, instead of confessing this story to the FBI or the Justice Department, Ellen decided it would be best to reveal this in Mrs. Foss's sixth grade class. Did I miss anything? Flying monkeys?"

Veronica should have been shocked, but she wasn't. The whole thing was more sad than anything. Ellen hadn't been in her right mind lately—the alien sighting being exhibit-A—but she had to admit this one was a doozy. Her heart broke for Maggie, who desperately wanted to believe in those around her after a tumultuous year in which her world flew off its axis. No kid should have to go through that.

She turned to Maggie, and chose the soft approach, "Maggie, honey, I understand that Oma believes the things she said, but she's gotten a little older and her mind isn't quite what it used to be."

"What she said is true," Maggie stood her ground.

Principal Sweetney growled, "Are you behind these photos, TJ?" She pointed to printed-out copies that featured a young Ellen with Adolf Hitler.

TJ looked at Maggie, as if to say *I'll back you up to the point my Xbox is taken away.*

Maggie stepped in. TJ was her friend and she'd have his back all the way to the electric chair. Veronica loved the loyalty aspect of her personality, but just not at the moment.

"TJ didn't doctor any photos," Maggie stated firmly.

"Then who did?" Principal Sweetney came right back at her. Veronica hoped Uncle Phil and Aunt Val had a second guest room. More suspensions were pending.

"They're authentic," Maggie said. "We had to go into New York City to get them from a safety deposit box at Oma's bank."

Veronica almost hit her head on the roof. Her compassion had limits. "And how did you get to the city?"

Maggie shrugged like it was no big deal. "We took the train with Oma."

Veronica was too horrified to say anything, choking on her anger. But she'd have *a lot* to say the next time she talked to Ellen ... not to mention the few choice words for Mrs. Rhodes about Sunshine Village's security.

Zach jumped in, or more specifically, he jumped down TJ's throat. "Who gave you permission to go into the city!? I hope you enjoyed your time at Sunshine Village, because you're going to be old enough to live there when your grounding is over!"

Maggie theatrically sighed. "I don't know why everyone is sweating the details. If Oma was willing to risk her whole reputation on this, then what she said was obviously important. We don't have much time."

As mad as Veronica was, she wanted to hug the desperation out of Maggie's voice.

Principal Sweetney wouldn't know a soft approach if she ran it over with her car. "Maggie! This is ludicrous. The woman is obviously off her rocker. So zip it!"

Maggie stewed, and a hostile silence filled the room.

Until Ben Youkelstein broke the stalemate. He cleared his throat and said, "I think Maggie is telling the truth."

CHAPTER 9

Veronica didn't know this Youkelstein fellow, but figured he must be courageous. He was headed for a couple weeks at Uncle Phil and Aunt Val's, yet he forged ahead.

"It's the symbol she showed," he stated. "The only time I'd come across it, was in regards to a man who was connected to the highest level of the Nazi hierarchy. And I was told the next time we saw that symbol, it would be the sign that the Reich was about to rise again."

Youkelstein looked at Sterling for help, but received none. "Mr. Youkelstein has a great imagination, and unfortunately I think my friend Ellen has joined him in his fantasy world. I believe she has deep rooted delusions caused by her traumatic incarceration at Terezin, and as her mind continues to crumble with age, they are beginning to spill out of her subconscious."

Youkelstein began pacing, using his umbrella as a cane. "She worked with Maggie on this report for almost two months. If Ellen Peterson were crazy, then she wouldn't be able to maintain the same story for such a long amount of time. And her facts were historically accurate. Such as the day she arrived in Maine, November 29, 1944, being the same day that a German U-boat surfaced in Hancock Point, Maine—two German intelligence officers made it onto US soil that day, but were captured and quickly executed. In retrospect, I don't think these men were spying, as they were charged with, but creating a diversion so that the Apostles could find safe passage into the United States."

Sterling laughed condescendingly. "What Mr. Youkelstein isn't telling you is that he wrote books in which he made the case that numerous Nazis war criminals escaped capture after the war, such as Himmler and Rudolph Hess. I think it's likely that Ellen read his book and concocted this story based on Ben's conspiracy theories. He preyed on Ellen's failing cognitive abilities to promote his agenda."

"Even if your theory was given credence, it doesn't explain the symbol," Youkelstein argued. "I never told anyone about that, much less published it."

"Knowing the lengths you'd go, I wouldn't put it past you to have planted the idea in her mind."

"I thought her mind was mush? And you didn't think that way when we were tracking down Mengele or Bormann, even though others claimed to have proof of their death. You once had the same passion to bring justice for the survivors. Did you forget what it was like at Terezin!?"

"You don't have a monopoly on the pain, Ben. These ghosts you chase are all dead now. Even if they did escape justice, they're now facing the ultimate jury," Sterling responded, pointing upward. "All that your ghost-chasing does is remove credibility from the work we've done. I continue to help the survivors and their lineage by supporting politicians like Jim Kingston, who will fight for their rights and make sure no such atrocities occur ever again. That is how the Reich will be kept down."

"I'll trade credibility for justice any day!"

"And you certainly did trade your credibility—Himmler … Hess … Müller—you never met a Nazi you didn't think was still alive! I'll bet you think Hitler is sipping on a Mai Tai in Brazil, as we speak."

"I hope you were paid handsomely when you sold your soul."

"You can continue to chase ghosts if you'd like, Ben, but I have a candidate to elect," Sterling got the last word. He performed a fancy pirouette with his chair and wheeled toward the door. This was not the gentle, self-deprecating man Veronica remembered. But then again, most people get a little cranky when they spend time around her mother.

Veronica noticed that Zach was eying Sterling as he moved toward the door. He had remained quiet throughout the showdown, but he seemed like the type who was always soaking in information like a sponge. As Sterling wheeled by him, he finally spoke, "For a man who has put in so much time and energy toward Kingston's election, and some would say his closest adviser, I find it interesting that you'd have the time to come down here this morning on the account of a *crazy old lady*."

Sterling looked back at him with a competitive glare. "Maybe you can co-author Ben's next conspiracy book and sell the movie rights to Oliver Stone," he said, and again headed toward the door.

There seemed to be too many cooks in the kitchen, so Veronica's mother let everyone know who was in charge, "Freeze! Nobody is leaving this room until I say so!"

Everyone stopped. With order temporarily restored, she answered the ringing phone on her desk. More angry parents.

Veronica moved to Zach. "Who are these people they're talking about—Himmler, Hess, Müller?"

"I thought you said you were a history major?"

"Art history. I can tell you about 19th-century neoclassicism, but I get Thomas Jefferson confused with George Jefferson."

He smiled. "Well, according to your daughter's Heritage Paper, Müller had a child with Maggie's great-grandmother. Which I think makes him Maggie's crazy Nazi step-great-grandfather."

She smiled back. "You'll have to show me some of the photos—especially the ones your son helped Maggie create with Photoshop."

Zach gave her a touché nod. "Long story short—Müller was head of the secret German police called the Gestapo. They were best known for terrorizing German citizens who were considered disloyal to Hitler. Himmler was the architect of the Holocaust. Many said he made Hitler look like a pussycat. And Hess was Hitler's Deputy Führer, who helped him author his book *Mein Kampf,* which outlined many of his philosophies, including a *slight disagreement* he had with the Jewish population. It wasn't on this year's summer reading list. I think it's a seventh grade thing."

Veronica sighed. "Between Ellen and the old guy with the umbrella, I hope somebody puts me out of my misery when I start seeing dead Nazis … or aliens."

Principal Sweetney slammed down her phone and jumped right into another lecture, "As you might have figured, in this world of instant information, I've got a bunch of parents on my hands who are instant pissed off."

Her scowl fell on Maggie, who didn't give an inch. She stood even taller, as if her sole regret was having only one life to give for her Heritage Paper.

"Oma told the truth. I followed the directions given by Mrs. Foss, and just because you can't deal with the truth doesn't make it wrong."

Then she did the shake of her head with her eyes closed, which was her way of informing everyone that they were morons.

Part of Veronica wanted to cheer for her. Her daughter was the pre-Carsten version of herself—the rebellious girl who used to fearlessly lead her friends to neighboring Sleepy Hollow, to search for the Headless Horseman—and hoped she'd continue to live life with that zest. But she also had never been so mad at her. The contradictory life of the mother of a twelve-year-old, she guessed.

Principal Sweetney didn't look impressed. She turned to TJ, "Any last words?"

TJ just looked at the floor. He was taking the fifth. There was no way he was dragging down his friend with him.

Veronica felt compelled to throw her little girl a life raft. "I agree with Mr. Sterling, from the standpoint that Ellen's experience in the concentration camp likely led to dark fantasies. And combined with the onset of dementia, they turned to wild tales. But Maggie and TJ did nothing wrong. They followed directions, and I think it's clear that they didn't make up these stories to get a reaction."

"I agree," her mother said, causing Veronica to do a double take. Agreement was not usually a dynamic of their relationship. "Because of these mitigating circumstances, I will allow Maggie to redo her Heritage Paper without penalty, preferably focusing on a different relative, and present it to the class at a later date. I will take it upon myself to send out emails to the parents, explaining the situation with Ellen's health, and that we don't support Nazi or anti-Semitic propaganda, nor will we subject their children to it in the classroom ever again."

Everybody accepted their light sentences from the judge … except Maggie. "That's bullshit! It was the best presentation in the class."

"My decision is final. And watch your language, young lady."

A tear started to slip down Maggie's cheek and she angrily wiped it off. "I won't redo it."

"Then you'll receive an F in Social Studies and repeat the sixth grade next year."

"I'll sue you!"

Principal Sweetney didn't seem to take the threat of litigation too seriously, not even acknowledging her. "Anybody have anything else to add?"

Her eyes went to Youkelstein, and she picked right. "I think you're making a grave mistake by underestimating this threat."

He turned to Veronica and she almost jumped back upon witnessing the fire in his eyes. "This plan has been secretly plotted for over half a century by the highest ranking members of evil, and anyone with knowledge of the details could be in grave danger. Ellen said in the video that their twisted plot is in its final stages, and that is why she chose now to go public. If those behind this plot believe Ellen told details to Maggie and TJ, they could be in danger. As could anyone they might have told, like friends, siblings, or even yourself, Ms. Peterson. This group will not allow anyone to stand in their way."

Principal Sweetney replied, "I suggest you take up an investigation of these Nazi ghosts on your own time, Mr. Youkelstein … and your own dime. It has nothing to do with this school."

The ringing of her phone interrupted the confrontation. After listening for a moment, she responded sharply, "He left here twenty minutes ago—no he's not with me."

When she hung up, the color drained from her face and Principal Sweetney turned back into a worried grandmother. "It's Jamie—he never showed up for Career Day."

CHAPTER 10

Ben Youkelstein remained calm in the sea of panic. If there was anything he felt comfortable doing in this world, it was tracking down a predator.

The general consensus of the others was that one of two things occurred. The best case was that Jamie, stung by his punishment, ran away to make a statement.

The other scenario, and the more troubling one, was that Jamie was abducted by the Apostles. Every brittle bone in Ben's body told him that Ellen was telling the truth, meaning the children were in great danger. But he doubted that Jamie was "taken." This group thrived for decades by fitting into the background, and they weren't going to start seeking the spotlight as they closed in on their goals. Police involvement and Amber Alerts didn't fit their profile.

After Principal Sweetney called the authorities and began the process of locking down the school exits, Ben wandered off on his own to find the boy. He figured if he could find Mengele in Bertioga, then this should be a piece of cake. With Aligor's stinging words still lodged in his craw, he moved as swiftly as his ancient legs would allow across the school grounds, leaning on his trusty umbrella.

He first crossed paths with Aligor Sterling at the Terezin concentration camp in Czechoslovakia. It was December of 1944 and Ben was at his lowest moment. Aligor saved his life that time. When Ben met up with him years later, Aligor would change it.

He could feel the cold steel flow through his veins when he thought back to that time. It seemed like just yesterday when the Gestapo raided his Munich apartment, and he and his fiancée, Esther, were transported to Terezin. The Nazis also took his parents. His mother died of typhus in Westerbork, a transit camp, while his father, a well-respected doctor in Munich, was taken directly to the extermination camps on the charges he provided medical assistance to communists and Jews.

At first, Ben found the experience at Terezin strangely rewarding. The conditions were bad—in 1942 alone, almost sixteen thousand residents died of starvation—but Terezin provided a sense of community and he felt it an honor to be surrounded by such creativity and culture.

Terezin was where they took the "privileged" Jews. It was full of artists, writers, and scientists. There were so many musicians that four concert orchestras operated at the camp and several stage performances were put on each year. Ben and Esther even tried their hand at acting. The Jewish elders took it upon themselves to make sure all the children continued their education, and many chipped in to help teach them.

Thoughts of the children still burned the pit of his stomach. Of the fifteen thousand children who passed through Terezin, only about a thousand survived, which was probably an optimistic estimate. But that was just a small portion of the death at the camp, as most of Ben's friends were either transported eastward to Auschwitz for execution, or succumbed to the conditions at the camp. He was one of the rare survivors, but sadly, Esther was not.

From the moment she was taken from him, Ben wanted to join her in death. The only reason he was still alive was the slave labor he performed, whether it be splitting mica rocks, or spraying German military uniforms a white dye to help camouflage Nazi soldiers on the Russian front. But he'd been stricken with typhoid fever, and a sick man had no value to the monsters. It was a certain death sentence, but a sentence he welcomed.

That was when he met a young man who arrived at Terezin in late November 1944. His freshness reminded Ben of himself when he'd first arrived. And like him, the young man was also a medical student who was the son of a doctor. But he nursed Ben back to health with his friendship, not medicine, and more importantly, built back his will to live. He used to make Ben vow that when they got out they'd seek revenge on the Nazis.

Ben couldn't picture them ever getting out, but didn't want to squash Aligor Sterling's idealism. It's what kept them both alive as long as it did, he was convinced. But then a miracle did happen, or so he thought. On February 5, 1945, Himmler allowed the transport of twelve hundred Jews from Terezin to Switzerland in an agreement with Swiss President Jean-Marie Musy. Ben would later find that Himmler did this as a PR move, hoping to save himself, with Germany's war effort on the brink of collapse. He'd always been convinced that Himmler had survived the war, and Ellen's tale validated his thoughts.

Ben remained in Switzerland following the war. He resumed his medical studies and eventually became a forensic surgeon. He settled into a prosperous life with a fulfilling job and a supportive wife. But he still craved justice—he couldn't let it go. And that's why he felt compelled to pilgrimage to Israel in 1960 for the war crimes trial of Adolf Eichman, one of the chief executors of the Holocaust, who had been captured in Argentina after years on the run. It was there that Ben again crossed paths with Aligor, who'd made a similar journey, fueled by the same pain. It had been fifteen years since they'd last seen each other, but to Ben it seemed like five minutes.

Aligor had also completed his medical degree after the war, but never became a practicing physician. He still healed wounds, but in a different way. His wealthy and influential family migrated from Prague to New York. Aligor's father, Jacob Sterling, a concentration camp survivor himself, opened an organization called Sterling Center, to further Jewish causes and keep history from repeating itself. By the time of the Eichman trial, Aligor had taken over the leadership of the organization. And while his father's mission statement was to always look ahead, Aligor knew the only way to future peace was to get justice for the atrocities of the past. And during their chance reunion in Jerusalem, he'd found a partner in this quest.

After a series of small but satisfying captures, they hooked their first big fish—Hitler's private secretary Martin Bormann, who supposedly had died while trying to escape Berlin. Aligor used his many contacts to track him down in the remote, treacherous hills of southern Chile. Bormann's final words had stuck with him for all these years. And after today's events, they took on greater meaning.

With over forty years of hindsight, Ben would admit the prudent thing to do would've been to keep Bormann alive. If his claims about Himmler were just a con to buy time, as both he and Aligor were convinced they were, then what was the harm of finding out for sure? But there was something about the arrogance in his voice, and how he talked down at them, just like the guards at Terezin did—the animals that killed Esther in cold blood. They snapped, and by the time Ben pulled Aligor from beating Bormann's bloody body, he'd already been dead for five minutes. They took his head as a souvenir. Ben considered it a symbol of justice.

Over the years, some got justice in a courtroom for the world to see, while others like Mengele, the "Butcher of Auschwitz," received a more personal brand—they left his stroke-ridden body in the Brazilian surf like floating garbage.

Up ahead he noticed the young boy's head peeking out of a slow moving car. It was moving toward the exit of the school grounds. Ben walked, slow but steady. He moved under a Career Day banner and toward the car, which had stopped to allow a group of students to cross the street. He moved to the open window of the vehicle and placed the pointed tip of his umbrella at the neck of the driver.

"You're not going anywhere with that child."

CHAPTER 11

In the midst of the chaos, Veronica realized that Jamie was in the clutches of a gun-toting lunatic. This news gave her a surprising sense of peace.

She had sought out Eddie for help, but when he was nowhere to be found, she put two-and-two together. Jamie must have conned Eddie into giving him a joyride in the police cruiser.

She took the lead, running ahead of the group. She asked a few people if they'd seen a police car, and was pointed in the right direction. But what she found was not very comforting.

Youkelstein was about to stab Eddie with … his umbrella?

"You're making a big mistake, Grandpa," she heard Eddie roar.

Veronica ran as fast as she could. "Eddie—it's a misunderstanding!"

But Eddie was tough to cool down once he arrived at a boil. And he must not have gotten the memo on the fragile hips of the elderly, because he got out of the car and shoved Youkelstein to the ground. He knelt down and held his gun to Youkelstein's mustache.

"You are about to die of natural causes, old man—two shots to the head!" Eddie continued like a crazy man.

"Eddie … no!" she screamed again.

He glanced up and saw Veronica. He must have realized how absurd it looked to be pointing a gun at a ninety-year-old man who attacked him with an umbrella, because he returned the gun to his holster.

Veronica arrived, out of breath. The others slowly formed behind her, her mother coughing up her smoker's lung.

"We had reports that Jamie was missing," Veronica stated vaguely, not going into the whole Nazi story. She had no idea how she'd explain to Eddie what Ellen confessed to in the classroom. Either she was lying, a lying Nazi, or had lost her mind. Eddie would accept none of the above.

Before Eddie could question her, Aligor Sterling spoke up, "Lieutenant Peterson—I see you're doing prep work for our meeting today."

Eddie actually smiled, noticing Sterling's presence. "I guess you could say that, Mr. Sterling."

"Meeting?" Veronica asked.

"It's nothing," Eddie deflected.

Sterling disagreed. "By nothing, Lieutenant Peterson means he's been selected to lead the NYPD security team to protect Jim Kingston tomorrow night when he gives his acceptance speech in New York. It's a historic occasion, and I'm sure a great honor for Lieutenant Peterson and his fellow NYPD officers."

Veronica looked proudly at Eddie. "Why didn't you say something?"

"I'm just doing my job—it's no big deal," Eddie shrugged it off, as he did with any praise.

Veronica knew the real reason he didn't say anything. It was the idea that he received special treatment because he was Harold Peterson's adopted grandson. It was the same reason he turned down a lucrative detective job to work undercover in a seedy section of the Bronx.

Eddie was the son of Greta Snyder, while his biological father was a drug dealer who used to beat Greta. That was, until he was confronted by a police officer named Harry Peterson Jr., the son of the legendary NYPD detective. Harry Jr. explained that it was in his best interest to hop on the next bus out of town, to never be seen again, and Eddie's father agreed.

Harry Jr. nursed Greta back to health and their relationship soon blossomed into a romance, which led to a rocky marriage and a half-brother named Carsten. But any dreams of a happy family life drowned in the pool of Harry Jr.'s blood on their kitchen floor. With their parents gone, Eddie and Carsten were raised by Ellen and Harold Sr. They were the only true family Eddie ever knew. He took the name Peterson and even followed Harold Sr.'s footsteps by joining the NYPD.

"That's great, Uncle Eddie," Maggie exclaimed and gave him a hug around his midsection.

Aligor Sterling broke up the party, announcing that he'd had enough "nonsense" for one day and was leaving. But before he did, he looked to Veronica and said, "Ms. Peterson—it's bad enough we have a daily reminder of the ghosts from the past. Please don't let people create new ones for you."

His eyes wandered to Youkelstein as he said it.

Zach was again quietly assessing the situation. And as Sterling wheeled toward his limo, he asked, "Are you sure your sudden loss of interest isn't because any connection between your agency and Ellen, an admitted Nazi, will hurt the Sterling Center's credibility, and more importantly, impair your candidate's chances of winning tomorrow's election?"

Sterling looked smug. "My house is in order, Mr. Chester. Can you say the same thing?"

Zach said nothing.

"Say hello to your wife," Sterling said as he wheeled away.

Low blow, Veronica thought. She'd seen a whole different side of Sterling today. The Nazi hunting, skull displaying, condescending side. It wasn't a side she cared for.

Suddenly two men with semi-automatic rifles appeared out of nowhere and moved in on Sterling.

Veronica instinctively began to scream out a warning. But realized that Sterling and the machine-gun guys were on the same team. They circled him, and helped him into the limo. Veronica was amazed she hadn't even seen the guards, who had melded into the tree-lined campus.

Zach dusted himself off from the cheap shot and forced a smile. "I think he's still a little upset over that story I did on them. I implied that they sometimes bent the rules to get justice, which he took exception to. But he has much bigger enemies than some small-time journalist. Those guys with the scary looking guns are his security detail. They are former Mossad intelligence agents from Israel. Sterling gets about as many death threats a day as the president and he's betting that semi-automatic beats anti-Semitic every time. Probably a wise choice."

Before Veronica could process the words, she had another crisis on her hands. Eddie was up in Zach's grill, demanding, "What do you mean she's an admitted Nazi?"

Zach was saved by the ring of Veronica's phone. When she checked the caller ID, she muttered, "Ellen, you've got some splainin' to do."

But it wasn't Ellen on the other end. It was Kathy Rhodes, the president of Sunshine Village. "Is this Mrs. Peterson?"

"Yes it is," Veronica replied, wondering if this time it was aliens, Nazis, or maybe some new fantasy.

"I'm afraid I have bad news. Ellen was found dead in her room this morning. I'm so sorry."

Veronica gulped hard. It took her back to when she was delivered the news about Carsten. At least Ellen was able to get her secrets off her chest before she went; Veronica got the idea that Carsten died with many of his. Particularly that woman upstate he never told her about.

"I understand," Veronica somberly replied. And now came the hard part—handing the phone to Eddie. He was the one who had to make the call to her about Carsten. She couldn't even imagine how hard it must have been for him. And while Ellen might not have been a ray of sunshine, she sure was to Carsten and Eddie.

Eddie grabbed the phone and answered it as he always did, "Peterson here."

As he listened intently, he seemed to shrink. He normally kept his emotions locked away, choosing to cover them over with a rug made of the unflappable, offbeat jokester. Veronica had never seen him cry before. Not even at Carsten's funeral, where she could tell he felt it was important to keep it together for Maggie and Jamie. But on the rare occasion when Veronica witnessed his emotions seep out, they were raw and primal, just like now.

When the call ended, he wound up and threw Veronica's phone at the trunk of a large oak tree, shattering it into pieces.

CHAPTER 12

The trip to Chappaqua took only ten minutes. Eddie provided them with an official escort, complete with lights and sirens. Veronica wasn't sure what the hurry was. She'd identified one dead body in her life and that was enough for her. It's not like you could bring them back.

She trailed close behind in the Tahoe with her kids in tow. Zach and Youkelstein also joined her carpool, probably too afraid to ride with Eddie in his current mental state.

They drove up the tree-lined driveway to Sunshine Village. Eddie cut the sirens on the police cruiser, presumably out of respect for his elders.

Geyserland, as Eddie referred to it, was an impressive park-like campus built around a man-made lake, reminding Veronica of a rural New England college. Groups of "active" elderly were scattered around the grounds, power-walking or feeding the geese, as if they were auditioning for the cover of next year's brochure. The many residents inside who were crippled by depression or hooked to ventilators never seemed to make the brochure.

The lobby looked like that of a swanky hotel, featuring a large open area that was crammed with fake ferns and furniture that always appeared to be brand new.

A peppy teenager working the front desk explained to them that Mrs. Rhodes would be with them in a moment. It was obvious to Veronica that their arrival had been anticipated. The only other time they were granted an audience with Mrs. Rhodes was during the sales pitch. Once they signed on the dotted line, she had no time for them. Even when they demanded to talk to her personally about the security after the "aliens" incident.

Veronica noticed a sign in the lobby for the *Sunshine Village Holiday Sale*. It reminded her of how rapidly Ellen went downhill. Veronica's grandparents on her father's side were the same way. One day they were traveling to France like some infomercial for retired life, and the next thing they knew they were practically paying rent at the hospital.

Carsten and Eddie had dragged Ellen here kicking and screaming, literally, almost two years ago. It hurt them to do so, but it was clear she could no longer live by herself in the New York apartment that she'd called home for almost forty years. First, she fell down the stairs and broke her ankle. And after surviving that, she ended up getting robbed at gunpoint by a couple of crack-heads while on her way to the grocery store.

But once she lessened the kicking and softened the screaming, Ellen took to the place, or at least tried to make the best of it. Maybe it was out of respect for Carsten and Eddie, or more likely, she hoped to get released based on good behavior so she could return to the city. But regardless of her motives, she got involved in the sale her first year, knitting numerous sweaters for the event, despite throbbing arthritis in both her hands. She even played the lead in the spring play. But in June of that year, Carsten died. From that point on, it seemed as if this day was inevitable.

Veronica suddenly felt Maggie missing. Her eyes roamed the room, searching for her. She'd reached her limit of missing kids for one day.

She quickly located her—practice makes perfect—surrounded by a mob of older gentlemen, standing around a pool table and pretending to play. During Maggie's many trips here for her project, she'd become the most popular person in the place. Veronica noticed her working the room like she was running for office, which she probably would one day. She had few friends at school, but she was Miss Popular at Sunshine Village.

Veronica just shook her head—Maggie didn't come with an instruction manual.

Not to be outdone, Jamie was playing the role of Maggie's running-mate. The residents were doting on him like he was their own grandchild, taking special notice of his police uniform. He loved making people smile—easily his best quality.

As for the rest of the group, Youkelstein was welcomed as if he were a new resident being dropped off by his family. Zach remained pleasant, but quiet. His serenity contrasted with Eddie, who was violently pacing and badgering the teenage girl behind the counter with questions she wasn't qualified to answer.

A few tense minutes later, Mrs. Rhodes arrived. She was in her fifties and wore a tailored suit. During their first meeting she had the bubbly-real-estate-agent thing going, but today she played the somber funeral director. Veronica saw a talented actress who could replace Ellen in this year's spring play.

She used all the soft words—peaceful, passed-on, left us—the same ones that were attempted by the doctors when Carsten died. But there was nothing peaceful about a thirty-six-year-old man dying of a stroke in a seedy Poughkeepsie motel, leaving two children without a father.

Mrs. Rhodes walked them down the cramped corridors. Veronica always felt like a giant when she came here. Everything was made to the scale of the shrinking residents and it felt like she would scrape her head on the roof, despite being just five-six. The familiar trip brought them to Ellen's room, which like her apartment in the city, was an overpriced closet.

Veronica wasn't sure why they were brought here, other than a subtle hint to remove Ellen's things ASAP so they could move the next resident in. She expected some sort of chalk outline or police tape, but it was just a lonely room.

"An orderly found her this morning in her bed, she must have left us some time last night," Mrs. Rhodes said, pointing to the bed that had been neatly made up.

The room looked the same as it always did—miserable. The small television on which Ellen watched her beloved Yankees play was still there. It was one of few surviving items from the "coffee pot fire," in which she'd accidentally left it on and almost burned the place down. Two of her favorite items—a tacky couch and the laptop computer that Carsten gave her—did not survive.

Veronica walked to a bookcase, which still held the many framed pictures of Ellen's husband Harold and son Harry Jr. According to Zach, she went out of her way to absolve Harold from any Nazi knowledge in the presentation, but Veronica still wondered what he would have thought about her claims of having a child with the Gestapo guy, or Hitler helping to raise her. Probably the same thing they did—sadness, at what her once sharp mind had been reduced to.

Carsten often claimed that Ellen had quite a sense of humor and optimistic outlook before Harold died. Veronica would need to see that to believe it—he had already died at the time she began dating Carsten. The ironic thing was the last time Veronica picked up Maggie, on Sunday, Ellen seemed the most at peace she'd ever seen her.

"So you're saying she died of natural causes?" Eddie asked in his investigator tone.

A serious look came over Mrs. Rhodes' face. "That is why I wanted to meet with you—I think you should come with me."

They followed her into the hallway, the cryptic reply piquing their interest.

They continued following in lockstep behind Mrs. Rhodes, and passed into the *Long Term Care* facility, which for all intents and purposes was a hospital. But not one that the patients left. Ellen called it a hospice without morphine.

Mrs. Rhodes whisked them into a small examination room. Ellen's body was lying on a table, with a sheet covering her to her neck. *A little notice would've been appreciated!* Veronica turned to block Maggie and Jamie from having a vision of their dead Oma permanently scarred into their minds. Despite Youkelstein's warning about their safety, she sent them off to play by themselves in the hallway. Her initial fears at the school had waned. Being in this place reminded her how frazzled Ellen's mind was at the end.

Ellen was laid out on the cold slab and looked like Ellen always did, still dressed in her favorite nightgown. But from Veronica's angle, it looked like a thin smile had escaped her lips. No doubt she was enjoying all the drama that she'd caused—she loved being the center of attention.

Standing beside the table was a man in a white lab coat. He introduced himself as Dr. Bondy, and then stated, "It's my belief that Ellen committed suicide."

There went the pleasantries. "What do you mean suicide?" Eddie shot back.

The doctor remained oblivious to Eddie's threatening tone. "At first it seemed like a typical death of natural causes. We see it all the time here. Just a peaceful passing. But when I began examining her I smelled it."

CHAPTER 13

"Two smells really," Dr. Bondy went on. "The first was hydrocyanic acid coming from her mouth. But it was the other smell that really clued me to the cause of death."

"Other smell?" Zach asked.

"The smell of almonds."

The strange looks staring back at him jolted Dr. Bondy to explain, but he kept his methodical pace. "My grandfather served in World War II and worked at the camps that were used to house the German war criminals after the war ended. These cowards often sneaked cyanide in with them. It was stored in glass vials the Germans called *Zyankali*, which they often hid in their buttocks—not a pretty image, I know. My grandfather used to tell me about the smell of almonds coming from the ones who were able to commit suicide. He wouldn't even let my grandmother cook anything with almonds because he associated it with the stench of death."

"So, you're saying that Ellen committed suicide by taking a cyanide capsule?" Zach asked.

Before the doctor could even answer, Eddie jumped in, "That's ludicrous—where the hell would a woman in her nineties get her hands on cyanide!?"

The question seemed logical, even if its messenger appeared anything but. The doctor moved to Ellen's body and proceeded to pry open up her mouth like a dentist. As disgusting as it was, human nature made them take a whiff of the almond smell.

"My theory is that she placed the capsule in this bridge," he pointed to Ellen's extensive dental work. "Then she said her prayers and goodbyes, or whatever her last thoughts pertained to, and chomped down. At least that's how the Nazis used to do it. It's the way Himmler killed himself."

There's that name again, Veronica thought. She caught a glance of Youkelstein, who had penned a book about Himmler surviving the war. So maybe he didn't take the easy way out after all. This was all very confusing.

Dr. Bondy continued, "Once she bit into the capsule it wouldn't take long. Just a slow series of strenuous breaths, maybe for thirty seconds or so, and a pulse for another minute. She definitely didn't suffer."

Eddie was pacing the room like a psychotic lion. "I think you've been watching too much CSI! I'm interested in the truth, not theories from some hack who works in an old folks home."

Bondy shrugged. "I'm not saying this as fact. We'll have to wait for the pathology tests to come back, which might be a few weeks. Along with testing these," the doctor held out his palm, revealing a couple of small tablets. "They were found in her bridgework. My guess is that tests will show them to be cyanide."

Zach seemed focused more on the 'how' than the 'if.' "Someone must have smuggled them in—do you have a list of all visitors?"

Veronica had a crazy thought about Maggie, but quickly dismissed it. She would never do something like that, even if Ellen pushed her for it. And how would she get her hands on something like that?

Mrs. Rhodes called on her assistant to get the records of Ellen's visitors. She would leave no stone unturned in trying to avoid a lawsuit.

Eddie wanted to settle out of court—as in right here, right now. "And I'm going to have to talk to the person who worked the front desk last night to see if there were any suspicious visitors."

"Ellen revealed certain secrets today, that in context, make her death suspicious," Zach added.

Eddie flashed him a look to kill. He'd been filled in on the details of the Heritage Paper presentation prior to the trip over, and didn't take it well.

"I don't know what these secrets are," Mrs. Rhodes said, for the first time appearing flustered. "But Ellen was not of sound mind, and tended to make up grand stories—like the aliens. It's very natural when the mind begins to slip."

Eddie wasn't listening, "I'm also going to need to see the security tape."

The assistant returned with the list of visitors. Eddie ripped the paper from her hand and began examining it. Two obvious names—Eddie and Maggie—dominated the list. They were the only visitors besides Veronica in the last month ... except one.

Aligor Sterling.

"That's an interesting piece of information that Mr. Sterling forgot to mention this morning," Zach said. "And what makes it more interesting, is if Sterling knew Ellen planned on making her admission public, then he possessed a motive to silence her. A lot is riding on this election for him."

Eddie scoffed, "That's ridiculous. Besides, his visit came two weeks ago. Why don't you leave the police work to me, Nancy Drew."

"I'm just saying it would be convenient for him if Ellen was permanently muted. I have no idea what happened, but the fact is, Ellen likely died by cyanide poisoning. Which begs the question—what kind of person can get his hands on cyanide? Probably someone with a lot of connections like Aligor Sterling."

"You don't know the cause of death. The tests haven't even come back yet."

"I'm just giving the opinion of an unbiased observer. I have no dog in this fight, unlike yourself."

"What's that supposed to mean?"

"You have a motive to protect Sterling—to save your cushy security job for Kingston."

Eddie jumped at Zach. He grabbed him by his tie and yanked him in his direction. He was about to start the pummeling when a shrill shout sliced through the room, stopping everyone in their tracks.

"Stop fighting!"

Maggie stood in the doorway, her face flush with anger. "You are acting like a bunch of children! Oma would be disappointed—now follow me."

For some reason it didn't seem like they had a choice, so they fell into line behind the twelve-year-old. Except for Eddie, who stayed behind like a pouting child to continue badgering Dr. Bondy and Mrs. Rhodes.

Maggie maneuvered them through the *Long Term Care* facility and out a sliding glass door that led to a courtyard. She trudged over the grounds until she came to a weathered maintenance shed. She went directly to a man in a flannel shirt who was old enough to pass for a resident. Maggie called him Red, and ignored his stench of gasoline and freshly cut grass to embrace him in a hug. She then introduced Red as the head of landscaping at Sunshine Village.

"What can I do for you, Mags?" he asked.

"I need to borrow a shovel."

Could this get any weirder, Veronica wondered. But on second thought, she really didn't want to know the answer.

Maggie flung the shovel over her shoulder and led them to a desolate, wooded area on the campus grounds. Without a word, she began to dig.

The group was too entranced to say anything, or offer help. About a foot deep in the hard November ground, Maggie put her shovel down and struggled to pull out an object that was covered in a plastic garbage bag.

Zach and Youkelstein proved that chivalry wasn't totally dead, helping her bring the object to the surface *At least it's not a body,* Veronica thought. Hoped.

When Maggie tore off the garbage bag, Veronica was stunned. It was a painting of a young man draped in a fur coat, with long 1970s rock band type hair escaping from underneath a beret.

Veronica moved closer to examine the painting. It could be a fake, but something told her it was the real deal. *And Mama Sweetney said those art history classes would never pay off.*

"You recognize it?" Zach asked.

"Yes—it's Raphael's *Portrait of a Young Man.* It was looted from the Czartoryski Museum in 1939. It's arguably the most famous still-missing painting from the Nazi art plundering during World War II."

Youkelstein joined her in examining it. "My Lord," he uttered, focused on the inscription. Veronica cringed. *Who would do such a thing to this valuable painting?*

The writing was in German, but Youkelstein translated. "It says: To my beloved Ellen on the birth of your Josef. He will be painted one day as the leader of the world, and his painting will be titled The Chosen One." He paused for dramatic effect, before adding, "And it is signed by Adolf Hitler."

Oh, him. Veronica guessed that if he was willing to destroy a race of people, desecrating a painting likely wouldn't have caused him any sleepless nights.

"I'm not a handwriting expert," Youkelstein said, "but I've seen that bastard's writing more than my own. I'd bet my remaining years that it's not a fake."

Maggie turned to Veronica. "Oma said I should show you this painting if she died unexpectedly. She said you would know what to do with it."

"How did you ..." Veronica began, but her words trailed off. She knew the answer.

"We got it from her security box at the bank when we picked up the photos you yelled at me for before." A sheepish grin came over Maggie's face. "Oma really didn't see aliens that night—it was just an excuse to bury the painting."

Ellen *was* crazy, but not crazy the way they thought. She was crazy like a fox. But she was wrong about one thing—Veronica had no idea what to do.

Zach noticed something. "Look—there's a note taped to the back."

Youkelstein pulled the note off and read it. "It says to deliver the painting to Flavia's Art Gallery in Rhinebeck."

CHAPTER 14

Arriving at his office just beneath the clouds, Otto peered down at the magnificent skyline of New York City. It was as if he were levitating above the great metropolis. *No wonder people think I have a god complex*, he thought to himself with a grin. But reaching the top of the world was only the first step—a journey sixty-plus years in the making—it was now time to run it.

He felt a tremble go through his body, and noticed his hands shaking. He didn't know if it was from the overwhelming anticipation, or just the effects of his advanced age.

The last few days had been the most stressful of his life. Whether to remove Ellen from the equation was the toughest decision he'd had to make since being anointed the leader of the Apostles—it was as if it were a final test. But Ellen had spared him the gut-wrenching choice, by choosing to take her own life—her loyalty shining through one final time.

When Otto heard the news, the first thing he thought of was the Führer. He always had a special spot for Ellen, but the Führer understood the importance of making the ultimate sacrifice to reach necessary goals. He had predicted this day many years ago, and now he'd taken Ellen home so she could join him in viewing their great triumph.

Thoughts of his mentor momentarily calmed Otto, and stopped the shaking. But as he studied his wrinkled hands, he realized he no longer recognized them. That was the cruel part of the aging process—he remained trapped within the excruciating knowledge of his deterioration. He envied Ellen, and her alien sightings, unaware that her mind had turned to mush.

In his mind, he was still the dashing young spy of yesteryear. His legend grew to the heights of the Loch Ness Monster within Nazi circles. Nobody could ever identify the mysterious Otto, but they knew he was present, camouflaged seamlessly into the background.

And perhaps his greatest secret was that the renowned Nazi spy wasn't even German. He grew up in Dublin as Petey O'Neill. He'd come a long way from that street-hustling kid in Ireland, who was only a toddler when his brother was killed during Bloody Sunday. At the mere age of ten, Petey carried out orders to kill a British intelligence agent—disguised by his youth, they never saw him coming—to achieve justice for the brother he never really knew.

The British came after him mercilessly. This was no surprise, since the British never understood the concept of mercy, and his life in Dublin was effectively over. In order to save his last remaining son, Petey's father moved his family to the States—Brooklyn, to be specific.

Petey never fit in his new surroundings. Ironic, since his natural ability to assimilate into any situation is what made him such a lethal spy. As he entered his teens, he grew to hate America, and especially the Jews who controlled his father's job. The one he slaved at over a hundred hours a week—until one day when they decided they didn't need him anymore, and killed him and Petey's mother.

By his mid-teens, Petey was orphaned and passed around from neighbor to neighbor. He did find comfort in the Good Book. Not the Bible, but a visionary work by an up-and-coming German politico named Adolf Hitler, called *Mein Kampf*. It was as if he'd understood Petey's pain. A pain that he could only numb by running—he channeled his tortured emotions into becoming the top high school track athlete in New York. Just the thought of those days bemused Otto. He patted his old legs, wondering if they were napping and would wake up in time to sprint to the finish line.

Many in his Brooklyn neighborhood, made up of hardworking Irish, Germans, and Italians, raised money for the local track star, so he could attend the 1936 Olympics Games in Munich. Jesse Owens stole the headlines at the Games that year, but nobody ran faster than Petey O'Neill. He ran all the way to a new life. He wouldn't return to America for nine years.

While at the Olympics, he posed as a British diplomat in order to gain a meeting with his hero. The Führer was impressed by Petey's ability to avoid his security, which, combined with his desperate need for English-speaking spies, made him an ideal choice to become a German intelligence officer. It was an offer he couldn't refuse. Petey might not have been blood German, but his loyalty to the Führer was unmatched, and he was willing to go to any length to prove it when challenged, which the Führer constantly did.

He was assigned to Reichsführer-SS Heinrich Himmler, who many considered the second most powerful man in Germany, and unquestionably the most ruthless. Petey was sent to Britain, where he enlisted as an agent in the British SIS named Peter Jansen. Mixing trickery with charm, and his debonair nature—he still believed the James Bond character created by Ian Fleming, whom he crossed paths in British intelligence circles, was based on him—he moved quickly up the ladder.

When war broke out in 1939, Peter Jansen was able to pass important strategic information to Himmler, including the British plans to defend Belgium and France. With each piece of classified information he turned over he grew in stature and responsibility.

His signature moment came in May of 1941, although he wouldn't realize the significance until much later. He was to establish communication between the Duke of Hamilton and his German contacts, to create a secret meeting in which Hitler's right-hand-man, Rudolf Hess, would travel to

Britain as an envoy of peace. Peter Jansen tipped off the SIS about this meeting, allowing the British to capture Hess.

Of course, it wasn't Hess who had parachuted to what he thought was the Duke of Hamilton's residence. Nor was the man who spent the rest of his life jailed in Spandau Prison after being convicted as a war criminal at the Nuremberg Trials.

The Führer was so impressed by the Hess operation that he began affectionately referring to Petey as Otto, because he "carried the spirit of the 'Iron Chancellor' Otto von Bismarck," who was credited with the unification of Germany. It also catapulted him into his most trusted inner circle—a group of twelve men and women anointed as the Apostles. The group's name was a sign of both the Führer's contrarian side and gargantuan ego. He didn't lack for either. But its formation showed a pragmatic side that was not normally his strength.

The purpose of the Apostles was to carry on the workings of the Reich if the war effort failed—a fact that all German leaders grasped long before the stubborn Führer. It was a plan that Otto unknowingly set into motion when he helped remove the real Hess from Germany. Hess was accompanied by a child named Josef, who was entrusted with returning the Reich to its rightful place. Hess would serve as the child's father in their new home, while the plane was flown by a brilliant German intelligence officer, who would play the role of Josef's mother.

And while the plan was enacted over the next six decades, the chaos of April 30, 1945 in the Führerbunker was a constant reminder to Otto that things don't always go as planned. It was a day that almost derailed the entire operation before it began. But even with the many bumps in the road, including the many issues concerning Josef, they were now on the threshold of regaining the kingdom in the most glorious fashion.

He looked down again at his shaky hands that held his cell phone. He understood now why they shook. He dreaded making this call.

The Candidate answered on the first ring.

Otto didn't mince words. "Your grandmother has gone home."

He could hear the choke in the Candidate's breathing—he knew how much she meant to him. But like a great leader, he rallied, "She sacrificed her life for future generations."

"And her sacrifice went beyond what we expected. She did it on her own."

The Candidate sounded surprised, but relieved. He had argued passionately against silencing Ellen. Like those before him in his family, he was both stubbornly loyal and optimistic to a fault. But he also had the highest of leadership qualities, which Otto had spotted long before the Candidate understood his gift, so it didn't surprise him that he eventually signed off on what was best for the group.

The Candidate spoke assertively, "Her behavior was erratic at the end. Did she talk to anyone about the Apostles? Are there any other trails that need to be covered?"

"Her only contact was with Maggie, whom she was helping with a school project. We can question the girl, but Ellen's faculties had slipped greatly at the end. She couldn't differentiate between the Apostles and aliens."

A long silence ensued, before the Candidate said, "It's time for the children to come home. I was the same age as Maggie when I was brought in. With the kingdom within our sights, I think the timing is ideal."

With that, the Candidate hung up the phone.

CHAPTER 15

Theodore Baer ended his phone call, pondering the news he just heard. He looked around his penthouse suite, which served as both the studio for his syndicated radio show and his campaign headquarters. It was the first time he'd been alone since he began his shotgun candidacy for the presidency on Labor Day, just two months ago. It was both a relief and a surprise not to see any campaign managers, pollsters, or whoever else was trying to attach themselves to his backside.

He moved to the window and looked down at the city below, reflecting on how this all started, back at the University of Maine. A much simpler time in his life where he hosted his first radio show on a college station. It was called *The Teddy Baer Show*, but was anything but cute and snugly. His passionate opinions got him suspended from school on more than one occasion, including the infamous term paper he wrote that compared George Washington to Adolf Hitler, which he'd meant as a compliment to both men.

Following graduation, he moved to a small station in Portland, Maine. His communications professor, Emil Leudke—the one who pushed him to do the college radio show—was such a believer in Theodore that he left his professorship to become his producer. It was the late 1970s, fresh off the wound of Vietnam, and America was being held hostage—overseas by the

Iranians and at home by a gas shortage. The nation was sick, and like any ailing soul, it desperately sought a cure.

His message resonated in a big way—rebuilding a self-sufficient America that wasn't reliant on foreign oil or trade, and didn't involve itself in international skirmishes that drained its blood and treasure like Vietnam. He shouted to anyone who would listen that America should once again claim independence from the rest of the world, even if his critics, the dreaded internationalists, called him a radical.

If he was, he figured he was in good company. George Washington had warned the nation in his Farewell Address about the dangers of permanent foreign alliances, and the current conflict in the Middle East was another example that his warning should have been heeded. Washington believed in building a self-sufficient America, and becoming unnecessarily entangled in the battles of others worked contradictory to this goal.

Adolf Hitler believed in this same concept of self-sufficiency, or what the Germans called *autarky*. He sought economic self-reliance, just like Washington, especially when it came to raw materials. Baer was convinced that the reason General Washington sat in the pantheon of history, while Hitler lay in the bowels of infamy, was that the German leader didn't stick to the principles of *autarky*. Instead, he chose to seek world domination and all the pitfalls that went with such a strategy.

Baer peered down at the ants below. The same way the "unbeatable" Jim Kingston and his political machine once looked at him. But as the historic election approached, Theodore Baer owned a slight lead in the polls, even after yesterday's controversial comments.

His independent candidacy was initially treated as a publicity stunt. And they were right—Baer knew he couldn't beat the machine. Republican or Democrat didn't matter to him—same disease, different doctor—but it was a chance for him to get his licks in, especially during the debates, and it sure wouldn't hurt the ratings of his syndicated radio show *The Baer Cave*.

But then the Republican nominee was caught celebrating Labor Day weekend at his Florida estate with his pants down—literally—and that was only the half of it, as his partner in crime turned out to be his running-mate. This made them not only endless fodder for the late night television comics, but more importantly, unelectable. With the election only sixty days away, too late to contain the damage, Theodore Baer suddenly didn't seem such a bad alternative for the anti-Kingston crowd.

Baer then received another dose of election magic, when tensions intensified in the Middle East, moving to the brink of war. Kingston's biggest contributor and supporter was Aligor Sterling, head of the Sterling Center, the world's biggest sponsor of Jewish causes. And he also happened to be his uncle—the brother of Kingston's mother—so it wasn't like he could just cut ties with him if he wanted to.

So despite the electorate being heavily against America joining another conflict in the Middle East, Kingston promised to commit a full arsenal of US troops to a potential war, and to protect Israel at all cost. With Sterling his de-facto campaign manager, he had boxed himself into a political corner. By Halloween, Baer went from a novelty act to ten points up in the polls.

The door of the suite opened and Emil Leudke walked in—a lone friendly face in a sea of ass-kissing. Emil put his phone away and headed toward him, showing urgency in each step of his old legs. After yesterday's incident, they no longer felt able to speak freely in front of the campaign staff. So Emil had gone into the adjoining suite to call him.

Baer smiled for the first time in days. Age had slowed his mentor's body, but not his mind or his passion for the cause. And he was still the best-dressed and most debonair man in the room.

Emil handed him a piece of paper, which he looked quizzically at. "What's this?"

"This is your first act of being presidential, Teddy. It's called an apology—just look into the camera and try to look like you mean it. They've all done it—Nixon, Reagan, Clinton."

"Not you, Emil—have they gotten to you, too?"

"You know as well as I do what an important moment in history this is. We can't take any chances—losing this election is not an option."

The words were not necessary—Emil had been preparing him for this moment since he was a teenager. He always believed he would be president one day.

"What happened to that great advice you've been giving me since Maine? About never apologizing to anyone for what I believe."

Emil just pointed at the piece of paper—it wasn't negotiable.

There was no time to debate. The show was one minute away. Baer sat behind the boom microphone with an enormous mural of a grizzly bear in the background, the symbol of *The Baer Cave Show*. The cameras were positioned for his simulcast on GNZ. Emil began counting down.

Being the first presidential candidate with a built-in media outlet was a unique circumstance. It gave Baer a daily pulpit from which to preach to the voters. But as his critics liked to point out, it could also serve as a noose to hang himself, and yesterday that's exactly what he almost did.

The comments in question were in response to Kingston's ad campaign that compared Baer's isolationist strategy to that of those who appeased Hitler in the 1930s.

Baer responded on air that he believed Hitler's one big mistake was not following a similar strategy as the *Baer Plan for America*. That he should have built on the successes he had in the economy, education, and the arts, which history had chosen to ignore. And by doing so, he would have let the Russians and the Western Allies fight to the death, as they eventually did in the Cold War, while Germany continued to thrive in its isolated existence.

Aligor Sterling, responded by going on the national news and reminding America that Hitler didn't make just *one mistake*, he made *six million mistakes*, as in the number of murdered Jews. It was damaging.

Watching Sterling's comments in his office, Baer angrily quipped that the *other mistake* Hitler made was not taking care of Sterling when he had the chance—Aligor Sterling had survived a concentration camp in Nazi Germany. One of Baer's staffers, a Kingston spy, secretly taped the comment and leaked it to the media. It might have been unethical, but it worked. His lead shrunk by epic proportions.

A loud bear growl shook the room—the famed intro to *The Baer Cave*.

"I told you, I told you, I told you," Baer began the show with his usual high-energy rant. "I told you the Kingston machine would pull out every dirty trick to win this election, so that they can keep you living in fear. So they can send your sons and daughters to bleed in a foreign desert.

"But the main difference between Jim Kingston and myself is that I don't send a twenty-year-old kid with a tape recorder to do my dirty work, just like he wants to send your twenty-year-old son or daughter to do his dirty work in the Middle East. And here's another thing—I meant *every word* of what I said yesterday. I *do* think this would be a better world if Aligor Sterling were gassed in a concentration camp. What he and Kingston are planning, by sending your children to die for decades as part of their war machine, and creating more dependency on foreign nations, is no less despicable than any act of the Nazis!"

Baer sneaked a peak at the cringing Emil. He could visualize the pollsters going into seizures in the next room. He shrugged at Emil, as if to say he couldn't help himself—it was in his nature.

CHAPTER 16

Zach didn't need his journalism degree to figure out that Veronica was tense. She was gripping the steering wheel so hard he thought she would break it. The trip to Rhinebeck would be just over an hour, but he got the feeling that it would seem much longer than that.

Her children were in the back seat, along with a ninety-something Nazi hunter. And behind them, in the hatchback, was a priceless stolen painting. Just your typical road-trip upstate.

Zach focused on Youkelstein, thinking back to the story he did on him and Sterling a few years ago, titled *Shh It's Nazi Season*.

The Nazi hunters weaved an interesting story, although they were vague on certain details, and danced around Zach's questions about their rumored vigilante style of justice. On the record, they claimed that whenever they'd tracked down war criminals, they'd always handed them over to the proper authorities. Zach wasn't buying it, but still marveled at their passion, and it's not like he could evoke sympathy for the butchers who may have ended up on the wrong side of their sword.

As Zach peered out at the monotonous row of barren trees that lined the Taconic Parkway, he felt a certain twinge of excitement. He'd had too many days lately where he knew how the next twenty-four hours were going to turn out before they ever happened. Raising TJ was all about schedules and pickups, which he worked around to write his bland stories for the small paper that was currently employing him.

So perhaps him "tagging along" on this journey was another chance to chase the big story, which led to the question: *Is it a big story?* Zach wasn't sure, but saw two possibilities—one was that it was a hoax of crop circle proportions. He doubted that one. TJ was good with altering photos, but not that good. The more likely scenario was that Ellen was telling the truth as she saw it. Of course, her cognitive abilities were very much up for debate. Like a good reporter, he would observe, seeking the truth without pride or prejudice, and remain open-minded until facts were validated.

He thought of Sara, who always told him he was afraid to take a side. She said he used journalism as an excuse to avoid life—observing, but never living it. Sometimes he wished she'd done a little less living, and then perhaps she might still be there for their son.

Veronica turned to him. "Do you really think Aligor Sterling could have given Ellen those cyanide tablets?"

"I don't know, but the guy does have a lot to lose in this election. And if he thought Ellen's connection to the Nazis was a threat to Kingston winning, who knows."

Youkelstein cleared his throat and spoke up from the backseat, "I've known Aligor since 1944. We've had our differences over the past few years, but he saved my life. He saves lives, not takes them."

"Except for when you two played judge, jury, and executioner. My mother always told me that if you stoop to someone's level, then you turn into that person," Zach challenged.

"Those Nazis weren't human lives. They were rabid animals that laughed when they shot Esther right in front of me. She was my soul—and when your soul is ripped from you, Mr. Chester, then you can talk."

They had more in common than Youkelstein would ever know. Only Zach's soul wasn't ripped away by soldiers wearing swastikas, but by a drug that proved just as crippling.

He looked back at Youkelstein. "Okay, Mr. Nazi Hunter, how about cluing us in on what's going on here?"

"I'm as much in the dark as everyone else."

"You just happened to have written books that claimed Himmler, Hess, and other members of this so-called Apostles group had survived the war, and then you received an invite to the Ellen Peterson 'Nazi coming out party'? That doesn't sound like a coincidence to me."

"The only connection I can make is from when Aligor and I interrogated Bormann in South America, many years ago."

"And this would be Martin Bormann, who according to the official record was declared dead when his remains were discovered buried at the Lehrter Bahnhof railway station in West Berlin, and later confirmed in DNA evidence and dental records?"

"'Ah, the official record. It sounds plausible to me that these skeletal remains just suddenly showed up there in 1972, twenty-seven years after his disappearance."

The coy smile told Zach that Youkelstein knew exactly how Bormann's body wound up there.

"Official record aside, when Aligor and I tracked him down, he told us he had correspondence that proved Himmler was both alive and part of this Apostles group."

"If you believed he could track down Himmler, it might have made him useful to you. I'm guessing that he would have told you whatever you wanted to hear at that point, hoping to buy himself some time."

"That was our belief, which was why we didn't pursue his alleged correspondence."

"And it's interesting that you never mentioned any of this in your books."

"The books you speak of were forensic investigations, which detailed how numerous Nazi criminals, including Himmler, used doppelgangers to survive the war and conspired with Western powers to do so. I had evidence to prove that Himmler survived the war, but I could never confirm his whereabouts, or determine exactly what happened to him. As a journalist, I'm sure you understand this standard."

Zach did. He also understood how to dig for the answers he needed. "Sterling mentioned that he believed your books put ideas in Ellen's head, which was already spinning with alien theories."

"Aligor is the delusional one. Not Ellen."

"Regardless of the mental state of those involved, I think you wanted to validate these ideas of Apostles and the rising of the Reich, and you found Ellen as a willing partner. By her publicly telling this tale, she is helping to reinforce your theories."

"Blast my tactics, but don't ever attack my sincerity. I've dedicated my life to justice, not publicity!"

"But justice isn't cheap, and keeping alive the myth that a Darth Vader figure like Himmler is alive can bring publicity, along with funding from your fellow conspiracy theorists."

Zach used his phone to pull up the Internet. He googled Himmler, which took him to the archived front-page headline *Death of Himmler* that ran on May 25, 1945 in the *Daily Mirror*. He held up the photo for Youkelstein to see. "I'm no expert, but he sure looks dead to me. Do you really think this guy is still alive?"

"First of all, Himmler was born in 1900, so I truly doubt he'd still be alive. But since you brought up the newspaper article, does it mention that the corpse's legs were muscular, contrasting with Himmler's frail physique, which was backed up by testimony of those closest to him? Or that many of Himmler's closest friends didn't recognize the photo in the paper? In fact, the British wouldn't allow his mistress, Hedwig Potthast, or his brother Gebhard, to view the body. And anyone who's had a mustache as long as Himmler would have a pale area of skin when it's shaved off, which wasn't present on the corpse."

"All things that can be explained away by the context of the time. It was twenty days after the war had ended. The whole place was chaos. Does it really surprise you the examination wasn't done in optimal fashion?"

"That's the thing, Mr. Chester, the examination of Himmler ranked as one of the most meticulous postmortem examinations of any historical figure. They noted every lesion, scar, and needle prick on the body. Now please click on the photo from the *Mirror*."

Zach followed his orders, and the photo of the dead man enlarged to fit the entire screen.

"As you can see, the eyes are level and bridge of the nose is straight. The tissue of the lower third of the nose deviates to the right. Much different from the real Himmler."

"Maybe the structure of his face was altered when he entered the camp."

"There is overwhelming evidence that no torture took place at the camp, but if it did, I was still able to get my hands on Himmler's dental records. His last visit was November 1944, six months prior, and his teeth were in perfect shape. When I compared them to the postmortem X-rays, it would seem that either Himmler had a case of the fastest spreading gum disease in history, or more likely, it wasn't Himmler who committed suicide in that camp."

Zach realized he wasn't going to win this debate, so he got back on track, "Okay, I'll concede the point that Himmler survived the war, and that he might be a member of the this group called the Apostles. But what does it all mean … and where do we go from here?"

"It means that they were acting in concert. And I believe we're going to Rhinebeck."

"Any idea what this symbol might represent?"

Zach held up a piece of paper that he'd scribbled the symbol on during Maggie's presentation. *v^988v^*.

"I wish I knew. The images around the number look like horizontal lightning bolts—as you know, the SS symbol was double lightning bolts, so there might be a connection there. As far as the number, I've run numerous scenarios in my head, but have hit nothing but dead ends. Thanks to Ellen's confession, we know that Bormann, Himmler, Hess, Müller, and Ellen were five of the twelve. I think we must figure out who the other seven were, and decipher what aliases they used, or are using, since the war—only then will the symbol be clear."

That seemed like a pretty tall order to Zach, and one that was unlikely to be successful.

Veronica must have been thinking the same thing. "All these men must be dead by now. So even if they survived the war, what's the difference?"

Youkelstein answered, "Think about what the original Apostles did. At the time of their deaths, Christianity still wasn't a dominant religion by any means. But they had planted the seeds. And Constantine, the Roman Emperor, years later took the fruit of that tree and declared Christianity the law of the land. By learning the identity of the Apostles who planted the Nazi seeds, it will lead us to the modern-day Constantine. He or she will be the one who will execute their takeover plan … and is the one we must stop."

"And where would we even start?" Zach wondered aloud. He looked back at Youkelstein, who answered Zach's question with a sideways glance.

He looked at Maggie.

CHAPTER 17

Veronica pulled off to the side of the road. The sky was bleak and she even noticed a couple of snowflakes float by. It was as if it were a sign that she should turn the vehicle around and not stop until she was curled up beside a fire in her living room.

But Ellen had hooked her with the bait. The Raphael appeared authentic, and if it wasn't, Ellen sure went through a lot of trouble to find a good knockoff. Not the work of your average dementia sufferer.

"I promised Oma that I wouldn't discuss the memoir," Maggie said, sounding like a prisoner of war.

Veronica realized the men were in over their heads in dealing with her daughter. So she took a deep breath and said, "Sweetie, Oma has gone to a better place, so nothing she told you can hurt her anymore. But if we don't find out what is going on here, more people could get hurt, and that's the last thing Oma would want."

"Oma said the reason I can't say anything is to protect her family, which if you haven't forgotten, is also *my* family. We have to trust that she's going to lead us in the right direction."

Dead or not, Ellen Peterson was pissing Veronica off. "Trust a woman whose entire life was a lie? If she really wanted to protect her family then she wouldn't have pulled this stunt!"

"It's not a stunt. And so far everything she's said has come true."

Maggie had a point. But protecting her children was Veronica's sole mission, and Ellen had compromised it.

Zach must have felt her angst spilling over because he stepped in, "Maggie, it's very important we locate this memoir you worked on with her. It would help us a lot if you'd tell us where it is."

"I don't have it!"

"Maggie!" Veronica shouted out. "Where is the memoir!?"

"I swear I don't have it," Maggie squeaked and began to tear up. "There was only one copy and Oma didn't tell me where it was. She even burned the computer I typed it on."

The coffee pot fire. Crazy fox strikes again.

Veronica backed off, knowing that Maggie would just shut down if this turned into a screaming match.

Zach took over the questioning, assuming the good cop role, "I believe you, Maggie. But perhaps you remember some of the things she dictated to you when you typed it. Names, places … anything."

"She didn't use the real names. Or say what the plan was. And she left it open-ended; she said it would be up to us to write the ending. Hopefully a happy one."

"I'm not following," Zach said, his voice remaining calm.

"Oma was worried if I knew the real names and aliases of the Apostles, then it would put me *and them* in danger. So she dictated it to me in code."

"So if the memoir is written in code, then Ellen and the other Apostles would be the only people who knew what it meant," Zach followed up. "I'm not sure how it would be relevant to us, since nobody would understand it except for the inner circle."

"No—I taught her how to use the 'find and replace' option on the computer, so she could put the proper names into the final version. She was able to convert all the code names to the real ones before she printed it. She said it would be a historical record that she'd release when the time is right.

And like I told you, only Oma knows where the printed copy is or when she plans to release it."

"You can't release something when you're dead!" Veronica interrupted.

"Everything she said has come true, so I'm not going to start doubting her now," Maggie shot back.

"She's not here anymore—I'm sorry, I really am, but this charade is over, Maggie."

"If it's such a charade then why are we going to Rhinebeck?"

Good question. "Maybe I'll turn the car around and we won't."

Good cop Zach again interjected, "Do you remember any of the code names she dictated to you, Maggie?"

"I told her to assign a letter like X or Y to each person, but you know Oma, she had to be complicated. So she used her own set of code names— some were short like James and John, but others were weird."

"Weird how?" Zach inquired.

"Long ones like Thaddeus and James the Less, or something like that."

Zach and Youkelstein traded glances. Youkelstein began scribbling furiously on a piece of paper. He then held up his pad that read:

1. Peter
2. Andrew
3. James
4. John
5. Philip
6. Bartholomew
7. Thomas
8. James the Less
9. Matthew
10. Simon the Canaanite
11. Judas
12. Thaddeus

"Were these the names?" Youkelstein asked, showing Maggie the pad.

"How'd you know that?" she answered like he'd done a magic trick.

"These are the names of the original Apostles, the followers of Jesus Christ. Bormann had told us that Himmler's code name was Thomas, but I didn't see the context back then."

Zach looked skeptical. "We can play the cryptology game all day, but what we really need to do is locate the memoir."

Then something hit Veronica. "It's in our backyard. Maggie buried it this morning. In the time-capsule, you told Eddie that the memoir was in there."

"Let's go back," Zach said with eagerness in his voice.

Youkelstein seconded.

Maggie rolled her eyes, as if to indicate that she couldn't believe the adults were of the same species as her. "Do you think Oma was that stupid? I didn't bury an important historical record in our backyard like some dead bird. I just said that to throw people off the right track."

"To throw who off?" Veronica asked. "We were the only people there."

"Oma said I shouldn't trust anyone, even those closest to me."

"Ellen said you shouldn't trust *us*? She was a Nazi for God-sake," Veronica lashed, immediately regretting the comment.

"Maybe so, but she was also right," Maggie fought back. "Oma was trying to keep us safe. But knock yourself out … go dig up our backyard. And then we can go tear apart her old room at Sunshine Village, or maybe we can get a court order to dig up the grounds. I'm just a kid, you geniuses can figure it out."

Veronica did another slow burn. She remembered something she preached to Maggie and Jamie about if they didn't have anything nice to say, not to say anything at all. And since nobody had anything remotely pleasant to communicate at the moment, no more words were uttered until they pulled into the small Victorian downtown of Rhinebeck.

With a quick check of the rear-view mirror, Veronica noticed that Maggie was staring blankly ahead and gnawing on her lower lip. It was her pet move to indicate anxiety. Jamie pulled on his ear, Picasso batted his tail against the floor, and Maggie gnawed on her lip.

"Mags, it's not too late to turn around and go sell the painting on eBay. Hitler autographed … I'll bet that would pay for a lot of double sprinkle ice cream cones at Carvel," Veronica attempted to comfort.

Maggie smiled. Not at another poor attempt at humor by her mother, but it was a smile of relief—knowing there might be another living organism on the planet who believed her, or at least had her back. It was the best response Veronica could hope for these days. Not those big belly laughs from when Maggie was a toddler that she missed so much.

She parallel-parked the Tahoe on Main Street and entered Flavia's Art Gallery, not sure what to expect. Maggie and Jamie trailed her, carrying the Raphael, one on each end like it was a couch. A clerk pointed them to Flavia.

When Veronica saw her, she almost fell over.

CHAPTER 18

Veronica had never felt such rage pulsing through her veins. And she wasn't sure why. At the end she made up any excuse not to be with him. Their love had long fizzled and they'd entered that zone they never thought they would enter—staying together for the kids—even if they never had an official conversation about it.

Flavia appeared older than Veronica, probably in her mid-forties, but it was only a small victory. She was a striking beauty.

"Can I help you?" she asked, and flashed the most perfect smile that Veronica had ever seen. Although, it probably wouldn't look so good with a few missing teeth, she thought.

"I'm Veronica Peterson … Carsten's wife."

Flavia took a step back and froze. They stared at each other, remaining as still as the many sculptures that filled the gallery.

"Do you two know each other?" Zach asked the obvious.

"Yeah," Veronica began, "Flavia was the one who …"

She caught a glimpse of Maggie and Jamie, still holding on tightly to the priceless painting, and looking intently at their lunatic mother. They worshiped their father, and she wanted them to hang onto that myth for the rest of their lives—no different than Santa Claus, even if Santa ran around behind Mrs. Claus back and once socked her in her rosy cheek.

"Why don't we talk in my office?" Flavia read the situation perfectly. There would be no winner in a public display.

Veronica followed her into a cramped office and closed the door behind them. Flavia offered Veronica a seat, but she chose to stand. If she asked her to stand, she would have sat. The return of her old stubbornness made her feel nostalgic.

Even the name Flavia sounded exotic—just the opposite of Carsten's simple family life with the cookie-cutter wife and two kids. At least she didn't have to wonder what he saw in her.

When Veronica hired that investigator to follow Carsten—she still couldn't believe she did that—the PI asked her if she wanted him to dig further, such as name, address, and whether or not she had a spouse. But Veronica declined. The pictures of the two of them sneaking into motels was enough. Veronica didn't want revenge—just a boring divorce. But before she could summon the strength to address him, their split became permanent.

"Did Carsten tell you about us?" Flavia got right to the point.

Veronica was thrown off by the honesty. "No."

"We decided it was best not to tell anyone. It was too dangerous to involve others. So if Carsten held his end of the bargain, how did you find out?"

The part he failed to live up to was their wedding vows. "I had you followed," Veronica said and felt guilty about it. She didn't know why—she was the victim here.

Flavia took a seat behind her cluttered desk. "Wow, he really had you pegged."

"Excuse me?"

"Carsten and I spent a lot of time together. He opened up to me about a lot of things, including you. Said you changed over the years. That you weren't the same girl he'd married."

"I'm surprised you had time to talk."

Flavia's face turned quizzical. "What exactly do you think went on between me and your husband?"

"Don't try to play innocent—I saw the photos."

"I don't know what photos you're talking about, but I doubt they show me and Carsten engaging in inappropriate behavior … at least not the kind you're thinking of."

Maybe not, but you didn't have to be a genius to figure out what went on once they entered those motel rooms together. Besides, what hurt Veronica the most was the way Carsten looked at Flavia in the photos. It was the way he used to look at her—when they were in love. What defines cheating has always been a big fat gray area.

"What your husband and I were doing is none of your business. What *is* relevant is that I respect people's marriages, even a complete unmitigated disaster like yours was."

Flavia stood and clanked around the office in her expensive heels. The rest of the ensemble didn't appear to be cheap, either. It looked like she leaped off the cover of some fall fashion magazine—a shiny silk blouse and a beige, knee-length pencil-skirt.

"So what inspired you to come face me, Veronica … after all this time?"

It was obvious that Flavia had no idea as to why they were here. So Veronica played along, "I was curious about the change in my husband's demeanor at the end of his life. And since he didn't talk to me, I figured I'd go see the one person he did discuss things with. And I'm glad I did, because I learned that I was the one who changed, not him."

"Have you met your therapist's benchmarks yet, so that we can end this meeting?"

"Not until you tell me how you met my husband. And if you weren't screwing, I think I have the right to know why he was sneaking around with you in those motel rooms."

"Like I said, it's none of your business. Not that it would change anything, anyway."

"It might not be my business, but your business is art, correct?"

She looked confused. "I own this gallery, so I think that goes without saying."

"Have you ever heard of a painting called *Portrait of a Young Man* by Raphael?"

"I've heard of Raphael, of course, but not that specific painting. I've never claimed to be an aficionado. My gallery is made up mostly of contemporary work by local artists. Monet and Raphael don't usually grace our walls."

"*Portrait of a Young Man* was stolen by the Nazis. It's been missing since 1939. But today it came into my possession, along with this."

Veronica handed over the note that instructed them to come here. Flavia studied it, as if trying to detect a hidden meaning.

"My coming here has nothing to do with Carsten and whatever you did or didn't do. I didn't even know your name before I arrived. I'm here because of Ellen Peterson—she's responsible for that note."

"The woman who raised him? He talked about her a lot. How did she know about me?"

"I was hoping you could answer that. She was found dead this morning at the retirement community where she lived. But not before she alleged to be a Nazi who was part of a group that had infiltrated America after the war. So how about you stop playing games with us, Flavia?"

She returned to her chair, appearing to be troubled by the words. "I never met Ellen."

"But you know about her from Carsten."

"And she obviously knew about me."

"Why did Ellen send us to you? There must be a reason."

Her voice dropped to a whisper, "I don't know, but there are people willing to go to great lengths to make sure this group Ellen speaks of remains a mystery."

"Who are these people?" Veronica pushed.

"The same people who killed Carsten."

CHAPTER 19

A dazed Veronica watched her children assist Zach and Youkelstein, carrying the painting into Flavia's office like pallbearers.

Veronica was trying to wrap her mind around what Flavia just told her. The first part—that Carsten might not have had an affair, not physically anyway. Even if true, Veronica didn't take this as good news. The affair was the event that allowed her to distance herself from his death. Just because their marriage was, to use Flavia's words, an unmitigated disaster, didn't mean she wasn't hit with an overwhelming feeling of loss when Carsten died. But the photos of him and Flavia entering that motel were like a force field that allowed her to exchange her pain for anger, which was a much more tolerable emotion.

The other part was harder to grasp. *The same people who killed Carsten.* And while most thirty-six-year-old men don't drop dead of a stroke, it's not like it never happened, and foul play was never even suggested.

After shutting the door, Zach and Youkelstein performed an "unveiling." They removed the garbage bag that covered the painting. Flavia studied it closely, and pointed to the scribbled ink. "Is that really Hitler's signature?"

"I believe it is," Youkelstein spoke up.

Flavia locked eyes on him. "And you would be?"

"Dr. Benjamin Youkelstein."

"What kind of doctor deals with Hitler's signature?"

"I'm a forensic pathologist. But I dabble in historical justice."

She chuckled. "I dabble in historical justice myself, Dr. Youkelstein. And I must confess that I do know who you are. I've read much of your work."

A satisfied grin came over his face. Veronica was once again reminded that boys might get older, but they never outgrow the urge to impress a pretty girl.

"How do we know it's not a fake?" Flavia asked. "The painting, the signature, or both?"

"We don't," Veronica said, feeling a surge of competitiveness. "But I'd be willing to bet that it's the original."

"Carsten mentioned you were an art history major. He wished you hadn't given it up. People should never give up their passions," she stuck Veronica with a few more needles, then added, "So if this is the real deal, it must be worth a small fortune."

Veronica took a deep breath, suppressing her urge to lash back. "Hard to tell if being underground has damaged it, and if so, how much damage there is. I also don't know if the signature of such an infamous figure adds or subtracts from the value, but yes, it's safe to say it would be worth quite a bit."

"I guess I'll hang it with others," Flavia said with a casual shrug.

Zach joined the conversation, "You're going to hang a stolen painting in your art gallery … are you mad?"

Flavia looked at Zach like he had just walked into the room. "I don't think we've been introduced," she said and extended her hand. "Are you a member of the historical justice team like Dr. Youkelstein?"

"No, my name is Zach Chester," he said and clasped her hand. "I'm a journalist. I used to write for *Newsbreaker*."

"I used to fit into my prom dress. I'm only interested in who you are today."

"I'm just a guy telling you I don't think it would be a good idea to hang a stolen painting in your gallery."

"I didn't say I would hang it in the gallery. I said I would hang it with the others."

Before anyone had a chance to grasp the comment, a man in a dark suit burst through the door.

Veronica jumped—were they about to be busted by police for being in possession of the stolen painting? Or was it the Apostles, who were going to kill them all because they now knew too much? Veronica stepped in front of Maggie and Jamie—nobody was going to hurt her kids.

But when Veronica's eyes focused on the man, she realized who it was.

It was Eddie.

In a suit.

Veronica had never used the words 'dapper' and 'Eddie' in the same sentence. But wow! And he brought with him a trail of cologne. His shaved head glowed like he'd shined it.

He had told Veronica that he wasn't going to follow a wild goose chase to Rhinebeck. But his protective instinct must have led him here.

The kids looked thrilled to see him, but Flavia not so much. She had pulled out a handgun from her desk drawer and held it on him. The Nazi ghosts had spooked her more than she initially let on.

Veronica mediated a peace settlement, "He's with us—it's okay."

Eddie smiled, seemingly oblivious that she had just been seconds away from putting a bullet in him. "I'm Lieutenant Edward Peterson—I'm in charge of security tomorrow for Jim Kingston, who if you haven't heard, is running for president. I'm kinda a big deal."

"Am I a threat to the potential future president?"

"You do pose a national security threat—nations have gone to war over women much less breathtaking than yourself."

"Does that line ever work?" Flavia asked.

"Normally I would have clubbed you over the head and dragged you back to my cave. But you struck me as sort of a classy chick."

Eddie's gaze finally left Flavia's glow, and made its way to Veronica.

"I have a meeting with Kingston," he explained the suit.

"You look good," she told him

"I think it really hugs my boobs," he replied with a laugh, before morphing into Serious Policeman Eddie. "I stopped by to visit the girl who works the front desk at Sunshine, but she wasn't home. Roommate told me that she often stays with her boyfriend in White Plains. I'll stop by tonight."

Veronica nodded, but knew the answers they needed were far beyond the pay-grade of the girl who worked the front desk.

Eddie returned his attention to Flavia. "So do I get a tour, or am I going to have to take out my badge and abuse my police power to get it?"

"I would be honored, but only on the condition that I can take all of you to lunch."

"I stopped allowing beautiful women to buy me meals—it was taking up too much of my time—but I'll make an exception this one time."

Veronica thought she was going to be ill.

Flavia locked the precious painting in her office, and began leading them around the gallery. The men followed her like Picasso would a bird, and hung on her every word. Even Jamie, which broke his mother's heart. Maggie must have sensed that Veronica could use some comfort because she clung closely to her as they toured the gallery.

Veronica wished she could say that the gallery was tacky or cheap, but it wasn't. It was the place she always dreamed of starting, but never had the guts. As the tour continued, she began to feel slightly better. She always had changed personalities when she was in an art gallery or museum. It gave her a sense of peace. But finding complete solace would be a challenge on this day.

Maggie also seemed to decompress a little as she soaked in the many paintings and sculptures, hopefully her mind off Ellen and the Nazis. Veronica was proud of the love for art she'd passed on to her daughter. She grabbed her hand and they began discussing some of the paintings that lined the walls.

But once they left the gallery, Veronica's sense of peace vanished. Every motherly instinct she had began to scream that her children were in danger.

CHAPTER 20

Lunch would be at The Tavern at the Beekman Arms, located about ten minutes up Route-9, along the Hudson River.

Despite the November chill, Flavia drove her Jeep with top down. Youkelstein, risked pneumonia to ride with his new BFF.

Eddie took Jamie off her hands for another ride in the "cool" cop car—this was turning out way better than Career Day for him. The three cars lined up in a row like a funeral procession. Veronica hoped it wasn't a sign of things to come.

The restaurant was located on the vast grounds of a historic hotel, which displayed a collection of WWI fighter planes that attracted Jamie's attention. The interior featured overhead beams, an open-hearth fireplace, and an intimate bar.

The hostess provided a scripted speech about the extensive history of the Beekman Arms as she brought them to their table. Veronica thought about playing "top this" with the story of the Hitler autographed Raphael, but didn't want to rain on her parade.

When the hostess suggested a viewing of planes while they waited for their food, it set Jamie off. "Oh, Mom, can I please go see the airplanes ... pretty please." He folded his hands into praying formation. "Pretty please with sugar on it."

"Perhaps after we eat."

"I'm still kinda full from that great breakfast you made this morning."

"We had cereal for breakfast."

"Can I *pleaaase* go see the airplanes."

Veronica knew the kids needed a break. The tension was starting to rub off on them. Children take their cues from the adults, even if they act like they don't know them sometimes. But at the same time, the warning signs about impending danger were multiplying. And Flavia's words were still lodged in her mind.

The same ones who killed Carsten.

"Maybe Uncle Eddie can take you," she said with a hopeful look in his direction. They weren't going anywhere alone.

"I think I should stay here," he said.

She'd hit his most touchy nerve. Eddie wore an eternal chip on his shoulder, always insecure about being good enough. And now she'd reduced him to babysitting duty while the "grownups" figured out how to save the world. She couldn't believe she did that.

Zach picked up on things. The observer. He volunteered to escort Jamie.

Eddie suddenly changed his tune. Veronica wished he would pick a lane and stay in it, but then he wouldn't be Eddie. One minute the childlike jokester, the next a raging bull.

"I'll go," he grunted.

"It's not a problem—I need to stretch my legs anyway," Zach said.

Jamie was on board, but not Maggie. She felt ownership of this Nazi scavenger hunt. She was the leader, no matter how old she was. Ellen had picked her.

But Veronica also knew that behind those old eyes was an unnerved twelve-year-old. Even Harry Potter needed to be twelve once in a while. Since Carsten's death, it was like she was caught in limbo between childhood and adulthood.

"Mags, why don't you go play with your brother," Veronica prodded. She didn't budge.

"Mags—I'm talking to you."

"I need to be here—why don't *you* go look at airplanes."

It wasn't so much the words, but the jolting tone that almost knocked Veronica off her seat. But before she could respond with words she'd likely regret, Eddie jumped in like the chubby, infantile angel he always defaulted back to. He got up and said, "C'mon, Maggot, I'll race you."

"You run like you have a refrigerator on your back, Uncle Eddie."

He grabbed her and slung her over his shoulder. She fought at first, but then let out a smile. The look on her face was priceless.

Thanks, Eddie ... again.

But before they exited, Zach made one last attempt, "Why don't you stay, Eddie. It's better that you're involved in these conversations. Being a cop, you might be able to decipher this mess."

Eddie's smile turned to a competitive scowl. "Who's going to protect the kids ... you?"

CHAPTER 21

Since Eddie and Zach couldn't properly determine who the alpha male of the group was, they compromised, deciding to both accompany the children.

It left Veronica and Flavia together, with Youkelstein acting as the referee. Before the bout could begin, a friendly waitress took orders for appetizers. Youkelstein got the onion soup gratin, while Flavia ordered the prosciutto and melon with extra virgin olive oil. Flavia seemed to Veronica like one of those people who would breezily order for the group in a trendy Manhattan restaurant. Even when they lived in the city, the Petersons were always more of a pizza delivery family.

Flavia ordered a bottle of Pinot, and Veronica finally found something they had in common—they both needed a drink.

As their appetizers arrived, and more importantly, the wine, Flavia stared them down with a look of mistrust. But her skepticism might have been prudent. For all she knew, they could have been the ones who "murdered" Carsten and were trying to elicit information from her before delivering her the same fate.

As Youkelstein sipped his soup, he shared the details of what Ellen had said on the video during Maggie's presentation. Hearing it out loud made

Veronica choke on her crab cake, and she needed a gulp of wine to wash it down.

But Flavia didn't seem a bit surprised. She turned to Youkelstein. "It makes me think of your book, Ben: *Smoking the Doppelganger*. A very catchy title, I might add—very sixties."

Youkelstein proudly mentioned that the book was still a hit on Amazon, despite being published over forty years ago.

"So did you find it informative?" he asked, unsteadily raising a spoonful of soup to his mouth.

"I would have if you had remembered to finish it."

"What do you mean?" he replied, a bruised ego showing through.

"I was impressed by the detailed forensic analysis. And I was very open to your theories, especially since I'd never thought of what happened to those dead Nazis. I went in with no preconceived notions—I didn't even know who most of them were. And you made an overwhelming case based on evidence, which swayed me to your thinking."

Youkelstein braced for the but. Authors never seemed to lose their insecurities.

"But you didn't answer the question of *why*, or at least project a hypothetical of what you believe became of them. So you left me hanging. All of these men you mentioned, like Himmler and Hess, were the types who believe they were put on the planet to do grandiose things. If they escaped, as you made a strong case for, I find it hard to believe they spent the remainder of their lives selling insurance in Santa Fe. You didn't complete the thought."

Veronica was stuck on something she mentioned. "You said you never thought about dead Nazis before—what suddenly sparked your interest?"

"Let's just say that the painting you brought me today wasn't the first of its kind to come into my possession."

Flavia turned back to Youkelstein. "So do you believe what you witnessed today represents the final chapter of your book? Maybe that's why you got the invite."

"Perhaps."

"Another issue I had was that the book didn't cover the one missing Nazi I was most interested in—Heinrich Müller," Flavia continued.

Veronica summoned the notes in her head from Nazi-101 class this morning. Müller was the Gestapo Chief.

Who had a child with Ellen!

The child who was the Chosen One.

The aliens are cleared for landing.

"Despite claims of my grandstanding, or those who say I've never met a conspiracy theory I didn't believe, I have always based my findings on facts ... which is why I didn't satisfy your need for an 'ending.' I have never come across any evidence that Müller survived the war. He was last seen in Berlin on April 30, 1945 with his communications director, Christian Scholz. There have been rumors, such as the Russians had captured him and he worked for the KGB, and similar ones about the US and the CIA. But good money was always on Müller being killed in the Battle of Berlin."

"What would you say if I told you I know for a fact that Müller survived the war?"

"After my experiences this morning, I wouldn't doubt you for a moment."

Flavia took another sip of wine. "What do you say we go pay him a visit?"

CHAPTER 22

Zach was convinced that Maggie Peterson was the key to unlocking this mystery. She would be his inside source, even if she didn't know it. And it wasn't a coincidence that he agreed to accompany her outside.

He took a seat beside Maggie at a patio table. It had a view of the grounds, which reminded him of a country club he worked at while growing up in Michigan. He watched as Eddie and Jamie trudged toward the WWI plane exhibit. Then Eddie turned around like he'd forgotten something.

"C'mon, Maggot," he shouted.

She didn't move a muscle.

Zach had the opportunity to observe Maggie during the numerous times she'd come over his house to play nerd with TJ. They didn't have many conversations, since he was the adult—*the enemy!* But he'd learned enough to be familiar with her world-class stubborn streak.

Eddie began marching back toward their table. Jamie was right on his heels. The little guy could smell trouble like a shark could sense blood. And he seemed to thrive on it.

Zach was struggling to get a read on Eddie. At first he wanted no part of leaving the restaurant, acting like he was being demoted to the kiddie table. Then in his next breath, he turned into Maggie and Jamie's personal Secret Service team.

"Let's go, Maggot," he barked. "It's for your own protection."

Not even a twitch.

Jamie decided to toss some gasoline on the fire, "C'mon, Maggot—let's go see the airplanes before they fly away!"

This brought the statue to life. "I told you not to ever call me that!"

"Call you what?" Jamie replied with the most innocent of looks.

"Maggot," she informed him with an earsplitting screech.

Jamie laughed as he pointed at her. "You called yourself Maggot."

Maggie's face turned bright red. "Only Uncle Eddie calls me that!"

Eddie flicked Jamie's ear. "Ouch," the boy said, baffled by the response.

"Only I call her that," he re-asserted his authority and returned his attention to the girl. "C'mon, Maggie—stop being such a wuss."

"I'm going to stay here," she stated. The terms didn't sound negotiable.

This set Eddie off again. He was the jolly mall Santa Claus until someone disagreed with him. "I wasn't asking, Maggie—now come on!"

"You're not my father."

Zach winced; she was bringing out the heavy artillery. Eddie's anger began to overflow ... but this time it was directed at Zach.

"If you think you're going to walk into their lives and then leave when you feel like it, you're going to have to answer to me."

"I don't know what you're getting at—I'm just trying to help out."

Eddie got up in his face. "I did some checking up on you. Seems like you have a reputation for not protecting those close to you, and leaving when it's convenient."

Zach kept his cool. The guy obviously was trying to bait him and he wasn't going there. Eddie wasn't the one who had to endure those painful visits to Bedford every weekend. He never left.

"Like I said, I'm just trying to help out. I didn't mean to step on your toes."

"I'm here for the long run to protect this family. It's how my brother would want it."

"Did he tell you that?"

"What's that supposed to mean?"

"Nothing—I'm just not a big fan of speaking for the dead. I think they can speak for themselves."

With a sharp jab of the hand, Eddie struck like a cobra, grabbing Zach's tie and pulling him close enough to smell lunch. Zach realized if he didn't take the bait, then Eddie was intent on starting the confrontation, regardless.

"Don't mess with this family!"

He whipped out his gun and jammed it against Zach's temple.

As Maggie and TJ might say, or rather, type—*OMG!* The patrons at the neighboring tables began wildly scattering.

Maggie looked horrified, but Jamie seemed enthralled by what might happen. The kid was a little scary.

Then Eddie surprised Zach again.

He lowered the gun and handed it to him. He read Zach's confused look and barked, "If someone comes after her, what are you going to do—stab them with your pen?"

Zach forced a nervous smile. "I once had an editor who said I could bore someone to death."

Eddie turned his back and headed off with Jamie.

CHAPTER 23

A scared looking waitress took their order. Zach got the traditional club sandwich, while Maggie ordered the vegetarian lasagna.

"I didn't know you were a vegetarian," Zach tried to make conversation, acting like the whole gun incident never happened.

Maggie didn't seem as affected—maybe it was just a typical day out with Uncle Eddie—but what he thought was a mundane comment raised her ire. "How would you? You don't know me."

She had a point.

A long awkward pause hovered, before Maggie said out of the blue, "My mom likes you."

Zach tried to mask his surprise. "She said that?"

"No—it's just that she gets all weird when you're around. Gets all forgetful and stuff."

He forgot the basic rules of a twelve-year-old—never let your guard down, and never underestimate their powers of perception. And sadly, eliciting memory loss from Maggie's mom was the best response he'd gotten from a female in a while. Maggie seemed to be gauging his potential response, and he felt he needed to clear things up, whatever those things were.

"We just have a lot in common. Kind of like you and TJ."

"What could you possibly have in common with my mom?"

"Well, we're both raising twelve-year-olds. And as much of a special treat you might think that is, you aren't always a picnic."

"What happened to TJ's mom? He never talks about it."

"She got sick."

"Is she in the hospital?"

"Something like that."

Another awkward silence filled the air until the waitress returned with their meals. She dropped off their food and scurried away before Wyatt Earp and Doc Holliday made a reappearance.

"So you're a big Jim Kingston fan?" Zach asked, pointing at the T-shirt that Maggie broke school rules to wear. Using the old baggy-sweater trick to fool her mother.

"I'm a supporter, not a fan. A fan is someone who paints their face when they go to hockey games."

"Okay, what do you *support* about him?"

"For starters, he's the only candidate who's backing our friends in their time of need."

Wow, twelve years old, Zach thought, when he was her age all he wanted was a BMX bike.

"But I remember you mentioning that you volunteered for his campaign last summer, and there wasn't any potential conflict then."

"I'm big on environmental issues—I think it's our job to leave the earth a better place than we found it, and Jim Kingston believes that. I think Theodore Baer's policies are selfish and shortsighted."

"You're deeper than most kids your age."

"My mom says kids who grow up in the city are like five years older than the average kid." She shrugged. "So who are you voting for?"

"To be honest, I'm not a fan of either guy. But I still have twenty-four hours to figure it out. I usually work better when I'm up against a deadline."

She didn't seem thrilled by the response, but moved on. "Do you believe what my Oma said?"

"I think she believed what she said. And I'm convinced that Sterling believed her, or he wouldn't have shown up."

She sighed. "Get off the fence. Did you believe her *or not?*"

"I'm a reporter. My job is to observe and report the facts."

"Are you sure you don't want to change your order to waffles?"

Good one—underrated sense of humor. Like her mother.

"Okay, I believe the part about your Oma being taken in by the Nazis. And I trust your mom's analysis of the painting. That is important, because it's physical evidence that links Ellen's relationship with Hitler, and gives credence to her claim that she had a child with Müller."

"But?" she read his doubts.

"I'm not sure I believe the whole Apostles thing. If there ever was such a group, I doubt it ever materialized into anything significant. I think your Oma was looking to validate the importance of her existence as she neared the end, so when she read Youkelstein's book about some of these Nazis possibly being alive, her imagination began to run and she created a history that never existed."

"She was telling the truth," Maggie remained steadfast, and irritably dug into her lasagna.

Zach shrugged. "Her timing is a little suspicious, to say the least."

"The timing makes perfect sense. If Theodore Baer gets into power tomorrow, then our freedoms will slowly be taken away, allowing the Nazis to move in."

Zach's face creased in skepticism. "She told you that?"

"No, I figured it out on my own. But there's still one part that doesn't make sense."

"And that would be?"

"The part about her son Josef being the one chosen to lead them back to power. It makes no sense. It would be like Kingston or Baer naming Jamie as their running mate."

Zach looked out at the grounds where Eddie was giving Jamie a piggyback ride. Zach was pretty sure that Jamie would make a more capable vice president than Officer Eddie.

"So you *don't* believe he was chosen?"

"I didn't say he wasn't chosen, I said it didn't make sense," she replied with a frustrated sigh—the grownup just wasn't getting it. "I think to get to the bottom of this we have to answer the question *why* he was chosen."

For most kids, losing their father at such a tender age would have knocked the passion out of them. But Maggie was still oozing with idealism and an overactive imagination that only a novelist could love. Zach got the idea that Ellen took advantage of these qualities, and part of him felt bad for the girl.

"Listen, Maggie, parents often glorify their children. And when children die at a young age they practically saint them. In the video, Ellen alleged that Josef died before he was able to fulfill his promise. I think she made him out to be this Chosen One because it raised him to heights his short life was never able to reach."

Zach thought of his stillborn daughter, Abigail, who would have been TJ's twin sister. Like most parents, Sara assumed that Abigail would've gone on to do great things if she had lived. Maybe. But nobody truly knows where life will take you. Maybe Abigail would have acquired the same sickness of addiction as her mother and ended up a junkie. The scenario was just as likely. Klara Hitler probably thought that her little Adolf would achieve great things. Or at least not become a mass murderer.

"But she didn't glorify him. She knew he wasted his life, and she blamed herself."

"Maybe she used the burden of being 'chosen' as an excuse for his demise?"

Maggie looked out at Eddie and Jamie rolling around in the grass, despite Eddie wearing an expensive suit. At that point, she decided to talk to herself because she seemed to be the only person who understood Maggie Peterson.

"Why was he chosen?" she asked.

CHAPTER 24

Otto sat beside the Candidate in the back of the stretch limo as they moved through the thick Manhattan traffic.

The Candidate's father, Josef, was originally chosen for this role, but greatness clearly had skipped a generation. His father never possessed his charisma and courageous vision. You're either born with that or you're not. Otto hadn't seen such a combination since the Führer—a comparison that gave him chills.

Otto viewed the landscape outside his window. He laughed to himself at the contradictions of this strange wasteland called America. A society that demonized the Führer's racial philosophies, yet built their dynasty on the ethnic cleansing of the Native American and the slave labor of Africans stolen from their homelands. He wondered how their celebrated Manifest Destiny was any different from the Führer's quest for territory called lebensraum.

The Führer understood that certain races were genetically superior to others. And Otto had observed the appeasement of the lesser races divide the United States, weakened its core, and made its structure vulnerable. But he wasn't complaining—it's what they had been counting on all these years.

There was a time when he doubted if this moment would ever be presented to them. As decades passed, and with his aging troops growing restless, he knew he'd have to spark their opportunity himself. And to do so, he re-created the spark that ignited Germany—the Reichstag Fire.

The fire was purposely set by members of the Nazi Party, made to look like an attempt by the communists to overthrow the German government. It was an act that woke up the nation from its slumber and caused then-chancellor Paul von Hindenburg to put out a decree nullifying many of the key civil liberties of the German citizens. The country had remained in a malaise since WWI, too busy feeling sorry for itself to reclaim its birthright of world domination. But the Reichstag Fire on February 27, 1933 restored Germany's fight, and led to the rise of the Führer.

As the new century began, America had slipped into a similar malaise. But unlike Germany, it was based on a different emotion—overconfidence. The United States believed themselves to be an impenetrable fortress, and it was Otto's challenge to alter their mindset.

He'd heard of a group that resided within Germany, which had picked up their battle to fight off the attempts by the Zionists to seek world domination. But while this ragtag militia was based in Germany, they weren't of German descent. *The German people couldn't even fight for their own causes anymore,* Otto sadly thought. This was a group of Arabs—a race he believed to be far beneath the Germans. But when he traveled to Hamburg to meet with their leaders in an apartment the group rented at Marienstrasse-54, near the university in the Harburg section, Otto found what they lacked in genetics they made up for with fearless delusion. Just the men to deliver a modern day Reichstag Fire.

The leader of these genetic mutants was a hypnotic brainwasher who hid in the caves of Pakistan. He had already done the legwork, setting a plan into motion where a cell based in Hamburg would hijack commercial airliners and crash them into symbolic US buildings and monuments. While Otto doubted their ability to pull off such a grandiose plan, he didn't doubt their commitment to the cause.

Otto had observed the US enough to know its greatest strength was also its biggest weakness. When attacked, it would predictably fire back with all its might. But in doing so, it would create an opening for its enemies. It reminded Otto of a celebrated boxing match he attended during his youth in New York, where the German, Max Schmeling, used a similar strategy in defeating the American negro Joe Louis, once again proving the superiority of the German race.

On June 3, 2000, Otto used his many contacts around the world to assist top cell members in moving to Prague, and would later help their entry into the United States, where they'd enroll in an aviation school in Venice, Florida. Otto didn't try to conceal the alias he'd used during his post-war years in the United States—he officially ceased being Otto in 1945—and even went out of his way to make sure his involvement was discovered if the mission was successful, which he did in very *traceable* emails. Only if they failed, as he expected, would he be forced to remove all links that could connect his alias to these savages. One way or another they were going to meet their maker that day.

In the days and months following the attack, the response was as expected. First, the US began restricting rights of the people just as von Hindenburg had done in Germany. Then they threw a wild punch—a convoluted and vague plan termed the War on Terrorism—leaving themselves open for defeat. When this war turned into a protracted struggle it tore at the US's resolve. Little did they know that it was just the appetizer.

And now the main course was about to arrive. Otto smiled at the Candidate and said, "Destiny has arrived."

CHAPTER 25

Jim Kingston, the Democratic nominee for president, looked out of the tinted window of the limo and almost laughed at the scene taking place before his eyes. Limos carrying both candidates were jockeying for position outside of the Sterling Center. With one day to go, even parking spots were a fight to the death.

Kingston exited his vehicle and waited for Aligor Sterling to be helped out. Kingston considered him his secret weapon in this battle, and anyone who underestimated him based on his age or physical handicap, did so at their own peril. Aligor had more energy than men half his age, and even found time to attend a presentation this morning at a school to support an old friend.

He looked out to see Theodore Baer standing in the distance, along with his longtime henchman, Emil Leudke. Baer's silver hair matched his silver tongue—the one he used as a weapon to spew his 500-watt personal attacks. He always looked so innocent—the cuddly Teddy Baer—but looks could be deceiving. And like Aligor, Leudke was still a worthy opponent, despite his advancing age. He was the one most responsible for Baer's meteoric rise, and some would say that he was really the one running for president. Kingston always pictured Leudke talking into his protégé's earpiece like a scene from the *Manchurian Candidate.*

When the two candidates shook hands a fireworks display of flashbulbs went off like it was the Fourth of July. It was like a duel from the Old West where two gunslingers were going to step paces at sunset and solve things the old-fashioned way.

Aligor was completely against what Kingston was about to do ... which was to stand side-by-side with his bitter rival and admit to the world that they were wrong to place that staffer in Baer's camp to tape his off-the-record conversation, even if he technically knew nothing about it. He doubted any campaign manager in the world would think this was a good idea.

Kingston knew he could have taken the easy way out. The tape actually helped him—moving him five points closer in the latest polls. But then again, he could have taken the easy way out in the entire election. All he had to do was sidestep the war issue—say he didn't deal in hypotheticals. That he would hope to broker peace, but would never rule out force if necessary. Political talk. Election speak.

In another time, Kingston might have taken that path. Throughout most of his youth he was rudderless. But when his father died at a young age and he was forced to be the "man of the house," his perspective completely changed. Like turning on a light switch, he suddenly knew who he was and where he must go. And tomorrow he was confident that he would arrive there. 1600 Pennsylvania Avenue.

The four men moved into the high-rise that was the headquarters for Sterling Center. They emerged an hour later and Kingston stood before a microphone and apologized for his campaign's behavior, taking full responsibility for what he called an "underhanded tactic."

When asked by the media why he took this unprecedented step, which was likely to his detriment, Kingston looked into the camera with his honest, pale blue eyes and said, "This is an election about one issue—the future of America. Will it be a courageous leader in the world, or will it build fences and hide from it? The American people have the biggest decision of their lives tomorrow, so I think it's important to move past this pettiness, and get to the important issues that face the voters ... the future of the world is in their hands."

CHAPTER 26

Veronica's mind continued to wander as she drove the winding countryside of Rhinebeck. Just a few hours ago, her biggest problem was the chaos of trying to get her kids to school. Now she was following the woman who may or may not have had an affair with her dead—murdered?— husband, on her way to visit some infamous Nazi who she'd never heard of before this morning, and who must be well over a hundred years old.

Never a dull moment.

The light drizzle turned into pounding rain. Veronica turned on some music. She wouldn't be so cliché as to play "November Rain" from Guns N' Roses, and instead went with "Living on a Prayer" by Bon Jovi. It was a perfect description of how they were rolling at the moment.

Flavia pulled into the entrance of the St. Marks Cemetery. After parking the Jeep, she got out and began walking toward the headstones. When Veronica chose to follow, she felt another chill. She hoped it was just the cold rain, but suspected it was a warning she wasn't heeding.

Youkelstein seemed the most excited of the group. He had a bounce in his step as Flavia held his hand and led him over the wet ground. He finally got to use his umbrella for its intended purpose, and like the gentleman he was, he held it over Flavia's head.

How cute.

Eddie caught up to Veronica and put his protective arm around her. She'd yet to tell him how sorry she was for his loss of Ellen. But this wasn't the time. As long as they were involved in this—whatever this was—he'd put on his tough-guy policeman facade.

Veronica just stared ahead where Maggie was quoting FDR, while Jamie was stepping on the back of her shoe and then acting like he had nothing to do with it. The normalcy made her smile … but it was short-lived. Flavia stopped behind a large marble headstone that read:

Gus Becker
April 28, 1900 - May 14, 1981
A beloved servant of God.

Flavia rubbed her hand over the top of the headstone, cleaning off the accumulating raindrops. "I'd like everyone to meet Heinrich Müller—the former head of the German Gestapo."

CHAPTER 27

The pitter-patter of raindrops served as eerie background music as Flavia spoke.

"My first time in Rhinebeck was during the reading of the will. At least that's what I thought. But the moment I set foot onto the creaky floors of the farmhouse, memories returned from my childhood. I knew I'd been there before.

"I had been flown in from my home in Florida—the whole thing was a whirlwind, and confusing for a teenage girl. I was given a letter dictated by Gus, prior to his death, explaining that my mother had helped him out when he was down on his luck, and he was repaying the favor by leaving me the farmhouse. As the story went, he had worked with my mother prior to his relocating to Rhinebeck to take the position of Chief of Police. Unfortunately, he had a stroke in 1963 that paralyzed him, and I learned that my mother was one of his few friends and colleagues who continued to visit him, and had brought me along on a few of the visits.

"He mentioned that he'd been saddened greatly by her death, and worried how her loss would affect me as I grew up. He said he followed my life from afar and hoped the farm could bring me peace, as it had for him.

"As I read the letter, the childhood trips to Rhinebeck with my mother returned to my consciousness. Including one specific memory—Gus Becker had a son. I was sure of it. But when I brought this up at the reading of the will, wondering why he didn't leave the farm to him, they looked at me like I was crazy. I was told that he had no son—or any other family, for that matter."

"Did you question it further?" Zach asked.

"I was always the kid with the overactive imagination, so I thought it was possible that I'd imagined him. Or perhaps it was a caretaker who I had mistaken for his son. Regardless, I wasn't concerned with why he left me the farm. Truthfully, I really didn't want anything to do with it."

"But you never sold it."

"There was something about the place. I can't explain it, but I could never pull the trigger. I remained in Miami, where I had lived my whole life, but visited a couple times a year. The place was a money-pit—I rented it out once, but being a long-distance landlord became too much of a hassle."

"What made you make the move here permanently?"

"The worst year of my life. The divorce was hard enough, but then my father revealed to me that he had cancer—the late stages that had spread to his liver. He had very little time left, but those last days of his life changed everything for me."

"How so?"

"He confessed that he and my mother weren't who I thought they were. That they worked for the CIA … they were spies. He revealed that my mother, Olivia, had worked on a case that was so highly classified that she couldn't even discuss it with him. And he believed that case was directly tied to her death, which had been made to look like a car accident. But what he told me next floored me."

"More so than your parents being spies?"

"While working on this sensitive case, my mother became pregnant. My father claimed he wasn't really my father, at least in the biological sense."

Flavia appeared to be momentarily overcome with emotion, but continued, "He died days after his confession, not even enough time for it to sink in. I no longer had a mother or father, a husband, or even a past. The only thing I had left was the farm. I went straight from the funeral to the airport, and headed to Rhinebeck to 'sort things out.' It's been over five years and I still haven't used the return ticket."

"Your father was probably on heavy medication when he told you those things," Veronica offered, for the first time feeling some empathy with Flavia.

She nodded. "I had thought the same thing, and began to put the past behind me ... but then I received an anonymous letter. It was from someone claiming to have worked with both my parents, and it backed up my father's statements. But it went a step further—this person had worked with my mother on that secret case."

Youkelstein had put it together. "The reason it was so secretive was that she was working with Heinrich Müller—he was employed by the CIA following the war, after being captured by the US. There were always rumors. The CIA file on Müller was released under the Freedom of Information Act in 2001. It declared no connection to him, but as a rule, I tend not to believe those who lie for a living."

"So you think the CIA killed your mother to cover up her work with Müller?" Zach asked.

"I believe her death was related to Müller, but I don't think it had anything to do with the CIA, nor did the anonymous source. The letter stated that when Truman left office in 1952, he released Müller from his 'sentence.' Müller hated Eisenhower, the in-coming president, and it was mutual—they never would've lasted together. It was the last time anyone officially saw or heard from him. And it's doubtful anyone would go looking for him, since nobody wanted to be connected to the Müller hot potato. There was no evidence that any such person had ever worked there."

"But Olivia Conte did," Zach said. "And she continued to visit him after he left the CIA."

"I had no idea who Heinrich Müller was when I received the letter. I knew very little about the Nazis, other than the basic war movie stuff, so I went to the library and took out every book imaginable. It didn't take me long to link the photos of a young Müller with those of a pre-stroke Gus Becker."

"I can't believe the government let that murderer walk free in exchange for information," Youkelstein bristled, looking physically pained.

Before they could ask more questions, Flavia was on the move again, as if she didn't want to be spotted at the gravesite. They followed her over the soggy ground like they were hypnotized. This was her show.

She strutted through the cemetery, the wind blowing her heavy, damp hair. She remained undaunted, continuing her ghost tale while on the move, "I learned that Gus Becker arrived in Rhinebeck in 1952, the same year he was supposedly released from his CIA commitment. I have no idea why he chose here, but I've found that he never lacked for planning or organization, so there was likely a reason.

"As head of the Gestapo, he had been in charge of creating false identities for the Nazi hierarchy, which became extra important at the end of the war, when they weren't so proud of those SS numbers anymore. So it's no surprise his identity was perfectly crafted, and included an impressive résumé in law enforcement.

"Gus served as head of the Rhinebeck Police Department from 1952 to 1963, before he suffered the stroke that left him in a wheelchair, and without the ability to speak. While on the force, he even used the same card system he'd made infamous when he headed up the Gestapo, which permitted a quick identification of every German citizen and their threat level to Hitler's government."

They passed St. Marks Church. "Following his stroke, Gus dedicated most of his time to the church," Flavia said, pointing at the old, wooden structure.

"That would add up—Heinrich Müller was an ardent Catholic," Youkelstein stated.

"He would be present each Sunday, regardless of his handicap or failing health. He donated a large portion of his life savings to the church, and even purchased a van for the parish so that handicapped people like himself could attend each Sunday."

"Are you trying to say that this made up for what he did?" Veronica asked, irritated.

"No, I'm telling you that the ones who appear the most innocent sometimes can be the most deadly. Like wolves in sheep's clothing."

CHAPTER 28

Veronica gripped the steering wheel as Bon Jovi's "Runaway" played. It was the first good advice she'd gotten all day.

They drove past Victorian homes with piles of leaves dotting the spacious front yards, before eventually turning onto a secluded, dirt driveway. They passed a weathered, red barn that sat peacefully next to a calm pond. The rural landscape was very Norman Rockwell, not to mention a good spot to hide out if you were a Nazi war criminal.

Flavia parked her Jeep in front of a cozy-looking farmhouse with an inviting front porch, which was shouting distance from the barn. Eddie skidded to a stop beside the Jeep, tossing dirt and gravel in all directions, and receiving a giggle from Jamie. In more sedate fashion, Veronica placed the Tahoe behind the police car.

"This place is beautiful," Zach gushed, stepping out of the vehicle.

"It looks peaceful, but the ghosts are just resting," Flavia said. Veronica couldn't decide if she was attempting to be funny or cryptic.

After helping Youkelstein out of the Jeep, their guide was on the move again. She began walking toward the horizon at a brisk pace. The group followed her. The rain had stopped, but the terrain was still muddy.

As they got further and further away from the house, the barn began to look like the tiny red dot of a laser pointer, and Veronica started to become unnerved.

Even Eddie looked a little apprehensive, his hand positioned in striking distance of his gun. Zach tried to give Veronica one of his comforting smiles, but she saw right through it. She grabbed Maggie's hand and found it clammy—a rare sign of nerves. The only ones who seemed to be enjoying the experience were Youkelstein and Jamie.

Flavia stopped suddenly. There didn't seem to be anything special about where she stood, an open field a few acres from the barn. She knelt down, balancing on her heeled shoes, and wiped away some hay. It exposed what looked like a sewer or drainpipe.

"I stumbled upon this when I first moved in—and I mean literally stumbled. I'm a Miami girl, so I was born in heels, but I found they don't work too good on a farm, especially when I caught them in this thing and almost broke my ankle."

She attempted to dislodge the protective cover atop the sewer. When frustration grew, she turned to Eddie. "Officer, I know you don't want to chip a nail, but can a girl get a little help?"

Eddie jumped. But if he didn't, Veronica was sure the other males would've stampeded over her to perform the manual labor for the princess. After a couple of grunts, he removed the metal grill and they stared down into a dark nothingness. Always prepared, Eddie pulled out a flashlight and shined it down what looked like a mineshaft. The light reflected off a ladder that was attached to the sidewall, leading into the abyss.

Flavia cautioned, "We have to go down about a hundred feet in the dark, if you're afraid of heights, the dark, or the Boogie Man, I suggest you wait up here." She paused for a moment, but nobody stepped back.

She looked at Youkelstein, who leaned fraily on his umbrella. Just the walk across the yard had worn him out, and his breathing was labored. "Ben, it might be best for you to stay up top."

A gleam formed in his eye. "I have a feeling I'd regret not seeing what's down there for the rest of my life."

Veronica was impressed by the John Wayne act, but wasn't sure how long that life was going to be if he made a habit of climbing into caves. But she could tell that there was no way he could be talked out of it. So one by one they descended into the dark. Veronica instructed Maggie and Jamie to go between her and Eddie—she would keep them as close to her as possible.

Just when she started to get the sinking feeling that there was no end, she heard Flavia's heels click on the ground, followed by the sound of Youkelstein's umbrella pecking at the terrain. When she reached the bottom, the darkness had turned to light—Flavia had lit torches that lined the walls. The flames illuminated the jagged stalagmites of the musty tunnels.

It reminded Veronica of Howe Caverns, a tourist trap near Albany that was made up of subterranean caves. And like Howe Caverns, the temperature was mild, regardless of the weather outside.

Eddie took control, doing a head count like a camp counselor, and asking, "Is everyone okay?"

Nobody responded, but Youkelstein didn't look too good. Everyone stalled to give him a minute to catch his breath.

Once he was stabilized, Flavia hurried down a winding cave corridor. She continually warned, "Watch your heads," as she expertly maneuvered through the caves. Veronica actually found the caves peaceful.

But then the tranquility was shattered.

Maggie screamed.

Everyone scattered as a bat flew past them.

Veronica took a deep breath. *Be calm for your children. That's what Carsten would do.* She put her arm around an embarrassed Maggie and pulled her tight to her side.

"Bats are cool!" her brother tossed a little salt onto his sister's wounded pride and began chasing after the bat until Eddie horse-collared him.

After putting their hearts back in their chests, they soldiered on, struggling to catch their breath in the thin air. Their path ended at a thick, steel door built into the cave wall. It looked like an airtight door that might be found in a submarine. This time Eddie didn't need to be asked, he twisted a steering-wheel-type device on the door like he was making a hard left turn. After some more grunting and groaning, the heavy door unlatched and opened inward.

This room was not dark, in fact, it was glowing. Veronica took one step inside and her mouth dropped.

CHAPTER 29

Veronica wandered toward the glow. It looked like a miniature version of pictures she had seen in her textbooks.

"The Amber Room," she exclaimed with astonishment.

"I figured that an art history guru like yourself would know better if it's the real deal," Flavia answered. "I found the materials stored underground here in sealed crates. I didn't know what it was at first, but when I figured it out, I tried to put it together just as it last looked in the photos."

Jamie made a mad dash toward one of the chairs, but Veronica grabbed his arm, stopping him in his tracks. You can dress them up, but you just can't take them to a lost treasure once described as The Eighth Wonder of the World, she thought with a shake of her head.

"Be careful," Flavia warned. "The amber is very brittle."

"Just amazing," Youkelstein chimed in. "Shortly after the German invasion of Russia, the Nazis gained control of the treasure. They maintained it at the castle of Königsberg, until January of 1945 when Hitler gave the order to move it. So the treasure was loaded into crates, which were last seen at a railway station in Königsberg. There were rumors it was put aboard the *Wilhelm Gustoff*, which was sunk by a Russian submarine. Some believe it never left Königsberg, which was destroyed by the Royal Air Force that April, while others believe it was burned by the Red Army."

"Wow—raise your hand if you had Rhinebeck in your missing treasures pool," Zach quipped.

Veronica lightly ran her hands over the porcelain fixtures. "I mean, it could be the real deal, but I'm a student, not an expert."

"Well, consider this to be your final exam," Flavia said. "These caves are filled with paintings and other works of art that were stolen by the Nazis during the war. But for obvious reasons, I've never had the opportunity to authenticate them."

"What was your reaction to finding this cave, and all it entailed?" Zach asked like a reporter.

"Like I said, I wasn't a Nazi expert when I moved here. And while I have a good eye for art, I am no historian. I thought they must be Gus' secret art collection—he'd given many paintings to St. Marks, so I knew he'd been a collector. I thought it would be a nice tribute to him to hang them in my gallery."

Youkelstein looked shocked. "You hung priceless stolen paintings in your art gallery!?"

"Obviously I didn't know they were stolen. At least until a customer complimented me on my exhibit to honor paintings stolen by the Nazis. She was also impressed with how exact my replicas looked."

"So let me get this straight," Zach interrupted. "You claim to have stumbled upon this cave after moving here full-time, but you had owned this place for over twenty years. So how did these artifacts remain in such pristine condition?"

"I'm sure the subterranean conditions down here helped, along with the lack of light. And I certainly wasn't the one who constructed these airtight rooms. I believe someone was taking care of the art for all those years after Gus' death. The cave had a curator."

"Any idea who that would be?" Zach asked.

"Yes, I think it was Ellen."

"What makes you think that?"

Flavia began walking away. "You need to follow me."

CHAPTER 30

Part of Veronica wanted to hightail it home. She was kicking herself for taking Ellen's bait. Her only objective was to protect Maggie and Jamie. And by bringing them here, she feared she'd done the opposite.

But the other half was intrigued by the stolen art, and was attracted to the mystery. The old Veronica was shining through the cracks.

Maggie must have noticed her inner turmoil and nudged up beside her. "You okay, Mom?"

"How could I not be? I'm surrounded by all the things I love—you and Jamie, amazing art, Uncle Eddie … okay, two out of three isn't so bad."

They had a good smile at that one—no comedian cracks this time.

The motif inside Flavia's farmhouse was sort of an eclectic mix of Miami Vice and Colonial Williamsburg, but of course it worked.

Flavia disappeared into a long hallway, leaving the rest of them standing in a rustic kitchen that featured a tempting wine bar. The hallway was lined with paintings and Veronica couldn't help wonder if they were also stolen. Flavia returned minutes later, carrying a pile of papers and envelopes and dropped them on the kitchen counter, reminiscent of when Veronica scrambled to pay the bills at the end of each month.

"These are letters between Gus Becker and Ellen Peterson," she announced.

Veronica picked up the first one, dated March 28, 1953. The letter was addressed to Philip and signed by someone named Andrew.

"I don't understand," Veronica said. "These aren't from Ellen."

"Yes they are," Youkelstein said, pulling the letter close to his face. "Philip and Andrew were names of Apostles. They are using their aliases."

"When I first found them, I was confused myself," Flavia explained. "I thought that perhaps Andrew and Philip were lovers who owned the farm prior to Gus. But then one day someone showed up to connect the dots."

"Carsten," Veronica blurted out.

Flavia nodded. "He traced a return address on one of the envelopes he'd discovered in the back of Ellen's closet when they were moving her to Sunshine Village. He wasn't sure what he was looking at either, but when we cross-matched them to the letters I'd found, we realized that we now had both ends of the letter chain. It became clear that Philip was Heinrich Müller/Gus Becker, and Andrew was Ellen. We assumed they had a secret love affair, but little did we know how much further it went."

Eddie didn't want to hear of any affair, or anything that would disparage his memories of Ellen and Harold Peterson. He stormed out of the room, almost knocking Zach over in the process.

Veronica thought to go after him, but thought better of it. She returned her focus to the letters, and when she began to read, she realized that when it came to the Peterson family, Eddie was the least of her worries.

CHAPTER 31

<u>*March 28, 1953*</u>

Philip,

I can't tell you how much your letter made my blood pulse. I have not heard from you in eight years. You always taught me about the importance of faith, but your capture after the war tested mine. I'm sure that working for the Americans could not have been easy for you, but at least you were safe and able to continue to fight the Russians. They are truly the most dastardly of all the earth's creatures.

The plan has carried on in your absence. Thank goodness that the Korean conflict has finally ended, so we can move toward the endgame. Josef is now fourteen and living with the family that was created to care for him. But I must tell you that our son has his mother worried. I'm told his indiscretions are a unique American phenomenon called teenagers. But on the rare occasions I'm able to visit with him, I see trouble in his eyes. I think he needs you ... his father.

My next words are the ones I've avoided since receiving your correspondence. I have married. A good man named Harold—an honorable police officer like yourself. He knows nothing of the group or why we were sent to America. We don't share the same fire as you and I did, Philip, but he is sturdy and the best friend I could ever imagine. We have a son named Harry Jr., who is now four years old. I can only hope that one day he will get to meet his brother Josef.

I can't wait to wrap my arms around you once again. Although, I know secrecy will be paramount for any such meeting.

Love always, Andrew

October 6, 1959

We did it, Philip! We married off our son. What a grand day! I never thought it possible that all the still-living Apostles could be in the same place at the same time. I joked with Bartholomew during dinner that it was our version of The Last Supper, and he responded that he was just glad that no secrets were revealed with so much champagne being consumed. Harold mentioned you when we returned to the city. He was very impressed with the security you provided for the wedding, especially how well organized it was. I could imagine the two of you being great friends under different circumstances. Unfortunately, he can never know who you are. Who we are!

I can only hope this union sets Josef in the right direction. Thaddeus looked beautiful and now that two Apostle families have joined, we are prepared to take our rightful place. I felt Peter beaming down on us. He must have been so proud—he's the one who anointed him the Chosen One, and despite Josef's many stumbles, I still believe in Peter's prophecy. And now we will become grandparents! I wish we could celebrate such a proud moment together, but I understand the situation, as we all do. I was relieved that they had the ceremony before she showed too much. That could be quite a scandal in the high society Josef has now joined. But anything to take the focus away from their true identify is a blessing.

December 1, 1963

I haven't been able to bring myself to write you, Philip. But I'm so relieved that you're finally out of the hospital. I feel the need to be by your side, but we both know that's not a possibility. Harold has focused on my recent depression. He doesn't know I was down about being unable to help my Philip.

Otto found evidence that traced your stroke to Thomas. I know this is not a surprise to you, or any of us. But this was just the tip of the iceberg when it came to Thomas' sins against the group. As we might have suspected, he was plotting his takeover since before the war ended, and was responsible for your capture by the Americans, while also plotting with Judas to murder Peter. Trust was always Peter's downfall, and both of us did warn him of Thomas' true intentions. I know it's no consolation to you, Philip, but we brought you some semblance of justice. Thomas is no longer a threat to us, or anyone.

The recent news of the death of President Kennedy was shocking. It made me think of his mother—I can't even fathom what it must be like for a mother to witness her son being murdered. It made me feel blessed that Josef is alive and healthy, although his relationship with this Olivia woman worries me. I am not one to argue against a mistress for a powerful man, but having a child is complicated and dangerous, as you know, especially with her working for the Americans. But I am glad you have got to spend time with Josef these last few years, and I must say I am excited about our new granddaughter, even if I have reservations about the mother. Get well, my love.

Veronica glanced at Flavia. Her ice princess persona was beginning to melt. Her mother was the Olivia that Ellen spoke of, the mistress who was to have a child with Josef. That would make Heinrich Müller her grandfather, and it suddenly made more sense as to why he left the farm to her. It would also explain the trips her mother made to Rhinebeck and her recollections of Gus Becker's son—he was Flavia's father.

Which meant that Flavia and Carsten did have something in common after all—Ellen Peterson was their grandmother.

CHAPTER 32

Veronica's journey through history brought her to the 1970s. A time of bell-bottoms, shag carpets, and much tragedy for Ellen Peterson. The loss of her children caused a seismic shift in Ellen's thinking.

September 26, 1972

I'm sorry that I haven't written in so long, Philip, but I hadn't the strength to lift a pen. The death of our son has sent me into the depths of despair. I need to be in your arms—it's the only tonic that could possibly ease the pain. It hurt me so much that your condition wouldn't allow you to attend our son's funeral.

I feel you are the only person I can trust now. Every motherly instinct I have is telling me that someone from within the group was responsible for his death. I am the first to admit that his worst enemy was himself. The drugs, the floozies, and his utter lack of ambition and self-discipline, I feel are a reflection on me as his mother. I failed him. The group failed him.

I am suspicious of all the Apostles, Otto included. But I will act like a grieving mother until I get more proof. What type of vicious animal would shoot a man right in front of his son?

August 4, 1975

Maybe I deserved this, Philip. But I would have rather been hit by a lighting bolt than lose another son. I tried to shield Harry Jr. from the secrets of the Apostles, but I couldn't protect him from his own violent and self-destructive nature. I've been thinking a lot about 'nature versus nurture' since Harry's death, wondering if I passed these genetics to both my children. The police say she killed him in self-defense and I have no reason to doubt that. I knew what he had become, I wasn't naïve, and it happened long before that night. It is part of the dark cloud that has been following me since we came to America. And now both my children have been the ones to pay the price. Harold Sr. is devastated. Some days I worry that he will harm himself. He is oblivious to the dark legacy I've brought to my children.

I will spend the remainder of my days on this planet protecting the family that I have left. It will be our secret that I no longer support the Apostles. My only dedication now is to raise my grandson Carsten, and his half-brother Edward. They are my last chance to bring light into my darkness. You must do the same for our granddaughter.

Veronica made eye contact with Flavia from across the room. Her humanity was coming more into focus each moment, even if Veronica didn't want to admit it.

And Veronica actually found some sympathy for Ellen. She had dedicated the last part of her life to protecting Carsten from the truth of his heritage, only to have him find a box of letters in the back of a closet, sending his curious mind on a dangerous mission. That's the thing about being a mother—you can do all the right things and offer fortress-like protection, but in the end, the world can be cruel and random, and there is nothing you can do to stop it. Veronica looked at Maggie and Jamie, and realized no matter what she did, she couldn't guarantee their safety. She felt helpless.

Zach addressed Flavia, "You said you cross-checked these letters against the ones Carsten Peterson had found. The ones that Müller wrote to Ellen. Can we see those?"

"I don't know where they are. They were in his possession the last I knew, but they weren't on him when he died, and were never found, as far as I know."

"We need to re-construct Carsten's last day. That's our best chance to lead us in the right direction," Zach said, sounding assertive.

Veronica didn't think Maggie or Jamie should be reconstructing the day their father died, and sent them out to "play" with their Uncle Eddie. Jamie was itching to join his police partner ever since Eddie bolted from the house, and eagerly ran to the door. Maggie didn't go willingly, but after a spirited debate she relented. She was picking her battles carefully.

"It was the first time I'd seen Carsten scared," Flavia said softly. "He informed me that we'd stumbled into a dangerous situation and that he no longer wanted me involved. I fought him, of course, but he was a stubborn one. Seeking help, he went to his boss at Sterling Publishing, Aligor Sterling, who as you know, is an expert on the subject."

The comment almost sent Veronica through the chimney. Flavia read her look. "It's not what you think—Sterling told him that he couldn't help him. So Carsten took up the search alone and began confiding in a mystery source he'd found through his research. And before you even ask me, he refused to tell me the name of the source."

Just the mention of Sterling seemed to irritate Youkelstein, who "pulled an Eddie" and stomped angrily into the next room.

"Where did he go on that final day?" Zach asked.

"He left to meet his source in Poughkeepsie. I should have followed him, and I've regretted not doing so ever since."

"What was the game plan after Carsten met his contact?"

"We were supposed to meet up later that night for a strategy session at the motel room he was using in Poughkeepsie. But when I got there ..."

Flavia didn't need to finish the sentence. She began to tear-up and Veronica did the same. She wasn't sure if she was crying for Carsten or because Maggie and Jamie had to grow up without a father.

"And that's where the trail ends?" Zach asked.

"Not exactly," Flavia said, and once again had the group's full attention. "I found a note in his pocket before the paramedics arrived. It listed a meeting in Bedford, New York with someone named Rose. I have no idea if it was a first or last name. It was dated from the previous day, but contained no details."

"Was this Rose his contact? The one he went to meet in Poughkeepsie?"

Flavia shrugged. "I have no idea. Like I said, he didn't tell me the contact's name. And with all the aliases these people use, who knows if Rose was the real name, or even if it was a man or woman. I don't even know where I'd start looking."

After a brief silence, Veronica spoke up, "I know who Rose is, and she didn't meet Carsten in Poughkeepsie. She hasn't left Bedford in thirty-five years."

CHAPTER 33

Otto sat by the open window, gazing out into the boundless water. The cold breeze made the curtains dance and goose-bumped his arms. It reminded him that winter was on its way. Perhaps his last winter. But no doubt his most glorious one.

He returned his attention to his favorite poem, *Nibelungenlied,* which he had read throughout his life prior to entering battle. In it, the dragon-slaying hero Siegfried is stabbed in the back by Hagen of Tronje. Otto remembered reading it for the first time back in Brooklyn. The words articulated how he felt—stabbed in the back—and he wept that night, knowing that there were others out there who shared his pain.

It reminded him of the young German soldier, who also broke into tears upon feeling a stab in the back. Adolf Hitler sat blinded in a Munich hospital in 1917—wounded in battle—when he learned of Germany's defeat in World War I.

When his sight returned, he was appalled by what he saw. The German state was being run by those who sabotaged them during the war. The Jewish elite controlled businesses, yet he rarely witnessed them sacrificing their lives on the front line. They were profiting from Germany's defeat. They began robbing the German people of their natural intellectual leadership and enslaving them. He also understood that the oppression in

Germany was not an isolated incident, but part of a bigger Zionist conspiracy to dominate the world.

And the only way to stop this world domination was through revolution. And that was exactly what Hitler did, returning Germany to its rightful place in 1933. He fought against the saboteurs of Germany—the Jewish elites and Marxists, and their enablers in Europe and the West—and while he lost his courageous fight, it was only temporary, as Otto had continued the quest. And with the revolution entering the final stages, Otto could feel the Führer's presence. He was not alone.

The shrill ring of his cell phone interrupted the reminiscing. He released his arthritic hands from the sides of his chair, which he had gripped in anger while thinking of the turbulent days at the end of the war, and answered.

"They are headed to Bedford Hills ... to see Rose Shepherd," the voice spoke with urgency. "Do you want me to stop them?"

Otto pondered this development for a moment. He was always at his best when plans went awry and he was forced to improvise. "No—that won't be necessary. Rose will come through. She always has before," he said and ended the call.

Otto suddenly felt a large hand caress his shoulder. He looked up to see the Candidate. He had been so engrossed in his call that he hadn't heard him enter.

Destiny had arrived.

CHAPTER 34

As far as Veronica knew, Carsten never had any communications with Rose Shepherd as long as they were married. He never even brought up the subject. *Yet on the day he dies, right before meeting his "contact," he goes to meet with her?*

It made no sense.

Or did it make perfect sense?

They'd have to go to Bedford to try to get their answers.

But not everyone would remain on the Nazi Ghost Ship. Eddie refused to go within five miles of Rose Shepherd, and had a good excuse to jump ship—a security meeting for tomorrow's election. Mr. Big Shot would be hanging out with Kingston, the mayor, and the police commissioner, to name a dignified few. Veronica feared his big break would be marred by Ellen's claims this morning. She hoped it wouldn't cost him the gig, but was aware that no politician wanted the stigma of a Nazi connection.

Flavia also turned down an offer to sail the "good ship" to Bedford Hills, choosing instead to return to her gallery. She claimed the Nazi ghosts had caused enough damage in her life, believing they were behind the death of her mother, and refused to chase after them.

After a quick break so that the children could use the bathroom and the adults could return phone messages, they were back on the road.

Youkelstein remained stationed between Maggie and Jamie in the backseat. He was talking to himself, analyzing the letters, and trying to match them to the list of Apostle names. It was established that Ellen was Andrew, and Müller was Philip. But he was now confident that Peter was Hitler, Judas was Bormann, and Thomas was Himmler. And they knew that Thaddeus was the one who married Josef.

But by the time they hit the Taconic Parkway he'd fallen asleep. Veronica noticed a lot of elderly folks napping during her visits to Sunshine Village, and a common theme she noticed was shallow breathing. It was like they knew they only had so many breaths left and didn't want to waste them. But not Youkelstein. Even his breathing was passionate.

He didn't even twitch in response to the sibling battle breaking out around him. Veronica decided not to reprimand them, finding the sound of normalcy to be calming.

My kids are actually acting like kids!

As they merged onto I-84 East, the mood relaxed. Jamie joined Youkelstein in a matching coma, and Maggie was using her iPod to block out the lesser species. Zach had signed on the Internet to search for all the information he could on Rose Shepherd. His mood seemed to sour the closer they got to Bedford. Veronica didn't blame him—the story of Rose Shepherd wasn't pretty.

When they first started dating, Carsten had told her that his parents had died in an "accident," which she assumed to be a car crash. But as their relationship took a turn for the serious, and they found they had that rare "can tell each other anything" dynamic—the one that often fools couples into making vows and having babies—he told her the real story. That his mother was taking medication for depression that caused her to go into a state of paranoia, and made her think his father was a burglar, resulting in her accidentally stabbing him to death.

Carsten blamed the charges against his mother on it being a different time, when not much was known about mental illness. He contended the

District Attorney made a mistake by putting her in a jail when she really needed to be in a hospital to get treatment. A mistake that cost his mother her life.

It was a gut-wrenching story.

But not completely true.

Veronica had been married to Carsten for almost eleven years when the incident took place in the kitchen of their Upper East Side apartment. The night their arguing crossed the line. The funny thing was that Veronica used to brag to their friends about how she and Carsten "never fought." *Probably because she always gave in to his every whim,* she thought in retrospect.

She couldn't pinpoint the exact time when he changed. There wasn't any one incident. His long nights at the office were not out of character throughout their marriage, but he'd turned distant, and started not coming home for days.

Their arguments went from non-existent to constant, each one escalating in ferocity. And that night it happened so fast that Veronica never saw his fist coming toward her, dropping her to the cold, linoleum floor. That's what she most remembered—how cold the floor felt.

The next day she told a mother at Maggie's school that she was taking a box off the top shelf of their closet and accidentally dropped it on her face. Suddenly she was one of *those* people. They were one of *those* couples.

He said it would never happen again.

And it didn't.

But his look remained a haunting reminder. The one where it looked like he needed every muscle in his body to restrain himself from doing it again.

All of this led her to re-examine his father's death, eventually leading her to the microfilm room at the New York Public Library. She'd never questioned it before—it was a touchy subject that Carsten would never bring up. But after their own violent altercation in a kitchen, questions had arisen in Veronica's mind.

By all accounts, Harry Jr. was a model husband and a doting father to their son Carsten, and Eddie, who was Greta's child from a previous relationship. But according to the police report, Greta claimed that something snapped in him one day.

He started drinking heavily and would go into random rages where he'd hold rambling conversations with himself. This correlated with violent attacks on the job, leading to reprimands and suspensions.

Greta alleged that he'd threatened to kill her and the children on numerous occasions over the past month of his life, and that night he looked like he was going to live up to his word. During a scuffle, with his hands gripped tightly around her neck, cutting off her air, she reached for the nearest object. It turned out to be a meat cleaver, and she thrust it through his chest.

And the worst part—

It happened right in front of Carsten and Eddie.

They weren't tucked away in their room like Carsten had told her.

The next days' headline in the *New York Globe* was *Mrs. Cleaver* with a picture of Greta being hauled away in handcuffs. Not exactly one for the family scrapbook.

The arrest was controversial. Groups for battered women came to Greta's defense, while the police tried to spin their fallen brother as heroic, and depicting Greta as a deranged woman with a checkered past.

Rumor was that the DA planned to drop the charges as soon as the furor died down and the police found a way to save face. But Greta Peterson never left her jail cell. While awaiting her preliminary hearing, she was strangled to death by her cellmate.

Her cellmate was named Rose Shepherd.

CHAPTER 35

The gray autumn sky had faded to black. It was a few minutes before four in the afternoon, but this time of year it got dark early. *Just what this amateur horror film needed,* Veronica thought.

Bedford Hills Correctional Facility was a block-shaped building surrounded by barbed wire fencing. It looked like a typical prison, but in the quaint, historic hamlet of Bedford Hills, it seemed as out of place as a snowmobile shop in Malibu.

As they moved through a guard-gate and headed toward visitor parking, Veronica was tempted to turn the vehicle around and dash the ten miles to home sweet home.

Jamie and Youkelstein were still out like a light, and Maggie remained lost in her iPodian world. Veronica expected Zach to be the rock he'd been all day, but he looked like he was about to be ill. Prisons could do that to people.

"Are you okay?" she asked him softly.

He didn't respond. He was lost in thought and staring at the large structure in front of them.

"Zach?"

"Oh … I'm sorry … you were saying?"

"You're supposed to wait until the second date to start ignoring me," she said with a grin.

Still no response. But then it hit her why. Bedford was the largest *women's* penitentiary in the state of New York. Over eight hundred inmates were incarcerated inside the facility.

Zach's wife was in prison.

"I'm sorry, I didn't connect it," she immediately apologized.

"It's not your fault. It wasn't your crystal-meth lab."

"It's not too late to turn around."

"Don't worry about it. I bring TJ up here every weekend. I should be used to it by now, but there is just something about this place that gives me the creeps. Once I get inside, I'm usually okay."

"That's why you moved to Pleasantville and took the job at the local paper, isn't it? To be close to Bedford."

"It's important that TJ continues a relationship with his mother. They have a great program here to promote closeness between the inmates and their children. Eighty percent of the inmates here are mothers."

"I never really thought about that."

"They offer programs that allow TJ to stay with a volunteer family overnight, and he can then visit his mother for extended hours during the day. It's run by this great woman named Sister Goulet. She's kind of a legend in these parts—she should be sainted."

"I think I read about her in the paper."

He smiled proudly. "That was my article. Of course, I also wrote one about the inadequate facilities—not enough heat in the winter and no ventilation in the summer. And how the bathrooms didn't meet minimal health codes. But I regret writing it, I don't want to hurt Sara's chances of parole."

"If you don't mind me asking, how long is her sentence?"

"Eight years, up for parole in three. She just completed her first year."

Veronica thought that perhaps Zach should be the one up for sainthood, but he was philosophical about it, "Sister Goulet reminded me that many of the women in here have been bad citizens, but still are good people and great mothers. I like to believe that Sara fits that description. Nothing in life is black and white."

The superintendent of the prison was waiting for them. Zach was the one who called ahead to request the visit, and after his articles they were ready to put on their best face when he came calling. The other reason for using Zach's name was so they didn't raise any suspicion as to why the daughter-in-law of the woman Rose Shepherd murdered would be attending.

The superintendent was a woman named Nina Flores. She led them through a security checkpoint, in which Youkelstein's umbrella was confiscated with the promise of a return upon their departure. Without his cane, Veronica helped him walk down the bleak corridors. She got the sense that he would've preferred Flavia.

Ms. Flores was putting on her best foot forward, but Veronica could still sense a little coldness directed at Zach. They first stopped off at the office of Sister Goulet, whose demeanor was the complete opposite. She greeted them with warm hugs and smiles.

After the introductions, and some brief small talk, they continued the journey to a large room that resembled a nursery, painted in pinks and blues. It was the playroom, filled with children and their jailed mothers—a few of the inmates were pregnant. There was even a pre-natal room with a wading pool.

Sister Goulet suggested the children stay there while the adults go to see Rose Shepherd.

Jamie was attracted to the toys, and didn't need to have his arm twisted. Maggie, on the other hand, would rather have been put in solitary lock-down. She looked like she was about to deliver a right hook to the sister's midsection. But showing another mark of her potential sainthood, she somehow convinced Maggie to stay behind without a fight.

Rose Shepherd was a local quasi-celebrity because she was the oldest incarcerated female in the United States. Ninety-nine years old.

Veronica was expecting the traditional jail cell with steel bars. But that wasn't where Rose Shepherd was spending the late winter of her life. A large window allowed visitors to view into her room as if she were on display in a zoo. When Veronica peeked in, she noticed what looked like an apartment with a couch and television. No windows to the outside world, but frankly, the place would've gone for about five grand a month in Manhattan.

Ms. Flores, likely fearing a Zach Chester exposé on preferential treatment of murderers, explained, "Ms. Shepherd is almost a hundred years old. It just isn't plausible to have her living with the normal population."

A guard opened a heavy, air-pressured door. Ms. Flores walked them in and Veronica almost choked on the heavy scent of perfume.

The sight before her was odd. Rose Shepherd was sitting on a couch with a blanket over her legs, reading the latest Nora Roberts romance novel. And she looked like she'd dressed for the occasion. Or maybe she was dressed for the Governor's Ball. She wore a blue, silk dress. Her face was heavily made up, her lipstick was bright red, and her hair was dyed a yellowish blonde and styled in a way that reminded Veronica of a Flapper-cut from the Roaring Twenties. About as far away from an orange jumpsuit as you could get.

She also wore a heavy necklace that hung below the neckline of the dress. Veronica found an object around her neck sadly ironic, since the thing that connected them was the fact that Rose had strangled Greta Peterson to death. She also found it lax in regards to Rose's personal safety, since it was well known that she had made numerous suicide attempts during her stay at Bedford.

Ms. Flores told them not to be flattered, as the stylish prisoner dressed to the nines every day, despite rarely seeing a visitor. She then left them alone with a warning that the guard was right outside the door. Veronica wasn't sure if the warning was for them or Rose.

Veronica studied the woman who she never met, yet had altered her husband's life more than she ever did. And despite all the pain that Rose had caused Carsten, he came to visit her on his last day of life.

CHAPTER 36

Rose didn't acknowledge their presence, as her nose remained glued to the book she unsteadily held. Veronica noticed magazines scattered across the floor. All of them were of the celebrity gossip type. The catchy theme of *Entertainment Tonight* played in the background at earsplitting volume.

Veronica approached the prisoner and introduced herself, trying to match the loudness of the television. Rose looked up at them in a childlike way. They didn't register to her, but she looked happy to see them nonetheless, and announced, "Welcome to the Grand Hotel!"

This should be good, Veronica thought. She was admittedly no Mike Wallace and opened the questioning with, "I love your dress."

Rose smiled. Her teeth were whiter than Veronica expected. "It's my wedding dress."

Veronica had researched Rose Shepherd backward and forward, so she knew she had never been married. But then again, in her mind, she might have been.

Veronica's eyes swept the room once more. The choice to come here seemed right at the time, but now she wasn't so sure. The room was full of entertainment—TV, movies, books. So she tried to play off that. "You look like a movie star."

The comment seemed to awaken Rose. "Ever since a little girl I wanted to be an actress. I always wanted to see my name up in lights like Jean Harlow," she replied enthusiastically. Zach clicked off the television so they could better hear. She didn't seem to notice.

The answer matched Veronica's research. According to a 1976 *TIME Magazine* article in which Rose gave her only interview about Greta's murder, she mentioned that the Shepherds came to New York following World War I. As a young woman, Rose caught the acting bug, and while she never became the next Jean Harlow, she did earn a small role in a 1949 off-Broadway play.

In the 1950s she moved behind the camera—another one of her passions—and opened her own photography shop on the Upper West Side. Her big break came when she was chosen as the photographer for the wedding of Aligor Sterling's son. Aligor was so impressed with her work that he hired her for all photography work for Sterling Publishing. By most accounts, she spent the next decades living out the successful life of a professional single woman in New York. There was nothing in her past that would foreshadow a violent future. That's what made what happened next so perplexing.

She was arrested in May of 1975 for blackmail and extortion. It wasn't a crime that made headlines like the *Mrs. Cleaver* stabbing had, months earlier. Rose Shepherd claimed to have come across information of a sensitive nature that she felt could hurt Sterling Publishing, and tried to extort money from Aligor Sterling in exchange for her silence. He alerted the authorities and cooperated in a sting operation. When she tried to blackmail him on tape, she was arrested.

The content of the "sensitive" photos was anybody's guess because the court sealed them. But no action was taken against Sterling, so Veronica figured they might have been embarrassing, but weren't illegal. The bigger question was what would cause a sixty-something woman to suddenly turn on her biggest client and blackmail him? It seemed like she was biting the hand that fed her. But then things took an even more bizarre turn. While in prison awaiting her trial, she strangled her cellmate.

Likely feeling guilty over their mother's murder, Aligor Sterling offered the Peterson children lifetime jobs at his company. Carsten took advantage of this opportunity and moved quickly up the ranks. But Eddie had always dreamed of following the family tradition of working in law enforcement, and never took him up on it. Veronica wondered if the security job for Kingston had some connection to that original offer.

Rose's eyes returned to the television. Zach turned it back on just in time for the anchorwoman to deliver a story about a one time A-list actress who had fallen on hard times and reportedly attempted suicide.

"I feel so sad for her," Rose surprisingly blurted out. "She was forced to go through life under the glare of the spotlight, I know exactly how it feels. I once tried to kill myself because a boy broke my heart. I just wanted to make the pain stop."

Rose pointed out the scars on her wrist to confirm her suicide attempt. The scars were faded with time, but it was obvious that her unstable behavior began long before she shared that cell with Greta Peterson.

"I want to ask you about a day last year when a man named Carsten Peterson came to see you," Veronica said.

Her eyes glazed over as she stared at the television screen. Veronica asked again, louder this time, like she was talking to one of her children.

Rose looked up with a baffled look. "I don't know—who is he?"

"You killed his mother," Veronica said directly.

Rose remained entrenched in her own little world, showing no outward emotion. "It's so sad when a child has to grow up without a mother."

Veronica was losing her cool, but luckily the unflappable Zach stepped in, "Rose—I'm trying to figure out how a woman in her sixties with a no criminal record, wakes up one morning and decides to blackmail one of the world's most powerful men ... who also happens to be her meal ticket. My guess is that it was about more than the money. Maybe you should think about cleansing your soul before it's too late."

Her eyes un-glazed, and she was suddenly in the moment. "I didn't blackmail anybody."

"A court of law didn't agree with you."

"That's not true, the blackmail charges were dropped. The only thing I was convicted of was murder," she said, surprisingly coherent.

"Only? Let me guess, you didn't do that either."

"They had Jew lawyers to say I did. They were very powerful men."

"So you're saying that Sterling conspired to frame you for murder. Why would he do that?" Zach pushed on, needing to take advantage before she drifted back into la-la land.

She clammed up, looking nervous. The woman was ninety-nine, serving a life sentence without parole, what did she have to lose? "*Shh*—the Jews can get you anywhere," she whispered.

Veronica found it peculiar that a man who ran an organization dedicated to Jewish causes would hire someone with such views, no matter how talented a photographer she was.

Zach pleaded with her, "Please, Rose, it's very important."

"I found out things about him," she said quietly like she was worried Big Brother was listening. Everyone inched closer. "I came across things."

"What things were those?"

"A good girl never kisses and tells."

Veronica was pretty sure that she was implying that she'd had an affair with Sterling. As Maggie might say—*super gross!*

"I was the only non-Jew associated with Sterling Publishing. Do you think he really hired me because my photographs were so special?"

Veronica was curious what Mr. Conspiracy Theory, Ben Youkelstein, thought about this, as he'd been mysteriously quiet during the interview process. She wondered if they might have crossed paths at some point, both working for Sterling.

But his only question for her was, "You said you tried to kill yourself over a boyfriend when you were younger. What was his name?"

She flickered a reminiscing smile. "Henry Wolf. He died in World War II, and I could never marry another man … including Aligor."

Veronica had no idea what Ben was getting at, but it appeared that it would be the final question. Before they could dig deeper into Carsten's final visit, Rose Shepherd drifted off to sleep.

The interview was over.

CHAPTER 37

Lieutenant Edward Peterson passed through the heavy security outside Jim Kingston's property. He drove through the gates, passing formal gardens that could have moonlighted as a state park, as he pulled his police cruiser to a stop in front of the mansion. It combined Tudor and Elizabethan revival styles and overlooked the Long Island Sound from its perch in Kings Point. "A man of the people," Eddie said to himself with a laugh.

He was greeted by Kingston's security detail. Since Bobby Kennedy's assassination in 1968, presidential candidates had the right to file for protection with the Federal Election Commission. But Kingston pointed out that it would cost the taxpayer about 50k a day to protect him, so funding his own security scored him some points with the voters.

Eddie was escorted through the grand doorway, into a low-beamed entrance room that contained a fireplace so big you'd have to chop down half a forest to get a good fire going. There, he was greeted by Aligor Sterling, who was flanked by a balding man with a whiny voice that Eddie recognized from TV as Kingston's campaign manager. A bunch of Sterling's ass-kissing assistants were also on the welcome committee.

Sterling immediately took control of the room. He might not have been officially in charge of the campaign, but everyone knew he had the most clout. He ordered the group to follow him, and they obliged.

Eddie trailed the group into the two-story Great Room. It was a "stop you in your tracks" room with a grand staircase leading up to a carved balcony. Enormous bay windows provided a magnificent view of the Sound and the beautiful cliffs of the north shore of Long Island.

Sterling wheeled to the window and gazed out. Eddie followed him. It seemed implied that he was supposed to, but he wasn't sure. After this morning's events, he was unclear if he remained in good standing.

"It's a beautiful view isn't it, Lieutenant Peterson," Sterling said. His tone differed from the cheery salutations at Jamie's school.

"Breathtaking," Eddie replied.

"You can see my estate from here," Sterling said, pointing at an enormous manor across the water on the hamlet of Sands Point.

"It's nice and all, but I'm not sure it compares to my rent-controlled one bedroom in the Bronx. Best fire-escape in the neighborhood," Eddie tried to joke.

Nobody laughed.

"Did you know that Sands Point was the inspiration for the fictional East Egg in the *Great Gatsby*, while Kings Point inspired West Egg. Did you read *Gatsby*, Lieutenant Peterson?"

"My rule is if it don't have a centerfold then I don't read it. Although, I once convinced Kristi Wallace that I read Shakespeare so I could get in her pants back in high school."

Sterling ignored him. "Jay Gatsby looked out from West Egg at a light at the end of a dock on East Egg. To him, it represented hope. It represented dreams."

"Sounds like a real page turner."

"You see, we are now very close to reaching that light. Tomorrow Jim Kingston will complete the journey to that dock, and will arrive carrying all of our dreams. Do you understand?

Eddie nodded. The message was clear—nothing would stop their dream.

Having made his point, Sterling was on the move again. They passed through a formal dining room and into the library. It featured a large mural of mythological sea creatures on one side. The other side of the room was lined with bookcases. A floor-to-ceiling window provided a view of the expansive front lawn. Eddie focused on the leaves swirling in the wind, which was how his stomach felt at the moment.

Jim Kingston sat behind a large mahogany desk, his ear locked to a landline phone.

The room was filled with his top aides, along with the mayor of New York and the NYPD police commissioner. Eddie was met with a cool reception from all.

Kingston hung up, apologizing for the delay, mentioning that he was talking to his running mate, Senator Langor from Florida. He rose to his feet and approached Eddie. He greeted him with a handshake and pat on the back.

Kingston returned behind his desk and addressed the group, "The reason Eddie is here, along with Mr. Mayor and Mr. Commissioner, is we've agreed to coordinate our safety with the city of New York when I give our victory speech tomorrow night at the Waldorf. As you know, Lieutenant Peterson has been chosen to head up the efforts of NYPD."

Eddie was given the floor. He nervously stammered through the detailed plan they'd been working on for months. The most interesting would be the Long Range Acoustic Devices used to listen in on people's conversations from as far away as a helicopter.

They would also use traditional tactics such as concrete barriers, while sectioning off areas around the Waldorf with barbed wire. NYPD would be stationed on horseback, bicycles, and in unmarked cars with blacked out windows. A makeshift holding cell had been set up at Pier-57 for those they apprehended.

Eddie began to get his sea-legs and his confidence rose. He skillfully detailed his coordinated efforts with the Technical Assistance Response Unit, who had been filming people in the area for the past week.

Kingston asked the group for feedback and it was negative. Not at the tactics themselves, but Eddie's presence. A bespectacled pollster warned of plummeting Florida numbers if word got out that Ellen Peterson's adopted grandson was involved in any way with the campaign.

The campaign manager called for Eddie's ouster. He then turned to the police commissioner and added, "And it's not like he earned the position because of his great résumé—he was chosen because he's a legacy of Harold Peterson."

Eddie bit his tongue—he could never escape his family history.

Aligor Sterling spoke up, "It was my decision to bring Eddie on because of my fondness for his brother, Carsten Peterson, who was a loyal employee of mine for years. But I must concur with the others ..."

Kingston had the final word, "Eddie isn't going anywhere. He is here for *my* security. Aligor picked him because loyalty is a family trait of the Petersons. And when someone starts shooting at me, I want a loyal man in charge of protecting me."

CHAPTER 38

Veronica remembered the last homework assignment she helped Maggie with. It was a math assignment about the lowest common denominator. She wasn't much help—math wasn't really her thing—but now she was starting to better understand the concept of LCD. And in this case the lowest common denominator was Aligor Sterling.

The last non-relative to visit Ellen was *Sterling*.

One of the few non family members invited to Maggie's presentation was *Sterling*.

Carsten brought the letters between Ellen and Gus Becker to his boss...*Sterling*.

Rose Shepherd was in jail for blackmailing *Sterling*.

They sat quietly in bumper-to-bumper traffic. Maggie and Jamie were both giving her the silent treatment. Maggie's angst was a result of being forbidden from the meeting with Rose Shepherd. But Veronica didn't care if she didn't speak to her for the next fifty years, she would protect the myth of her father and shield her from her family history of violence.

Jamie, on the other hand, was ticked off because he wasn't allowed to stay and finish a video game he was playing with one of the children of the inmates. Their tactics weren't working—Veronica was enjoying the rare quiet time.

Keeping with the theme, Youkelstein was silently reading in the backseat. Zach turned back toward him like he wanted to ask him a question and noticed his book. "Where'd you get that?"

"I carry a copy with me at all times."

"Why on earth would you do that—you do know that book claims the personification of the devil as the symbol of all evil assumes the living shape of a Jew?"

"I carry it because I never want to forget."

He held up an aged hardcover that displayed a menacing portrait of a youthful looking Adolf Hitler. The title *Mein Kampf—My Struggle*—was draped diagonally over Hitler like he was wearing a pageant banner.

"It's currently banned in France and Germany," Youkelstein added. "I don't agree with that. I think it should be required reading in all schools throughout the world. It's important for children to learn that such a level of hate exists, and how dangerous it can be when mixed with elements such as opportunity and charisma."

"And what made you suddenly need to remind yourself again?" Zach asked. "You would think our adventures today would make you unable to forget."

"Rose Shepherd's accommodations."

"You mean that furnished apartment that was disguised as a jail cell?"

"Yes, it reminded me of when Hitler was arrested for the Beer Hall Putsch in 1924—when he and his cronies tried to take over the government in a coup."

"I know what the Beer Hall Putsch is—I just don't know what it has to do with Rose Shepherd's room."

"Hitler was jailed, but not in a normal prison cell. He stayed in two adjoining luxury rooms like a four-star hotel and visitors could come freely. It's where he dictated *Mein Kampf* to Rudolph Hess. It made me wonder if there are answers within these hateful diatribes."

Zach looked skeptical. "Any luck?"

"Even if Himmler was the most powerful force within the Apostles, Hitler was still the original architect of the plan. And unlike Himmler, who operated under the surface, Hitler always laid out his ideology for the world to see. *Mein Kampf* is a prime example of this. He wore his emotions on his swastika'd sleeve. And in doing so, left the blueprints for the Apostles."

"Did he by any chance leave a map to the bad guys?"

Veronica could tell that Zach was losing patience with Youkelstein's cryptic responses.

"For starters, I realized that *v^988v^* is not a code or puzzle piece in a treasure map. We were looking too deep. They didn't need a stealth code to hide from capture. They were the only ones who knew the code—it was the most selective of clubs. It's probably more of a rallying call, or a mission statement, than the secret code we've been making it out to be."

"I was focusing on a date," Zach said. "I thought the numbers might add up to a date of significance. That is how the military came up with the 21-gun salute—they added up the numbers from the year 1776."

"That is a myth—the salute was instituted long before 1776. A petty point, I know, but one that reinforces the point that what is accepted as historically accurate is often untrue. This makes *Kampf* an important guide for us, since the words come right from Hitler's mouth, and can't be diluted by storytellers. In it, he writes of '*A Thousand Years of Reich*.' He served from 1933 to 1945, twelve years, so *988* is likely referring to the remainder of the thousand years they are trying to recapture. And if you re-hook the horizontal lightning bolts that surround the number, you will have recreated the Nazi symbol of a swastika." He scribbled it on the inside cover of the book, connecting the lines of the swastika. "That is what this is all about, returning the Reich to its position of power, as promised by Hitler himself."

Veronica had stopped listening. She doubted that Zach and Youkelstein were on the path to the right answers, mainly because they were taking the wrong classes. They were studying literature, history, and symbology, when they really needed to be taking math.

She continued to drive toward Manhattan, to have a discussion with the lowest common denominator.

CHAPTER 39

As they pulled up in front of the glimmering skyscraper on Park Avenue, Zach felt an old familiar rush. He'd been lost at sea, wallowing in self-pity, but now felt as if he were rowing ashore once again.

He thought back to when he interviewed Aligor Sterling in the same building on the 60th Anniversary of the end of the Holocaust. Little did he know that there might be a modern-day story of danger and intrigue inside those walls.

As he'd told Maggie, Zach had his doubts that this was a big story, at least in the way Ellen and Youkelstein thought it was. But nevertheless, Sterling was still a huge player in this election—many believed him to be Kingston's "voice"—and there was no denying he was his biggest financial supporter. At the very least, his conduct was suspicious.

Veronica had been a rock all day, but Zach noticed that her emotions were starting to fray. And when she spotted Sterling's limo pulling up to the sidewalk, she looked like she was going to erupt. She got out of the vehicle and headed right for him, machine-gun-wielding security be damned.

Sterling looked surprised by the crazed woman rapidly walking toward them, as he was being helped from the limo. But when he realized it was Veronica, he told his men to stand down, and offered a friendly greeting. He took Veronica's hand and said, "Twice in one day—what do I owe such an honor?"

"We have a few questions concerning Ellen Peterson," Zach said, right behind her.

He looked at his watch. "Very well, we can meet in my office. I'm just returning from a security meeting for tomorrow's victory."

He smiled pleasantly like he was running for office himself, but his smile suddenly sank into the sea.

He saw Youkelstein.

"I must be dead," Sterling snipped, "because I know Ben Youkelstein only chases ghosts."

Youkelstein looked ready for a fight. "I find it much more honorable to chase ghosts than to whore myself to television cameras and the publicity machine."

For a moment, it looked like the former friends were going to have a physical altercation. Yoda on Yoda violence. But Sterling was savvy enough to know that Theodore Baer's people would love to get a shot of him coming unglued on Election Eve. So he backed down.

Youkelstein retook his vow to never again step foot in Sterling House. He limped away, rhythmically pounding his umbrella cane into the cement sidewalk.

Sterling ignored the tantrum as he ushered his guests toward the entrance. But Zach realized Veronica was stuck in a quandary. She wanted to shield Maggie and Jamie from any discussions involving their father's death, but also needed to keep them close.

Sterling offered his security detail to watch them. But with her trust level of Sterling at zero, that wasn't happening. Maggie initially fought for inclusion, the first words she'd spoken since leaving Bedford Hills, but she was no match for her protective mother. Seeing that it wasn't going her way, Maggie offered up a potential solution—to catch up with Youkelstein and stay with him. She probably saw an opportunity to pick his brain.

Veronica didn't trust anybody at this point, but she seemed resigned to the fact that this was the best possible solution.

Sterling took money out of the pocket of his suit-jacket and handed it to the children. "There is a great ice cream shop down the street, why don't you take Ben and get something you like."

The mention of ice cream sealed the deal, and the kids were racing toward Youkelstein before the adults could change their minds.

Veronica's face reeked of apprehension as she watched her children run away from her.

CHAPTER 40

Whenever Veronica couldn't make a decision, whether it be one with life-changing implications or as simple as what dress to wear to a party, Carsten would always tell her to trust her gut. And when she did, the right answer always seemed to present itself.

All day the gut was very clear—keep Maggie and Jamie as close to her as possible—but for some unknown reason she didn't listen this time.

Maybe it was because of Zach's presence. He had a way of making her feel like everything would be all right. For the first time in a long time, she didn't feel like she was totally on her own. Maybe it distracted her from the inner voice.

They followed Sterling and his guards into the open plaza that led into Sterling House. The granite park was normally a quaint place, but tonight a small rally was taking place in support of Kingston, filled with energized college kids handing out pamphlets.

Sterling was proud of the plaza. It was created back in 1950 with the intention of it being a gathering place, especially for displaced European Jews and Holocaust survivors who ended up in this new crazy world called New York. His face lit up when he described letters he'd received from married couples who had met there. Including one couple who'd just celebrated their fiftieth wedding anniversary.

He was equally proud of Sterling House. He said it was important for the building to symbolize the Jewish people as strong and resilient, as they healed the wounds of their battered self-esteem following the war. But also a reminder of the past, as it included a black marble scroll with the names of Holocaust victims engraved on the side of the building.

Despite his claim of being short on time, Sterling took a few moments to talk to the Kingston supporters. Veronica was getting jumpier by the second, needing to get to her kids.

They eventually moved inside the lower level of the building. Sterling bragged that over five million pounds of bronze was used during construction, as they rode an elevator to the top floor. Veronica hadn't been in the building since she'd picked up Carsten's belongings after his death, and felt a similar discomfort. When they exited the elevator, they followed Sterling into a lavish office that overlooked Manhattan Island, the guards remaining outside.

No sign of Bormann's skull.

As Sterling wheeled behind a desk, he noticed Zach looking at the pictures hung on the office walls. "That's my father Jacob Sterling," he said, pointing proudly at the picture of the balding man in a suit, sporting horn-rimmed glasses and a gray mustache.

"My father came from a wealthy family in Prague. He didn't have to work a day in his life, but he chose to become a doctor to help those in need. He worked in the Jewish ghettos of Prague, helping the most weary and poor, and he never took a dime in his life from his patients."

Veronica's mind infested with conspiratorial thoughts, centering on Sterling's eagerness to separate her from her children, and now seemingly stalling, when he previously claimed hurry.

"Then when the Nazis took over," Sterling continued, "he was arrested for treating Jewish patients. I was a medical student at the time. We were sent to separate concentration camps, and I feared it would be the last time I'd see him. My father wisely used his wealth and connections to get my mother and two younger sisters out of the country to flee from their inevitable capture. Then, after the war, we were able to rejoin them here in America."

"From the looks of things, America has been good to the Sterlings," Zach observed.

Sterling smiled. "America is the land of opportunity. And we took advantage of that opportunity to give back to those who were oppressed. My father started his publishing business for the sole purpose of telling the stories of those who suffered in concentration camps. The ones who weren't as lucky as us. He wasn't going to let the world forget."

"You've definitely succeeded in that area," Zach said in a conciliatory tone.

"It's an ongoing fight, which is why we expanded the business to include the Sterling Center, which promotes Jewish causes throughout the world. And when my father died, back in the 1960s, I took over the entire business."

He caught himself. "I'm so sorry—I'm babbling—you said you had some questions for me?"

He sat with a satisfied look—the lights of the city reflecting off his old face. Veronica wanted to grab him and shake the truth out of him. But Zach gave her his calming "follow my lead" look.

Her gut told her to follow. She wasn't going against it again tonight.

CHAPTER 41

Zach took out a flip-pad and pen. "Your were the last non-relative listed as visiting Ellen's room at Sunshine Village. Could you tell me the nature of your business?"

"She called me and asked if I'd stop by."

"What was her reasoning for such?"

"Ellen and I had known each other for years. I believe her purpose was nostalgia. When you get to our age, memory lane is a long and winding road."

"Did she talk about taking her own life at any point during your conversation?"

His face saddened. "Ever since Harold died, some years ago, she had often mentioned a desire to join him. But after Carsten's death, she really got bad. It always came up with her."

"And what did you tell her?"

"The usual—I moved her mind to happier thoughts." He pointed to a large family portrait on the wall. "I'm up to fourteen grandchildren and six great-grandchildren. It's the thing that keeps us going at our age. She was excited about the project she was working on with Maggie. She talked about it at length, although she left out the part about her alleged Nazi connection."

"So you were unaware of Ellen's Nazi claims, which would create a lot of bad PR for you and your candidate?"

"No, I had been made aware prior."

"I thought you said you didn't know?" Veronica responded in an accusatory tone.

"No, I said Ellen didn't mention it during my visit."

Zach continued to push forward, "So with this knowledge, maybe you found it convenient to help out a friend who wanted to die, by slipping her some permanent-sleeping pills. It might benefit both your interests."

The accusation reddened Sterling's face. "I certainly did nothing of the kind. If I wanted to stop Maggie's report, I would have. I think you are chasing ghosts just like Ben, willing to exploit a woman who was not in her right mind."

Veronica was focused on how he'd "been made aware" of Ellen's past. She knew it was through Carsten when he'd brought him the letters. But she conceded that if Sterling wanted to stop the Nazi connection from getting out, he could have silenced it without incident. The murder route didn't seem prudent. People don't become as successful as Aligor Sterling by playing such high-risk/low-reward odds.

"So you're saying that you had nothing to do with Ellen Peterson's death?" Zach asked.

Sterling shook his head. "After putting together a record of sacrifice for a half-century, wouldn't you find it odd that suddenly at my late stage of life I'd put all that at risk?"

"What I find *odd* is how Rose Shepherd, a woman who seemed to live a nondescript life, and whose only brush with the law was a citation for nude sunbathing in Central Park in 1957, seemingly woke up one morning and decided to blackmail one of the world's most powerful men, claiming to have sensitive information that could hurt Sterling Center."

"Rose Shepherd was a fine photographer. She first worked my sister's wedding and I fell in love with her talent."

"She made it sound like there was more you fell for than her photography."

"I don't deny the affair, but that's not why Sterling Publishing hired her. Her work spoke for itself. I was surprised by her claims against me. I was forced to act, so I worked with the police. It was a sad day for me. Further inspection found that Ms. Shepherd always lived above her means and had visions of grandeur—making financial gain a possible motive. Perhaps that is why she pursued me romantically when she didn't like my kind."

"Your kind?"

"We later discovered a history of anti-Semitic views and behavior. So in retrospect, her actions toward myself and Sterling Publishing made more sense than originally thought."

"Even if she was a racist blackmailer being driven by monetary gain, murder seems like a pretty big leap," Zach challenged, sounding skeptical.

"I'm not a trained psychiatrist, but I do know that Greta Peterson gained much notoriety for killing her husband—Mrs. Cleaver and all that business—which probably aroused Rose's obsession with fame. I think that was the common theme of both crimes, no matter how different they appeared. Rose Shepherd was unstable and saw that killing Mrs. Cleaver could bring her the headlines she craved. And sadly, it did."

"What was it that she claimed she had on you? The documents were sealed by the court."

"She threatened to go public with her claims that the Sterling House was built on blood money. According to Rose, we would allow Nazi war criminals to walk free in exchange for a large monetary payment. This was a false accusation, of course, built on wild accusations and unsubstantiated rumors. But our enemies would've tried to use it against us, regardless, so we thought it was best for the organization to have sealed any documents that spelled out her accusations against us."

Sterling reached into a desk drawer and pulled out a photo. He handed it to Veronica.

She studied it, recognizing a young Aligor Sterling and Ben Youkelstein with arms around each other in a concentration camp. Their faces were thin and gaunt, and they looked like two scared boys.

"It's the only picture I keep in my desk. Any thoughts that Ben, myself, or anyone who went through what we did, could ever accept a penny of Nazi money is ludicrous. Some might not like the way we administered our brand of justice, but to say it was for sale, was, and still is, hurtful."

"Why were the blackmail charges against Rose Shepherd dropped?" Zach asked.

Sterling appeared surprised by the question. "Since Rose was already going to spend her life in prison, we felt justice had already been served. It also made it easier to have the aforementioned records sealed, including the tape recordings made during the police sting, and avoid a public hearing on the matter."

The guy had all the right answers. But Veronica still needed the one answer she came for. To the question that changed her life. Her gut was still screaming at her to get to Maggie and Jamie, so she had no more time to waste.

"Did you kill my husband?" she asked directly. "We know Carsten came to you with the letters that connected Ellen to the Nazis."

"As far as I know, Carsten died of a stroke and Ellen is believed to have taken her own life, so I'm not sure why you speak of their deaths as if they were criminal. But yes, Carsten did come to me with correspondences he claimed were between Ellen and Heinrich Müller. And I helped him prove their authenticity."

Veronica began rising off her chair in anger, but Sterling put up the stop sign. "After the letters proved to match Müller's handwriting, Carsten asked me, as a so-called Nazi hunter, to try to use my connections to dig deeper into it. But shamefully, because of the potential bad PR for my center, I declined. I did send him to someone who I thought might be able to help. I loved Carsten—I would never harm him."

"And who did you send him to?"

"Ben Youkelstein."

CHAPTER 42

Maggie and Jamie held their half-eaten cones in their hands as if they were gold. Maggie initially claimed they couldn't leave the area without permission, but after a little ice cream Youkelstein was convinced that they would've willingly followed him to the depths of hell. A place that was not unfamiliar to him.

After exiting the cab, he led them over the cobblestone street to his SoHo apartment. His legs felt like they were going to give out, but he was fueled by adrenaline. He was so close to solving the puzzle.

They entered his apartment building, which was an abandoned warehouse before he renovated it in the mid-1970s. He and his wife lived there until she died, seven years ago—a kind woman who embraced the burdensome challenge of following Esther into his heart. He loaned the other apartments, with no charge, to many of the great artists he'd met in Terezin, who'd made the pilgrimage to the United States following the war. Most of them had sadly passed on, so their children currently occupied the apartments. His business manager constantly scolded him about the free rent.

A service elevator took them to his top-floor loft. With its wide-open space, it still had a warehouse feel. A very popular style with the many artist types who "discovered" SoHo back in the 1970s.

The children were awed by the size of the place. "This is *way* bigger than our apartment ... I mean our old apartment." Maggie said.

"It's as big as my school!" Jamie added with exuberance.

And Youkelstein needed every inch. Books were scattered everywhere, a slide projector was set up on one wall, and a huge map of Germany circa 1945 filled the entire wall behind him. Maria, his longtime assistant, tried to clean it up during his frequent travels, but since he forbid her to touch his cluster of notes that were scattered across the floor, she rarely made a dent.

The children were met by his fluffy white cat. He explained that he'd gotten Leo after his wife died because he needed someone who would always agree with his crazy theories like she always did.

"My dad died," Maggie offered, probably detecting his sadness in his voice when he discussed the loss of his wife. "It really sucks when people die."

Plato or Aristotle couldn't have articulated it any better. The girl had a way of getting right to the point, a skill many twice her age had yet to master. "I'm sure your father is in heaven."

"I don't think so," Maggie replied.

"And why's that?"

"Because it can't really be heaven unless the whole family is together. So I think he's waiting for us. Kind of like on Christmas morning when the parents get to go down and see the gifts first, but nobody is allowed to open the gifts until the kids get there."

"That's an interesting way to look at it, Maggie. I'm sure one day your family will be together again," Youkelstein said.

"Hey, do you still get Christmas presents even though you are *soooooo* old?" Jamie asked.

Maggie rolled her eyes in disgust. "He's Jewish—they don't celebrate Christmas, stupid."

Jamie scrunched his face in thought. "If you don't get Christmas, why would you be Jewish?"

"It wasn't a choice," Youkelstein answered. "It was the destiny I was born into."

"I'm sure glad I'm not born Jewish," Jamie said, letting out a theatrical sigh of relief.

"You are part Jewish," his sister replied, incredulously. "Oma is Jewish, so that makes Dad half Jewish, which makes you a quarter Jewish."

"Does that mean I only get part of my Christmas presents?"

Maggie just shook her head in disgust. But Jamie had already moved on. His attention locked on an object that took up most of a dining room table. "Cool—what's that?"

Youkelstein maneuvered to the table and proudly stated, "This is a model of the Führerbunker."

"The what?" Maggie asked.

He took a moment to explain the glorified air-raid shelter the Nazi elite used as a hideout in the last days of the war. Despite grand descriptions from the Nazi spin-doctors, the bunker was nothing more than a claustrophobic tube in which its occupants had to duck debris when a bomb struck nearby. The lower part, where Hitler resided, was made up of fifteen rooms that were divided by thin partitions and connected by a narrow central passageway. The feared Reich went down with nothing more than a whimper, hiding like rats. A concept Youkelstein once took great satisfaction in, but now with the puzzle pieces coming together, he was questioning their true motives.

"It made no sense that Hitler would be here," he said to nobody in particular. "He should have been close to the command center at Zossen, south of Berlin. It never made any sense."

"What didn't make sense?" Maggie asked.

"Nobody in this room is making any sense," Jamie added.

Class was now in session and Professor Youkelstein was presiding. "Hitler made all the wrong moves at the end of the war, to the point most observers believed he'd been rendered insane. He was sick, yes—he suffered from debilitating Parkinson's and syphilis. And he was never the most grounded fellow. *But crazy?* I'm not so sure.

"He did make a convincing case to those around him that he'd lost his marbles. He would give an order to send a tank brigade to Pirmasens, then change his mind and send it to Trier, and then to Koblenz. And as erratic as that seemed, the final result would have been the same, regardless—they were all suicide missions! I should have seen it before," Youkelstein's voice turned anguished and he pounded his fist against the table.

"Seen what?"

"That he'd already put into motion his escape plan—the Apostles. Even when he declared Himmler a traitor for negotiating peace with the Allies in the last days of the war, that was just another con to throw his enemies off the trail. He was crazy … crazy like a fox."

"That's what they said about Oma. But I still don't get it," Maggie said, growing frustrated.

"It was right in front of my face and I didn't see it," Youkelstein said and moved to a contraption sitting on an end table, and clicked a button. The out-of-date slide projector shot a large photo of Martin Bormann on the wall.

Jamie must not have been impressed, because he declared himself "bored" and began chasing the cat.

"Who is that?" Maggie asked. She wasn't going anywhere—he had her full attention.

"Martin Bormann was Hitler's secretary and some would say closest confidant after Rudolph Hess left. He was a cruel murderer, even by Nazi standards, and a professional weasel whose claim to fame was the trust Hitler put in him. Without Hitler he was nothing, and now it makes sense."

Youkelstein reached into a drawer and pulled out the gold cross with $v^{\wedge}988v^{\wedge}$ engraved on it.

Maggie inched back. He'd scared her. "Oma said only Apostles have those—you're one of them!"

He flashed a comforting smile. "No, my dear, I got this from Bormann. I'd always assumed he was on the run from the authorities like the rest of the Odessa rats running around South America, but he was on the run from something more deadly. If he was a member of the Apostles, why was he unable to make safe passage into the US like the rest of them?

"That's why he planted that skull in Berlin, hoping to be declared dead. That is why he created false sightings in places like Chile and Argentina— not to throw off the authorities, but to divert Himmler. That is why fear filled his eyes—because if we were able to locate him, then Himmler had already found him."

"But why would Himmler be after Bormann? They were on the same team."

"Himmler was anything but a team player, and Bormann knew things that could threaten Himmler's power within the group."

"What did he know?

"That Himmler was the one behind the murder of Adolf Hitler."

CHAPTER 43

Maggie sat beside him. Trusting him again. "My history teacher said Hitler shot himself in the mouth while chewing down on a cyanide tablet. And his wife overdosed on pills."

Youkelstein cringed. "Did your teacher explain to your class that the blood on the wall of the room was A2, which correlates with Eva Braun, not Hitler?

"Did your teacher explain why no signs of a gunshot residue or cyanide poisoning were found in Hitler's corpse?"

Maggie shrugged.

"Did your teacher explain why the body of Eva Braun had six steel fragments lodged in her chest and severe injuries to the thorax, that even the most novice forensic doctor would recognize as a death from shrapnel injuries? And last I checked, no recorded suicide ever occurred from shrapnel wounds.

"And did your teacher explain to you how a man who had such severe Parkinson's that he walked by throwing his torso forward and dragging his legs behind him, and shook constantly, somehow held a gun in his mouth and bit on a cyanide capsule at the same time?"

Maggie sighed. "Hey, don't shoot the messenger."

Youkelstein had written a book over twenty years ago that laid out his theory of how Hitler was murdered, but only today could he connect a motive. In the end, Himmler attempted to negotiate his safety with the Allies, but it became clear that they would never consider him anything but a war criminal, and he was forced to take the Apostle escape hatch to ensure his survival. But he wasn't going to play second fiddle to anyone, especially the young child that Hitler proclaimed to be his chosen successor—a bizarre and reckless decision likely driven by the syphilis that was eating away at his brain. So Himmler began a plan of divide and conquer within the group before the war even ended. To control the Apostles he had to remove its leader. He needed to kill Adolf Hitler, and Bormann, who was always willing to attach himself to the winner, was his handpicked man to do it.

Youkelstein explained to Maggie that the expectation was for Hitler and his new wife, Eva Braun, to commit suicide on April 30, 1945. At 3:30 in the afternoon, following Hitler's marriage to Eva and a long ceremonial goodbye, their 'much publicized' and 'expected' suicide was to take place. So much so that Hitler's physician, Dr. Haas, had even tested the cyanide on Hitler's dog Blondi. But they never were going to kill themselves.

"Which means that someone was going to have to do it for them. The SS guards who protected the lower bunker—the ones controlled by Himmler—locked the doors, supposedly to provide privacy for the Hitlers to end their lives. This left only Goebbles, Bormann, Hitler, along with his driver, Lidge, and Dr. Haas.

"Hitler was unceremoniously strangled to death in his room. For her part, Eva tried to fight off her husband's attacker, which is how her blood got on the wall. She was helpless to stop it, before being whisked away. A doppelganger was then buried in her place.

"The dental records proved that the corpse burned in the garden was indeed Adolf Hitler. But the cause of death never added up. Those who found him recorded the smell of almonds coming from in his mouth, but when his organs were sent for further testing, no cyanide was detected in his tissues—an obvious attempt to stuff poison into an already dead Hitler's mouth to make it appear to be a suicide. But by that time, nobody really cared about the how and why, all that was important was that the monster was dead. There was no clamoring for further investigation.

"But when Bormann peeled away the layers, even a dumb block of cement like him was able to figure out that he was being set up to be Himmler's patsy, and he made a run for it. That is why he never joined the other Apostles in the States ... not because he was a casualty of war."

Maggie appeared unimpressed. "Hitler was murdered by his own people, fine, whatever, but it doesn't solve our problem. I think we should concentrate on what made him choose Josef to be his successor. One minute you're saying it was because he was crazy, and then you tell me how he was pretending to be nuts to pull off an escape—it's the same stuff they tried to say about Oma. Make up your mind, which is it?"

She had a point, and she wasn't finished. "You know what's also weird? That they killed him, but they didn't kill his wife ... at least not the real one. Did you ever try to find her in one of your Nazi hunts?"

He clicked a picture of Eva Braun onto the wall. It was a glamour shot from 1945 when she was in her early thirties. No, he hadn't looked for her. *Why would he?* She wasn't a Nazi criminal—just some dimwit who obsessed on fame, which she gained for being the Führer's girlfriend, but not until after her presumed death.

Then it hit him.

Youkelstein headed for the door. He realized that he'd already found her.

CHAPTER 44

Veronica didn't take a breath until she exited into the plaza outside of Sterling House. She sucked in the sharp night air, burning her lungs like it was a punishment for not listening to her gut. She had to find her children. They were with him.

Youkelstein.

He knew the whole time!

Zach caught up to her as she headed toward the busy Park Avenue and delivered more bad news. He made a few phone calls, confirming that on the day of Carsten's death, Ben Youkelstein was a guest lecturer at Vassar College—*in Poughkeepsie!*

Could Youkelstein be involved with these people? *But why?* Theories filled her head—none of them good—but she didn't have time to think about it now. She had to find Maggie and Jamie.

She felt like the surrounding skyscrapers were about to crash down on her. She began running down the busy sidewalk, yelling, "Maggie! ... Jamie!" Nobody even made eye contact with her. It was the way New Yorkers dealt with the abundance of mentally ill who flocked to their streets.

She began grabbing Wall-Street-looking types and demanding cooperation. She shoved wallet-sized photos of Maggie and Jamie in their faces. They pushed her away.

Her instinct was still to call Carsten. This is when she needed him most. He would've grabbed her face with both hands, as he'd always do. Then he would convince her that they'd find them. And she would believe him.

But Carsten wasn't available to take her call.

And the guy who might be responsible for his death had their kids. She just stared at her phone, hoping Carsten would call from the Great Beyond and make this right for their children.

And then it did ring.

But it wasn't Carsten.

Even better.

It was Maggie!

Veronica kept strong during the call, holding back her true emotions, and the 'running off without permission' lecture. Maggie went on a tangent about Youkelstein having a eureka moment while they were eating ice cream, and he needed to get to the Führerbunker right away, which apparently was in his apartment because that's where he took them. He then left just as abruptly, leaving Maggie and Jamie stranded on a street corner as he jumped into a cab and sped off. Not ideal, and likely to get him passed over for any future babysitting gigs, but all Veronica cared was that he was away from them.

Maggie didn't know the address, other than she thought it was in SoHo, based on what Youkelstein told the cab driver on the way there. Maggie offered to ask some strangers, but Veronica strongly instructed—more like threatened—them not to talk to anyone or give any appearance of being alone.

She had a better idea—she'd call Eddie at his precinct. But with all the commotion, she'd forgotten that he was still en route from his security meeting with Kingston. Luckily, she was able to get Eddie's longtime partner in crime, and occasional partner in fighting it, John Marquez. Eddie and Marquez considered themselves family. He quickly located Youkelstein's address.

Zach offered to drive. He was probably scared of Veronica's emotional state, as was most of Park Avenue at this point. She collapsed into the passenger seat and thanked the same heavens she'd been cursing this past year. She even had a few good thoughts for Ellen, remembering that she was the one who'd purchased the cell phone for Maggie, in the face of her heavy opposition.

When she spotted her children sitting on the street corner, looking more bored than frightened, Veronica could no longer keep her cool. She practically leaped out of the vehicle and ran to them. She squished them both in a hug and refused to let go.

They had no idea where Youkelstein went. "Just the way he rolls," Maggie said with a shrug. But Veronica knew there was more to it. Carsten had seen at least two people before his mysterious death—Youkelstein and Rose Shepherd. There had to be some connection.

CHAPTER 45

Rose Shepherd looked up from her romance novel and smiled at Otto.

"I hear you had visitors today," he addressed her pleasantly, as he stepped into her room.

Even though she was closing in on the century mark she was still childlike. Just like the first time he'd met her back in 1936. "Oh my gosh, yes I did, Otto. I did good, you would've been proud of me. They asked about Greta Peterson, and her son coming to see me, but I told them I was framed by Jew lawyers—doesn't that sound like something my love would say?"

"Your loyalty has always been a key element in the success of the Apostles. You should never be underestimated."

Her look changed from child-like to competitive. "Like those women at Berghof always did. Like that jealous Angela Raubal, who couldn't stand that he dumped her daughter Geli for me."

The Führer actually had Geli, his half-niece and lover, killed for insubordination when she threatened to expose certain secrets after he left her, but Otto didn't want to ruin the more romantic tale, and kept quiet.

"And Gerda Christian," she went on with a frown. "She said I was just a vacuous showoff with a passion for bad clothes and cheap films, hardly suitable for the leader of the Third Reich. But my love told her off ... said that I suited him just fine."

Otto agreed that Eva Braun was never as stupid as people made her out to be. In fact, she did most of the manipulating in her relationship with the Führer. And her biggest weapon of manipulation was the suicide attempt.

Her first attempt was in 1932 when she shot herself in the neck. Then in 1935 she made a second attempt by taking pills. After Raubul's "suicide," the Führer wanted to move past any scandal that might stunt his still-growing power, especially with the whispers that he was behind her death. So Eva's tactics often worked, meaning she usually got what she wanted.

And what she wanted was often expensive. The Führer bought her a villa in a Munich suburb, a Mercedes, and provided both a chauffeur and maid. By 1936 she'd become a fixture at Berghof, his grand estate in the Bavarian Alps. He was always worried about her safety, so he hid her out, so much so that most of the German people were unaware of their relationship until after the war.

But while she wasn't the simpleton that many portrayed her to be, Otto would never have described Eva as being deep or profound. Her life was basically that of leisure, even during the war, in which she was oblivious to most of what was going on around her. She spent her days exercising, reading romance novels, and watching films. Unlike most Germans, she was free to read European and American magazines.

But as dysfunctional as their relationship was, Otto thought that in many ways it worked. They had what the Germans called *gemütlichkeit*—a coziness. It was something Otto never found in his own life.

"It's been a long journey for us," he said.

Her smile seemed to go back in time. "I remember the first time I met Adolf back in 1929, when he called himself Herr Wolf. I was a lab assistant for Heinrich Hoffman, the official photographer of the Nazi Party. It was just like a movie—I was up on a ladder and he came in to a great view of my legs ... he always loved my legs."

She giggled as she told the story once again, and probably for the last time. Otto must have heard it two hundred times throughout the years.

"I can see it like it was yesterday. He wore this big felt hat with his light-colored English coat. He told me I had the dreamy beauty of a farmer's daughter and that I had the same eye color as his mother."

Her face turned dismayed. Otto knew that even in the best relationships the thoughts always turned to the end. As was common with Eva, the smile faded away and she returned to her sad sulk—her carefree giggles were often a cover for her inner torment.

Otto noticed that she was wearing her wedding dress today. Normally a symbol of the beginning of a journey, but for Frau Hitler, it was an emblem of the end.

"All the women of Germany would've given their lives to be with him, but he chose you," Otto tried to comfort her.

Her smile returned, like a weak pulse, but it quickly faded. "He deserved a better ending. Not in that dreadful place. All I can remember is the smell—the smell of death. And I'll never forget the sight of the Goebbles children, their bodies piled in that room. I could never understand how a mother could do that to her own children."

The comment took Otto back to that fateful day. Upon arriving at the Führerbunker, he found that their plan had gone terribly awry. The Führer was dead, Bormann and the pilot Baur were nowhere to be found, and Otto's contacts were telling him that Müller had been captured by either the Russians or Americans. Nobody was sure—the entire country was in the fog of war. Berlin was nothing but chaos—every man for himself as Stalin's troops marched in.

What he did find was an inconsolable Eva Braun. She was telling bedtime stories to the bodies of the six children of Joseph Goebbels, all poisoned to death by their mother, Magda. Otto needed to think fast. He decided to bring Eva with him, more out of respect for the Führer than his better judgment, and headed northward to the coastal city of Flensburg. He wouldn't regret it.

Flensburg was crawling with Allied troops, so Otto made the risky move to take Eva across the border into Denmark, where they found a deserted farmhouse. He spent seven long days holed up with Eva Braun and her nonsensical conversation. But they also formed a bond that would last the rest of their lives.

On May 10 they crossed back into Germany to meet up with Himmler. Otto always had a laugh at how history recorded Himmler as taking the southern route and being caught by the bumbling Brits, before supposedly committing suicide. That route was a certain death trap, especially with Eisenhower's obsession with the Führer's redoubt in the Bavarian Alps. For the tale to be true, one must believe that the world's most conniving plotter didn't have a post-war plan. But Himmler made sure his doppelganger was on that route. He was the one captured by the British and splashed across the world's newspapers upon "Himmler's" suicide.

Ironically, they used British built planes from the Air Squadron 3KG200 to flee Germany. It was no coincidence that Himmler had used his SS powers to move the planes to Flensburg near the end of the war. They flew to Britain where they hid amongst the mass celebration of the Allied victory. In Britain, they mastered their new identities and received enough plastic surgery to make a Hollywood actress envious. When the time was right, they moved to the United States without receiving a second look.

Rose remained nostalgic. "I want to thank you for taking me with you, Otto—the United States was good for me. I missed Adolf, and my sister Gretl, but for the first time I really became who I was supposed to be. Not somebody's girlfriend or somebody's daughter. I was Rose Shepherd."

Otto almost laughed out loud at the contradiction of someone who "found themselves" while using a false identity. Spy humor. He could relate.

He couldn't deny that playing Rose Shepherd was Eva's greatest acting job. It came quite naturally to her—her whole life was an act—and she pursued it professionally in the late 1940s and into the 50s, even getting a couple of roles in off-Broadway plays. And if she wasn't in front of the camera, she was behind it. Her friends in Germany had called her *Rolleiflex Girl,* after the popular camera of the time. She did her own darkroom processing and most of the color stills often seen of the Führer, along with the campy home movies that showed him in the Bavarian Alps, were the work of Eva.

And even though she had many doubters within the Apostles, she proved her importance when she volunteered to silence Greta Peterson— sacrificing her own freedom so that Greta couldn't share the secrets of the Apostles with the world, as she planned.

Otto knew that time was getting short. "I believe we must part ways now, Eva."

Her expression was of acceptance. She nodded slightly, and said, "My mother only made it to ninety-six. I beat her by three years." She smiled. "I already died at thirty-three ... at least that's what people think."

He removed the glass vials of cyanide from the pocket of his overcoat and handed them to her. She stared at the vials for a moment and then looked up at him.

"Would it be okay if I finished my book first? I only have one chapter left."

He had no worries that she wouldn't go through with it. And he wanted to be far away when her body was discovered, anyway. Before he left, she removed her necklace and handed it to him.

It was a gold cross with v^988v^ on it and her apostle name *James The Less* carved in the back. Otto put it in the pocket of his coat. They traded final smiles as he left, and then Eva Braun returned to her book's final chapter.

***

Eva finished her novel. In the end, the two lovers found each other after years of being kept apart. She saw it as another example of art imitating life. She set the book down on the nightstand and placed the glass vial in her mouth. She bit down, eager to join her love in eternity.

She soon found herself in the Alps on a chilly autumn day with him beside her. His arm was wrapped around her as she snapped photos of the leaves as they blew off a tree in the distance. And when the final leaf released from the tree, her story had come to an end.

CHAPTER 46

Veronica read the signs.

Jamie bouncing off the walls. Maggie whining.

She knew exactly what this meant—it was nine o'clock and they hadn't eaten since lunch, which according to Veronica's watch, was three lifetimes ago. They needed to eat or this was going to get ugly.

Zach remained behind the wheel, and had his own parental radar working. Without prodding, he suggested they grab a bite at "the best restaurant in New York."

Veronica was surprised when he drove off the island of Manhattan. She was expecting a swanky uptown eatery Zach might have frequented when he worked for *Newsbreaker*. Twenty minutes later they arrived at the Palisades Mall in West Nyack, and Zach announced they were going to the Rainforest Café. This was a big hit with Maggie and Jamie, whose surliness instantly turned to glee. It was their favorite.

Zach explained that he often took TJ here, and Maggie once mentioned her fondness for the themed restaurant on one of her visits. Veronica was impressed.

They moved past all the typical mall stores until they arrived at the restaurant, where they were greeted by trumpeting elephants, squawking birds, and erupting volcanoes. They were seated beside a robotic, chest-pounding gorilla that Jamie thought resembled Eddie. They ordered a "Paradise Pizza" for everyone to split, but Maggie had to be different and got an order of "rasta pasta."

Shouting over the simulated thunder, Maggie and Jamie asked if they could check out the large marine aquarium built into the back wall. But before Veronica was able to instruct them that they wouldn't be allowed out of her sight until they turned fifty, they were already halfway to the fish tank.

She began to order them back to the table, but Zach encouraged her to let them go.

Veronica gave in. But that didn't mean she wouldn't keep one eye on them at all times. They did look like they were having fun, though.

Zach sipped on his fruity drink, and intently viewed the landscape.

"What is it?" Veronica asked.

"Nothing Nazi related. I just see all these young families and couples, and it makes me think how simple things were back then."

"If it makes you feel any better, I went on my first date last night since Carsten died, and it was one big awkward mess."

"Wow—congratulations." He caught himself. "On the date part, not the mess."

"Thanks, but I didn't get promoted to department manger, I just took in a film festival with a guy I met in one of my classes at Pace. I went back to school to get my masters."

Zach tried to hide his reaction, but he wasn't a very good actor, so she answered the question he wanted to ask, "He's twenty-three."

He smiled. "You gotta be young to keep up with you. I don't think I've had a day this crazy since, well ... I don't think I've ever had a day like this."

"Just a typical day in the life of a single mom," she said, returning the smile. She appreciated his demeanor. Eddie would have made a clawing motion, including sound effects, and called her a cougar.

"So how did you meet Carsten?"

"College—NYU. He was a business major from an upscale Nazi family," she made a bad attempt at humor—she could-a sworn she used to be somewhat witty. "We dated all four years and we were married soon after. Then Maggie came along and I haven't had a good night's sleep since."

"Kids change everything," he said with the look of experience. "Sounds like he'll be a tough guy to replace."

"You don't replace the past—you just look to the future. And hope one day you don't learn that the past is plotting to kidnap your children and take over the world."

He laughed. "Having met your mother and Maggie, I think it's safe to say you're the funny one in the family."

"I'll take that as a compliment … I think. How about you and your wife?"

"I'm originally from Michigan, but my first job out of college was with the *Arizona Republic* newspaper. I couldn't get access to the Detroit Lions games in Phoenix, so I would go to a local sports bar to watch them. Sara was a waitress there. Long story short, we fell in love, got married, had TJ. We moved to New York when I got the job with *Newsbreaker*. You can read the rest in the police reports."

Veronica was half listening—maybe less than half. An older man had moved behind Maggie and Jamie and for a brief second she thought it was Youkelstein.

It wasn't.

Zach read her mind. "I know you think that Ben is involved in this somehow, and that he might have something to do with your husband's death. But I don't think so."

"According to Sterling, he knew about the letters, and he was in Poughkeepsie the day he died. What else could that mean?"

"I admit that it's suspicious behavior, but Sterling is the one with the motive, and I think he wants us to believe otherwise. He has all his life's work and fortune invested in this election. And don't forget, he also knew that Carsten had those letters. And he was the one who met with Ellen a couple weeks ago, so he likely knew what was going to go down at Maggie's presentation."

Veronica again looked at her children, who appeared mesmerized by the fish. She figured Jamie was plotting ways to poison them, while Maggie was complaining about some oil company that was threatening that specific species of fish into possible extinction.

"They're not in danger," Zach said, eying the children.

"How can you be serious?"

"I believe Ellen is telling the truth that there was a group called the Apostles, but I think it was just a last ditch effort to save the collective asses of the Nazi leadership that died out years ago. I don't believe the part about reclaiming power."

"But you have to admit that it's interesting timing with an election coming up. If you're planning on taking over the world, snagging the job of President of the United States seems like a good stepping-stone."

"That's an interesting angle, the same one your daughter has, but Kingston and Baer aren't exactly Hitler's kinda guys. Hitler was an expansionist, to say the least, and Baer is by any definition an isolationist. And Kingston is willing to go to war to protect a Jewish state … need I say more?"

Veronica took another glance at Maggie and something clicked. Maggie was a passionate environmentalist long before she knew what the word meant. Veronica remembered one time in the third grade when she came home crying because a classmate called her a tree-hugger. Veronica told her that trees and hugging were two of the best things on the planet, so it couldn't be a bad name. And since those were the days when she let Veronica hug her, they pretended to be trees and hugged. Veronica realized this wasn't about political ideology—this was about trees. And that's why she knew danger was lurking in those trees.

"To fulfill my science requirement at NYU I took a botany class."

"And this has something to do with what's going on?" Zach asked, looking confused.

"We studied trees. And it's related because this thing is all about family trees."

She pulled a pen from her purse and began scribbling Ellen's genealogy on a cocktail napkin. Ellen had children with two different men—Harold Peterson and Heinrich Müller—creating two lineages. She had two children that they knew of—Chosen Josef and Harry Jr. From the letters, they'd learned that she had at least three biological grandchildren—Carsten came from the Peterson lineage, while Josef, of the Müller branch, had a child named Flavia with his mistress, along with another child with his wife, whose identity they'd yet to learn.

Veronica began crossing off names of those who were deceased. Sure, some of the deaths were natural, especially those of advanced age, but many were suspicious. Harry Jr. and Greta were murdered. Flavia's mother died suspiciously. So did Carsten and Ellen.

It was like when those gypsy moths eat away at a tree until it's completely dead, and in this case it was a family tree they were destroying. And while Veronica only got a 'C' in that botany class, she did learn enough to know Maggie and Jamie were in danger.

CHAPTER 47

Ben Youkelstein needed to get inside to talk to Rose Shepherd. She'd left out an important detail during their first meeting—her real identity. The murder of Greta Peterson now made perfect sense.

He cursed himself for not putting this together sooner. The Wolf reference—Hitler's early alias—was a clue she handed him on a silver platter.

Through the darkness outside the prison, he saw a man leave the premises and walk briskly toward an awaiting vehicle.

It couldn't be, he thought.

But that was just wishful thinking.

And it changed everything.

He waited for the man to drive away, before heading inside. He called for Nina Flores, but was told that she'd left for the evening. He then asked for Sister Goulet.

The person behind the desk informed him that she was in a meeting, and wouldn't be available for a half hour. He couldn't wait that long, so he made up a story that he'd left his wallet behind in Rose Shepherd's room earlier this afternoon, and hoped to retrieve it. A reasonable request, he thought. But like most of modern society, the prison was a bureaucracy and Rose Shepherd would have no visitors without being cleared.

He thought to mention that he believed Rose Shepherd was actually Eva Braun, and her murder of Greta Peterson was connected to a group called the Apostles, who were plotting to raise the Reich from the ashes. But he figured that would just get him a one-way ticket to the psych ward. He had too much to do to spend his final days in a straitjacket. So he impatiently waited.

Thirty minutes later, Sister Goulet met him with a smile. He told her his "lost wallet" story and she led him to Rose Shepherd's prison suite.

When she opened the door the smell of bitter almonds attacked his senses.

Rose Shepherd was sprawled out on the floor in front of her favorite chair. The television was blasting out the ten o'clock news with wall-to-wall coverage of tomorrow's election. Sister Goulet rushed to the woman on the floor.

Youkelstein didn't move. This time he was sure that Eva Braun was dead.

CHAPTER 48

By the time they hit the Saw Mill Parkway, Veronica could smell home. They were so close. And while she craved it, the kids *needed* it. They were riding high after their pizza and sugary drinks, but she knew it was fleeting, and their crash was imminent.

While children might be the most resourceful creatures on the planet, and were able to rinse horrible events from their consciousness like shampoo from their hair, they were still slaves to structure. And as their crankiness heightened, Veronica knew that she needed to get them to bed and pray they didn't have permanent nightmares.

The last leg of the trip was to pick up TJ at Zach's neighbors. Zach immediately rushed to his son and wrapped him in a big embrace. TJ looked confused by it, but Veronica wasn't.

As she neared home, she could practically feel the warm fire she planned to build, and curl up next to it with a good book. But something didn't feel right.

The first bad sign was that the lights were on at her mother's house. She was normally in bed by ten. Veronica did remember her mentioning something about a school fundraiser, so maybe she'd just returned home. She hoped.

But when she noticed the lights on inside her house, along with Uncle Phil and Aunt Val standing outside the front door, Veronica knew something was very wrong. She parked the car and rushed into the house, finding it looking like tornado footage. Broken glass, furniture turned over—the place had been ransacked.

Her mother was crouched by a smashed television on the floor like she was contemplating giving it CPR. "What happened?" Veronica asked, horrified.

"I just returned from my fundraiser and I noticed a strange car—a Jeep—in your driveway. But I didn't want to pry because I thought it might have been that boy you went to the movies with and didn't want to be one of those overprotective mothers."

"I think it's a little late for that."

"I heard a crashing sound, so I turned on my floodlights. That's when I saw the man in your backyard. I grabbed a baseball bat, but by the time I got out of the door, the Jeep was hightailing it out of here. The lights must have spooked them."

"They could've had guns, Mom—what did you think you were going to do?" Veronica admonished. The mother/daughter roles had reversed. A fitting ending to this bizarre day.

"When it comes to my daughter and grandchildren, I don't worry about my safety."

Her words were firm, but Veronica could tell her mother was shaken. It was a rare sight.

Veronica did a sweep of the house. While things were smashed and broken, very little was taken. Her jewelry was still there, as were most of the valuables. The only thing she noticed missing was Maggie's computer. She didn't need to be Sherlock Holmes to figure out that the intruders were looking for something specific.

She immediately called Eddie. Her voice cracked as she described the scene. The day just kept getting worse.

"I was headed over there anyway. I just dropped by to pick up some of Ellen's things at Sunshine. I should be there in ten minutes," he said, providing a small level of comfort.

She moved downstairs and was cut off by an angry Picasso, who was demanding his bowl of dinner, or "cat crack" as Maggie called it. She took a moment to feed the king, without so much as a "thank you" meowed in return.

Veronica's next stop was her still brightly lit backyard. She noticed that Maggie was observing an area that had been dug up. Veronica joined her daughter, and realized the intruder had removed the time-capsule she'd buried this morning.

But upon further inspection, it was clear that Ellen had beaten the Nazis to the punch once again.

"You never saw what was in there, did you?" Veronica asked, as she eyed the box in Maggie's hands.

"No—Oma put it together and I just buried it."

The only thing in the box, besides books and paperweights to give it the impression it was full of goodies, was a note that read: *Did you really think I'd make it that easy for you? If you want the book you're looking for, the only way will be to face me like real men.*

A thin, wry smile escaped from the corner of Maggie's lips.

"What is it?" Veronica asked, reading her look.

"I know what Oma meant when she said *facing* her to get the *book*."

"Is it something that you can let your mother in on?"

"I helped her set up a Facebook page so that we could communicate directly for our project, and we could store the scans from her photos."

Veronica didn't know much about Facebook. She gave into the pressure a few years ago and signed up, but as her marriage crumbled, and her husband ended up dying, it became really annoying to look at her "friends" happy lives that they were constantly posting about, so she shut it down.

"Only Ellen can get into her page, right?" Veronica asked.

"Unless someone else had her password," Maggie said with a big smile.

CHAPTER 49

There was no reason to call the police.

This was not a burglary. At least not the typical kind the police could help with. And while the police in town were very good at certain things—like breaking up high school keg parties—Veronica figured international conspiracies and Nazis weren't really their thing.

So they waited for Eddie. At that point they could discuss the next steps, and check out what Ellen was hiding on her Facebook page. In the meantime, Veronica took care of some much-needed business. First of which was to get rid of her mother, along with Uncle Phil and Aunt Val.

Once that was taken care of, they changed into more comfortable clothes. Maggie put on her pajamas, while Jamie finally shed his police uniform, changing into an oversized, hooded Yankees sweatshirt that Carsten gave him on their last Christmas together.

Veronica changed into her own comfortable sweats, which she wore with running shoes. She then started a fire in the fireplace.

Next, they all chipped in and tried to clean up some of the wreckage. Luckily all the broken stuff was just that—stuff. The really important items like photograph albums, DVDs of the kids being born, and the last connections to their father, weren't touched.

A knock pounded the door. Veronica expected Eddie, but remembered he would never knock. When she looked through the peephole and realized who it was, she filled with anger. She swung open the door. "What the hell are you doing here?"

"I have uncovered new information," Ben Youkelstein said. "We need to talk."

"Yes we do," Veronica fired back. She sent the kids to their room. No arguments this time.

"I really need to tell you what I've learned," he eagerly repeated.

"Is this something you *just* learned or something you learned a long time ago, like how my husband came to you with Ellen's letters? Did you think to bring that up when Flavia mentioned he was meeting his contact at Vassar … it was you!?"

His face went blank. "Veronica, I can explain."

"How could I trust anything that ever comes out of your mouth after all your lies? Get out of my house! And for your sake you better hope I don't find out you had something to do with Carsten's death, or I will hunt you down like those Nazis you chase."

"But Veronica …"

She didn't want to hear it. "The police will be here any minute, so I suggest you go … now!"

When the door slammed shut, it sent the tears rolling down her face. As if she sensed something, Maggie hurried down the stairs and went right to her with a hug, and whispered, "I wish Dad were here,"

"Me too," Veronica said, and for the first time in a long time she meant it.

Fifteen minutes later, Eddie arrived, still in his suit from the security meeting. Veronica brought him up to speed on everything that happened since he left Flavia's. Which was a lot. As if trying to avoid the reality of the situation, he turned back into carefree Uncle Eddie.

He tousled Maggie's hair and asked, "How you doing, Maggot?"

"I'm okay."

He surveyed the room. "Where's your brother?"

"Upstairs playing video games. You know him—he's a *vidiot*. Good thing they didn't steal his Xbox or he woulda had a mental breakdown."

Eddie thought for a second, once again the serious policeman. "Everybody should stick together right now. Have him come down here."

But before anyone could move, the doorbell rang. Eddie pulled a gun from his waistband. Veronica doubted the "bad guys" would ring the bell.

Eddie moved to the door and whipped it open. He jammed his gun into the temple of the man standing there.

Zach stood frozen, gripping tightly onto TJ's hand.

"Eddie … no!" Veronica screamed out.

Eddie looked like he wanted to shoot him, but grudgingly accepted Veronica's plea—sort of. He forcefully pushed Zach to the floor.

Zach ignored the police brutality, picked himself off the hardwood floor and ran to Veronica. "Are you okay?" he asked.

"If you told me you were coming I would've cleaned the place up a little," she tried to joke. "What are you doing here?"

"I had this sense that you were in trouble."

Veronica just stared at him. Her knight in shining armor … or at least her knight now dressed in sweater and jeans.

"That's real convenient," Eddie shattered the nice moment.

"What is?" Zach asked.

"Is that the same 'sense' that told you to stowaway on the trip to Rhinebeck?"

"I don't know what you're talking about."

Eddie eyed Zach up and down with suspicious eyes. "I just think it's interesting how you keep showing up. At the school this morning with a coffee … pushed your way into the principal's office … and here you are again. And what a coincidence that while Veronica's house was being broken into, you took her out for dinner and tried to convince her that there was no danger."

"You think I'm ... that's crazy!"

"Who else would have knowledge of this time-capsule buried in the backyard, or the information on Maggie's computer?"

"Why would I do such a thing?"

"A down-on-his-luck reporter who sees his opportunity to get back to the top. How much did they pay you?"

"C'mon, Eddie, we're all tired here," Veronica tried to play peacemaker. "You're making wild accusations."

"I don't think they're so wild. His kid just *happens* to end up in the same class as Ellen's granddaughter, and his wife *happens* to be in the same jail as Rose Shepherd?"

Zach turned to Veronica. "You don't believe this, do you?"

Veronica stood paralyzed. She didn't know what or who to trust anymore. She asked her gut, but it didn't have time to answer her.

Because all the lights in the house went off.

She heard footsteps upstairs. Too heavy to be Jamie's.

And there was more than one set of them.

The Nazis were back.

CHAPTER 50

Veronica reached into a drawer of an end-table and pulled out a flashlight. Just where Carsten left it back when the table resided in their New York apartment, in case of an "emergency." She assumed this would qualify.

She clicked it on, surprised the batteries still worked, and a stream of light sliced through the room. It reflected off Eddie's bald head like a spotlight. His gun was drawn and eyes were on-point. He grabbed the flashlight away and shut it off with a look of disgust.

The footsteps got louder.

Veronica needed to get up there. She didn't care if she had to take on the 82nd Airborne to save him, and would gladly trade her own life. She began to race for the stairs, but Eddie grabbed her by the back of the shirt and pulled her back, kicking. There would have been screaming, but she couldn't afford to make any noise.

"You're going to get yourself killed," he whispered.

To quote her daughter—*woopdy-do*

"And you're going to get Jamie killed," he added.

That one did the trick.

Eddie moved the herd behind a turned-over couch. He took Veronica's half-finished coffee and tossed it on the fire, extinguishing the remaining light in the room with a crackle. The darkness grew thick.

More footsteps upstairs.

Eddie joined them behind the couch. He was the leader—they all appeared ready to follow, no questions asked, even Maggie. He reached under the pant leg of his suit and pulled out second gun. He glared at Zach. "Can you be trusted?"

"He can be trusted," Veronica answered for him.

Her word was good enough for Eddie, and he handed Zach the gun. Wasting no time, Eddie moved to the stairwell with weapon outstretched. He stopped at the bottom, contemplating his next move. Veronica looked on helplessly.

More footsteps.

This time quick movements. Like mice scrambling across the kitchen counter in the middle of the night.

Then Jamie screamed.

Veronica's heart dropped to the floor and Eddie rushed up the stairs. "Freeze—police!"

A gunshot rang out.

Veronica couldn't take it anymore. She grabbed the flashlight and ran as fast as she could. She bounded up the stairs, almost tripping over Eddie, who was sprawled across the floor at the top of the stairwell. She pointed the flashlight at him, realizing he'd been shot in the shoulder.

He pointed with his non-wounded arm. "They went that way—they have Jamie."

Veronica followed his point—*Maggie's room!*

She bolted into the room, and noticed the open window. Veronica ran toward the cold air that was seeping into the house. The motion-light illuminated the backyard and she saw two men with ski masks and semi-automatic weapons dashing across the yard like a prison break. They'd shimmied down the gutter, just as Maggie often did.

They were also carrying something else.

Jamie!

Veronica knew her only chance was to cut them off at the pass. She ran back toward the stairs. That's when she heard the crashing noise coming from downstairs. And she realized something.

They weren't running *away* after escaping out Maggie's room—they were coming back for what they'd left behind.

Maggie!

Veronica moved past Eddie, who handed her his gun as she went by. "Don't do anything stupid," he cautioned while grimacing in pain.

To a mother trying to save her kids, there was no such thing. When she reached the bottom of the stairs, the sight in front of her was every horror movie rolled into one. A shadowy figure in a ski mask held Jamie in one hand and a gun pointed at the head of Zach, who was trying to protect Maggie.

"Let the girl go and you might live," one of the intruders commanded Zach.

"She's not going anywhere," he countered. Very brave—but also very stupid. TJ already lacked a mother; he shouldn't have to grow up without a father. This wasn't his fight. Not to mention, his bravery might be putting Maggie and Jamie in further peril.

Veronica was stealth for a split second. They didn't know she was there, and she was plotting a way to whisk away her kids and make a run for the Tahoe. But Jamie blew her cover.

"Mom," he exclaimed, pointing at her. "Help!"

All guns were now pointed at Veronica. She directed Eddie's gun back at them. It was comical—a group of professionals against a woman who didn't even know how to work Jamie's Super Soaker squirt gun. She couldn't even blame them for laughing at her.

"Get the kids and let's get out of here," the leader said, not even acknowledging her.

Veronica wasn't letting them go without a fight. She fired the gun at the leader. She wasn't sure where the shot went, but sounded like it headed into one of the walls. It barely got her a second glance.

In one swift movement, one of the intruders cracked Zach over the head with his gun handle and grabbed Maggie.

She was kicking …

And screaming!

Veronica screamed, too, *"Noooo!"*

But like a flash, they were out the door and barreling down the driveway in a SUV that had been hidden in the woods. *How long had they been waiting there?* They probably left the vehicle when they had broken in earlier, knowing they would need to return.

Eddie ran out behind her. He'd done a homemade bandage job on his shoulder. "Which way did they go?" he called out.

Veronica just pointed randomly down the driveway, tears streaming down her face.

"The kids will be safe, I promise you," he said as jumped into his police car and rushed down the driveway, lights flashing.

Suddenly Veronica's tears dried up in the cold air. Her motherly instincts took over again. She had to get her children back. She got in the Tahoe and raced after them.

CHAPTER 51

Youkelstein lay still under a blanket.

When Veronica banished him from her home, he'd remained hidden on the property. But after Eddie Peterson arrived, he moved his hiding spot to the back of his squad car. From there, he witnessed the whole thing unfold.

The children appeared to be in imminent danger, but Youkelstein knew they wouldn't hurt them.

They couldn't.

When Eddie ran out of the house, Youkelstein scrambled under the blanket and lay on the floor of the backseat. The car burst out of the driveway, jarring his old bones. He was in great pain, but gritted his teeth, knowing this might be his last Nazi hunt, and his most important. Ever since he spotted the man coming out of the prison tonight, he knew they were on a collision course. And as Eddie powered his vehicle after the kidnappers, Youkelstein got the feeling this chase would lead him to the confrontation he sought.

He could hear Eddie talking into a phone. Youkelstein knew that Veronica needed to hear this with her own ears, since she'd understandably lost trust in him. So he twisted and contorted his body the best he could in the tight crevice between the seat and floorboards, and struggled to release his phone from his front pocket. It was like trying to dance in an air conditioning duct.

He somehow removed the phone without alerting Eddie to his presence, and made the call. He used the option that allowed those on the other end to hear what was being said, but muted any response. It was a one-way conversation.

"Do you have them?" Eddie barked into the phone. He briefly waited for a response, before adding, "I better not see a scratch on them—handle them like they're priceless jewels."

Eddie listened to another response, then said, "I'm sure they are scared—just tell them to be calm and their Uncle Eddie will be there soon."

When he didn't get the answer he wanted, he grew irritated. "Maggie can be such a baby!" He took a couple of deep breaths to calm himself. "Listen, make something up. Tell her that Veronica is on her way. I'll be there in a few minutes."

Eddie instructed the caller to meet him at Underhill School. And minutes later, they pulled into the dark parking lot of the deserted school. It was quite a different atmosphere from this morning when it was buzzing with parents and children.

He showed off his shoulder-wound to his fellow swine, who had removed their masks. "It hurt like a bitch—but it had to be done to make things look good," he said.

Maggie was demanding to see her mother as she was put in the back of the police car. Jamie went more willingly—the car was as seductive as ice cream for him.

The scene reminded Youkelstein of his friends being forced on those eastbound trains. He couldn't allow Eddie to take the children away. If he didn't act now, they might be lost forever.

After being in such a cramped space, his legs were completely numb. He got about halfway to the captors and collapsed onto the blacktop.

Once Eddie realized who it was, he began laughing like a bully. He approached and gave him a kick in the ribs. Youkelstein curled into the fetal position. It was like he was back at Terezin when the Nazi guards used to beat them. Not just to inflict physical pain, but to humiliate them.

"Did you come to harm the children?" Eddie asked.

Youkelstein remained quiet. He learned at a young age that you couldn't argue with a monster.

Another kick to the ribs.

He felt the blood fill inside his throat. He doubted he was getting out of this alive. He began hallucinating and swore he was looking at Siegfried Seidl, the brutal dictator of Terezin.

"I will protect these children at any cost—and nobody will ever harm them … do you understand?" Eddie exclaimed.

After all these years, Ben Youkelstein finally understood everything.

CHAPTER 52

Veronica drove as fast as she could, but her children just kept getting further away.

Her lone saving grace was that Eddie was on the heels of the SUV as it sped down Bedford Ave. And he was likely doing police things she would've never thought about—make and model, calling for backup.

She wasn't sure why she even kept driving—she would never catch them. And what would she do, anyway? But she'd keep going until her last breath. It was get to Maggie and Jamie or die trying.

Her phone rang. She didn't recognize the number—probably one of the local politicians bugging her again with the election nearing. She had no plans to answer, but then she got the crazy idea that Eddie might be using a different phone. Or maybe it was the kidnappers demanding a ransom. She changed her mind.

"Hello ... hello."

No reply.

She was about to hang up when she heard the voice on the other end. It was muffled, but she recognized the voice.

It was Eddie!

Strangely, he wouldn't answer her, but was talking to someone.

"Do you have them?" she heard Eddie ask.

Who had who? Was he talking to the kidnappers? Had he called her on a backup phone to put her fears to rest?

"I better not see a scratch on them," he demanded. "I'm sure they are scared—tell them to be calm and their Uncle Eddie will be there soon."

Thank God for Eddie—the protector. Her fears momentarily calmed, but then things changed.

"Maggie can be such a baby!"

"Listen, make something up. Tell her that Veronica is on her way. I'll be there in a few minutes."

Veronica couldn't breathe. She felt like she'd been punched in the stomach. There had to be a mistake.

She drove as fast as she could to Underhill School. Eddie obviously didn't know she was listening. Someone else must be helping her.

She skidded to a stop in the back of the school's parking lot. In front of her was a man curled up in a puddle of blood.

It was Youkelstein.

She spotted Jamie and Maggie in the back of Eddie's car. Their faces were pressed up against the window. They saw her—Maggie was screaming "Mommy!" at the top of her lungs. She was scared.

I'm coming!

"Eddie, stop!" she shouted.

He rolled down the window of the police car. "Get out of here, Veronica—you don't understand."

He was right—she didn't.

"What's going on!?" she desperately called out.

"One day you'll understand. The children will be safe. I promise you I will keep them safe," he said, as he drove away.

CHAPTER 53

It all happened so fast that Veronica wasn't even sure what just occurred. But she knew someone who did.

Youkelstein was alive, but badly hurt. She touched his midsection and his face contorted in pain. She wasn't a doctor, but was fairly certain he had broken ribs. She feared potential internal injuries.

This beating would have tested the limits of a healthy person in their prime, but at Youkelstein's age, and with his frailty, she knew it could prove fatal. He needed medical treatment ASAP.

She thought to call the police. *But where would she even start? And could she trust them?* Eddie was a well-connected NYPD cop who'd been given the plum assignment of providing protection for a presidential nominee on election night—a candidate who's safety might now be in question, based on these developments.

Her one ray of hope was Eddie's final words to her—that he would keep the children safe. She could only hope that Eddie knew the kids were in danger and forcefully took them so he could safely hide them, knowing she'd never allow it. Her gut mocked that theory.

She helped Youkelstein into the car. One minute he was lying to them about his knowledge of the letters and his meeting with Carsten, and now he was risking his life trying to save her children. He was a mystery wrapped in a riddle. And she had a sudden interest in that "new information" he wanted to discuss earlier … but first things first.

She couldn't risk taking him to the hospital, so they returned to Veronica's house. Zach and TJ were still there, along with her mother. When she hugged her, Veronica broke down, and began sobbing in her mother's arms. Not even after Carsten died did she let it out like this. She tried to be so strong then—for the kids—but now they were gone, and so was her strength.

Veronica didn't have time to explain the situation, Eddie's involvement, or anything Nazi related. Her mother read her thoughts—that she needed to be alone—so she took Youkelstein to her house, to give him some basic medical attention.

That left Zach and TJ.

"I hope you know I had nothing to do with this, Veronica. That stuff he was saying was completely false," Zach said.

"I believe you," she replied.

What she really needed was for Zach to play the role of Carsten. Patiently holding her steady until she could get herself together. She knew that to find Maggie and Jamie she would need a calm, clear mind.

After a couple deep breaths, she said, "It's Eddie—he took the kids."

Zach took a step back, shocked. "Eddie? What are you talking about?"

She told him the whole story—beginning with the mysterious one-way call, and ending where Eddie told her she didn't understand.

She still didn't.

Veronica walked to her closet and took out a heavy jacket. She put the coat on and headed toward the door.

"Where are you going?" Zach asked.

"I don't know—but I have to find them."

"Listen, going on a wild goose chase isn't going to help anything. And it might hurt your chances. We need to take a step back and take a logical approach."

His voice was calm. And even though his words were in conflict with her motherly instincts, she knew he was right. "What do you suggest?"

"I think we need to keep following Ellen's clues."

"But the next clue was on her Facebook page, and only Maggie had the password."

TJ was standing quietly nearby. His terrified look had vanished, and he was now smiling like the cat that got the canary.

"You got something to add?" his father asked.

"Yeah—I know the password."

CHAPTER 54

With all the Peterson computers smashed and/or stolen, Zach made a quick trip home to get his laptop. Once he returned, TJ went to work—signing on Facebook and filling in Ellen's user name and password.

The page was very bare. No profile picture, and the only information she listed was *Current City* as New York, NY, and *From* New York, NY. She could never bring herself to admit she lived in Chappaqua. But as they'd learned, she was really not from either place. She came from somewhere much darker.

She had one "friend" named Mags P, who also had no profile picture or other friends. For Maggie, this wasn't that far from the real thing. Neither Ellen or Mags P "liked" any pages that might draw attention, and the only communications on their *Wall* or *Direct Messages* was about the Heritage Paper project, communicated directly to each other.

Ellen did list her favorite book as her memoir called *The Last Leaves of Evil*, with the notation that it was "coming soon." But as far as they could tell, there were no clues as where to locate it. And there was no electronic copy hidden on the Facebook page, as they'd hoped. Veronica wondered if there was a hidden message that Maggie might have been able to decipher. But just the thought of her daughter almost brought Veronica to her knees. She fought it off, needing to remain strong.

The one fertile area of their search was the *Photos* section. Ellen had posted a life's worth of pictures that spanned almost a century. TJ stated defensively that he didn't alter them in any way, but did help to scan the old photos. This time they believed him.

TJ clicked on an icon titled *Family Photo Album*. A picture might be worth a thousand words, but these pictures rendered Veronica speechless.

Zach was less affected—he'd already seen a few of them during Maggie's presentation, lessening the shock value—and he took over the wheel from TJ. The first photos were of Ellen and her mother, Etta. The photos were black and white with the typical quality of a 1920s photo. They chronicled a journey from a beautiful young woman to a gauntly sick one who was knocking on death's door.

Next up were shots of a young Ellen with Adolf Hitler, who was dressed in his military uniform. A comment under the photo read: *The Alps: 1936*. The mountainous scenery behind them was breathtaking, as she stood with Hitler's arm draped around her. Veronica tried to shake the cobwebs out. It was too far beyond her realm of comprehension to even grasp.

Zach continued to click through the photos. Many of Ellen with Heinrich Müller during their time in Germany. It looked to be at the same location in the Alps, again providing the postcard-esque scenery. There were a few more of her and the head of the Gestapo being lovey-dovey—holding hands and kissing. A few when Ellen was pregnant with Chosen Joe.

"Ellen mentioned in the presentation that she and Müller had fallen in love when he was assigned by Hitler to head up her security. She said she regretted that he was married, but not enough to stop the affair," Zach said.

Next came the photos of the newborn. Like any new mother, there was no shortage of baby photos. Most were of Ellen holding the infant in her arms, wrapped in blankets. Others featured Müller, the proud papa, holding the child. And not to be outdone, there were a couple of Hitler awkwardly cradling the child to his chest. Seeing the mass-murderer holding an innocent child was both strange and chilling.

The next album centered on Ellen's time in the United States. Zach found particular interest in a picture of Josef at his wedding in 1959. According to Veronica's calculations, he would be about twenty at the time. She remembered Ellen stating in the letters that she hoped the marriage would help him get his life together. The ceremony looked to be lavish, and his wife was a Nordic beauty.

Like many of the clues that Ellen had left for them, the pictures were both fascinating and shocking, yet didn't seem to help them get any closer to the answers they needed. They didn't even know the aliases of these people in the pictures, so how could they track them down? Veronica thought Ellen could have at least had the courtesy to tag the names.

The photos that followed were the polar opposite of the happy wedding photos—they were from Josef's funeral. His wife was still beautiful and svelte, but appeared to be about fifteen to twenty years older than at the wedding.

Ellen was dressed in black from veil to shoes. She displayed the same despondent, sad expression that Veronica remembered from Carsten's memorial service. It was hard to find sympathy for her at this moment, but as a mother, Veronica felt her pain. The thought of losing a child was indescribable—she again fought to block thoughts of her own missing children.

After passing through the sea of sadness, they arrived at happier times. Ellen's marriage to Harold Peterson, and holding Harry Jr. as a baby, just as she held Josef. No Hitler this time.

The photos kept coming—Harry Jr. and Greta's wedding, with Greta in a dress that would make Hugh Hefner blush. Veronica studied the happy couple, and wondered again what caused Harry Jr., her children's grandfather, to change so dramatically, so quickly.

Others included a proud-looking Ellen with her arm around Harry Jr. in his police uniform, upon graduation from the academy. Another of Ellen with her guys, Carsten and Eddie, at a Yankees game—they were maybe ten, eating cotton candy and flashing youthful smiles. The final picture was of Ellen and Maggie together at her room at Sunshine Village, which could have been taken in the last few days or weeks. Circumstances aside, it was a really good photo of the two of them. Getting Maggie in front of a camera, and then to smile, was quite a challenge.

As night drifted toward morning, Zach continued to beat a dead horse, searching every inch of Ellen's account. He didn't have any quit in him, she'd give him that.

Veronica got TJ set up in Jamie's bed. He was acting unaffected, but she could tell he missed his mother. Maggie and Jamie struggled without Carsten, and not to pat herself on the back, but the mother was the comfort—the one who gave the feeling everything would be all right. The hug from her own mother was what was keeping Veronica going tonight.

Tucking the boy in felt right. She needed to feel like a mother again. She was supposed to protect them, but now they were God-knows-where with Eddie and whoever he was working for. Her heart broke once more.

She turned out the lights and wandered into Maggie's room. It felt so lonely. Maggie normally kept it so neat, but the burglary had left clothes strewn all over the floor and her beloved easel tipped over. Veronica sat on the bed for a moment, feeling an intense exhaustion take over her body. She tried to fight it—she had no time to sleep—but the Sandman proved too strong.

It was still dark when she awoke. Her watch said it was almost four in the morning. She hoped for a dream, but the post-disaster look of Maggie's room made her scramble to her feet. She didn't know where to go, or what to do, but she knew she needed to keep moving.

She checked on TJ, who was sound asleep, snoring away. She then went downstairs to find Zach still stubbornly staring at the computer screen.

He turned around at the sound of her entering. But he wasn't jumpy. And actually had a smile on his face.

"What is it?" Veronica asked.

"I found it—Ellen did leave us a clue."

CHAPTER 55

Otto peered out over the great city, taking a rare moment to enjoy the heavenly sunrise over the Atlantic. There wouldn't be many more moments of reflection until the job was complete. Today was a day he'd anticipated for as long as he could remember—the day America would succumb to the Achilles heel of any democracy … an election.

His eyes moved from the ball of fire rising in the sky, to the endless ocean that acted as its footstool. The Americans always arrogantly believed the great ocean was their shield. Wars might take place in Europe, the Pacific, or the Middle East, but never would the Great Democracy be threatened on its own turf. But they should have studied the lessons that the Germans learned after Word War I—that the deadliest enemy was always within. Germany was stolen by the saboteurs within its borders, not by England or France.

His eyes moved to the southern tip of the island, where the attacks took place. He still couldn't believe those savages were able to pull it off, even with his help. It was all it took for the natives to trade two hundred years of freedom and ideals for security. They chased mythical enemies around the globe, opening America to the threat within its own borders, just as he thought they would.

Otto flashed a rare smile. Today was the culmination of the struggle. But in the end, he knew they wouldn't be able to complete their mission without the right leader—the Candidate.

The Führer might have been presumptuous in his anointing of Josef, but he was correct in his selection of the proper bloodline. The minute that Otto met Josef's son, he knew he was the one who would lead the revolution. He was a natural born leader, matching what the Führer had famously written: *The spark of genius exists in the brain of the truly creative man from his hour of birth. True genius is always inborn and never cultivated, let alone learned.*

There was no more time to waste on sunrises, no matter how stunning. Otto took the elevator to the ground floor, where the limo was waiting for him. After informing the driver of his destination, they were off, beating the heavy morning traffic.

They drove through the Brooklyn Battery Tunnel, before exiting at Hamilton Avenue. A few turns later they arrived at the entrance of Green-Wood Cemetery.

It was made up of five park-like acres. It would be hard to find a more attractive place to be buried. Its inhabitants included Boss Tweed, Horace Greeley, and Charles Ebbets, of Brooklyn Dodgers fame. But the only people Otto cared about were John and Eleanor O'Neill, his parents.

The limo pulled to a halt and Otto entered into a sun-drenched morning. His driver offered help, but this was a private time for him and his parents. He slowly maneuvered over the grounds by foot.

They were not buried in an elaborate mausoleum like those responsible for their death, but under two crumbling stones.

The term "murder-suicide" wasn't en vogue in 1933, and technically, his father did shoot his mother and then put the gun in his own mouth. But Petey knew the real culprits were the Jews who oppressed his family, and sucked the will to live from them. He held them responsible for their murder, even if the enabling American law enforcement didn't see it that way.

With the memories lingering in the morning air, Otto told his parents how the Candidate would get them justice, even if they weren't around to witness it. He felt the strong sun beating on his face, and took it as a sign of their approval.

Otto meandered back to the limo, before heading for the next order of business. As they maneuvered from the BQE to the Long Island Expressway, Otto made the call.

"Today you take your place in history," he began.

"According to the polls, the size of my defeat will be the only thing that will be historical."

"Nonsense. Your candidacy is going to shape the ideals of the world for the next thousand years."

"Last I checked, the world wasn't built on ideals—it was built on kingdoms of wealth."

"Subtlety has never been your strong suit. The money has been put into your account in Switzerland."

"All of it?"

"One billion dollars."

He laughed shamelessly. "That should buy a lot of idealism."

With that, they hung up. It would be the last time Otto would talk with Theodore Baer until the election was over.

CHAPTER 56

Veronica's mother always told her that everything would look better in the morning. And like most of her mother's motivational clichés, they were usually on target, even if she'd never give her the satisfaction of admitting it. But Veronica did give her mother the ultimate compliment—she taught it to her own kids.

But then one morning everything didn't look better.

Carsten was dead.

It was a similar sun-filled morning to today. But what she would never forget was Maggie and Jamie's faces. And as the words came out of her mouth, she felt an insidious numbness like she was the one who'd died. She had that same feeling this morning.

Veronica had surprisingly kept it together last night. She knew it was her only chance to get them back safe and sound. One of Carsten's favorite catchphrases popped into her mind—*pressure either crushes you or turns you into diamonds.*

She entered Jamie's room, checking on TJ. She looked at the small child snoring away in the miniature race car bed. It devastated her to see TJ lying where Jamie should be. They both should be snuggled in their own beds.

"TJ, sweetie, time to get up for school."

He turned away from her and buried his head under the pillow. She was momentarily glad to know it wasn't just her kids who refused to wake up.

She lightly shook him. "Five more minutes, Mom," he mumbled.

"Okay, five more minutes," Veronica replied and patted him on top of his head.

She followed an enticing smell downstairs and into the kitchen. It was starting to feel like a typical morning in the Peterson house. At least what used to be a typical morning. Zach was finishing a masterpiece of scrambled eggs and sausage. Carsten was the king of breakfast, and ever since he died the Petersons became a cereal and toast family. It was nice to have breakfast back.

Zach, who had been home to shower and change out of yesterday's suit, looked no worse for wear after his all-nighter. He wore a blue and white striped button-down with sleeves rolled up, and khakis, looking more business casual today.

He had left a note that instructed Veronica to dress professionally for what he had planned. So she wore a turtleneck sweater with a plaid skirt just above the knee. Her cognac-colored, knee-high boots matched her leather jacket and tote bag. No concert shirts today.

Zach dished three plates of eggs and sausage, and asked, "Is he up?"

Veronica sped by him and began dishing Picasso's "cat crack." The furry fellow seemed to want to have a heart-to-heart about the recent lack of attention, but there was no time this morning.

"He said five more minutes."

Zach chuckled. "He'll five-more-minutes you until noon if he has his way."

"He's yet to deal with my patented Chinese Water Torture knocking method."

"We tried water-boarding in our house—didn't even budge."

The small television on the counter played the local news—the election was dominating the coverage. The latest development was a follow-up to

Baer's controversial comments yesterday. A term paper had shown up on the Internet that Baer had written in college. In it, he compared Hitler to George Washington. You couldn't make this stuff up.

Baer just finished giving a news conference where he played it off as misguided youth that had nothing to do with today's election. He was probably right, but regardless, he'd lost almost eight points in the latest poll and was losing steam in the key swing state of Florida.

She buttered a bagel, took a swig of orange juice, and headed back upstairs to torture the hostage. But when she entered Jamie's room, TJ was nowhere to be found.

It was a nightmare that Veronica kept reliving. She was about to scream down to Zach when she heard running water. She moved down the hall and found TJ brushing his teeth in the bathroom. She let out a sigh of relief, but thought it wouldn't be long before she started seeing aliens.

She forced a smile at the boy, who must be wondering why the crazy lady just bolted into the bathroom, almost causing him to swallow his toothbrush.

"Oh, you're up—good. You're in luck, you were about to get the Chinese Water Torture knock."

He smiled shyly. "Maggie tells me about that—she says it's rough."

Veronica stood proud. Her reputation had spread to the masses. But then she gulped at something else he mentioned.

Maggie.

She's gone!

Veronica gathered herself enough to say, "Your dad made some eggs if you're interested."

"Cool."

That was the deepest conversation they'd ever had. Either out of habit, or pulled by a strange force, Veronica made her way into Maggie's room. The smell of her missing daughter turned her heart into the dirty, slushy ice on the street corner that people crunch with their winter boots. She felt like she wanted to curl up and die.

Then she heard a sound. It was coming from outside. This time it wasn't her paranoia playing tricks. She ran to the window, but couldn't see the driveway from that angle. She dashed back into the bathroom, again almost knocking over TJ, and opened the window. The morning temperatures were mild for November and the sun was bright.

What she saw was her Tahoe peeling out of the driveway.

Somebody was stealing her car!

When she looked closer, she realized it wasn't just anybody. Ben Youkelstein had just hot-wired her car—*could this get any stranger?*

TJ was now looking over her shoulder, and appeared to be enjoying the grand theft auto.

Veronica watched as her mother ran out of her house in a terrycloth robe, balancing a cup of coffee in her hand.

"You lied to me, mother!" Veronica shouted down at her.

"What are you talking about?"

"You said everything is always better in the morning."

CHAPTER 57

The modern American family sat at the breakfast table eating eggs and slurping orange juice.

A widow and her mother. A father whose wife was in jail, along with his sweet but anti-social son. Not to mention Picasso, the eccentric feline who was displaying his "catitude".

Then like the typical family, they'd spend their day trying to get their children back from the Nazis, and hope the ninety-something Nazi hunter didn't crash Veronica's car.

The first order of business was for Veronica's mother to give the blow-by-blow details of Youkelstein's maladies and how she heroically nursed him back to health. After what she'd just witnessed, Veronica thought she might have done too good of a job.

Youkelstein had filled her in on the details last night. She didn't look like a total believer, but agreed to take TJ to school today, and watch him afterward until they returned.

TJ didn't look thrilled by this. Like Maggie, he enjoyed his outcast status. And showing up as the personal guest of the school principal didn't exactly scream rebel.

"Dad?" he pleaded for help, but got none.

Principal Sweetney stood and dragged TJ to his feet. He looked like a hostage as they headed off for school.

That left just Veronica and Zach. But any thoughts that she might get a brief moment to finish her eggs in peace, quickly evaporated. The election coverage took a small break to mention a story about the oldest living inmate in the state of New York dying last night.

"Rose Shepherd was ninety-nine years old, and had been confined to Bedford Hills prison since 1976 for the murder of Greta Peterson. No cause of death was provided," said the helmet-haired anchor.

His female partner's look saddened, and said, "That's too bad," totally glossing over the fact that the dear old lady once strangled another woman to death.

Veronica and Zach looked at each other. Sure, she was well past her expiration date, and if we're all day-to-day, then Rose was minute-by-minute. But this couldn't be a coincidence.

After scarfing down the remainder of their eggs, they headed to Zach's car—a silver Audi—and took off for Long Island.

"A German car?" Veronica asked with a half-smile.

"All that stuff your friend Eddie said …"

"I was just teasing—I trust you. You wouldn't be here if I didn't. And for the record, I'm not sure I'd consider Eddie a friend at the moment."

Zach drove, while Veronica manned the radio. She searched for news on Rose Shepherd, but it was election, election, election. Things were not looking good for Theodore Baer, and the talking heads were predicting a landslide for Kingston. "Amazing what a difference twenty-four hours can make," one analyst said. "Tell me about it," Veronica muttered.

They drove onto Sprain Brook Parkway, before merging onto the Hutch. An hour later, they arrived in the quaint village of King's Point, which sat on the tip of the Great Neck Peninsula. It was filled with palatial estates, wooded parks, and breathtaking water views. It was also the home of the Heyman Funeral Home, which was located in an old colonial house with a white picket fence. Where suburbia comes to die.

While Zach was studying photo after photo last night, something had caught his eye—a photo from the funeral of Ellen's "chosen" son Josef.

On the surface, it wasn't very helpful—they didn't know Josef's alias, where he'd lived, and so on. But one of the mourners attracted Zach's attention. Not who he was, or what he looked like. It was what he held in his hand. A paper program. *In memoriam.* Using a trick TJ taught him, Zach was able to blow the photo to a larger size, while still maintaining clarity, so they could read the writing on the program.

It didn't give the name the deceased used, but it did give the next best things. Where it took place—the Heyman Funeral home. The city—Kings Point. And the date—September 18, 1972. When they checked, the place was still in business.

They were met in the lobby by a short, chatty woman named Maureen. When she inquired why they were interested in a forty-year-old funeral, Zach made up a story about finding photos in Ellen's room at Sunshine Village after her death. They were from a memorial service, and listed the date and location of the service, but no name. They wanted to give them to the deceased's family.

It was a flimsy story, but Maureen bought it. Funeral homes were probably not hotbeds for underworld conspiracies and she had no reason to be suspicious.

She led them to the Records Room, providing a quick tour along the way. *Just in case they die today,* Veronica guessed, which wasn't looking that far-fetched the way things were going. There were three chapels, all empty. This made Veronica feel better. *The less death today, the better.*

They arrived at a small office full of metal file cabinets. Maureen disappeared into a sea of files, while Veronica and Zach waited outside.

Maureen returned about ten minutes later. She had a smile on her face, but Veronica was wary of it. It was similar to Maggie's "gotchya" look.

"This isn't about a photo, is it?" she said, eyes latched onto Zach.

"Excuse me?"

"You're a reporter, aren't you?"

He hemmed and hawed, before coming clean. "Yes, why do you ask?"

"Because the only funeral that day was for Joseph Kingston, and I'm guessing that you're doing a story on his son, being what today is and everything."

"I'm not following," Veronica said.

"Joseph Kingston's son is Jim Kingston—you know, the guy running for president."

CHAPTER 58

Jamie fired the gun at the armed guard. Another direct hit. A second guard thought he could sneak behind him, but Jamie was too smart for that. He turned and fired—two more down—and he yelled out in exuberance. It was hard work saving humanity, but it sure was a lot of fun.

Maggie looked at him with big-sister disapproval. "You know Mom doesn't let you play that game."

Jamie didn't take his eyes off the eighty-inch plasma screen gracing the wall of the room. It's where he fought the battle for humanity on the game *Halo* that he played on his new Xbox, a gift from the kidnappers.

Jamie dramatically craned his neck, purposely hamming it up. "I just looked—Mom's not here. Too bad, so sad, for her."

"I'm not one of your stupid friends, so don't try to play me."

He let out a frustrated sigh. "I keep asking you to play multi-player."

"I didn't mean it that way. So you think just because Mom's not here you can get away with anything you want?"

Jamie killed a couple more Covenant Soldiers with a tactical grenade launch. He sighed again. "Why do you always try to ruin all the fun!?"

Maggie paced the room, looking for a way out. It might have been the most beautiful room she'd ever been in, but it was still a prison.

"Dad would know what to do if he was here," she grumbled, just loud enough for Jamie, the Master Chief of the United Nations Space Command, to hear.

"If Dad was here he'd be all—*go to your room, do your homework, go to sleep.* He'd never let us stay up all night playing *Halo* and eating M&Ms … and on a school night!"

Jamie continued having success, killing another cybernetically enhanced Super Soldier. He was also dressed for success, wearing the tuxedo their kidnappers left out for him. Maggie refused to put on the dress they provided her, choosing to remain in her pajamas with a pair of crocs, although she did put Jamie's oversized hoodie sweatshirt on over her top. She wanted to hide in it.

"You know that stupid game takes place in the 26th Century," she said. "So if we don't stop the Apostles, the Reich will only be halfway through their thousand years of terror by that time. That will be the real enemy taking over the earth."

"Don't you know I don't care what you say?" He put the control down for a quick moment and put his hands over his ears. "Stop talking! Stop talking!"

"If you like that Xbox so much, why don't you marry it?"

"Why don't you marry TJ?"

"Right after you marry Haley Burkhardt."

Jamie paused, looking defeated. "Hey—that's not a fair one."

"Can you just stop playing for a minute and help me figure a way out of here?"

"Don't you get it—I don't want to leave!"

She couldn't take it anymore. She grabbed the controller out of his hand, and threw it across the room. Without Jamie's expertise, the Master Chief was a sitting duck for the Covenant Soldiers and was ambushed.

"Hey—you made me die."

"If you don't help me, you really are going to die. We all will."

"Uncle Eddie said I could play the game."

"Uncle Eddie is a real asshole."

"I'm going to tell him what you said."

"I don't care."

Jamie jumped up on the bed and started screaming. "Uncle Eddie! Uncle Eddie!"

Maggie leaped on top of him and forcefully placed her hand over his mouth. But it was too late. The door opened and a man in a suit walked in.

But it wasn't Eddie.

It was Jim Kingston.

The next president of the United States.

CHAPTER 59

He looked the same as he did on the poster in Maggie's room. His thick hair was stylishly parted to the side, and his boyish face was offset by a rock-solid jaw that looked to be carved from stone. He sounded the same as he did on television, with a perfect balance of comfort and passion in his tone. But to Maggie, he didn't appear to be the same.

He looked at the bickering siblings and smiled. "I'm glad to see you've made yourself at home. This is now as much your home as it is mine."

"This is not my home," Maggie snapped back. "Where is my mom!?"

He looked her up and down. It made her feel icky. "The dress I gave you didn't fit? Or if you didn't like it, I can get you one you more approve of."

"I wouldn't like anything you gave me—where is my mom!?"

He smiled with amusement. It was condescending. He was everything she thought he wasn't. "I know politics is fickle, but yesterday you were wearing my shirt to school, and today you want no part of me."

"You're just a typical politician who never listens—where is my mom!?"

"Your mother is fine," he said and started to laugh.

"What's so funny?" Maggie snarled.

"It's just that you remind me of *me* at your age."

"I'm nothing like you."

"They called it stubbornness," he said, maintaining his smile—the one that always won over the voters. "But since I'm about to be elected president, they now say I have resolve. It's all in the eye of the beholder, I guess."

"You need a shower, you dirty Nazi," Maggie shouted at the top of her lungs.

The insult didn't dent his amusement. "I've been on the campaign trail for eighteen months, Maggie, so you're going to have to do better than that. In fact, I received a letter from the head of a certain terrorist group this morning who called me a *Jew Loving Dead Man*, and then went into explicit detail of how they were going to behead me. Makes the Cheerios not go down real smooth."

Maggie seethed. She remembered her mom telling her that *sticks and stones may break my bones, but names will never hurt me*, after some kids had picked on her and she came home crying. She really wished she had some sticks and stones right now to throw in Kingston's face. She wanted to hurt him.

He moved beside Jamie, who had resumed his game. "So how about you, Jamie?" he said and patted him on the head like their father used to do.

Jamie bubbled with excitement. "Xbox, M&M's, and no school—what's there not to like!?"

"So what game are you playing here?" he asked.

"It's *Halo*," Jamie stated enthusiastically, "It's an intergalactic battle in the future. I'm in charge of the good guys, we're fighting against the Covenant Soldiers—they're the bad guys. They're robots!"

"Wow," Kingston acted interested, "So are you winning the war?"

Jamie sighed. "I'm not going to lie to you, it's been a struggle."

"A great man once said—those who want to live, let them fight, and those who do not want to fight in this eternal struggle do not deserve life."

"So will you also be quoting Hitler in your acceptance speech tonight?" Maggie asked. "I think it would be fitting."

He looked impressed. "I didn't know they are teaching classics like *Mein Kampf* in school these days."

"Those who don't learn from history are doomed to repeat it."

"She always ruins all the fun," Jamie interrupted, and handed the future president a controller. "Here—let's play multi-player. I'm the Master Chief."

"Until the votes come in tonight," Kingston joked.

"You get to be Arbiter."

"Arbiter?"

"The leader of the Alien Elite—they broke away from the Covenant. We are going to fight together to take them down."

"Arbiter was given the rank by the high prophet because it was a time of extraordinary circumstances," Maggie added, "You know, he was *chosen*."

Jamie became annoyed with the distraction, tapping Kingston on the arm to get his attention. "Your weapons are holstered on your back. You have grenades and a whole bunch of other cool stuff." Then he had an epiphany, "Oh, I totally forgot, in this version there's this cool weapon where you can make the enemy believe the wrong stuff. I love tricking people and then taking their stuff. *Halo-2* didn't have that feature."

"Sound familiar?" Maggie asked.

Kingston didn't respond, he was too busy being educated by Professor Jamie. "Watch—I'm going to fire my assault rifle at that bunch of grunts."

The grunts crashed to the ground. "I killed them!"

Jamie noticed on the split-screen that Kingston's man, Arbiter, was in trouble. "Put up your bubble-shield! Put up your bubble-shield on your vehicle!" Jamie exclaimed. But it was too late. Kingston's vehicle was blasted to high heaven by the Covenant Soldiers. He wasn't as good at saving humanity as he was in his commercials.

"You'll do better next time," Jamie said in a consoling tone.

Maggie added, "The Covenant Force that fights against humanity is united under the worship of the Forerunners, who believe they are superior to the humans and ordered their destruction ... sounds a little like ... um ... you know ... Nazi Germany."

Kingston looked to his more receptive audience. "Jamie—I'm going to tell you about a similar fight between good and evil back in the 20th century. The good guys were called the Reich and fought against the evil Bolsheviks and the Zionists. But while the Reich soldiers were off fighting to protect their homeland, the Zionists hid within the homeland that they shared and pretended to be loyal, but were really working for the bad guys to cause the Reich to lose.

"The Reich fought back behind a brave, young Master Chief they called the Führer. But by that time, the Bolsheviks and Zionists had grown too strong. A great war broke out, and while the Führer fought courageously, his enemies were too powerful. With the Führer out of the way, the Zionists fought a civil war with the Bolsheviks to gain ultimate control of the world, called the Cold War. And when the Zionists triumphed, and became the world's lone superpower, they controlled all the money and food, leaving the world at the mercy of the Global World Order they created."

"So the bad guys won the war?" Jamie asked, confused.

"The war is still going on, Jamie. The Zionists didn't know the Master Chief of the Reich had planted the seeds of trees that would bring them back from the dead. And the once barren meadow slowly grew into a forest. And today, each beautiful leaf on those trees represents their glorious return."

Maggie felt sick. "FYI—the reason the Covenant Elite came over to the good side was because they realized that the Covenant had lied and were really the ones who were trying to destroy the world. And they will win in the end, because good always overcomes evil, even the kind that is hidden behind a lie."

"Did you learn that in school?"

"No, I learned it from my Oma, Ellen Peterson. You know … your grandmother."

She paused for a moment to let him know she'd put it all together. "I know you are the son of Josef, the one Hitler chose to lead the Reich back. But there's one thing I haven't figured out."

"Which is?'

"Why was your father *chosen*? It just doesn't make sense."

"I'll explain that to you when you are old enough to understand. Then you'll be able to fully comprehend your legacy."

Maggie viewed the branches of her family tree in her head. "I have no connection to you or your father, so I don't understand what legacy I would have. Our only link is Oma."

"Ellen is of royal blood, which makes us both part of a royal bloodline. She was a great woman who sacrificed for us all."

"Oma was some sort of Nazi queen or something?"

"The royal blood chooses you, Maggie, not the other way around. It takes a while to embrace it. I know this because I fought against it for years. But you must understand that people will try to harm you because of your heritage. So you must be prepared to protect yourself."

"Sounds like more Nazi lies. Who is writing your material … Goebbles?"

Kingston looked impressed at her knowledge of Hitler's Propaganda Minister. "The fact is my father was killed by these Zionists, as was *your father* …"

"My father would never be part of this!"

"You're a smart girl, Maggie, do the math."

She began running for the door. "I'm calling the police!"

"The police are already here," Kingston announced, and shouted for Eddie. He entered on command. "What's the problem now, Maggot?"

"What are you, some kind of SS Officer?"

"Is that anyway to treat your uncle?"

"Fuck you! Is that better?"

"Watch your mouth. These people are just trying to protect you."

She lost it. She ran to Jamie and took the controller out of his hand and threw it at Eddie. Then the Xbox. Jamie started screaming, but she didn't care. She picked up the glass dish of M&M's and threw it at his forehead. It was a direct hit. Eddie was knocked to the ground and candy spilled everywhere. Maggie ran to him and started kicking him with the tip of her crocs. She picked up the M&M's scattered at the floor and hit him in the face like she were spraying him with bee-bees. Then something made her pause.

Eddie would never let her get away with this. He was pissed, and his forehead was bleeding, but he couldn't do anything. He couldn't touch her. She was royal blood—whatever that meant—and he was just a working stiff for the Nazis.

Another piece of the puzzle fell into place, causing her to stop the candy Blitzkrieg. She'd figured it out, but he hadn't. They never told him, or more likely they lied to him. "You don't know, do you?"

"Know what?" he asked, half angry, half dazed.

"Rose Shepherd—the one we went to visit today—she's one of them. They killed your mother!"

Eddie glared at her, stunned. His eyes trailed to Kingston, who looked away like a coward. Eddie's look changed from surprise to sadness, and then to anger. But there was nothing he could do.

Silence filled the room, until a distraught Jamie shouted, "Maggie, you always ruin all the fun!"

CHAPTER 60

Kingston's mansion in Kings Point was only five minutes away. Yet Veronica knew the likelihood of the future president keeping kidnapped children in his home the day of the election was minuscule. And the possibility of him revealing their location to her was zero. But it still seemed like their next *illogical* step.

Any attempt to get there by car would be near impossible. The small town was packed with heavy security, clashing supporters and protestors, and practically every news outlet in the world. So Veronica began to run toward the mansion.

Zach caught up to her and made a convincing argument that her mad dash might garner some unwanted attention from the security force. She thought of those guys outside of Sterling's with the machine-guns, and knew he was right.

So they walked. Veronica's fashion slavery was backfiring, as the boots were killing her feet. But she figured they might come in handy when she put her foot into Kingston's ribs. And Mr. Head of Security, Eddie Peterson, better be wearing a cup when she got a hold of him.

As they walked, Veronica mentally untangled the branches of Ellen's family tree; from the dark roots to the blooming of the new buds, Maggie and Jamie.

"So if Joseph Kingston was the Chosen One, then Ellen was his mother and his father was … " she blanked. All the Nazis were melding together in her mind.

"Heinrich Müller—head of the Gestapo—captured by the CIA after the war, and later became Gus Becker," Zach informed.

"Why couldn't she just have told us this in the first place, instead of sending us on this crazy chase?"

"Because nobody would believe her. If she made such a claim against Kingston, it would've been laughed off as the ramblings of a crazy old lady. She was counting on a respected journalist getting the proof she needed, to give her claims credibility. Only then could it be stopped."

"Don't hurt yourself patting yourself on the back."

"I didn't mean me—I think she meant Maggie."

Veronica looked surprised, as Zach continued, "I also think Ellen wasn't just trying to stop it, but to also protect her family in the process. She didn't want Kingston to be harmed. I think she considers him to be a victim of all of this. Just like her other children, whose heritage led to their demise."

"If she wanted to protect her family, then why put Maggie in harm's way?"

"I don't know, but I get the feeling that before this day is over we're going to find out."

"Do you still think Kingston isn't connected because his political views differ from Hitler's?"

"I guess I forgot something else that Hitler said—that the great masses of people will more easily fall victim to the big lie than the small one."

Veronica nodded. And noted for future use, that one of the first signs you're with the wrong man is when he starts quoting Hitler. "Is there any reason I should believe you this time?"

"You shouldn't, but I'm all you have right now, so I have desperation on my side."

They pushed their way toward the gates. Veronica thought maybe if she could see the house, she could feel the presence of her children. She was banking on one of those special innate powers to finally kick in—the ones she thought she'd naturally obtain upon becoming a mother—but no such luck.

Zach suggested that before they start banging on the gates and demanding entrance, they regroup to come up with a more plausible plan, or at least one that would reduce their chances of being shot by security. Veronica didn't want to leave at first, but eventually agreed.

They re-traced their steps to Zach's Audi. Veronica's feet felt like someone was driving knives into them, but that wasn't even close to the sharpest pain she was feeling at the moment. They drove to the Great Neck Public Library. It was housed in a modern-looking stone building that was located a couple of miles from the Kingston mansion.

On the short ride over, they looked up Joseph Kingston on the Internet. All the information they found was in relation to his more famous son. This past Father's Day, Kingston gave a speech at the Merchant Marine Academy in King's Point, about his father and the qualities he believed he'd ingrained in him. For most candidates, the family rhetoric could be taken with a grain of salt, or in some cases a salt mine, but Veronica believed every word in this case, especially the parts about his father instilling loyalty into young Jim. This family had been loyal to each other for generations, never divulging their secret.

On the official Jim Kingston website there was an entire page devoted to his family. One picture stood out to Veronica. It was of a twelve-year-old Jim Kingston with his father. They were sailing on a boat in matching striped rugby shirts. The mother in Veronica was attracted to the father/son dynamic. But the cynic in her saw a politician trying to exploit the heart strings.

With little information on the Internet about the elder Kingston, and since the local newspapers only archived articles on their websites going back fifteen years, Veronica and Zach headed for the microfilm room in the library. They weren't so much interested in information on his father's life—they were more interested in his death.

According to a local newspaper, Joseph Kingston, 33, of Kings Point was gunned down at the local marina after getting off his boat on a September afternoon in 1972. There were no witnesses, and no arrest was ever made. Veronica winced at the gory picture of Chosen Joe, sprawled out on the pavement in a pool of his own blood.

"Notice the shirt," Zach said. "It's the same one he had on in the photo on the website. I think there *was* a witness. I think young Jim Kingston witnessed his father being murdered when they returned to shore that evening."

"Maybe that was his fishing shirt, or his favorite. My kids would wear the same clothes for a week if I'd let them."

"With all the father/son photos he could have used on the website, he picked one related to the boat his father was murdered by, wearing the same shirt. I think it's a symbol."

Veronica thought he was reaching, but nothing would surprise her at this point. Zach scrolled through the next six months' worth of articles that followed the murder. Microfilm was a slow and tedious method of getting information, but Zach plowed ahead skillfully.

There were plenty of related articles over the remaining months of 1972, but none of them shed any light on the motive, and despite a couple of locals being brought in for questioning, no real suspect ever materialized. There were rumors in some of the gossip pages that the murder was connected to the terrorist group Black September that had been responsible for the murder of eleven Israeli athletes at the Munich Olympics, just weeks earlier. That they had targeted Joseph Kingston for marrying into a prominent Jewish family.

The marriage reference sent Zach off in another direction. "They love society stuff out here," was all he said.

He searched until he found what he was looking for—the society section of a 1959 paper. It was coverage of the wedding of Joseph Kingston and Erika Sterling.

"I should have identified her as Erika Sterling from the photo on Ellen's Facebook page," Zach said. "Besides the visibility of being the mother of a presidential candidate, I had attended a couple fundraisers that she was at."

"Stop being so hard on yourself. That wedding photo is from over fifty years ago. How were you supposed to recognize her?"

The only photos that Ellen had posted on her page were of the bride and groom. But the newspaper had complete group shots of the wedding party and assorted guests.

"In the letters Flavia showed us, Ellen mentioned that Josef's wedding was the only time that all of the Apostles were in the same room," Zach said, intently studying the photos. "We're probably looking at some of the most notorious war criminals in history, including Himmler and Rudolph Hess, hidden right in plain sight. And there's our old friend Gus Becker," he said, pointing at the screen.

Veronica picked out Erika Sterling's brother, Aligor. "I don't get it. I thought he might have been responsible for Ellen and Carsten's deaths to protect his legacy, but I never thought in a million years that he'd be part of this group. He dedicated his life to getting justice for persecuted Jews, and he was in that concentration camp with Ben."

"Just like Ellen was," Zach said. "And I don't think it was a coincidence that he paid her a visit the last week of her life."

As did Eddie. Veronica now saw those visits in a different light.

She again looked at the close-up shot of bride and groom. Veronica couldn't shake what Ellen wrote in the letters about this wedding "merging" two Apostles families, which allowed the Apostles to associate closely without suspicion.

She now feared that the strategy for growing the family business had changed from merger to acquisition. And her children had been part of a hostile takeover.

CHAPTER 61

For Ben Youkelstein, it was a race against time. He needed to get to the children before they were taken away forever. He also had to stop this sham of an election.

He knew where he needed to go. The bigger challenge was his hand-eye coordination, which had admittedly regressed since he'd hit eighty. He rarely drove anymore, so trying to maneuver Veronica's large vehicle was a struggle.

Getting near Kingston's house was an even steeper challenge. He was forced to park about a mile away and walk. His legs often struggled to make it from bed to bathroom these days, but if this were the last thing he did on this earth, he would stop this horror movie from having a sequel.

He passed Kingston supporters, protestors, and media. But suddenly his slow journey was impeded, and his umbrella went flying to the pavement. Standing in front of him were two plain-clothes security guards. Modern-day SS stormtroopers dressed in brown uniforms with black boots. One of them smiled smugly at him, while the other picked up the umbrella.

"Sorry about that, old man," the smiling one said. The one who'd "accidentally" kicked it away in the first place.

His partner handed it back to him. "It's a long walk for an old timer like yourself. We're going to offer you a ride."

"I think I'll walk, thank you," Youkelstein said politely. "It's not often you see such sun this time of the year."

"I think you should reconsider," Smiley said.

"A car will stop beside you in thirty seconds, the door will open and you'll get in," said the one who'd retrieved the umbrella. With his bright blond hair, and being that he was a lapdog for the Nazis, Youkelstein thought they should call him the Golden Retriever.

True to their word, a stretch limo with dark tinted windows eased beside him and the back door opened. Youkelstein maneuvered his old bones into the car—no reason to put off the inevitable showdown. A hand reached out to help him—it belonged to an old friend.

"Hello, Ben," said the man he'd known for so many years as Aligor Sterling.

CHAPTER 62

They drove past the hordes of people outside the gates of the estate with help of the police escort. The gates opened and they pulled up to the grand front entrance.

Youkelstein and Aligor exchanged no words as they were whisked into the mansion.

"It's such a beautiful day, Otto," Youkelstein broke the silence. "I'm surprised you didn't choose to walk instead of ride ... in your chair."

"I don't know what you're talking about, Ben."

"I saw you leaving from your visit to Eva Braun's luxury cell, very much on your feet. And she only had one visitor in the log last night, who happened to sign in under the name Otto. It's a name that would be hard to trace, but one I'm quite familiar with."

Aligor didn't flinch. He just smiled. "And they say I'm the great spy."

Youkelstein wasn't as good at keeping his emotions in check. He always wore his fiery passion on his sleeve, and seeing his onetime kindred spirit here—up close—he felt a fire burn in the back of his throat. "I don't understand. You were there with me at Terezin! I saw you beaten by the Nazis until you spit up blood."

"I was in so many places and called so many names. I was once Petey O'Neill from Ireland, and then of Brooklyn. I was Agent Peter Jansen in the British SIS. And I've been known as Aligor Sterling since 1944."

Youkelstein would have thrown up, but he was certain he had no insides left.

"I won't rehash the story of the brilliant escape-pod designed by the Führer, codenamed Apostles. I'm sure you've gotten your fill of that the last few days. And your instincts were correct to believe in Ellen."

Aligor wheeled into a large office and the door shut behind them. He took a seat behind a large mahogany desk.

Youkelstein sat across from him. He looked right through his old friend, and out a large window behind the desk. It displayed a great view of the enormous front lawn, which led to the sturdy gates. Behind those gates was an unsuspecting world they were preying on.

"I was suicidal after Esther's murder and you saved me. You healed my soul."

Aligor smiled. "I saved your life in much more tangible ways than that, Ben. You see, my boss was the Reichsführer-SS Himmler. And as usual, he was only concerned with saving his own ass. So for PR purposes he worked a deal with Switzerland to release a number of Jews from concentration camps in December of 1944. Of course, he also got a nice sum in one of his Swiss bank accounts for his efforts. Himmler never did anything for free—even save himself. You weren't originally on that list, Ben, but I made sure you ended up being released."

Youkelstein wasn't feeling very grateful. "So everything has been a lie?"

"It became quite obvious that the war would end badly for Germany. So we were forced to put the Apostle plan into motion, and the Führer honored me by offering me a large role in launching the operation. My American cover was that of a young Jewish doctor from a wealthy family in Prague, who had been incarcerated by the Nazis. I've always been a firm believer in research—so I did time at Terezin preparing for my upcoming role."

Youkelstein wanted to stab him in his sardonic smile. Kill him in cold blood, just like the Nazis did to Esther. But it wouldn't help. Aligor was just a piece of the machine, and he had to stop the machine from rolling uncontrollably down the hill.

The room began to spin. The book-cased walls were whizzing by like he was looking out the window of a moving subway car. But it stopped just as quickly. Something had caught Youkelstein's eye, and the world froze. Like a hypnotic sleepwalker, he struggled to rise to his feet and shuffled to the large painting that hung on the sidewall of the office.

Aligor noticed the source of his attention, and glowingly stated, "It's the 1959 wedding of my 'sister' Erika and Joseph Kingston."

And to show off their macabre humor, the wedding photo was shot to the exact look of Da Vinci's painting of *The Last Supper.*

"It was the last time all of the original Apostles were together," Aligor said with a touch of nostalgia in his voice. "The only ones not present were that swine, Martin Bormann, and sadly, the Führer himself. It felt a little empty without him there."

Youkelstein's nose was now practically touching the photo, reviewing each person with diligence.

"All the way on the left," Aligor pointed from his seated position, "is our photographer, Rose Shepherd."

"Eva Braun," Youkelstein mumbled.

"Next to her is our head of security, Gus Becker, a police officer from Rhinebeck. Even in the United States there was a lot of threats directed at a wealthy Jewish family like ours, and Gus did a great job of keeping the event safe."

"How sad that Heinrich Müller was forced to do the grunt work at his own son's wedding."

"He was very proud of Josef, as were the groom's parents—the Kingstons. A blue-collar family from here in Long Island. Frank was a fisherman, while the groom's mother, Mary Kingston, was a brilliant pilot and intelligence agent who worked under me. She flew Hess and Josef to safety out of Germany years earlier. She was a vital member of the group, and it's sad that she didn't live to see this day."

Youkelstein remained fixated on Frank Kingston. It was Rudolph Hess.

"I must say, Ben, that your analysis in your book that declared the prisoner in Spandau a fraud, was right on the money. I was glad I pulled the strings to get you in there to examine him. The more conspiratorial you became, the more it hurt the credibility of your arguments, even if you did have evidence on your side."

Youkelstein always thought it was fishy that the prisoner refused to see his wife and son until twenty-five years after his imprisonment, but was willing to be examined by a forensic doctor for a book. He felt sick, realizing that those he hunted had mocked him.

"It was the easiest analysis I ever did. Apart from the fact that the flight plans, auxiliary tanks, and maps of the route didn't add up, Hess had received a rifle wound to the lung in World War I that was so severe that he spent a month in the hospital, yet the prisoner in Spandau had no scar on his chest. And perhaps the most damning evidence of all, was that many of Hess' fellow Nazis called out this stand-in as a fraud at the Nuremberg Trials. There is no doubt in my mind that it was an imposter—but I can't figure out why this man was willing to sacrifice his life for a lie."

"When he agreed to parachute into Scotland on May 10, 1941, pretending to be Hess, I don't believe he understood the long term ramifications. But he knew if he chose to talk, Himmler would be able to get to his family. They were all afraid of Himmler and his *sippenhaft.*"

Youkelstein's focus trailed back toward the center of the wedding table, zeroing in on the man pretending to be Aligor's father. When he pulled away the layers, Youkelstein felt like he had been set on fire. He couldn't believe it.

Aligor wheeled beside him, inches from the photo. "And of course you remember my father Jacob Sterling. I've never seen him look so proud as he did that day. But I guess it's normal for a father to feel that way the day he gives away his daughter."

Youkelstein peered at the man in the photo. He wore horn-rimmed glasses and looked different without his Charlie Chaplin mustache. He'd seen Jacob Sterling thousands of times—his picture still hung on the walls throughout Sterling Publishing—he'd even broken bread with him in his home. But he never looked at him like this. In this new light, the forensic surgeon in him noticed possible plastic surgery, but it was undeniably him.

"I sat right next to him when you invited me to spend the holidays when I first came to the States. I can't believe I celebrated the holiest of days with the devil himself!"

Himmler.

CHAPTER 63

Youkelstein continued to stare at the Nazi Last Supper in disbelief. He reached into his pocket and pulled out the pad in which he had scribbled down the Apostle names during yesterday's trip to Rhinebeck. He mentally filled them in. He now had a complete list from Peter to Thaddeus.

"I must disagree with you on Himmler, Ben, calling him the devil would be insulting to Satan himself. We never wanted him or Bormann to be involved, but he always had the Führer on his marionette string.

"He was a brilliant planner and economist, and while it pains me to admit it, the Apostles never would've survived to see this day if he wasn't at the forefront of our formative years. Our first step was to build a wealth worthy of a great empire. Nobody was better skilled at these tasks than Himmler.

"He also knew the best way to engage the enemy was to become the enemy. And by posing as Jacob Sterling, he became a beacon of the Jewish community."

"Why did you bring me into this? Nothing you did was without calculation."

"It was like a miracle when I ran into you at the Eichman trial. And certainly not planned. All the Jews there were so bloodthirsty, but you even more than most. I realized if I hunted down these vilified Nazis, then the Apostles' infiltration into the enemy would be complete."

"You used me."

"I gave you a platform for your revenge and you bit into it like a slobbering shark! And often we were on the same team. For instance, we both wanted Bormann dead."

"He was about to talk before you killed him. He had no idea he was speaking to an Apostle—he never knew the true identity of Otto, only a select few were privy to it. I thought your rage overtook you, but killing him was about revenge ... because he murdered your mentor."

"If not for the Führer, Bormann's own men would've killed him ten times over. He sent more people to death then imaginable, and whored himself to whoever was the most powerful man in the room. And yes, he did betray the Führer by joining forces with Himmler, and I vowed to get justice."

"You were surprised Himmler had devious plans? Killing Hitler might be his one redeeming quality."

Aligor glared at him—he'd hit a nerve. "Himmler's ego wouldn't allow him to play second fiddle. His plans were so grandiose and delusional that he actually sought a meeting with Joe Kennedy in early 1960, seeking to be his son's choice for Supreme Court Justice if he won the presidency. Jacob Sterling on the US Supreme Court, can you imagine it, Ben?"

Youkelstein shuddered with thoughts of the damage that Himmler could have caused from that powerful seat. But also saw how his craving for the spotlight had threatened the secrecy of the Apostles.

"When he was told there were no openings, he created one. In 1962, Supreme Court Justice Felix Frankfurter was forced to retire from the court after suffering a sudden stroke, but President Kennedy nominated Arthur Joseph Goldberg to fill the Jew seat vacated by Frankfurter. So Himmler declared war on the President and his family. He was clearly out of control at this point and putting the group at risk. And when we discovered that he'd murdered such a great leader, we had to act."

"You are saying Himmler was responsible for the Kennedy assassination?"

"I said nothing of the sort! The great leader I speak of is the Führer. To even compare his legacy to a lightweight like John Kennedy is blasphemy! And we both know the communists were behind that day in Dallas, Ben."

"So tell me how you killed the devil. After all the help I've provided you over the years, I think I deserve one last joy before my death."

"I will defer to the US Coast Guard on the official cause of Jacob Sterling's death, which they declared an accidental drowning," he said with a smirk.

"With all the time you spent around Himmler, I see you picked up his opportunistic traits. When he went overboard, it boosted you into a position of power."

"I always preferred to work behind the scenes, but with Jacob's death, and the age and health issues of the others, I was forced to take on a leadership position. And I thought it would just be temporary, until Josef was ready to take his rightful place."

"But the chosen one didn't turn out as planned."

"That would be an understatement—and it set us back a generation. Unfortunately, he became Americanized—the drugs, the women, and his overall reckless behavior. We all believed, or at least hoped, that marriage, along with the responsibility of his own child, would set him on the right path. But the decline continued, culminating with his affair with that CIA operative from his father's case, which resulted in another member of the bloodline."

"Flavia. Daughter of Josef and Olivia Conte."

"And thanks to Josef's loose lips—often fueled by alcohol—Olivia learned too much about our operation. And it was just a matter of time before she acted on what she learned. It was a messy situation. Eliminating a CIA member was a great risk, but we felt we had no other choice."

"Did Ellen know you had her son killed?"

Aligor's eyes shifted. Youkelstein could tell he wanted to avoid that issue. "While it was very clear that Josef would not live up to expectation, we found hope in his son. But we worried that Josef would drag Jim down with him, and we couldn't afford that. He was our final chance."

"I think 'final solution' would be a more appropriate term. By killing his father in front of him, and in doing so, painting the Jews as his killer … you created a monster! Or more accurately, *re-created* one."

"That's humorous coming from the man who believes in nature over nurture. You know as well as I do that Jim Kingston is a product of the bloodline. All I did was clear the path for him to accept his destiny."

Aligor *stood* and *walked* to the window. He stared through the thick bulletproof glass out at the energized crowd that had gathered just beyond the gates of the Kingston Estate. He cleared his throat and said, "And destiny has arrived, Ben."

CHAPTER 64

"So what is Kingston planning to do when he gets in office—nuke Israel?"

Aligor turned back toward him, looking mortified by such an accusation. "Of course not! You are a student of history, Ben, so you know that revolutions are not won with guns—they're won with the hearts and minds."

"The American people will see through your lies," Youkelstein shot back.

But when he glanced at the zealous crowds beyond the gates, he knew his response was laughable.

Aligor followed Youkelstein's gaze out the window. "We're just leading them where they want to go. Any poll will tell you the last thing they want is war—if Jim embraced that position the election wouldn't even be in doubt. But look at the people, Ben—the revolution has already been sparked!"

Youkelstein knew only a fool of the highest order could doubt the energy and passion he was watching from Kingston's supporters. And he was aware that Hitler didn't take power in Germany with tanks and bullets. Although, contrary to popular myth, he never received more than 37% of the vote in the 1932 elections. And he used underhanded tactics, such as threats of a military coup, to gain the position of Chancellor, which he used to vault himself to power in 1933. But by the looks of things, Kingston would need no such tactics.

Youkelstein also was aware that the Apostles would leave nothing to chance. And when Sterling boasted about the details of his "billion dollar bet" made on the election, he knew nothing could stop a Kingston landslide victory.

"So how were you able to spark your *so called* revolution?" Youkelstein took the bait.

Aligor returned to his wheelchair, eager to discuss. "We waited and watched. We had the ups and downs of any American family—sad deaths followed by happy births. And I won't kid you, when Josef and Harry Jr., both direct links to the lineage, failed tragically, it placed doubt in our minds. But Jim's rise returned our hope."

Youkelstein clenched his arthritic hands in anger.

"But it would take more than hope. As the 1980s came to a close, and the Berlin Wall fell, marking the end of the Cold War, I began to wonder if our time had passed. Müller and Hess had both died by that point, and Ellen was never the same after she lost her children. I looked to history, and realized that the great leaders understood how one small spark could turn into a blazing inferno. America understood this, which is why they withheld information about the Pearl Harbor attacks to wake the people from their slumber back in '41."

"You accuse me of creating elaborate stories to push my agenda, but I could never equal your imagination!"

"You really still doubt me, Ben? British intelligence agent, Peter Jansen, one of my many aliases, was the one who delivered them the news of the imminent attack a month prior. But my real interests lay with Germany, whose main objective was to keep the US out of the war. The Führer knew that the US could tip the balance, and he was right. I don't know if my information ever reached FDR, and doubt that it did, but someone in the hierarchy of government chose to sit on it."

"I'm not sure I understand what Pearl Harbor has to do with what you're attempting to achieve today."

"Because Pearl Harbor taught me that the only way to move Americans to action was an attack on their homeland. Just like the events of September 11, 2001."

Aligor savored the stunned look on Youkelstein's face. "Like I said, Ben, I'm a student of history. And like you, I believe in nature over nurture. There is a reason the US never learned from their past mistakes. For better or worse, they are genetically programmed to act in a certain way. So it was no surprise they reacted like a preoccupied grizzly bear when attacked, swatting at flies around the world, while the true enemy rose from within their own borders. And unbeknownst to them, a revolution had been sparked."

As Youkelstein scrambled to reconstruct the puzzle in his mind, Aligor continued, "Those who learn from history end up as the ruling class—those who don't, perish. The Führer learned this lesson the hard way. He should have absorbed the lesson of Napoleon's invasion of Russia, but he followed his passion right into the deadly Russian winter. He chose to listen to his heart instead of his brain ... very similar to yourself, Ben."

"I am nothing like that monster!"

"The Jews were the enemy of Germany, just like they are for America. And the people will cheer as President Kingston tears down the symbol of this embedded enemy."

"What symbol is this—another cross labeled in code?"

"No, this will be a living symbol ... Aligor Sterling."

"You?"

"The renowned Jewish leader will come clean about his actions in the planning and plotting of 9/11. And I have the evidence to prove it. An investigation will follow, which will reveal to the world that Israel not only had knowledge of the attack being imminent, but they withheld it, hoping to spark the US into helping to further their agenda in the Middle East and taking on Israel's enemies."

"More lies!"

"Maybe so, but they won't be coming from some radical Islamic cleric. They will come from the mouth of Aligor Sterling—the man who spent his life hunting down Nazi war criminals, and was a constant dinner guest of the Israeli prime minister."

Youkelstein felt sick. "So I presume after this alleged evidence against Aligor Sterling is revealed—to a crime no different than if Israel declared war on the US—Kingston will be forced to remove his support for the current conflict, despite his campaign promises. Just like Hitler, you will have created an enemy in the Jews. And you will have learned from Hitler's mistake, and choose to stand aside as your enemies destroy each other."

Aligor smiled like a teacher who'd just gotten through to his most difficult student. "This act of neutrality—citing George Washington's 1793 Proclamation of Neutrality as precedent—will create an isolated and vulnerable Israel. And without the specter of US intervention, the path will be cleared for its enemies to join together and rise up against them. Israel will be left a cornered animal with one last card to play in the name of survival."

"Nukes," Youkelstein said sadly.

Aligor nodded. "And with the Russian's economic relationship in the region, they will have no choice but to retaliate. And if America has reservations about entering the current struggle, I doubt their willingness would increase as the body count rises, and the radiation spreads.

"And as history tells us, the Russians don't need to have their arms twisted to join a war. The French and Germans will not have the internal support to back Israel—as their large Muslim populations will rise up in the streets. The only support will come from the British … based on their own self-interest, of course. So the Israelis and British end up fighting the

Russians. To the death. The Führer hated the Russians much more than the Jews!"

Aligor pushed out of his chair. He stood beside Youkelstein and draped his arm around him. In a different time, it would've been a portrait of friendship. But today, Youkelstein squirmed away.

Aligor remained undeterred, "I will take great pride in the destruction of the British, and this time the US will not be there to save them. You see, Ben, the British killed my brothers and the Jews killed my parents, and now I'm going to get justice. How does the saying go—killing two birds with one stone?"

"And once your enemies have destroyed each other, you plan to have the Reich move in and rule the world for the next thousand years."

"Which is precisely why we will protect Maggie and Jamie at any cost. We won't let you harm them, as you have come here to do."

CHAPTER 65

"So what's this, Obi-Wan, your light-saber?" the guard asked, stroking the umbrella.

"If it was, I would've killed you yesterday morning," Youkelstein replied, matching Eddie Peterson's smugness. He was his personal warden, watching over him, locked in a room inside Kingston's mansion.

Eddie laughed. "I've been shot, stabbed, and had my throat slit with the jagged end of a broken bottle. But I must admit, nobody ever came after me with a weapon as pathetic as an umbrella."

"Since it isn't a threat to you, perhaps I can have it back?"

"No, I think I'll hold onto it, Obi-Wan. Why do you have it, anyway? It couldn't have been a sunnier day."

"It helps me to walk. I guess I'm too stubborn to admit I need the help of a cane. It's not easy being in your nineties—too bad you'll never live long enough to find out."

Eddie laughed again. "You had your chance to take your shot. Now it looks like I'm going to outlive you."

"I didn't mean I was going to kill you—*they* will. Those without the blood are expendable. And when they start covering up their crimes, you'll be first on their list. Especially since you allowed Veronica to witness the kidnapping of the children, which put their entire operation at risk. Neither you or her will live to see the inauguration."

"Spare me the psycho-babble."

"You're already dead to them. Yesterday you were head of security and now you're stuck babysitting an old man and his umbrella. The important players have already left for the Waldorf."

"Your arrival changed the plans. They know they can count on me in an emergency—I'm a team player."

"Just like those SS officers who marched those innocent women and children to their deaths. Just doing their job ... following orders. And when it was over, like you, they all became expendable."

He swung the umbrella, striking Youkelstein in his broken ribs. The pain ripped through him, but he found the strength to laugh.

"What's so funny?"

"You have the same problem I do."

"I have a death wish?"

"Perhaps, but I meant you wear your emotions on your sleeve, which makes you easy to read."

"So you think you have me all figured out, old man?"

"This is all about you not being good enough. Your parents deserted you, and Harold Peterson is given credit for your police accomplishments. These Nazis were the first people to make you feel important, and they gave you a chance to finally match up to Carsten—the one with the royal blood."

"That's not true—Ellen always believed in me."

"Which makes it strange that you wouldn't follow the wishes she willed to Maggie. Unless your Nazi friends convinced you that *this* is what Ellen really wanted. That she no longer understood what she was saying, and needed to be silenced. At least it was a more peaceful way to go than the method Rose Shepherd used to quiet your mother."

Eddie swung the umbrella again, and connected in the same spot.

Youkelstein curled up on the floor, and weakly responded, "You will never truly be one of them. First, you'll be called on to do away with Veronica before she goes to the police, and then you'll be next. Save yourself."

He raised the umbrella again, "I said shut your mouth!"

"If you won't save yourself, at least save Maggie and Jamie. I see the way you look at those kids—you love them."

Eddie began to swing the umbrella again. This time at Youkelstein's head. But he stopped in mid thrust.

Youkelstein was right—Edward Peterson wasn't like them.

CHAPTER 66

Eddie moved across the upstairs of the mansion until he came upon the guard standing stiffly outside Maggie and Jamie's room.

"I need to talk to them—let me in."

The guard looked annoyed. "Your orders were to not leave Youkelstein. Where is he?"

Suddenly the guard's face contorted. His eyes dazed and he staggered a few steps before falling to his knees.

Youkelstein looked at the man he'd just injected with the tip of his "light saber," having surprised him from behind

"Hurry," he urged Eddie, noticing the guard beginning to twitch on the floor. He was the one who kicked Youkelstein's umbrella away outside. Smiley was no longer smiling. In fact, he was in the beginning stages of a deadly stroke.

Eddie pounded on the door. "Open up! Emergency! Guard down—guard down!"

The door flung open and a large man with a semiautomatic weapon stepped forward. With no hesitation, Eddie put a bullet into his head, and he fell like a rock.

Maggie began to scream, but Eddie muffled it with his hand. Jamie's eyes bulged out of his head, but it seemed to be more excitement than fear.

"We don't have much time," Eddie urged. "We need to get out of here."

Maggie wasn't going anywhere—not with him. She folded her arms and moved away.

"I messed up, okay? I told your mother I'd keep you safe, Mags, and I plan to keep my promise."

She gauged him for a long moment, searching for the answer. She appeared to relent, and approached like she was going to give him a hug. But then she threw a punch to his most sensitive of areas. "Don't ever do that again," she said.

Eddie bent over in pain, but nodded in agreement.

It turned out that Jamie needed the bigger sales job. He'd grown accustomed to the lifestyle of the rich and famous. Only when his sister threatened his life did he agree to go. But the boy refused to leave his video game behind. He found a white laundry bag in the closet, put the game inside, and slung it over his shoulder.

Eddie led them into the hall. Footsteps were moving in their direction. A shot whistled by them and a vase crashed to the floor.

Eddie returned fire and they could hear the guards fall to the ground. They then followed him through a maze of corridors until they arrived at the grand staircase.

As they stood at the top of the staircase, reality clicked in. The footsteps grew louder behind them. It was the guards on the upstairs level. Below, two more guards aimed their automatic weapons. Word had spread quickly.

They were trapped.

But Maggie had an idea.

"Uncle Eddie, you shouldn't be trying to protect us. We need to protect you."

"What are you talking about?" he snapped, as the two upstairs guards moved into their vision. He was the protector.

"Jamie and I are royal blood, remember? They can't shoot us. We are like …"

"A shield!" Jamie exclaimed.

Jamie handed Youkelstein the bag with the Xbox in it, and hopped on Eddie's back. Maggie wrapped around his shoulders from the front like they were slow dancing, her legs dangling down.

Youkelstein trailed close behind, as they started down the stairs. "Move back—precious cargo coming through," Eddie yelled at the downstairs guards.

They didn't drop their weapons, so Eddie shot at them. He hit one in the arm and his gun fell to the ground. The other, the one Youkelstein had nicknamed the Golden Retriever, put his down voluntarily. Smart puppy.

The guard looked confused, and shouted at the upstairs guards, "Hold your fire! Secure the children without force."

They reached the bottom of the staircase and stepped into the Great Room. Then eased toward the front entrance. The guards followed slowly. It was a game of chess.

Even if they made it out, the yard was littered with security. Sterling's personal security, who claimed to be ex-Mossad, Israeli loyalists, but Youkelstein knew that was a fabrication—they were nothing but SS in training.

Maggie again took the role of leadership—she was a natural. "Once we make it outside they can't do anything. The only thing that could hold Kingston back from winning at this point is a shootout in his front yard."

"Can't shoot kids and old people!" Jamie shouted out.

When they reached the front door, Eddie set them down. He began pushing the kids out the door. Shots rang out, and Eddie's white dress shirt instantly turned red. He had been shot through the chest and slumped to the ground.

Maggie shouted at Youkelstein. "Get down!"

He followed her orders. She then ordered Jamie to stand in front of him. They couldn't shoot Jamie.

Maggie knelt by Eddie. "Are you okay?" she asked.

"I'm fine, Maggot, but you need to get out of this house," he replied, his voice fading.

"Not without you."

He mustered strength. "I'm ordering you, Maggot—get out of there now!"

"You can't order me—I'm royal blood."

"What you are is a royal pain in the ass. Besides, I'm your uncle and that outweighs everything."

She was only twelve, but wise enough to realize that Eddie wasn't going to make it out alive. But she still had a chance to get out … if she hurried. The guards were moving closer, their rhythmic footsteps clicking on the floor. Youkelstein could swear they were goose-stepping.

Maggie's expression turned angry. A fire began simmering in her eyes. She noticed Eddie's gun on the floor and picked it up.

She could do anything she wanted and the lowly guards couldn't do anything back. It was intoxicating. *No wonder so many kings and queens had abused their power over the years,* Youkelstein thought.

She pointed the gun at the culprit—Golden Retriever.

"No," Eddie said with a weak voice.

"Family sticks together, right?" Maggie said, tears streaming down her face. "He shot you, so now I'm going to shoot him back."

"No," Eddie said, this time firmer. The red pool on his chest had grown from a puddle to a lake.

Maggie held steady, her stare never leaving Retriever.

"They think because you have a certain blood in you that you're like them, but you're not. That stuff doesn't matter. The person you are is because of how you were raised. You're mother and father are the two best people I know, and they didn't raise a killer."

Maggie held the gun firm. It was like she wasn't listening. The guards continued to move in, but not as confidently as before.

At the last second, she dropped the gun.

Youkelstein had no such reservations. He picked it up and fired a sizzling bullet through Golden Retriever's brain—it's not like he was using it, anyway. Not a bad shot for an elderly man with poor vision and shaky hands, if he said so himself.

The shot bought them a few seconds to make a run for it. Before they did, with one last gasp, Eddie ordered them to stuff his belongings—badge, wallet, handcuffs, and second weapon—into the laundry bag. There was no time for tearful goodbyes.

As they moved out the door another shot rang out. This one pierced Youkelstein's clavicle and he could feel the bone shatter. But he fought through the pain until he felt the sun on his face.

Once outside, Maggie and Jamie began running toward the front gate, yelling "Help!"

The scene was complete chaos. People pressing up against the gates. Helicopters flying overhead. Youkelstein moved after the kids as fast as he could, but collapsed midway through the yard.

Maggie and Jamie saw him fall. Maggie took Eddie's gun and began running at one of the heavily armed guards who was moving in on Youkelstein. Jamie followed his sister.

CHAPTER 67

"So did you vote today?"

"Huh?" Flavia spacily responded to her female assistant as they stood in her Rhinebeck gallery.

Before she could answer, a bell signaled the opening of the front door. Flavia sent a paranoid look in its direction, but a stream of sun burst through on a rare, sun-drenched November day, and spotlighted the familiar man.

False alarm.

"Are you okay, Flav?" her assistant asked again.

She wasn't sure. She hadn't slept since Veronica Peterson and her group had shown up here yesterday. She could feel the ghosts closing in on her last night with every creak of the old house.

Flavia shook the cobwebs. "I'm sorry. Just a little distracted. No, I plan to go after we close. The polls are open until eight, right?"

The man approached her. It was FedEx Steve. Just like every day, he wore his purple and orange pullover with baseball cap and a happy-to-be-alive smile.

"I almost didn't recognize you. You're usually dressed a little more Flav-ulous," he greeted her, before turning apologetic. "But that's not to say you still don't look great."

She smiled at him. He wasn't being flirtatious. He was just one of those serial complimenters. She wore a simple fall sweater and jeans, her hair was in a ponytail and she wore little make-up. Obviously, Steve didn't notice the dark circles under her eyes.

Flavia took the package, and after trading pleasant goodbyes with Steve, she carried it into her office and shut the door. She checked the postal mark—Chappaqua, New York. She removed the mailing tape with a pair of scissors, and opened the box.

The contents of the box consisted of a key that was attached to instructions, along with a neatly typed manuscript titled *My Family Tree— The Last Leaves of Evil. By Ellen Sarowitz-Peterson.*

The final item was a portable video player. On it, Ellen had loaded a video in which she methodically explained everything from the beginning, filling in all the blanks.

Ever since her father's deathbed confession, Flavia had felt as if her identity had been stolen. She had been lost. But suddenly she knew exactly who she was, and where she'd come from. She realized that the ghosts weren't chasing her—they were protecting her.

And it was clear what she needed to do next. She had to get Ellen's memoir to Jim Kingston before it was too late.

CHAPTER 68

Veronica had pushed her way to the front gate of the Kingston estate. She doubted her children were inside, but she was sure that Jim Kingston knew their whereabouts. She needed to talk to him.

But as the afternoon grew long, the gates opened and a stretch limo headed out. It stopped just outside the gate and a window electronically rolled down. Veronica strained to look in.

She saw Kingston sitting next to Sterling.

Kingston shouted out a statement to his supporters, who were surrounding the vehicle. A few reporters yelled questions to him, but his only response was a thumbs-up. He flashed his charismatic smile as the limo pulled away.

The obvious reaction would've been to follow Kingston, but something told her to stay. Zach read her eyes and agreed. *As if he had a choice.*

About an hour later, she appeared prophetic, when the most unbelievable thing happened. The front door opened and two small children ran out, followed by an elderly man.

Maggie and Jamie!

They were shouting, "Help!" at the top of their lungs as they moved toward the front gate. Veronica tried to will them to safety like she was using some Jedi mind trick. But it had the opposite effect.

Youkelstein fell to the ground and the kids stopped and ran to help him. "No!" Veronica shouted out. All that crap she taught them about helping others was coming back to bite her in the ass.

The security guards on the grounds of the estate—the ones with the machine-guns—began to move toward them. And Maggie was pointing a gun at them!

"No Maggie—run! Jamie!"

But as usual, her children didn't listen to her. And in this case, they did the most horrifying thing imaginable. They ran right at the guards!

Things then changed from scary to weird. Maggie began instructing the guards like she was their superior officer. The guards strangely followed her orders, helping to carry Youkelstein to the front gate.

The children kept getting closer. She wanted to reach through the gates and pull them through. When they arrived at the gate, Maggie ordered the guards to open it. With a little urging from her gun, they obliged. As happy as Veronica was to see her children safe, the sight of Maggie pointing a gun at someone was a frightening image. It was surreal.

When the gate opened, Veronica's kids kept it classy. Jamie stuck out his tongue at the guards, while Maggie flashed them the bird. But when they ran to her and she wrapped her arms around them, all was forgiven.

Only Zach's desperate urging snapped her back to reality. He hoisted Youkelstein over his shoulder, still gripping that damn umbrella. Veronica took the kids' hands and they ran all the way to the Audi. This time she couldn't even feel her feet. The pain had gone away.

Within minutes, they were driving west on the Long Island Expressway. It was rush hour and the LIE was a parking lot. But Veronica didn't care—her kids were safe. She didn't want the details of how Youkelstein got shot, especially any part that might have to do with Maggie and guns. It was too much to take right now. But she did notice that Eddie wasn't with them, and she had a pretty good idea what that meant. She wasn't sure what to think about Eddie right now.

Youkelstein had lost a lot of blood, but his stubbornness was intact. He fought any attempts to get him immediate medical attention, urging them to get to Manhattan as quickly as possible to try to stop Kingston. He didn't offer up any suggestions as to how they would be able to do that.

Zach compared notes with Maggie and Youkelstein. Maggie shared a conversation she had with Kingston during her capture, and despite his injury, Youkelstein was able to detail his meeting with Sterling, including the part about how he was really a German spy named Otto, and was about as Jewish as the Pope.

The rapid-fire discussion ping-ponged topics like Nazis, Israel, World War III, and 9/11—it was like Veronica was attending a conspiracy theory trade show.

But like most mothers, she was skilled at narrowing things down to just the important facts. Bottom line, Kingston and Sterling were the bad guys, and they had to be stopped to keep her children safe.

Attempting to drown out the heated conversation, she turned on the radio. It was now 6:30 in the evening and the exit polls in Michigan and Ohio were showing an overwhelming Kingston victory. Maggie informed the adults that these two states were in the heart of Baer territory. The election was starting to look like a landslide. But while Kingston might have been on his way to winning the election, he seemed to have lost the support of Maggie Peterson, who frowned upon hearing the report.

They crossed over the Whitestone Bridge. Nobody discussed where they were going—it was understood. They were headed to the devil's den. Veronica glanced back at her children and fury pulsed through her veins. The devil was about to face an adversary that could match his fire.

An angry mother.

CHAPTER 69

Lower Manhattan was packed to the rafters as darkness had settled in. The energy reminded Veronica of New Year's Eve in Times Square.

Youkelstein had come to the end of his road. He started losing consciousness and they decided to drive him directly to the hospital. He railed against it—it was like trying to get Picasso to the vet.

His physician was based out of Beth Israel Hospital on 16th Street. They stopped in front and Zach carried him in. He dropped him in the lobby without explanation and returned to the car. They then miraculously found a spot near the park at Stuyvesant Square—a place Veronica often took the kids when they lived in Manhattan—they left the vehicle there and headed off by foot.

Veronica, always prepared, fitted Maggie and Jamie with the jackets she brought with her when she left for Long Island this morning. *What an optimist,* she thought, but it's not like she had a choice—thinking any other way would've crushed her. Maggie's coat was a wool, pink button-down. She normally refused to wear it, or the cute matching hat that came with it. But she understood there was no way she was getting in the Waldorf in a pair of pajamas, and put it on without a fight.

Jamie, Mr. GQ, was more prepared for high society. He proudly wore the tuxedo that his new pal Jim Kingston had provided for him. He opted for fashion over comfort, but she wasn't taking no for an answer. The jacket was not optional.

They headed without a second look through the minefield of security and barricades for the two-mile journey from 15th Street up Park Avenue to the Waldorf. If anyone had a plan for what they were going to do when they got there, they'd yet to reveal it.

Their biggest weapon was Eddie's badge that declared him to be the head of NYPD's Kingston security task force. It worked like a charm all the way through the Waldorf's Park Avenue entryway, which they entered under the hotel's famed art deco grill.

Inside, it felt like the center of the universe. And in a way it was. Zach mentioned that he doubted it was a coincidence that the Kingston victory celebration would take place within blocks of some of the country's best known financial, political, and religious symbols, including Rockefeller Center, St. Patrick's Cathedral, and Times Square. *What better place to launch a takeover of the universe, but from its core?*

Now came the hard part. Their request to be cleared to go to Kingston's suite was met with suspicious looks. When they offered to call the presidential nominee, those looks turned to action. Security began moving toward them like they were John Wilkes Booth scalping theater tickets.

As the guards closed in, Maggie calmly spoke up, "Mr. Chester, can I see your phone?"

Zach flashed her a curious look, but reached into his pocket and pulled out his cell. The Waldorf staffer saw it as a possible weapon and shrieked. Security now came rushing towards them. Veronica knew when they checked the bag and found the gun and handcuffs that Eddie had left for Maggie, they'd be spending a long time in prison.

But Maggie remained undeterred as she punched in a phone number.

"Is this Jim Kingston?" she asked into the phone and awaited an answer.

Maggie listened for a moment, before replying, "This is Maggie Peterson. I'm down in the lobby being hassled by some of your security force. Can you call down and clear us to come up? We have a few things we need to talk about."

They were now surrounded—guns pointed at them. "Get down ... now!" yelled one. "Drop the bag," shouted another.

They followed orders and hit the cold floor. The buzzing lobby went silent and all eyes shot toward them.

The silence was shattered by the ringing of a phone.

It was coming from the hotel staffer. He answered it, did a few *a-hums* and *yes-sirs*, before handing it to the lead security guard, who repeated the drill.

"On your feet," the guard demanded, putting his gun away. The others followed his lead.

"What's going on?" Zach asked.

"I'm going to take you up to Senator Kingston's suite," the guard stated, matter-of-fact. He was now on his best behavior.

As they rode the gold and glass elevator to the 35th Floor, Veronica looked to her daughter with astonishment. "You have Kingston's cell number?"

Maggie smiled. "Actually he confiscated my phone at his house. So I dialed my own phone and he answered."

Veronica couldn't help but return a proud smile.

CHAPTER 70

They were led into the suite. It was crowded with a who's-who of supporters, many of them familiar faces. The first person that Veronica noticed was the vice-presidential candidate, Senator Langor from Florida, who was hard to miss with his tanned skin and snow-white hair.

The crowd was too glued to a massive television screen to notice their arrival. Not that anyone would know who they were, anyway. The background noise of the television declared another state—Missouri—and shaded the color-coded map blue for Kingston.

The cheering brought Kingston out of a connecting room. Sterling was by his side, in his wheelchair. According to Youkelstein, Sterling's legs were capable of running a half-marathon.

Sterling acted as if he'd caught a surprise glimpse of Veronica across the crowded room and wheeled toward them. Kingston followed, his patented smile plastered on his face. All eyes went to him. He shook Zach's hand like they were old buddies, before kissing Veronica on the cheek.

Maggie struggled away from any attempt at affection, but Jamie moved in for a hug as if Kingston were his new favorite uncle. Maggie grabbed her brother by the jacket and yanked him away, a not-so-subtle lesson about loyalty.

Veronica remained still. She didn't know what to say, and felt the eyes of the room on her. She uttered the first thing that came to mind, "You stole my daughter's phone, and we've come to get it back."

Kingston smiled and put his hands up like he was surrendering. "I'm sorry, Veronica—we don't want another Watergate here," he replied with a confident grin. "Why don't you come to my room so I can give Maggie her phone back?"

Veronica thought for a second. Should they be alone with him? But with all these witnesses in the next room, it was likely the safest place on the planet. She traded glances with Zach, and they agreed to follow.

On the way, Kingston pointed out JFK's rocking chair and General Douglas MacArthur's writing desk. The suite was steeped in history. Zach looked impressed.

Kingston's private room was filled with televisions, a wet bar, and a bathroom with a marble tub that Veronica wanted to take home with her. She expected Kingston to morph into some fire-breathing creature behind closed doors, but he kept his campaign cool.

"I made the wrong choice not to include you," he began. "It was wrong for my family to not be with me on this historical occasion. It felt wrong without all of you here."

Maggie screeched, "We're not your family, you scum-sucking Nazi!"

Kingston remained eerily calm. It was like he wasn't human. "Your energy is boundless, Maggie. I thought you would've been worn out after that theatrical display you put on at my house, but you remain an inspiration." His smile sobered. "The same display that got your friend Lieutenant Peterson killed."

Maggie looked like she wanted to go straight for his throat. Veronica could see it now, infamous assassins of US presidents—*John Wilkes Booth, Lee Harvey Oswald, and Maggie Elizabeth Peterson.*

"Eddie gave his life to stop you—he's a hero!" Maggie shouted.

"To stop me from what?" Kingston asked, feigning surprise. And not fearing that any of this conversation would leak through the soundproof walls of the suite.

"Now that we've escaped, we're going to tell the world what you are planning to do and you'll never get away with it. Oma chose me to stop it— so now I'm the chosen one!"

"Okay, Maggie, I'll play along. How would you *stop me?*"

"Oma hid her memoir, and only I know where it is. It tells all the secrets about the Apostles. If you don't resign your candidacy for president, we're going to publish it and then the whole world will know!"

Veronica could tell that her daughter was out on a limb with a bluff. At least she thought so. Things seemed to be changing by the second the last couple days.

Kingston looked smug. "Isn't there only one copy of that?"

"Yes ..." her voice trailed off.

Veronica grew worried—Kingston had something up his sleeve.

A buzzing sound interrupted them. Kingston pushed a button on the phone and a female voice came over the speakerphone. "Senator Kingston, I have a Flavia Conte for you."

Veronica cringed—she's one of them. *Kingston's half sister.* She should have never trusted her.

CHAPTER 71

Flavia glided in. Adding her presence to Kingston and Jamie, the room was now on charisma overload.

She was dressed down, compared to the previous day—a pair of snug-fitting jeans, sweater, and a bouncing ponytail. But the accessory that caught Veronica's attention was the document she held in her hands.

"Uh-oh," Maggie said softly.

"That's the only version you were talking about?" Veronica whispered.

Maggie nodded stoically.

"How can you be sure?" Veronica asked. "Ellen admitted to telling lies for sixty years, what's one more?"

"Because TJ made the cover—how could she copy that? She wasn't exactly Bill Gates with the computer."

Flavia handed the memoir to Kingston, and now Veronica was the one to say, "Uh-oh."

Flavia turned her head in her direction. It was as if she noticed her presence for the first time. "Veronica?"

"You lying ..."

"It's not what you think."

Veronica looked at Maggie, who for the first time looked overwhelmed. She silently stared out into space.

"Then enlighten me," Veronica said.

"I'm just following Ellen's orders."

"Following orders just like those Nazi soldiers?"

Flavia shook her head. "You just don't understand."

Those were the same words Eddie used when he took her children. Veronica wasn't seeking understanding, all she wanted was to take them home to a safe world.

Veronica took another peek at Maggie, who was now catatonic. So Veronica spoke the words she thought her daughter would say in this situation, "Whatever."

When Kingston held the memoir, he smiled with relief. He had been more worried than he'd let on.

He handed the document to Sterling—still in the wheelchair—who laid it out on his lap. He read the title out loud, "*My Family Tree—The Last Leaves of Evil*, by Ellen Sarowitz-Peterson."

He began examining the pages. "This could have ruined everything we worked for," he said with great relief.

"She was old—she didn't know any better," Kingston defended. "I'm just glad we were able to get it back before my enemies could use it against me."

Sterling flipped to the back of the binder, where he found something taped to the back cover. He pulled off the tape and handed it to Kingston. It was a disc.

"This should be interesting," Kingston said with an amused look and placed it into a DVD player. Flavia made sure the doors were locked and the room secure.

Ellen appeared on the screen, wearing her Sunday best, along with her usual scowl. Veronica tensed—the last time Ellen made a video they all ended up in the principal's office.

"Hello, James—this is your grandmother," Ellen began in her usual curmudgeonly tone.

"I spent the latter part of my life trying to protect my family from the dangers of our heritage. I'd seen too many lives cut short by tragedy. Your father Josef was a victim of it, as was my other son, the half brother you never met, Harry Jr. I tried to protect Maggie's father and others, but since we're here today, it means I've failed miserably.

"I suspect you are about to be elected President of the United States. And while this is a great achievement, it's not what defines you. It is what you do with this great responsibility that will. As a man once said—*sooner will a camel pass through a needle's eye than a great man will be discovered through an election.*"

"It's Hitler," Zach whispered.

Things had gotten so zany that Veronica's first impulse was to ask, "Where?"

"No—the quote about the camel's eye, it's from *Mein Kampf.* It's probably why he's smiling."

"That or he's just a sociopath and that's what they do," Veronica said back.

"So now begins the last revolution," Ellen passionately continued onscreen. "In gaining political power the Jew casts off the few cloaks that he still wears. The democratic people's Jew becomes the blood-Jew and tyrant over peoples. In a few years he tries to exterminate the national intelligentsia and by robbing the peoples of their natural intellectual leadership makes them ripe for the slave's lot of permanent subjugation

"Around people who offer too violent a resistance to attack from within he weaves a net of enemies, thanks to his international influence, incites them to war, and finally, if necessary plants the flag of revolution on the very battlefields.

"The ignorance of the broad masses about the inner nature of the Jew, the luck of instinct and narrow-mindedness of the upper classes, make people an easy victim for this Jewish campaign of lies."

Veronica was stunned. "How could this possibly be helping?"

"I have no idea," Zach whispered back. "But I do know she's regurgitating Hitler's words. Those were exact quotes."

That can't be good, Veronica thought with a hard swallow.

"If the Jew is victorious over other people of the world," Ellen continued with her rant, "his crown will be the funeral wreath of humanity—this planet will, as it did thousands of years ago, move through the ether devoid of men."

Veronica cursed herself for trusting these people—Ellen ... Flavia ... evil was in their blood.

"As you know, James, those are the words of a man whose beliefs you have dedicated your life to re-establishing, isn't that true?"

Kingston nodded his head as if Ellen was in the room with them.

"So if you believe those statements as fact, then *you* will be responsible for this 'Jewish Campaign of Lies,' and *you* are responsible for this 'crown,' which will be the funeral wreath of humanity. Because *you*, my grandson, are of Jewish blood. You are the great-grandson of Etta Sarowitz."

Veronica shared a look with Maggie, as if to say *Oma had it all the way.*

"You are a crazy old lady who doesn't know what she says," Kingston shouted at the screen.

"You can paint me as crazy if you like," she continued, as if they were having a real-time conversation. "But every word that was presented to Maggie's class, was completely accurate. While the Sterlings and others within the Apostles might be using Judaism as a cover for their true identities, my identity has always been true to my blood. I was wrong to keep this from you and your father, along with the rest of the Apostles— only recently did Aligor discover my true heritage. I thought by keeping it from you, I was keeping you safe, but I came to realize how wrong that was.

"And that's the reason he wanted to remove me from the equation. Because if you found out, then you might question your own beliefs ... especially when you find out that the Führer was well aware of my Jewish blood when he took me in and cared for me. That is why he kept me hidden in that bunker in the Alps. He said it was for my safety, which was partly true, but the main reason was that he was worried that if the world found out how he cared for a Jewish girl, he could no longer sell the myth of the Jews as a subhuman race. A myth that fueled his power. A power he needed like oxygen.

"One can detach themselves from large masses of unknown souls, but not from an individual connection. Six million is a statistic, but one person is a tragedy. The Führer treated me with the utmost care and delicacy, but he chose to delude himself about my true heritage. Maybe if he acknowledged it, he would have seen the Jewish people as living, breathing souls, and history would have turned out differently. Nobody will ever know.

"If you don't believe me, I suggest you ask Aligor about it. He can vouch for what I just told you. In fact, I have it on tape from our last meeting. And while you're at it, ask him how your father was really killed. The one who was chosen to lead the Apostles by the Führer, despite having the same Jewish blood as his mother."

Kingston looked at Sterling. He waved dismissively, as if to indicate that Ellen was off her rocker.

She continued, "I knew the Führer as well as anyone, and I know you, James. One of the things you have in common is neither of you carried these vile hatreds until you were young men. You weren't born with these beliefs. Your father's murder sparked your anger, just like World War I sparked his. But in the end, it was he, and he alone, who was responsible for what happened. Just like it will be for you, James. The question is whether you take action for the truth, or if you will continue to fall victim to the big lie."

The screen went blank. The room turned deathly quiet.

Kingston gathered himself. He tried to stand strong and look presidential, but he couldn't hide the fact that he was shaken by Ellen's words. He didn't look at Sterling as he walked to the DVD player and ejected the disc. He causally took it out and broke it in half.

He then began ripping the pages out of the memoir, and feeding them through a shredder.

"No!" Maggie yelled out and began running toward him. Veronica held her by the back of the coat. There was nothing they could do.

Kingston viewed the room, and announced, "Ellen was a great woman who sacrificed for us all. I'd hate for the world to see her in the throes of dementia. She obviously didn't understand what she was saying."

Sterling received a call on his cell, breaking the tension. He listened intently, then smiled. "Turn on the television," he instructed.

Kingston clicked it on just in time to hear the commentator emphatically state, "NBC News is declaring Jim Kingston as the next President of the United States in what is looking like a landslide of epic proportions!"

A loud roar went up in the adjoining room. Kingston moved behind Sterling's wheelchair and pushed him toward the door.

"So what happens to us?" Veronica blurted.

Kingston shrugged. "I guess it's up to you. My presidency is about giving power to the people, so you are free to go and live your life as you choose. Spread your lies if you like, nobody will believe you. And as for Maggie and Jamie, they will come to us on their own—they won't need to be forced—it's in their blood."

CHAPTER 72

With Aligor Sterling wheeling beside him, President-Elect Jim Kingston made the first stop on his victory tour. Starlight Roof was located on the eighteenth floor of the Waldorf, where a grand party was being held in his honor.

In the 1930s and 40s, the Rooftop was regarded as the world's most glamorous nightclub. It epitomized the elite, and its excessive parties were the stuff of legend. At the same time, across the ocean, the Reich had risen to become the ruling elite of Europe, and they ruled with the same decadence and glamour. This party was a sign that what was once great could rise again.

But as Kingston walked into the luxurious rotunda, he felt a threatening cloud hovering over him. Like a thunderstorm appearing on a perfect summer day. This should be a night to celebrate the crowning achievement of the Apostles, but when he looked up at the gilded ceiling he could have sworn he saw that dark cloud of doubt.

The partygoers didn't share his reservations. Wine was flowing and a band was belting out tunes from the Big Band era. Kingston almost expected to see Sinatra crooning on the stage. He pressed the flesh for over an hour with many of his biggest supporters, and began to regain his bearings. Before leaving, he took the microphone and to overwhelming cheers, announced that tonight marked, "A return of the good old days!" Little did they know how true that statement would be.

As Kingston left the room, he noted the twinkling of the stars through the two-story high windows that peered out on the glittering Manhattan skyline. It was like the heavens were sending their approval. And the feeling of impending doom waned.

Surrounded by his security team, Kingston and Sterling were taken down to the third floor, where they arrived at an ornate, silver corridor that passed under an arched ceiling. His mother, Erika Sterling-Kingston, met him there. Thaddeus. He greeted the still attractive, seventy-four-year-old with a deep hug and a peck on the cheek. She raised him for this day. It was a powerful moment between mother and son, but Kingston couldn't help feel that the picture was incomplete without his father by her side.

When they broke their embrace, Kingston hooked arms with her and walked her down the corridor. She whispered into his ear her hope that the next time he walked down an aisle it would be at his wedding. She was never a fan of his bachelor life, and felt it was now time to find his First Lady. Marriage and family meant everything to her, although she had never remarried herself after his father was killed.

Onlookers clapped for Kingston, echoing throughout the hallway. A grand piano belted out "Hail to the Chief." He felt at peace again—the thunderstorm had passed.

The ovations grew louder as they approached the Grand Ballroom, where he'd give his acceptance speech. But before entering, he needed a moment alone with Aligor.

"Yes, Mr. President," Sterling said with a big grin, liking the sound of the new title.

Kingston didn't share his jovial mood. There was still much work to do. "I want the children picked up once they leave here and brought back to the house."

"What about the mother?"

"You are going to need to silence her, and her reporter friend."

"Don't you think that will be dangerous, especially after the children were seen at the mansion?"

"I think it will be a love triangle, which will help us solve our Edward Peterson problem. He was in love with his dead brother's wife, but when she chose Zach Chester, he couldn't bear it and it led to a murder-suicide."

Sterling looked like he'd seen a ghost.

"I'm sorry, Aligor, that was insensitive of me. I'd forgotten about your parents."

"No offense taken, Mr. President. It was a long time ago. What about the children?"

"In the short term, we will put out word that they were guests at the mansion. Maggie invited you to her Heritage Paper project, where she informed you what a big fan she was of mine. So I made her dream come true by allowing her to visit her hero. Her devotion to me is well documented. And make it clear that they were just playing on the lawn, security was trying to stop them because they were worried about their safety. The guns weren't real. Obviously they didn't view me as harmful, as they sought me out tonight at the hotel."

"And in the long term?"

"In the wake of their mother's death, we will move to adopt the children. Maggie might resist initially, but she'll come around. Jamie will not be a problem."

"That would be great PR, but might be complicated. Veronica Peterson's mother and family members are very much alive, and might seek custody."

He patted Sterling on the back with a big smile. "We're the kings of the world, Aligor. We can do anything we want. I'm confident that you'll figure out how to make it happen."

Sterling smiled back, looking relieved. "I was concerned that you might buy the nonsense your grandmother was saying on that video."

"Like I said, she obviously was suffering from a form of dementia."

"What about Youkelstein? We tracked him to Beth Israel Hospital—he was admitted for a gunshot wound."

"Let him be—just make sure the bullet can't be traced back to our men. Nobody will believe the old conspiracy theorist, anyway. He has been screaming about escaped Nazis and the Fourth Reich for decades. He has no credibility, so let's not be the ones to give him any."

With business settled, Kingston entered the Grand Ballroom. It was four stories high and surrounded by two tiers of boxes like an Old World opera house. The normal seating capacity was fifteen hundred, but tonight well over two thousand had jammed in to celebrate the election of Jim Kingston.

Sterling wheeled onto the stage and announced into a microphone, "Without further ado, I'd like to introduce to you my nephew, my friend, and my hero—the President of the United States, Jim Kingston!"

Kingston leaped onto the stage, where he was met by Senator Langor. The Vice President-Elect knew nothing of the Apostles, or ever would. He was put on the ticket because they felt his presence would guarantee winning Florida, which most experts thought would be the key swing vote. Although, it turned out to be an unnecessary boulder in a historical landslide.

Kingston and Langor clasped hands and raised them over their heads as balloons began raining down from the ceiling. Their campaign song belted from the speakers—Springsteen's "The Rising." Never could lyrics be more appropriate.

When the room settled, Kingston stepped to the microphone. He looked out at the faceless crowd and felt the irony. The Grand Ballroom at the Waldorf was built as a re-creation of the court theater in Versailles. The same city where the treaty was signed in that train car. A document that attempted to destroy Germany forever.

But as he was about to reclaim their rightful spot, and do so in the same manner that it was taken from them—by sabotaging the society from within—he couldn't shake Ellen's words.

CHAPTER 73

Veronica's lungs felt like they were about to explode when she exited the Waldorf.

Did that just happen?

She gripped Maggie and Jamie's hands as tightly as possible, while Zach tried to hail a cab. A nightmare on a normal evening, but tonight it was a near impossibility.

A voice shot out through the brisk night, calling her name.

She looked up to see two members of Kingston's security team heading toward them. She instinctively stepped back.

"President-Elect Kingston instructed us to give you and Mr. Chester a ride to wherever you want to go."

Veronica wanted no part of any connection to Kingston, even if that meant she died of old age while waiting for the cab on the corner of Park and 49th.

"That's nice of you to offer, but I must decline," she said politely.

"We insist," the one said. The pleasant smile couldn't hide his devious eyes.

"I said no," Veronica responded, firmer.

She felt a sharp gust of fear blowing at her face. The crowded city street failed to provide comfort.

Another voice rang out in the night air. This one female.

"The lady said she wasn't interested."

Veronica looked to see Flavia gracefully bouncing towards them. The guards stared at her. Veronica wasn't sure if it was due to her words, or perhaps because all men stare at Flavia.

"We have orders," one guard said.

"Do you know who I am?"

"Yes, Ms. Conte."

"Good—now I'm giving you an order to leave the lady alone."

The guards reluctantly walked away, their black boots rhythmically clicking on the busy sidewalk.

Flavia approached with apology in her eyes. "Veronica—I just want you to know I only did what Ellen asked me to do. I think she believed if Kingston saw the video he might re-think his position. In no way am I working for them."

Veronica didn't trust anyone at this point, but she believed that Flavia was telling the truth. "I'm just frustrated—that memoir might have been our last chance to prove what they've done, and what they plan to do in the future."

Veronica felt a tear roll down her cheek. "And I won't feel that Maggie and Jamie are safe as long as they are in power."

Flavia looked like she wanted to hug her. Veronica wasn't going there, but she needed to hug someone. So she crouched down and pulled Maggie and Jamie into her arms.

She looked up at Flavia, who glistened like the Manhattan skyscrapers. It was like she was part of the sparkling skyline. "So what do we do now?"

Flavia's face turned stony. "*You* aren't going to do anything. *You* have two beautiful children to protect. *You* will not put yourself in harm's way—they need their mother. I will handle this myself—I'm done running from the ghosts."

"What are you planning?"

Flavia's voice fell to a whisper, making her hard to hear against the backdrop of honking traffic. "Same thing they did. Rise up from within their ranks, while pretending to be someone else. And I have an advantage—I'm royal blood, remember?"

Veronica was still having trouble grasping that Flavia was the president's half-sister, both fathered by Josef Müller aka Joseph Kingston. The Chosen One.

Zach continued to struggle with his taxi flagging, so Flavia relieved him of his duties. Veronica was surprised a twenty-car pileup didn't occur. She secured a cab in less than twenty seconds. Veronica just shook her head with envy.

She ushered her children into the back of the vehicle, joining Zach.

Flavia declined the offer to come with them. "You're driving back to Rhinebeck tonight?" Veronica inquired.

"No, I'm going to visit Ben at the hospital. I'll pull up a cot, and then head back upstate in the morning," she said. She then surprised Veronica by giving her that hug. Flavia didn't seem like the hugger type.

But as she watched Flavia disappear into the crowd, she realized that there was a purpose to the embrace. She pulled out an object that had been placed in her pocket. A key.

CHAPTER 74

The cab moved west on 49th Street. They had no firm plan as to where to go, but needed to get out of the city as fast as possible, and returning to Zach's Audi wasn't the best way to accomplish that.

As they passed Madison Avenue, Veronica noticed Zach sneaking glances in the rear-view mirror. "What is it?" she asked.

"They're following us," he spoke softly in her ear.

"Who's following us?" she whispered back.

"Those guards who offered us the ride—black Hummer, three cars back."

Veronica wasn't as subtle. She turned all the way around and noticed the vehicle swerving through cars to stay close. Luckily, their wannabe NASCAR cab driver, Albadejo, was disregarding the caution flag. But he still couldn't shake the Hummer.

"Oh my god," Veronica called out.

Not the smartest thing to say—she alerted Maggie and Jamie. She didn't have that "cool under pressure" switch like their father. Nor was she as savvy. Of course they weren't going to let them go. They had damaging evidence that could be used against Kingston, memoir or no memoir. Plus, this group already had kidnapped Maggie and Jamie once before. She couldn't believe she bought anything that came from the mouth of the man telling the biggest lie in the history of the world—Jim Kingston didn't believe in freewill.

Zach instructed Albadejo to turn right on Fifth Avenue, which he did, passing the glowing Saks Fifth Avenue. They would've yelled, "Step on it!" like in the movies, but Albadejo didn't need any encouragement.

Now Maggie and Jamie were in the act. They positioned themselves backwards on the seat. They were giving constant updates on the Hummer. "They're getting closer," Maggie informed.

"This is cool, Mom!" Jamie added.

They kept going up Fifth Avenue, running red lights, leading to horn-honking chaos at every intersection. The presidential security had turned Midtown into gridlock, but Albadejo remained undeterred.

They continued dashing uptown, strategically using the sidewalk when need be, cruising by 56th Street and Trump Tower. As they passed 60th street, Central Park appeared on their left like a dark emerald ocean.

When they hit 64th Street, Veronica thought back to their time living in the city—places she and Carsten went—and she realized sanctuary was right in front of them.

Veronica shouted for Albadejo to stop the cab. He jammed on the brakes right in the middle of the busy avenue. She then tightly latched onto Maggie and Jamie's hands and practically dragged them as she dashed across the street, narrowly avoiding oncoming vehicles. Zach paid the driver and followed at his own risk.

CHAPTER 75

The Central Park Zoo was located at 64th Street and Fifth Avenue. A tidy five-acre oasis in the park, filled with natural-habitat exhibits of animals, ranging from tropical to polar. It was one of Maggie and Jamie's favorite places, and tonight it was Veronica's.

It wasn't a plan without holes, but she hadn't heard a better idea yet.

The first flaw was that the zoo closed at five o'clock and was locked for the night. But it wasn't exactly Fort Knox when it came to security. People weren't normally inclined to break into a home when there was a good chance they'd be eaten by a polar bear. The front entrance featured a ten-foot, picketed wood fence that looked like the bars of a jail cell. Perfect for climbing.

Jamie didn't have to be asked twice, and scurried over. Maggie couldn't let her little brother get the best of her, and was right behind him. Veronica used a boost from Zach to help her over.

But as Zach began to mount the fence, a voice echoed, "Freeze."

Uh-oh.

All eyes went to the night watchman. Zach pulled out the gun that Eddie provided them—he wasn't messing around.

The night watchman threw up his arms in surrender. But Eddie's NYPD badge proved a more useful weapon, convincing the guard to open the gate without any shots being fired.

"You're not to let anyone else in under any condition, or mention that we are in here—this is a classified mission," Zach forcefully stated. "I can't go into details, other than to say that it's related to security for the new president."

"No problema," the night watchman casually replied, unaffected by the gun dancing in his sight line. But it was doubtful he could be relied on. Especially since he smelled like he'd just rolled around in a marijuana field.

Veronica led them into the zoo. It was almost dreamlike at night. It wasn't being lit by the moon, but the Manhattan skyline in the distance.

It was also pin-drop quiet, the exact opposite of the typical day trip when the hordes of children generally made more noise than the squealing seals. Veronica felt like the Ben Stiller character in that movie where he was the night watchman at the Museum of Natural History, when the place came alive at night.

As Veronica searched for the best place to hide, her stomach dropped. She heard footsteps coming.

The Gestapo.

She put her finger to her lips to indicate to Maggie and Jamie to be quiet. "Please go away," she said under her breath. She led them deeper into the zoo.

But when they reached the sea lion pool, they were busted. Living up to their chatterbox reputation, the sea lions began vociferously yelping.

Voices grew louder in the distance, and the footsteps quickened. They were getting closer! She recognized the night watchman's voice—then a gunshot rang out.

Oh shit.

Veronica kept the group running. They stopped for a moment to catch their breath in front of the polar bear lake, one of the zoo's most popular exhibits.

"Look, its Garth and Lilac," Jamie admired the long time zoo residents, who were pushing a thousand pounds. As was the norm, they looked annoyed to be there.

"We better go or we'll be polar bear food," Zach said. *And dessert for the Nazis,* Veronica thought as they headed off again.

The footsteps were nearing.

They dashed into the chilled penguin house—a place Jamie once had a New York sized temper-tantrum when he refused to leave, and the room had to be shut down for a half hour. They exited the other end and arrived at another fence. Their adrenaline carried them over, and they fled out of the zoo, back onto 65th Street, which cut through Central Park.

They retreated into the park, too afraid to look back. But Veronica swore she could feel their hot breath on the back of her neck. They came across a large pro-Kingston rally that was taking place in a section of the park called the *Sheep Meadow.* Veronica didn't care for the hero they worshiped, but there was comfort in numbers, and they were able to meld into the crowd.

The meadow was normally a great place to leisurely congregate. Veronica used to come with Carsten on sunny spring days with a picnic basket. Then when the kids were born, they would bring them along. But there would be no leisure tonight. Every person was suspect, and the enemy could be within … disguised in sheep's clothing. They had to keep moving.

They pushed through the thick crowd until they were blocked by *The Great Lake.* Since swimming wasn't an option, they took a westerly path.

They didn't stop until they arrived at *Strawberry Fields.* A pastoral setting with verdant lawns that was dedicated to John Lennon. A group was congregated there, but it was a smaller, more subdued crowd than at the

Sheep Meadow. It was a rally for peace. With Kingston winning, they believed war was imminent.

If they only knew!

Veronica and the others mixed into the group and even spent a few moments singing along to "Give Peace A Chance" as a guitar player strummed. When in Rome …

But the Gestapo didn't give it much of one. Veronica spotted them in the distance. It was the two guards who offered them a ride. But they hadn't been discovered yet, so it was time to move before they were.

"I think we need to split up the cord and the outlet," Zach said.

Veronica protested at first, but logic was on his side. It would make them less of a sitting duck. Being together might have provided a certain comfort, but it was also increasing the odds of their capture.

"I'll take Jamie and you take Maggie," Zach stated assertively.

Veronica contemplated the idea of letting her son out of her sights.

"Guys against girls!" Jamie shouted out.

There was no time to argue. Veronica had to make a decision right now.

Because they had been spotted.

The Gestapo was moving toward them.

CHAPTER 76

As they reached the corner of 72nd Street and Central Park West, Veronica began questioning her intuition.

One voice said that Zach was right—the prudent move was to split up the jewels. But her inner-mother was taking issue with the idea.

Before they went their separate ways, Zach whispered in her ear, "I will meet up with you at the West 110th Street subway station."

Veronica didn't know if it was the comforting tone of his voice, or the intoxicating smell of his cologne, or who knows, the way the planets were aligned, but as he pulled away she planted a juicy kiss on his lips.

Oops.

He looked stunned, but there wasn't time to plead insanity. She grabbed Maggie's hand and headed in the opposite direction, fighting every desperate urge to take another look back at Jamie.

Veronica found herself right in front of The Dakota, the apartment building where John Lennon had lived ... and died. And just a few blocks up Central Park West was the Museum of Natural History, another favorite of her children. Jamie loved the dinosaurs, while Maggie's favorite part was feeding the pigeons outside on the museum steps—she always had a thing for the outcast. Veronica had vowed to continue the city experience for the kids after moving back to Pleasantville, but this wasn't exactly what she had in mind.

She didn't know why Zach chose the meeting spot he did, but he appeared to be man with a plan. She tightly held Maggie's hand as they hurried down the steps of the subway station on 72nd street.

It seemed like hours until their train arrived. When it did, Veronica and Maggie found a seat in the back. The first thing Maggie said was, "You kissed Mr. Chester."

Veronica flashed a surprised look. "I did nothing of the sort."

"Mom …"

"Okay, fine—but it was just a small good luck kiss—like a family kiss."

"I don't know what family you're talking about, but if Uncle Phil ever kissed me like that I'd call the cops."

"It was nothing, Mags. Besides, he was the one who kissed me."

"Puhleeze … you totally made the move."

"Made the move?"

"He was just standing there and you planted one right on his lips."

"Let's drop it, Mags, we have bigger issues here."

Maggie wasn't easily moved off a subject matter she was interested in. "Did you kiss that guy you went out with the other night?"

"Not that it's any of your business, but no, I did not. It was just movie and a dinner—like friends. Who told you I went on a date?"

"Uncle Eddie," Maggie said, her look turning somber.

Veronica put her arm around her. After a lengthy silence, Maggie said, "He tried to do the right thing in the end. He saved us."

Veronica nodded. She still wasn't sure what to make of Eddie. But it was a debate for another day.

She was all for changing the subject to something that didn't include Nazis, Eddie, or dating, but Maggie had other ideas. "I'd give you my approval if you wanted Mr. Chester to be your boyfriend."

"Your approval?"

"You always say we're a team."

"I had no idea you listened to anything I said. And besides, Mr. Chester is married."

"Does it count if his wife is in jail?"

"It counts even more. Marriage is for better or worse, and the worse part is when things really count."

"Like when you and Dad used to fight all the time before he died?"

"We had a lot of issues we were trying to work out."

"Do you think you would've gotten divorced if he were still alive?"

Wow—where did this come from? Veronica had always wanted more mother/daughter heart-to-hearts, but she guessed her own mother was right when she warned her about being careful what she wished for.

"No matter what happened, it wouldn't have changed how we felt about you and Jamie."

"That's totally the way divorced people talk. So what were you guys so mad at?"

"Just typical married stuff—you'll find out one day."

"I think you thought he was having an affair with Flavia."

Affair? Veronica tried to think if she even knew what that word meant when she was twelve. She wanted to end the conversation, but was hesitant to, since Maggie might not open up again until college. She also didn't mind the temporary diversion from their current predicament.

"That's between your Dad and me, and it's going to stay that way."

"I don't know why you would think that—you're *way* prettier than her."

And with that one comment all the struggles were worth it.

"Kingston said Dad was involved in this thing," Maggie continued.

So that's what was gnawing at her. "No he wasn't, Mags. He was trying to stop it, just like we are."

Maggie's face turned as serious as Veronica had ever seen. "I was there, you know, when he did it."

"Did what?"

"When he … you know … hit you. I was hiding in the doorway."

Veronica never felt worse in her life. "Oh, Mags."

"Did he do it because he had Nazi blood in him? Will I do stuff like that because of the Nazi blood?"

Veronica pulled her as close as possible. "Your father was a good man. It was one bad moment in the fifteen years that I was with him. He loved us so much—and if he were here, he'd tell you that your future is completely up to you, not who you're related to."

She hoped.

Maggie looked encouraged. "Uncle Eddie said the same thing. He told me I don't have to be like them."

Carsten and Eddie—so different, but always on the same page when it came to family.

Despite the danger surrounding them, the conversation gave Veronica a sense of peace. It made her think back to when she read *The Diary of Anne Frank* back in high school. Veronica was taken by how such a young girl, despite being trapped in an attic while being hunted by the Nazi Gestapo, still could find hope in the most ordinary life events. And now Veronica, through her daughter, had done the same.

CHAPTER 77

Veronica viewed the other passengers on the train. She now understood the fear and paranoia those in Germany had of the Gestapo. Danger could be anywhere. The old lady, the young Asian couple, the Wall Street looking straphangers.

The enemy within.

She looked at Maggie, noticing that her head was drooped toward the floor. Usually she held it up so high and proud. Veronica wondered if she regretted opening up to her. It wasn't her style.

"What's wrong, Mags? We're almost there."

She sniffled. "I let everybody down. Oma gave me the responsibility to stop this whole mess and now the whole world is going to be ruined because of me."

Nice expectations to put on a twelve-year-old, Ellen.

"Honey, this isn't your fault. And don't be scared by all this war talk. Right now it's just that … talk."

"You don't get it, Mom … it doesn't matter if there's a war or not. If Sterling convinces everybody that the Jewish people were responsible for 9/11, then people will hate them here like they did in Germany. First they couldn't go to the same schools, and then they were sent off to concentration camps. Even if they don't take over the world, it will still be a really mean place to live."

The train stopped at 110th Street station. Veronica took a deep breath, grabbed Maggie's hand and led her off the train. The hand felt so small, like they'd gone back in time. Veronica's wary eyes viewed the train platform. *Would Zach be there? Or would the bad guys be waiting for them?*

The answer was neither.

Veronica stood with Maggie on the platform as the other riders dispersed in all directions. The station completely emptied out, except for mother and daughter.

Part of Veronica wanted to flee, but would it be safer somewhere else? And if they left, she might miss the chance to reunite with Jamie.

Footsteps echoed in the stairwell. She recognized them—her heart sank. *Had Zach set them up?*

Before she could even look up, the two guards from the front of the Waldorf ambushed them. It happened so fast, she didn't know what hit them, and they were holding Veronica and Maggie at gunpoint.

They needed a miracle.

And then one arrived.

It came in the form of a small boy in a tuxedo. Seemingly appearing out of nowhere, Jamie stood at the end of the platform. He had his hands behind his back like when he plays the "pick a hand" game. *Oh god, don't let him have a gun,* Veronica thought.

He smiled. "Catch me if you can," he said and began backpedaling, which wasn't very effective. The guard who had hold of Maggie took off towards him and easily caught up to the boy.

But there was a method to his madness. He had backed up to a turnstile. And as the guard leaned in to grab him, Jamie showed his hands for the first time. He didn't have a gun—but handcuffs—Eddie's handcuffs! With surprising speed, he cuffed the guard's hand and then clamped the other cuff onto the turnstile.

Maggie was already running toward the guard. She karate-chopped the gun out of his hand and it fell to the platform. But just as Veronica started warming to the idea of having a weapon of their own, Maggie chucked it as hard as she could into the tracks and announced, "I hate guns!"

The other guard held his weapon tightly to Veronica's neck and ordered, "Come back here or your mother dies." His words echoed through the empty station.

Veronica had other ideas. "Run—get out of here—don't worry about me—run!"

They didn't listen.

So what's new?

Maggie and Jamie began darting at the guard like planes to King Kong. Jamie was even making an airplane sound. Always pushing his limits, he buzzed Kong's tower.

In a moment of indecision, the guard played it halfway. He reached for the precious cargo—Jamie—while trying to hold on to his insurance policy—Veronica. It backfired. He missed Jamie, and loosened his grip on Veronica, allowing her to wriggle away.

She fell to the ground and Maggie pounced on her. Veronica was starting to wonder whose team her daughter was on. "Do the pencil roll, Mom. They can't shoot me."

Veronica really didn't want to test her theory, but they had no other choice. They rolled over the grimy platform, away from the guard. Maggie was clinging close to Veronica's body, as if she was a second set of skin. The guard couldn't get a good shot without hitting Maggie, so he set his sights on Jamie.

Then Veronica heard more footsteps coming down the stairwell. Reinforcements.

Damn!

They appeared with guns pointed, yelling, "Freeze!"

But their guns were pointed at the Gestapo guy.

They were the good guys!

NYPD!

And Zach was right behind them. He didn't waste time ushering Veronica and the kids out of the subway station and up onto the street.

"What just happened?" Veronica asked.

"I saw the guards heading down the stairwell into the subway station," Zach said. "So I found a couple police officers and explained that these goons tried to attack Eddie Peterson's family to get at Kingston. No more loyal bunch in the world than cops—Eddie was family to them. They didn't believe me at first, but I showed him his ID—said he gave it to me with instructions to find the nearest officer."

"Quick thinking," Veronica said. Obviously word hadn't spread yet of Eddie's demise. "So what's your excuse, wild man?" she asked Jamie.

"My job was to buy time until he could find the police," he said with a big grin,

"That was a little dangerous, don't you think?"

"Not really—they can't shoot me—I'm royal blood," he replied, nonchalantly.

"I forget sometimes," Veronica said as they hit 115th Street by foot. "So now what?"

"We find a place to hide until morning," Zach said.

"And where exactly would that be?"

Zach suddenly took a sharp right and bounced up three small steps to the front door of a three-story, walk-up brownstone.

"You are going to break into a house?" Veronica asked with surprise.

He smiled. "It's not breaking and entering if you own it."

CHAPTER 78

"I haven't had the heart to sell it," Zach said. "Kind of stupid, I guess, as if I can bring back the past."

Right now it seemed anything but stupid to Veronica.

"They'll figure it out sooner or later, but hopefully it'll buy us some time until morning," he said.

Zach went in first to make sure that 'sooner' didn't mean that they were inside waiting for them. When he deemed it clean, he allowed the rest of them in.

He began rushing around the first floor, making sure all the drapes were shut, his familiarity guiding him in the dark. He disappeared through doors into a black hole of darkness, but quickly returned with a couple of flashlights. Veronica couldn't get a good picture of the place in the dark, but it smelled musty, like it hadn't been used in a long time.

"We have to keep you guys hidden—you're the ones they're looking for," he addressed Maggie and Jamie, sounding apologetic

He guided them into a basement that might have even creeped-out Hannibal Lecter. Veronica ran into a spider web and needed to activate every restraint in her body to keep from screaming. Zach found the spot he was looking for and pulled up a small rug. He then pried open the floorboard, revealing a ladder that led down into a dark abyss.

Veronica had already seen this movie, but had a feeling that there would be no treasure waiting for them this time. Zach went in first, as if to prove it was safe. The kids trailed him down, while she apprehensively brought up the rear.

When he reached the bottom, Zach pulled a string and a light bulb flashed on. Nobody from the outside could see a light in this subterranean …

"Meth lab," Zach informed, not so proudly. "The guy who was supposed to be re-doing our basement built it, so he and Sara could work on their science project."

Veronica didn't know what to say, but was surprised by the candor. She gauged her children, taking notes for a future lecture on drugs—Maggie seemed to be aware of what crystal-meth was, Jamie not so much.

"I hate to do it to you guys," Zach said, "but to be safe, I think you need to stay down here tonight. I'll bring down a couple of sleeping bags."

Maggie wanted no part of it. Being cooped up with her "annoying little brother" was bad enough, but toss in some cobwebs and possible sewer rats, and the idea was utterly unappealing. Her eyes pleaded with Veronica.

She had another internal battle. And once again intuition won out. She stamped her approval and Maggie stomped her foot. "Mom!"

All the good progress down the drain. "It's just going to be a few hours," she tried to soften the blow.

Maggie folded her arms close to her chest—bad sign—and then did a theatrical turn away—really bad sign.

After getting the "prisoners" settled, Zach closed the floorboards and returned the rug, causing Veronica to feel ill. Burying her children alive in this tomb was beyond her worst nightmares. She kept telling herself it was for their safety. Her gut was starting to piss her off.

Zach led a shaky Veronica up the dark stairs and into the master bedroom. "Hey, it was only a kiss," she attempted humor as Zach headed for the bed.

"Only a kiss is like saying the Mona Lisa is only a painting," he joked back. At least she thought he was joking.

"I'm sorry about that—my emotions got the best of me," she apologized.

"Perfectly understandable—didn't mean anything."

"Actually it meant a lot at the time, but glad you weren't offended."

"The day I'm offended by being kissed by a beautiful woman will be the day I cast a vote for Jim Kingston," he said with a smile, but then turned serious. He pointed to the bed. "I suggest you hide underneath." He handed her Eddie's gun. "And keep this with you."

Veronica looked skeptically at the gun—she had the same disdain for them as Maggie, and proved inept with one when she tried to fend off the kidnappers from her children—but Zach's advice had gotten them this far, and she chose to hold on to it.

"Where are you going?" she asked him with a quizzical look.

Zach held up a laptop computer. "In the closet."

"One kiss and I've driven you to the other team?" she said with a grin.

He smiled. "I'm going to write the biggest story of my life. I've missed the morning deadline, and tomorrow will be nothing but *Kingston Wins in Landslide!* on the front page of every paper. But he'll only have one day to enjoy his victory when I'm done writing this for the Thursday edition."

He then barricaded himself in his closet with his laptop, while Veronica slid under the bed, holding the gun next to her like a stuffed animal.

Every creak of the old brownstone made her leap out of her skin. She again thought of young Anne Frank. This must have been what she felt like. Every noise or footstep could be the end—curtains always drawn.

To Veronica, it was a glimpse into the type of world Kingston would bring. A vision of fear. A woman under a bed clutching a gun. The press locked in a closet, typing in secret. Two children hidden under a floorboard in a damp basement that once was a drug lab. Not exactly in harmony with the hopeful themes from his campaign speeches.

The thoughts of Anne Frank made her think of her own daughter. It wasn't just a story of war; it was also a coming of age story. Anne was just a year older than Maggie when she first went into hiding. And all these years later, young girls had the same issues and angst. She wrote about boys and dreams, and of course, frustrations with her mother. And like Maggie, she was wise beyond her years, but not always as smart as she thought she was. They were just two children put in an impossible spot.

Veronica gripped the gun, remembering Anne's words: *It is utterly impossible for me to build my life on a foundation of chaos, suffering and death. I see the world being slowly transformed into a wilderness. I hear the approaching thunder that, one day, will destroy us too.*

Veronica understood the despair now more than ever, but marveled how no matter the circumstances, she always found hope. *And yet, when I look up at the sky, I somehow feel that everything will change for the better, that this cruelty shall end, that peace and tranquility will return once more.*

Veronica's brief moment of tranquility was broken by a noise coming from the next room. A footstep. Then another.

She gripped the gun.

The footsteps were moving toward her room. There were two of them. Moving closer. They tried to disguise themselves, but each creak of the wooden floorboards gave them away.

Then a voice rang out.

"Mommy, can we sleep with you? It's scary down there."

This time Veronica's gut told her to take her two children and curl up in the bed. To hold them and to never let them go. And when she did, she also found hope.

CHAPTER 79

A ray of sunshine glistened off Veronica's eyelids, and she forced them open. It was just one single strand fighting through the pulled shades.

She felt a huge sense of relief, just as she always did when she woke up from a bad dream. *But it seemed so real!* Carsten had died, and of all things, she moved back to Pleasantville next door to her mother. *Only in a dream would that happen!* But things got even weirder. Nazis were chasing them, and somehow her children were responsible for saving the world.

It was just a dream, she told herself, feeling safe as she lay in the king-size bed in her New York apartment, listening to the sounds of the city outside the window. She rolled over and found the bed empty. Carsten wasn't there, but she knew where he was—she inhaled the smell of breakfast coming from the kitchen. *It must be Sunday morning,* she thought, Carsten always cooked breakfast for her and the kids on Sunday morning.

But when the room came into focus, something occurred to her. *This wasn't her apartment!*

She tried to open her eyes again, only to realize they already were. She was in Zach Chester's townhouse, and since she met him in Pleasantville, it meant this wasn't a dream. She fought back a scream.

Maggie and Jamie were gone!

Still fully clothed from the day before, Veronica hopped onto the wooden floor. She looked under the bed and found Eddie's gun, just where she'd left it.

She grabbed the gun and followed her nose to the dark kitchen. What she found was Zach and her children sitting at the table and eating a candlelight breakfast.

"Mommy—you're up!" Jamie exclaimed.

She looked at Zach. "You cooked?"

He motioned her to the table. "I found some bacon and sausage in the freezer. Sorry, if you don't like breakfast meats, but that's all we had."

All Veronica really craved was a cup of the coffee. She poured herself a cup and asked, "So what did your editor say?"

"That I was certifiably crazy. He wouldn't print my story in a million years, and I should think about going to work for one of those conspiracy-theorist blogs."

Veronica had been afraid that would be the case, and it likely was what Kingston and Sterling were counting on.

Zach tossed her a printed version of his story and she read. When she finished the detailed account of the last couple days of her life, she set it down. "I don't believe it either—I can't blame your editor."

"I'm more interested in your opinion than some editor who is more worried about covering his behind, than exposing the truth."

Veronica grinned at the compliment. "I think it's not half bad considering the writer was jammed in a dark closet."

"Hey—Lincoln studied by candlelight."

"You're no Lincoln, Mr. Chester."

He smiled as he poured himself another cup of coffee.

"Seriously, I think it's good," Veronica went on, "but won't you get sued by Sterling? He'll deny he told you any of this stuff about his involvement with 9/11. Without the memoir we have nothing to back up our accusations."

Zach held up what looked like a cassette tape.

"What's that?" Veronica asked.

"Youkelstein taped his conversation with Sterling during his capture at the Kingston estate. He slipped it to me when we dropped him off at the hospital, but I didn't know what it was until I got a chance to listen to it last night. It came from his umbrella, which nobody thought to check—no wonder he keeps it close at all times."

Veronica looked impressed. "I'm going to have to put one of those umbrellas on my Christmas list this year."

Jamie began rattling off a laundry list of things he wanted for Christmas, while Maggie called him selfish and went on a tangent about kids in Africa who didn't have food or medicine. Things almost seemed back to normal.

"So did your editor change his mind when he heard the tape?"

Zach shook his head. "No, he said Sterling would just claim I created it. He had no intention of taking on a man who just won fifty states."

Veronica's hope washed away. Which made it all the more strange that Zach was smiling.

"My editor was right—no legitimate news organization would run the story. So I needed to find a media outlet willing to swim in the cesspool, lacking any journalistic integrity, and more interested in pushing an agenda than seeking the truth. Guess who that would be?"

"I don't know," Veronica said.

"That's easy, Mom," Maggie chimed in. "Talk radio!"

Zach nodded. "I pitched it to Theodore Baer. He's never been big on backing up sources, and after last night, he'll do anything to shift the attention from his landslide loss. So I'm going on the air with him when his show starts at nine … if that's okay with you?"

It was a risk, no doubt, but Veronica knew if they didn't get their story out, and quickly, they were goners. "Okay, but you can't use Maggie and Jamie's names. They stay out of it."

"Of course—I will not mention your family, other than Ellen."

Veronica believed him. "We better get going then," she said, caressing the key given to her by Flavia, "I need to stop off at the bank first."

CHAPTER 80

Theodore Baer had sent a limo to deliver them to his Midtown studio. He'd take no chances of Zach not making it—he needed a subject change, and bad.

They were ushered into the limo by a group of Secret Service agents. Baer wouldn't get to use them much longer, so he might as well take full advantage.

Once settled in the back of the vehicle, Veronica instructed the driver to take them to First Manhattan Trust on The Avenue of the Americas between 39th and 40th. The agents didn't seem thrilled with the change of plans, but must have been under orders to make Zach and his group happy.

They drove through the heavy morning traffic until they arrived at the historic limestone building that housed the bank. It opened at eight, and they were the first people in. Maggie informed them that it was the same bank that Oma brought them to get the Raphael painting, among other items. Veronica was still a little bitter over Ellen's reckless soirées into the city with her children, but chose to bite her lip. For now.

When they entered, Maggie ran ahead. Veronica ordered her to come back, her voice echoing off the cathedral-like ceiling. Maggie kept running ahead, not hearing her. Or more likely, ignoring her.

She headed toward a gray-haired woman, who wore a dark suit and a pair of eyeglasses with pink frames. Veronica had no idea why her daughter was running toward this woman, and she got the feeling that security was asking itself the same question.

"Mrs. Blythe!" Maggie shouted.

The woman recognized her. "Ms. Peterson, so nice to see you again. I'm so sorry to hear about your grandmother."

When the others caught up, Maggie did the introductions. Veronica learned that Mrs. Blythe had been in charge of Ellen's account for the last twenty years, and Maggie had met her upon Ellen's last visit.

More lip biting.

When Veronica began spouting information about the key to a lockbox, password, and other assorted privacy issues right in the middle of the bank, Mrs. Blythe urged them into her office. In private, she explained that the key and password were not enough to get her into the safe-deposit box. Only Ellen, or an "agent for the account" created by Ellen, could enter. Or, the executor of the will, but it could be weeks before the will officially went through probate. They didn't have that kind of time.

Luckily, Ellen had had the foresight to make Maggie an agent to the account. Although, with what Veronica knew now, she doubted Ellen left anything to luck.

Despite Maggie's chumminess with Mrs. Blythe, she still needed to prove identification. So Veronica hunted through her bag until she found Maggie's passport. She'd gotten it for the family trip to Europe that they never ended up taking. It was the trip to save the marriage, even though nobody ever admitted that was the reason.

Satisfied, Mrs. Blythe led them into a grand vault. There, she left them alone with Ellen's safe-deposit box. When they pulled it out of the wall, it was much larger than the shoebox size Veronica had expected. This box was large and rectangular. *About the size of a box that could store a priceless Raphael painting*, she thought.

The contents consisted of one bound document, a slip of paper, and what looked to be a small electronic device. Veronica picked up the document. The first thing she noticed was it was written in German. "It's titled, *Die Endlösung der Judenfrage*," she said to Zach in a puzzled tone, as she flipped through it.

The title sparked Zach into action, which surprised her. "Let me see that."

He intently scrutinized the words, before looking up with wonderment. "These are the meeting minutes from the Wannsee Conference from January of 1942. A copy was found after the war, and is displayed at a Holocaust museum, but this one has the infamous missing minutes that were blocked out of that version."

Veronica wasn't sharing the enthusiasm. "The Wannsee what?"

"*Die Endlösung der Judenfrage* is German for the Final Solution to the Jewish question."

"As in …"

"As in, the Germans wanted to displace their Jewish population, and the answer they came up with was extermination. But because the meeting minutes that were found didn't contain specific language about the death camps, certain neo-Nazi types have argued the Holocaust was a figment of a pro-Jewish media."

Zach zoomed to the spot he was looking for in the document.

"Yes—right here," he said, tapping his finger on the page. "Methods of killing … liquidation … extermination." Zach looked up, his face looked ill. "God, these guys were sick bastards."

And now they were after *them*. Veronica took a quick glance at Maggie and Jamie. They were racing each other up the long corridor of the vault. Jamie was more athletic than his older sister, but he was still wearing his tuxedo shoes and they were holding him back. Any advantage one might gain, the other would counter with sheer competitive will. Brother and sister acting like brother and sister.

Veronica's eyes returned to Zach, who was still buried in the document. "I didn't know you could speak German?"

"Our neighbors growing up in Michigan immigrated from Germany." He smiled. "If I told you, would you have put two and two together with my Audi and declared me to be conspiring with the enemy?"

Veronica smiled back. He always knew the right tone to take. "So what does this have to do with me? Why would Ellen give me the key to this box?"

"I have a theory. The most important player in regards to these lost minutes was Reinhard Heydrich. He represented Himmler at the meeting. Heydrich's direct understudy was Heinrich Müller."

"It's a small Nazi world."

"My guess is that Müller was the one who ended up with the document, which he gave to Ellen with instructions to take it to America and keep it safely hidden. I think he saw the original document with the missing minutes as a future piece of leverage if he ever got in a tough spot. That would appeal to his pragmatic side."

Zach placed the document back in the box with a sad shake of the head. "Ninety minutes—that's how long the conference lasted. Ninety minutes to decide to murder six million people—and half the time they seemed more interested in their cognac."

Veronica reached into the box and pulled out a small index card. On it was the First Manhattan Trust logo with the term *VSD*. Underneath *VSD* was a username and password.

Veronica had no idea what it meant, so she handed it to Zach. He looked equally confused. They called in Mrs. Blythe to explain, since it was a bank issued card.

"*VSD* stands for Virtual Safe Deposit," she stated. "Recent legislation has made digitally signed documents legally binding. To accommodate this, First Manhattan Trust became one of the first banks to offer an online safe-deposit box."

"So we go to the Internet site, sign in using our password, and that will take us to our virtual safe-deposit box?" Zach asked.

Mrs. Blythe nodded. "Yes—the great advantage is 24-hour access."

Zach and Mrs. Blythe briefly chitchatted about new bank technology. When she left, Zach pulled out his phone and brought up the Internet.

"I can't believe the kids' great-grandmother was so much more tech savvy than I am," Veronica bemoaned.

Zach put in the user name and password that was left for them in the lockbox. On the screen appeared the one document Ellen stored in her virtual safe-deposit box. Zach smiled, as did Veronica.

The memoir.

A second copy.

A second source to back up Youkelstein's tape.

There were two more items in the bin. One was a small booklet that looked like an address book. It was an inventory of precious art stolen by the Nazis. Some Veronica was familiar with, while others were obscure. She vowed to return the art to its the rightful owners, and knew just the person to make that happen.

The last item was a hand-held video player. Veronica placed the earbud headphones in and turned it on.

When she hit play, Ellen's face came onto the screen. She was wearing the same outfit she wore on the tape they viewed in Kingston's room. At first, Veronica thought it was a copy of the same video. A necessary copy, since Ellen accurately predicted that Kingston would destroy the video and the memoir. The old lady had been right about every move so far.

Veronica made eye contact with the dead woman. It was an eerie experience.

Ellen somberly began, "Veronica—this tape is for your ears and yours alone. Do not allow anyone else to view this video."

When she said it, Veronica felt a chill down her spine.

CHAPTER 81

Veronica wandered away from Zach and sat on a bench. She held the small video screen inches from her face, as if that would help her hear better.

"Now that you've found a copy of the memoir, I want to let you know I left out one important chapter. The reason I did so was that I believe you, as Maggie and Jamie's mother, are the executor of their heritage. Only you can decide what information will help them to grow, versus what will hang a burden on them. As my husband Harold used to say—pressure will either crush you or turn you into diamonds."

So that's where Carsten got that saying.

"If it were up to me, I'd choose for you to never inform them of what I'm about to tell you."

Veronica filled with fear. There was something about those piercing, pale blue eyes staring back at her. She took a quick look at a pacing Zach, whose natural curiosity was eating at him. Maggie and Jamie remained oblivious, still involved in the Sibling Olympics.

Ellen continued, "It is true that my mother, Etta, was a prostitute in Munich during World War I. It was there she met and became impregnated by a young German corporal. But it wasn't until I was almost fourteen that my mother, then bedridden and nearing death, revealed to me who my biological father was.

"During the creation of her Heritage Paper, Maggie kept asking me why my son Josef was 'chosen' to lead the return of the Reich. I never answered her. Because he wasn't chosen … he was born into it. He was an heir to the throne. And that's because I'm the daughter of Adolf Hitler. And that's the real reason he took me in and protected me."

Veronica felt like her head just exploded. *Did she just say what she thought she just said?*

Veronica rewound the video, but the result was the same.

I'm the daughter of Adolf Hitler.

She did it again.

Adolf Hitler.

Again.

Hitler.

When Veronica found her bearings, she updated the family tree in her head. If what Ellen said was true, Adolf Hitler and Etta Sarowitz had a child, Ellen Sarowitz-Peterson. That was what Kingston meant about royal blood.

The bloodline had thinned dramatically over the years, including young deaths for Josef, Harry Jr. and Carsten. And coming in contact with the lineage from the outside appeared to be just as deadly. It had befallen Greta Peterson, Flavia's mother … and Eddie. She didn't think that any of this was a coincidence.

Veronica looked into Ellen's eyes, desperately searching for some clue as if to say she's a little coo-coo for Cocoa Puffs. But there was none. And after the last couple of days, how could Veronica legitimately dismiss it?

She stared out at Maggie and Jamie, feeling helpless. She had tried to protect them from everything—took every precaution—but in the end there was an evil embedded inside them. Derived from a gene cesspool. They were descendents of the devil.

Ellen provided a moment for it to sink in, as if she understood what her reaction would be, before continuing, "There are four remaining members in the blood line—Maggie, Jamie, Flavia, and James, who I presume has been elected president. He has known the secret since his formative years, and I informed Flavia yesterday in a similar manner to this. I asked her to bring that video to James—a last ditch effort for him to come to his senses, which I'm sure failed.

"Otto, or Aligor Sterling as you might have known him, is the only other member of the Apostles who is aware of this secret. So whether Jamie or Maggie ever learns of this information, is completely up to you. But recently I've become worried that an outside force has discovered this secret, and in the future, will attempt to harm those in the bloodline. So telling you this is also a call for awareness on your part.

"I know what you must be thinking, Veronica, but I don't want you to jump to conclusions about any path Maggie or Jamie may take. History has already delivered its overwhelming verdict on my father, but what I can tell you is he was *not* programmed to become what he became. It was *not* genetic destiny, as most of the Apostles believe. Events shape our destiny, just as they shaped my father. His choices were regrettable, but not inherited.

"After burying my children, I vowed to spend the rest of my life protecting my family from these harmful secrets. Especially Carsten, who I never wanted to find my letters to Heinrich. Like his father, he couldn't handle it, and snapped. And that's why he did that to you—not a violent nature handed down through genetics."

Veronica looked quizzically at the screen—did she know?

"Yes, Veronica—he came to me that night and revealed his actions. I never saw him so ashamed, and he vowed that he would never raise a hand to you or the children ever again. I'm confident he didn't. You are too strong to have stayed if he did. You must trust me when I tell you he loved you and the children more than anything in this world."

Ellen was now crying on the screen. Veronica cried with her, as if they were sharing it.

From a distance, Zach looked like he wasn't sure if he should help or not. But she looked right past him toward Maggie and Jamie. They were now sitting on the floor with the bored looks of typical kids. No longer competing—united in their boredom.

Ellen looked as if she were drowning in regret. "Perhaps all this could have been avoided if I'd done a better job as a mother. You see, Veronica, mothers are the most powerful creatures in shaping the good of the world. I failed my children, which makes me realize how lucky that Maggie and Jamie are to have you. Despite our differences, I've always respected your stewardship of the children, and often envied it. I know you will bring out their goodness.

"But while I'm confident that they will forge their own path, I do see a few qualities in them handed down from my father." A lump the size of a basketball clogged Veronica's throat. *Not the words a mother wants to hear.* "I have seen his passion in Maggie, and I've noticed a similar charisma in Jamie. But remember, when guided the right way those qualities can be great attributes. Your children are a blank canvas, and you have always been a great artist. Godspeed, Veronica."

With those words, the video went dark. Veronica removed the headphones.

"Are you okay?" Zach asked in a hesitant voice, as he approached her.

Why wouldn't she be okay? No biggie—she just learned that her children were related to the devil.

Veronica wiped away tears. "I'm fine—she just had a few things she wanted to get off her chest about Carsten. Kind of a final goodbye."

Zach nodded, but she could tell he was skeptical.

Then Maggie's voice filled the vault, in her best twelve-year-old whine, "Are you almost ready, Mom?"

Jamie seconded, "Yeah, it's so boring here!"

Zach looked at his watch, "If I'm going to make Baer's show, we better get going."

Veronica agreed. But as she stood, she pretended to lose her grip on the device. She dropped it to the floor, but it was still breathing. So she "accidentally" stepped on it with the heel of her boot. She twisted her heel until she was confident it had no chance of ever working again.

She would take the secret to her grave.

CHAPTER 82

Veronica and the kids were dropped off in front of Beth Israel Hospital. The Secret Service showed some chivalry, helping them across the busy sidewalk and into the lobby.

A nurse led them to Ben's room on the third floor. They were met by Flavia, who informed them that Ben had a "rough night," but was much better this morning.

Veronica looked to Youkelstein. "You look much better this morning, considering."

His ashen face lit up. "Never underestimate the healing powers of a beautiful young woman."

He nodded in Flavia's direction. Veronica faked a smile and held back any urge to let him know she wasn't *that* young.

"He's just buttering me up so he can steal more money from me in cards," Flavia replied with a flirtatious wink.

Maggie walked to the bedside table and picked up the deck of cards. "What were you playing?"

"Strip poker," Youkelstein said, grinning. "I must admit I cheated, but it was well worth it."

Veronica cringed. She also wondered what Mr. Nazi Hunter would think if he knew he was flirting with Hitler's great-granddaughter. She doubted he'd be in such a jovial mood if she'd revealed the secret to him.

Veronica approached Youkelstein's bedside and reached into her bag. She pulled out an item and handed it to him. "I brought you a present."

He looked confused by it.

"It's the notes from the Wannsee Conference. You know, *Die Endlösung der Judenfrage*. I think what you'll find most interesting is it contains the missing minutes," she said like she was an expert on the subject.

He appeared awed.

"I also have in my possession a list of stolen Nazi art, and its location, that I will leave in your care to return to the rightful owners."

Youkelstein looked like he was on the verge of tears.

Veronica had one more thing for him—an apology. "I'm sorry for doubting you, Ben. Without you I'd never have gotten my children back. I owe you my life."

He waved his bony hand dismissively, almost yanking the IV tube out of his arm. "I didn't take it personally. My only agenda is to eliminate this evil from the planet, and so far I haven't been able to. Time ruthlessly moves on, and at my age I'm sadly running out of it."

CHAPTER 83

The loud growl of the angry bear shook the room.

Last night, Youkelstein had his assistant bring over a radio from his apartment so he could listen to election results. It was a bulky relic that looked like something a family would gather around in 1938, listening to *War of the Worlds*. He still hadn't accepted that television wasn't just a passing fad.

Theodore Baer aggressively took control of the airwaves with no hint of the humility that should accompany such a historic defeat. "My fellow Baer Cubs," he shouted. "They think they have defeated us, but little do they know the fight has just begun! We might have lost the battle last night, but we're going to win the war!

"They compare Kingston to JFK, but he will go down as the next William Henry Harrison." After a dramatic pause, he continued, "For those of you who weren't paying attention in history class, Harrison was the ninth president of the United States. He died thirty-seven days after taking office, giving him the distinction of having the shortest tenure as president of the United States. A record Jim Kingston will break!"

Veronica sighed. She couldn't believe the fate of the world was in the hands of this narcissistic loud mouth.

"And now that I have your attention, I want to introduce a guest who will further this topic. He has been working on an investigative report concerning Kingston that will blow your minds—so without further ado, I'd like to introduce *Hudson Valley Times* columnist, and former *Newsbreaker* correspondent, Zach Chester. But starting today, the only title he'll be known by is: Jim Kingston's worst nightmare. Good morning, Mr. Chester."

"Good morning, Theodore," Zach's voice filled the airwaves and it brought a smile to all faces in the hospital room. It was the first time they'd been out of the shadows in days, and it felt liberating.

"Please tell us, Mr. Chester, about your shocking story that will hit newsstands tomorrow."

"As some people might know by now, a woman named Ellen Peterson recently confessed that she was an intricate member of the Nazi hierarchy during World War II. And that she had arrived in the United States as part of an organized escape plan, which included twelve of the most loyal members of Hitler's inner circle, who called themselves the Apostles.

"Their mission was to plant the seeds of infiltration that would lead to an eventual return of the Reich. Through my investigation, I learned that some of the notables involved in this group were Gestapo Chief Heinrich Müller, Reichsführer-SS Himmler, and Rudolph Hess. Even Hitler's wife, Eva Braun, took part in the plot. They faked their deaths, using doppelgangers to cover their tracks. To paraphrase Mark Twain, reports of their demise were greatly exaggerated."

Veronica was impressed. Zach started a little nervous, but by the second sentence he sounded confident, and more importantly, believable. Well, as believable as he could sound making insane accusations.

Baer played devil's advocate, "But this Peterson woman had a history of being a nut job. Just weeks earlier she wandered out on a cold night because she saw aliens, correct?"

Zach didn't fluster. "On the surface, her mental state raises many questions. But we discovered a methodical road map of clues she purposely left behind. It would be impossible to form such a coordinated effort if she were mentally impaired. And earlier this morning I was able to review the contents of a safe-deposit box, which contained considerable evidence to back up her claims."

"Tell us about this group, the Apostles, and more importantly, how is this related to the election?"

"I think the most important fact would be that the Apostles were based on four elite families embedded within the United States. One of those families was named Kingston, another was Sterling."

"Whoa, whoa, whoa. Are you saying that Aligor Sterling, the great champion of the Jewish community, and dare I add, Kingston's biggest financial contributor, is a Nazi supporter?"

"No, I am saying that he is an actual card-carrying Nazi."

"And he's conspiring with the president-elect of the United States? These are some serious claims, but why should anyone believe you? I hope you have more to back up your claims than you've shown so far."

"I don't expect anyone to believe me. That's why I think it would be best for Aligor Sterling to tell the story in his own words. My guess is that he'll be a much more believable witness."

Baer acted shocked, but he knew very well that Zach had the Sterling tape. It was the only reason he allowed him on the show.

And they played it.

It began with Youkelstein's voice accusing Sterling of being a German spy named Otto. Sterling not only didn't deny it, but detailed how he infiltrated the Terezin concentration camp and befriended Youkelstein in preparation for his future existence in the United States. He referred to it as "research." The tape then morphed into a conspiracy theorists dream, including one of the world's biggest mass murderers—Himmler—rising up the financial ladders of the United States, under the alias of Jacob Sterling. And Gestapo Chief Heinrich Müller working for the CIA.

And the grassy knoll kept growing—Bormann, Rudolf Hess, and the rest of the Apostles were revealed. But Sterling's most disturbing claim was that he helped finance 9/11 as part of a strategy to blame Israel for the tragedy—in what he believed would spark a revolution, while he himself would serve as the sacrificial lamb.

When the tape shut off, Baer's voice was filled with smugness. Veronica's own satisfaction came from Zach keeping his word, by not mentioning Maggie and Jamie. They were so engrossed in their card game that they wouldn't have noticed anyway. Jamie's disinterest didn't surprise her, but Maggie had been front and center in this thing, and often the driving force. Maybe she realized the adult stuff couldn't compare to being a kid. Veronica sure hoped so.

"I applaud your courage, Mr. Chester, to come out against the powerful Kingston machine," Baer's voice roared. "But I'm sure you're aware that Aligor Sterling will deny that it was him on the tape. He will also attack your credibility—trust me, I know first hand—and he will focus on how your once promising career is now in the toilet, and accuse you of trying to make a big score at any cost. He will also go after the fact that your wife is a crackhead who is doing time in prison."

Veronica wanted to jump into the radio and knock Baer in the teeth. *That was a total cheap shot!*

But Zach stayed composed. "It was crystal-meth, not crack."

"Whatever—you see my point—can you prove that it's Sterling on that tape?"

"The tape was provided to me by Ben Youkelstein, his longtime partner."

"Who had a falling out with Sterling, so his motivation could be questioned. And like most of your sources, he was born during the Woodrow Wilson administration, so his cognitive abilities might come into question."

Whose side was he on?

"I'm sure you can get a voice expert to test it against Sterling's voice," Zach said.

"Funny you say that, because we had the world's premiere voice expert do preliminary tests on the tape, and their initial report is that it *is* a match."

"So you are saying it's a match?" Zach repeated. There was something about his voice—he was up to something.

"Did I stutter? We will do more extensive tests today, but in the meantime, I'd advise Mr. Sterling and Mr. Kingston to get a good lawyer. Good thing I didn't throw out my acceptance speech, huh?"

"Now that you've confirmed that it is indeed Aligor Sterling on the tape," Zach said, "there's one other part of it that I'd like to play."

"The more the merrier."

When Baer hit play, Youkelstein asked Sterling, "But for your plan to work, Kingston has to win—what if he loses?"

"He won't lose," Sterling said firmly, "I'm so confident I bet a billion dollars on it."

"What are you saying?"

"You know I never leave anything to chance, Ben. That's why I provided Theodore Baer a billion dollars in a bank account in Zurich. All he had to do to make his money was to make sure he didn't win the election, even if that self absorbed imbecile couldn't understand the implications of doing so. But while dumb, he still wasn't stupid enough to make those anti-Semitic comments the day before an election. And it wasn't a coincidence that his college term paper suddenly showed up."

"So the election is fixed?" Youkelstein asked, sounding surprised.

"You fix a sink, an election is bought!" Aligor shouted.

Ding, ding, ding ...

Baer had always bragged about not working with the standard five-second delay because he, to use his words, "wouldn't want anyone to wallow in ignorance for five seconds."

Guess he could throw out that acceptance speech, Veronica thought. She smiled at the radio, and she could feel Zach smiling back.

CHAPTER 84

As much as the last two days seemed as long as centuries, the day after the election flew by at warp speed. The fallout to Zach's appearance on the Baer Cave came with an equal swiftness.

Veronica spent the day at the hospital—it seemed like the safest place to hide out from the feeding frenzy. Youkelstein fell in and out of sleep, while Flavia continued to keep her bedside vigil.

Maggie and Jamie continued to act like kids. They played with blood pressure cuffs and stethoscopes. They laughed and fought, and then laughed again. It warmed Veronica's heart.

The CIA was the first to react to Zach's appearance on the Baer Cave, denying any involvement regarding Heinrich Müller, and pointing to previous inquiries and release of their documents on the subject. Veronica thought the haste of their response showed that they'd hit a nerve. Which meant she'd probably need to check her phone for bugs for the rest of her life.

The first arrest was Theodore Baer. And like the bully he was, the minute someone fought back against him he surrendered. He admitted to taking the bribe to lose the election, but denied any involvement in any bigger plot. He claimed to only have discussed the transaction over the phone with a man who called himself Otto. He agreed to testify against Sterling, hoping to save himself from being charged with treason and facing the death penalty. But conspiring to fix a presidential election wouldn't come without a lot of years behind bars.

After authorities grilled Youkelstein for hours in his hospital room, a search warrant was served on Kingston's estate. Eddie's body was found loaded in a sailboat, prepared for a burial at sea before the authorities could find it. The NYPD credited Eddie with uncovering the diabolical plot as part of his job as the head of Kingston's security team. The accepted theory was that Eddie was killed for what he'd discovered.

Sterling predictably denied that it was his voice on the tape, or that he was the mysterious man called Otto who'd paid off Baer. But according to news reports, when the FBI threatened to send him to Israel and let them interrogate him, he suddenly got very chatty and admitted his role in the Apostles and 9/11. He became the villain he always planned to be, just not the way he expected.

By mid-afternoon, Jim Kingston was missing and presumed on the run, which had to be a first in US election history. At three o'clock, Senator Langor held a press conference in his native Florida, to disassociate himself from any knowledge of Kingston and Sterling's plot, and took himself out of any consideration of becoming president, effectively resigning.

But as Maggie pointed out, he really had no position to resign. The US presidential election was not a popular vote, as many believe—it is decided by the vote of the Electoral College, which wouldn't cast their votes until December.

An emergency caucus was called. There were discussions of holding a "do-over" election, but nobody was sure if that was even constitutionally possible. *It was a mess!*

But there was some good news—while tensions were still high in the Middle East, it looked like war would be averted.

At four o'clock, Veronica's stomach began to grumble. The only thing she'd consumed all day had been coffee.

Flavia joined her in the search for food. But even though the bad guys had been rounded up and hauled away, Veronica was still hesitant to leave Maggie and Jamie behind. They had finally crashed, now sleeping side-by-side on a cot, and she didn't want to disturb them. Ben agreed to watch them. Veronica agreed, which would have seemed unfathomable just a day ago.

The two women found a secluded table in the hospital cafeteria and picked at pre-packaged salads in plastic containers and drank diet sodas.

Flavia eyed her intently. "Are you okay? You seem troubled by something."

"I'm just worried about Maggie and Jamie. It's not every day you learn your children are …"

"Hitler youth—like me?" Flavia said, matter of fact.

"I'm sorry, I forgot it also affected you. It must have been hard to learn that?"

She shrugged. "Not really. It's not exactly something I'm going to brag about, but it's not like I was diagnosed with a terminal disease."

Veronica looked surprised. "With all due respect, how can it not bother you? When you see the things that man did and then look at the history of violence that followed him from Harry Jr. to Ellen's other son to …"

Flavia looked annoyed. "Don't even say Carsten. That was one fight that got out of hand and you know it. He didn't invade Poland."

Did everyone know about their fight? "But if you would have seen the look in his eyes. Like there was something inside of him, urging him to do it again."

"I want to hit you right now, does that make me a bad person?"

"Thanks a lot."

"What I'm trying to say is, we all have good inside us. But we're also human, which means we're flawed and full of temptation. In the end, we will be judged by our actions and each individual is responsible for their own actions. It doesn't matter who your parents are, how much money you have, or if you were hugged enough as a child. It doesn't matter what our beliefs are, or ideals, or genetics, or any of it. I've given in to my dark side too many times to discuss, but it had nothing to do with being the daughter of a spy, or the great-granddaughter of a mass murderer. We all do the best we can, but that usually isn't good enough, so then we must ask for help."

"Who do you ask?"

Flavia pointed to the hospital chapel in the distance. "I ask Her to lead me from temptation and deliver me from evil. Maybe you should try it sometime—but asking for help wouldn't work with a narcissist like yourself."

"A narcissist?" Veronica replied, annoyed.

"It's all about you, Veronica. You really believe *you* are responsible for whether your children turn out good or bad. It might be noble to get them to do their homework and eat their vegetables, but in the end, they're the only ones who will guide their path."

"If trying to protect my children makes me a narcissist, then so be it."

"What you're trying to protect is your God complex, not your children. If it were true that life was predestined for them, then you wouldn't be the master of their future. But lucky for you, the genetics angle is nothing but nonsense, so you can go on deceiving yourself."

They quietly finished their lunch, as Flavia's stinging words set in. When they returned to the room, Maggie and Jamie were alone.

"Where is Ben?" Flavia asked.

Maggie handed them a note. It read: *I have so little time left in this world to fight for justice. I won't waste one more moment in this hospital room. Thank you for all your help—I will never forget it. Ben.*

"He just left?" Veronica asked.

"Just the way he rolls," Maggie replied with a shrug.

Veronica shook her head in disbelief—he had more energy than the rest of them put together. She looked at her watch. "We better be getting home—you two have school tomorrow."

Jamie did a dramatic sigh and fell on the bed. "Oh, Mom—you always ruin all the fun!"

"I don't know what you are so worried about, Jamie, you're suspended anyway," his sister taunted him.

Veronica had forgotten about that. She wondered if Principal Sweetney would commute his sentence for saving the world.

Yeah right.

Jamie buried himself in the blanket. "Not Uncle Phil and Aunt Val!"

"You're going to have to scrub the toilets," Maggie piled on.

It might be as close to normal as things ever got.

As they left the room, they were met by a surprise visitor on his way in.

Veronica gave Zach a big hug. "You did it," she said.

"*We* did—we all did it," he replied humbly. "But I think you should lay low for a few days. The media will be going full force on this story trying to make connections to Ellen, and there already is a video out there of Maggie running with a gun on Kingston's estate."

"You could stay at the farm," Flavia offered.

Veronica looked hesitant. One minute she was calling her names, the next she's offering shelter.

Zach agreed. "I think it would be a good idea. I'm staying in the city for a couple days to tie up the loose ends on this story, so why don't you take my car." He tossed Veronica the keys.

"I promise—no more lectures," Flavia said with a smile. It was the same as Jamie's—the one that was impossible to turn down.

Maggie, now in her second childhood, agreed. "C'mon, Mom—it'll be fun!"

Veronica wasn't concerned about fun—safe was what she was going for. "I just need to stop home to pick up some things and feed Picasso. Then we can go."

Maggie and Jamie jumped up and down with joy.

CHAPTER 85

Flavia walked past Stuyvesant Park, en route to her Jeep. Her feet were killing her, but she would never admit it was connected to her choice of footwear.

When she got in the vehicle, she removed her heels and flipped on the radio.

She still didn't know what to make of Veronica, but thought it would be nice to have some company at her lonely farmhouse, especially the sounds of children. She was about to put the key in the ignition to start her journey back home, when she felt the sharp pain in her neck. A pointed object penetrated her skin. She immediately grew dizzy and felt sick. The world began spinning.

She used all her strength to turn to look at the man who had hidden in the backseat. As her breaths became shorter, he explained to her why he was sucking the life out of her.

Her mind flashed to the first time her mother brought her to the farm in Rhinebeck, when she was just a little girl. It was the first time she had ever seen the fall foliage. She was amazed by the leaves falling from the trees. Their beautiful colors and how they so gracefully cascaded to the ground. She sat behind the barn and watched the leaves for hours.

And here she was, over forty years later, just as awestruck as the first time she'd watched them. Flavia watched every last beautiful leaf hit the ground, and when the last one floated softly to the ground ...

Everything went dark.

CHAPTER 86

Rush hour was the culprit in what turned out to be a two-hour journey from Manhattan to Pleasantville.

Veronica phoned in an order from Pleasantville Pizza on the way. Coffee for breakfast, hospital cafeteria for lunch, and a pizza dinner wasn't exactly the diet of champions, but at least it now looked like they might live long enough to develop diet-related, long-term health issues. And that was good news.

They ate with Veronica's mother, who actually agreed that it was a good idea to hide out for a few days at the farm in Rhinebeck. Her prisoner for the day, TJ, also joined them for dinner, as his father would be off breaking the story of the century for the next few days.

Once the kids were ushered off to pack for the trip, Veronica gave her mother all the details. Except for a small omission concerning the identity of Maggie and Jamie's great-great-grandfather. She also softened the blow on Eddie—sticking to the 'dying a hero' story.

Veronica couldn't believe that Eddie was gone. But she couldn't find tears right now for him. Like with Ellen, Veronica needed to sort out her feelings, but he did keep his promise—he kept her kids safe.

Veronica traded in her sweater and skirt for NYU sweatshirt and jeans. Jamie changed into a colorful flannel shirt and cargo pants that made him look like he came off the cover of a fall catalog. Maggie was back to her all black ensemble that she wore with her usual ponytail. The images of normalcy.

Veronica gathered children and toothbrushes, and then they were off, heading upstate in Zach's Audi. She clicked on 1010 WINS, the all-news station, as they knifed through the darkness of the Taconic Parkway.

Bad decision.

There was just no avoiding their current reality. The newscaster grimly reported the death of Jim Kingston. He was found in a Manhattan apartment building owned by Aligor Sterling, dead of an apparent suicide.

Talk about a reversal of fortune. One minute he was elected leader of the free world, and twenty-four hours later he was in a bunker taking his life, just like his great-grandfather—at least according to the history books. Whatever the details of either death, Veronica couldn't deny the trail of destruction that was handed down from generation to generation. She did the math. Kingston's death left three members remaining in the bloodline.

Veronica switched off the radio, and drove the rest of the way to the soothing sound of silence. They arrived at Flavia's around ten. Maggie and Jamie had been sleeping since they hit the Taconic, but awoke as soon as they hit the gravel of Flavia's driveway. Veronica parked the Audi behind Flavia's Jeep and they moved to the front door, carrying their overnight bags.

To Veronica's surprise, the door was open. "Hello," she shouted upon entering.

A note was left for them in the kitchen. Flavia had gone into town to check on something at her art gallery and would return shortly. It instructed them to put their items in the guest bedroom and make themselves at home.

The sleepy children dropped their bags in the kitchen and looked like their last fumes of energy were finally zapped. Pretty understandable—not their usual con jobs to get Mom to do all the heavy lifting for them. Veronica grabbed their bags and carried them into the guest room.

She heard the door slam behind her.

She turned and attempted to open it. It was jammed. She jarred it a few more times. It wouldn't budge. She had underestimated them once again.

"Maggie! Jamie! This isn't funny."

She heard Maggie scream and her heart jumped. Footsteps headed toward the door. Along with a rhythmic tapping she recognized.

She pounded on the door, "Let me out of here!"

"I'm sorry, I can't do that, Veronica," a man's voice said.

CHAPTER 87

"Ben, is that you?" Veronica asked. "What is going on?"

"Think of me as a gypsy moth, Veronica. I have come to defoliate your family tree of evil."

Maggie screamed out, "Mom—help!"

Her world began to spin out of control. She banged harder on the door.

"Your children are fine, Veronica. Let me set the scene for you. I'm holding Maggie down with the tip of my umbrella. I'm just going to lightly prick her with it and she will go to sleep. I am holding a gun in my other hand at Jamie's head, but I don't want to use it. I'm hoping he will cooperate and I will put him to sleep, also."

"No!" Veronica shouted. "I don't understand—why you are doing this?"

"Oh, I believe you do. And I think deep down you have the same fears I do about what the future brings for them. You know of their genetic makeup—they are the last leaves on the most evil family tree in history. The world cannot allow this disease to spread any more."

"How did you know we were here?" Veronica asked sharply.

"I was able to attach a little gadget to Maggie's cell phone when she visited my place, which allowed me to track her. Isn't modern technology fantastic? When I was a boy, the automobile was a luxury, and now the whole world is connected by a signal."

"Where's Flavia?"

"She can no longer hurt anyone. Same with Jim Kingston, who was struck down by a sudden stroke earlier today, even if they are calling it a suicide."

"My children are innocent!" Veronica shouted through tears, "Please let them go."

"We both know that isn't true. But let me tell you a story about someone who was innocent. My father was a doctor in Munich who helped those who couldn't afford medical treatment after World War I. It was there he came across a young prostitute named Etta who was impregnated by a German corporal. He threatened her with violence if she didn't terminate the child. But my father risked his life to help secretly deliver the child—a girl named Ellen.

"What he didn't know was that his loyalty had helped to continue a shark infested gene pool. I think you have most likely figured out what that young corporal's name was, Veronica. And how was my father rewarded for this? He was murdered by those with the same blood as your children."

Veronica kept frantically pounding the door, but it wouldn't budge. She tried kicking it, but the only damage she inflicted was on her own foot.

"If you do this, you are a monster just like those Nazis you hunted. Just like those secret police who tracked down Anne Frank hiding in that attic. Just like the ones who killed your father and fiancée. Just like the ones who loaded the trains with children and the elderly, and sent them to their death …"

She hoped to strike a nerve of guilt, but Youkelstein seemed unfazed.

"Mom—please!" Maggie called out again, and Veronica's heart almost exploded.

"The ironic thing, Veronica, is after all the evil I hunted down across the globe, your family came to me—when Carsten brought the letters between Ellen and Heinrich Müller. That in itself was quite an impressive discovery. But you see, one of the letters was dated April 20, and in that letter Ellen and Müller discussed the birthday of their son Josef's grandfather, who was an Apostle named Peter. April 20 happens to be the birthday of a certain former German leader. It allowed me to connect the dots.

"When I learned that Carsten's grandmother was Ellen, it brought me back to the story my father told me. I knew it couldn't be a coincidence, and I had to eliminate the tree at the roots."

"You killed Carsten!" Veronica shouted through sobs. She was now bull-rushing the door with no success.

"I enjoyed my time with Carsten. He was intelligent and passionate, much like his daughter. As was Ellen when I surprised her with a visit. But in the end, I had no choice."

"If it wasn't for Maggie and Jamie then the world as we know it would be gone. How could someone who did that be evil?"

Veronica's plan was to hold on as long as she could. An elderly man who suffered a multitude of injuries over the last two days, including a gunshot wound to the shoulder he held his weapon with, couldn't hold out much longer, could he? Even fueled by his thirst for revenge, he'd ultimately run out of gas and drop his weapon.

She hoped.

Keep him talking, she told herself. Play into his ego … his vanity.

But Jamie threw a wrench into her plan. "Hey Maggie, let's play the game we did at the subway."

"No, Jamie—no!" Veronica shouted out.

But it was too late—she heard his small feet running across the floor and yelling out a nonsensical, primal scream.

"No!" Veronica shouted again.

A gunshot rang out and she heard a body hit the floor. Maggie screamed.

Veronica dropped to her knees, yelling at the top of her lungs. But there was nothing she could do to drown her pain.

Footsteps moved toward the door once again. She scrambled back, but it was too late. The door swung open and a man stood before her.

She thought she must be dreaming, because when she looked at the man with a gun in his hand, it was Zach. She shook the cobwebs out.

Still Zach. *Was he in on this?*

"Are you okay?" he asked.

She didn't know what to say. But when Jamie bolted into the room with a smile on his face, she had her answer ... she was perfect.

"But how?" she asked, still in shock.

"There was something Sterling said on that tape Youkelstein gave me, which got me thinking. He said he would protect your children from Youkelstein, who came to *harm them*."

Before she could completely digest Zach's words, she heard Maggie's voice in the other room. But she wasn't sure she liked what was coming out of her mouth. "He's losing a lot of blood—we need to get him to a hospital."

Veronica couldn't believe Maggie was trying to help the man who tried to kill her. Youkelstein was not dead—he had been shot in the same shoulder as last night. But that was her daughter. Maggie wasn't evil; in fact, she represented everything that was good and hopeful in this world.

Youkelstein had other plans. As if he mortgaged every last ounce of strength in his body, he rose to his feet and mumbled something, the only word Veronica could make out was 'Esther,' and rushed toward Maggie with his umbrella pointed at her.

Veronica instinctively grabbed the gun out of Zach's hands and fired.

Youkelstein fell to the ground, dead.

Veronica threw the gun as far as she could and pulled her children into a group hug, trying to shield them from the horrible scene.

CHAPTER 88

Veronica Peterson's week from hell ended on a blissful Saturday afternoon. It was as if Mother Nature was signaling that things would be okay.

The Petersons' long journey back to normalcy was beginning with some good old fashioned yard work and leaf raking. But it predictably turned into the kids playing in the leaves as Veronica photographed them. She was trying to capture every moment of their innocence.

She had sent them to school on Thursday and Friday. Well, Maggie went to school, but the judge upheld Jamie's sentence. He spent his days at Uncle Phil and Aunt Val's, probably longing for a return of the Nazis.

Veronica got back to normalcy herself. That is, if you can call making funeral arrangements normal, along with wrapping up Ellen's affairs at Sunshine Village.

She still had mixed feelings about Ellen, but Flavia left this world with nothing but her respect—not that Flavia cared what she thought. Veronica realized that she never really hated her. She actually envied her, because she was a constant and painful reminder of the person Veronica used to be. The one that Carsten fell in love with. She vowed to never lose herself again.

Flavia also left her art gallery and farmhouse to the estate of Carsten Peterson. Leaving it to someone who brightened her life, as the farmhouse had been left for her. Veronica could see herself running the gallery, keeping Flavia's dreams alive, but also re-starting her own. She visualized Maggie working with her during her summer vacations from school, maybe even hanging a Maggie & Veronica Peterson original on the wall. And while logic told Veronica to run as far away from the ghosts as possible, her gut disagreed.

Next week would be the full-dress police funeral for Lieutenant Edward Peterson, who would be laid to rest as a hero. Journalists like Zach might see nobility in the quest for the truth, but Veronica thought the world was a better place when there were more heroes than scoundrels, even if that conflicted with reality.

She believed the same about Youkelstein, who was also being hailed as a survivor who sought justice. And since his body was laid to rest deep in the caves beneath Flavia's property, it likely would never be found, and Veronica and her children would never have to be questioned about the shooting or what led to it.

And Eddie's police family continued his legacy as the protector. They wouldn't allow anyone to get within a hundred feet of Veronica's house, or the children at school. This police protection wasn't for any reprisals or revenge from the Nazis or Kingston supporters—it was from the media. The last thing Veronica wanted was their association with Ellen to cause them to be dragged back into a drama they never asked for.

Veronica looked at her children through her camera lens. Jamie was running and jumping into the piles of leaves like he was performing a cannonball dive into a swimming pool. Maggie had bunched handfuls of leaves under her shirt. She yelled, "Look Mom—I look like a pregnant lady!"

Oh God—no! It's way too early to even start thinking about those things.

Veronica thought again of her natural instinct to protect. Did that mean that nature would eventually win out in the never-ending debate?

That's what scared her.

Did this mean Maggie and Jamie had a ticking time bomb inside them? Did she give birth to Rosemary's babies? According to many accounts, including Ellen's, Hitler didn't embrace his vile views until his teens. Before that, he was supposedly just a passionate artist with a temper—sort of like Maggie.

So every time Jamie poisoned a classmate's lunch or Maggie displayed a passion for politics, Veronica would wonder if it was the zest of youth, or a cancer spreading inside them. For a mother, it was eternal damnation—they might have caught the bad guys, but this would never be over.

She wanted to believe the Ellen view of nurture. That a mother could guide the child through the events that shape their life for the better or worse, and send them down the right path. It was an empowering viewpoint. Even if according to some, this made her a narcissist.

Flavia believed that neither nature nor nurture shaped children. While providing a good home and values might be helpful, in the end it's up to the individual to make the correct decisions on their actions. And there can be no predictive analysis of what those decisions will be when presented with the unpredictable choices life will present.

And it wasn't just Flavia who believed this. Veronica again thought of Anne Frank, who wrote: *The final forming of a person's character lies in their own hands.*

A car pulled up the driveway, stealing Veronica's gaze.

Zach and TJ.

TJ gave Veronica the abrupt hello of a twelve-year-old, then did a beeline to Maggie and Jamie. He dove into the leaf pile like it was the town pool.

Zach approached her with a big grin. "So, did you do anything interesting last week, Ms. Peterson?"

She smiled back at him. "I didn't think you'd have time for us common folk anymore, Mr. Big Shot. What's next—anchoring the national news?"

He maintained his contented smile. "No, I'm happy where I'm at. Once you hit the bottom you realize how silly all that stuff is."

He handed Veronica a bound document. "What's this?" she asked.

"It's a printed copy of Ellen's memoir. I erased the copy in the safe-deposit box."

"Why'd you do that? I figured you were going to publish it. You have my blessing as long as Maggie and Jamie aren't mentioned." She smiled, before adding, "And that you take us to the Rainforest Café with some of the royalties you earn, of course."

Zach shook his head. "All that would do is cause more burden for your kids that they didn't ask for." His face saddened as he looked out at TJ. "If anyone has learned about putting burdens on children, it's Sara and me."

He pulled out the tape Youkelstein gave him, and asked, "Do you think I'm a good reporter?"

"The best."

"Well, not as good as Maggie, because she asked the most important question in this whole thing—*why was he chosen?* And when I arrived at the farmhouse, I overheard the back-end of your conversation with Youkelstein. The part where he was outlining his motivation for what he was doing. I think he answered the question. In fact, I think Ellen already answered it for you on that video she left you—the one that died at the tip of your boot."

Veronica didn't say anything.

"I'm right, aren't I?"

She remained silent.

"A simple shake of the head will do. Or you can extend your arm and give me the heil sign."

She turned to him. "You can't say anything."

He tossed her the tape with a grin. "It's your secret. Nobody will ever know but you, me, and Grandpa Adolf."

Veronica looked out at her kids. Maggie and TJ were burying Jamie alive under the leaves, and he seemed to be enjoying it. She had explained to Maggie and Jamie that Youkelstein's words at the farm were just the desperate rants of a sick old man. Jamie didn't really understand any of it, while Maggie was predictably skeptical of anything her mother said.

Zach read the dread in her face. "It's probably not true, anyway."

"How can you say that? Why would he have taken her in if she wasn't his daughter?"

"Most people crave to have children, perhaps even the worst ones, so maybe he wanted to believe she was. And while it was true that Corporal Hitler was in Munich in late 1916 and early 1917 while recovering from a battle wound, making an encounter with Ellen's mother possible, the fact is, she was a prostitute who was likely with numerous men, and it's not like they were doing DNA testing back then. And while it's not scientific, I don't see any outward resemblance to Ellen or any of your children." He thought for a second, before adding, "Although, I once saw Maggie with a chocolate milk mustache after serving her and TJ lunch, and now that I think about it …"

She tapped him playfully on the shoulder. "Not funny."

"And remember that battle injury I mentioned? Well, it has been long rumored that it was a shot to the groin, and he lost one of his friends down there, which left him impotent. So it might not even have been physically possible."

"But everything else Ellen said turned out to be true."

"Even if it is, I think they're going to turn out great."

"How can you be so sure?"

"There's a precedent."

"Which is?"

"Luke Skywalker was Darth Vader's kid and he seemed to turn out okay."

The comment drew a smile from Veronica. That wasn't any easy accomplishment when it came to this topic. "That's true, but he did have a strange sexual tension with his sister."

"Yes, but if I recall correctly, Luke and Leia did end up saving the universe—sound familiar?"

As usual, it was the right words and the right tone. "So now that you're kind of a big deal, I hope you're not afraid to get your hands dirty—why don't you pick up a rake?"

His smile left. "I'd love to, but TJ and I have to get going. We're late for a visit with his mother."

Veronica put on her tough face and gave him a hug. "Thank you for everything—I hope it all works out for you."

After watching Zach and TJ drive away, Veronica's children began calling, "C'mon, Mom—come and play in the leaves!" Jamie yelled.

She looked at them and filled with the hope for the future that children so often bring out in adults. Once more, she thought of Anne Frank, who never got the opportunity to play in the leaves with her mother because of the Nazis. Her words flowed through Veronica's head as she approached the leaf pile. *This is not the end. It's not even the beginning of the end. But it is, perhaps, the end of the beginning.*

"Kids against adults!" Jamie announced. He threw a colorful collage of leaves at Veronica that glanced off her face.

She picked up a handful and fired them right back at Jamie. Then Maggie turned on her brother and dumped a bundle of leaves over his head. It was girls against the boy.

A full-scale leaf war broke out. Leaves filled the air, as did their laughter. After a few spirited minutes, Veronica rushed her children and tackled them into the leaf pile. She hugged them as hard as she could. She would have held them forever, but Jamie squirmed away.

He picked up a pile of leaves and tossed them as high as he could into the air. "Look—it's snowing leaves!" he shouted gleefully.

Veronica watched the leaves, as they seemed to fall to the earth in slow motion. As they did, she heard Anne Frank's words whistling through the wind: *Think of all the beauty around you and be happy.*

Veronica fixated on the leaves raining down upon the beauty that was surrounding her—her children—and when the final leaf hit the ground, she was ...

Happy.

ACKNOWLEDGMENTS

The Heritage Paper was the trickiest story I've ever written, due to its use of real life historical references. At the end of the day, it's a work of fiction meant to entertain, and certainly not a history book or official record, but I do think it's important to be as accurate as possible with these facts and historical figures. And I hope that was achieved.

The story is also loaded with conspiracy theories, many which are well known. While they are used as a vehicle to tell the story, in no way does it mean that I am endorsing them as true. I'll leave that up to you. My take on conspiracy theories in general, is that there's probably a 99.9% chance that they're *not* true. But it's that 0.1% possibility that makes them so enticing when it comes to fiction, and that small dose of possibility can draw us in and make for a fun ride.

Many of the referenced events in the book from World War II to 9/11 to potential conflict in the Middle East all have touched people in a real way in the non-fiction world we live in. And of course, the terror of Nazi Germany and the Holocaust, which is at the center of the story. So I'd like to ˙k everyone who provided feedback to me on those subjects, so that I ˥re that those events were referenced with the proper sensibility.

˥ to extend a special thanks to Jeff Finkelstein, for reading ꓶ provided me with a Jewish perspective of the story. Jeff is the president of the award-winning Customer Paradigm marketing firm, and a key contributor in the Adventure Rabbi program, which was founded by his wife, and best-selling author, Rabbi Jamie Korngold.

There is no shortage of theories and literature out there on the many war criminals that were mentioned throughout the book, as to what their true fate was. But if Ben Youkelstein existed in real life, much of his thinking and theories would be considered Thomasian, based on W. Hugh Thomas. Thomas is a forensic surgeon who wrote books questioning the deaths of Himmler, Rudolf Hess, and Adolf Hitler. His book on Hess "The Tale of Two Murders" led to the opening of a Scotland Yard investigation on the subject. Like I mentioned earlier, it's up to you to make up your mind on these sort of theories, so if you want to read Thomas' writings on the subject, his books can be found at Amazon and most online booksellers.

And a big thank you to the usual suspects who make up the best team any author can have. Carl Graves with another great cover, Curt Ciccone with his formatting expertise, and Sandra Simpson for her eagle eyes spotting my many mistakes. Christina Wickson typed the original manuscript, as she has with most of my stories, and I think deserves a medal of honor for being able to read my handwriting.

And last but never least, to my grandmother, Harriet Mays, who showed me that a person over the age of ninety can be as vibrant and curious as those half their age. Without knowing her, I would never have thought to create characters over ninety who displayed such energy and passion as they led the charge, and considered them realistic. Love you, Grams!

KEEP IN TOUCH WITH DEREK

website: www.derekciccone.com

Facebook: Derek Ciccone Book Club

Twitter: @DCicconebooks

Email: Derekbkclb@yahoo.com

CPSIA information can be obtained at www.ICGtesting.com
Printed in the USA
BVOW08s1213060416

443207BV00001B/73/P